Zomb
For The Fallen

Mark Tufo

CreateSpace Edition
Copyright 2013 Mark Tufo

Discover other titles by Mark Tufo
Visit us at marktufo.com
and http://zombiefallout.blogspot.com/ home of future webisodes
and find me on FACEBOOK

Edited by:
TW Brown
twbrown.maydecpub@gmail.com

Cover Art:
Shaed Studios, shaedstudios.com

Dedications:
To my wife: a thank you seems such a simple way to express my appreciation but it is all encompassing. For everything you do for my mind, body and soul - thank you.

I honestly can't thank my beta-readers enough, Vix Kirkpatrick, Joy Buchanan and Kimberly Sansone. That they give of their time (willingly) to help me put out a better book is mind-blowing. You three will always have my utmost appreciation.

To David Knuth, he gave an idea for a particular mode of transportation, I just wanted to give credit where it was due.

To all my readers who have sent me communication over the last year hoping this book would come to its fruition, I hope you enjoy it!

As always to the first responders and men and women of the armed forces, you have mine and my family's admiration and respect for all the sacrifices you endure to keep us all safe.

Acknowledgement page for all those who so kindly helped when I asked for a favor!

'Louise Thostrup, Aaron Altman, Amanda Burns-Austin, Amanda Felix, Amanda Perez, Amber Cichon, Ami LawLess, Amy McNea, Andrew Cross, Angel Campbell Welch, Angela Crabtree, Angela Gomez Ritchie, Angie Zuver, Anne-marie Stephens, Anthony Hoahng, Anthony Morley, Ariel Alvarez, Armand Rosamilia, Barbara Friskey, Barry Hruby, Becky Usherwood, Bill Allen, Bionicgargoyle Grrarg, Bob Simister, Brenda Spears, Brian Forsythe, Brian Kelly, Brown Lawrence, Bryan Shrove, Chris Decoteau, Christine Kelly, Christopher Dorrell, Christopher Scott Caldwell, Claire Rees, Combat Johnny, Consuelo Delgado, Dan Modzik, Danielle Dorsey, Dargan Franks, Darrell Dutton, Darren Bailey, Dave Heron, David Bain, David Marble, David Quincy, Debora N. Derr, Deborah Brayshaw, December Maglior, Diane Long, Diane Paster, Dieter Wheatley, Donald Fuchs, Elijah Wilson, Elizabeth McCurry Wilson, Emma Keogh, Felicia Braden Wahl, Finlay Grant, Gayle Davidson, Gem Preater, Ginger Dailey, Gypsy Rose, Heath Stallcup, Heather Willingham, Hector Cervantes, Honey Rand, Irene Dawn Guerrero, James R McCain Jr, Janet Dugas, Jason Blocker, Jason Wylie, Jay Parthenopaeus, JCastillo Lando, Jim Bouque, Jody McLee, John Kenkel, Johnn E. Houston, Joseph Fleischman, Joshua Kessler, Joyce Scott, Julie Greig, Kai Pao, Karl Adams, Kate Carlan, Katie Cadena, Katina Henderson, Kelly Rickard, Kim Corona, Kim McClellan Meyers, Kimberly Munsell, Lana Sibley, Lauren Worley-Coleman, Leann Brackney, Leigh Windridge, Lillian Patterson, Lisa Evans, Lisa Harper, Lisa M Jennings- Friloux, Lisa Marie Williams, Lisa Snyder-Phillips, Lisa Swarm, Lori Lynch Fontanez,

Lou Miller, Luci Tomaselli-Steffensen, Maria C Farber,
Mark Heath, Marrah Goodman, Matt O'Shields,
Matt Santiago, Melissa Joy Broderick, Michael Chance,
Michael Gunn, Michelle Thrasher, Nadine Price,
Nathan King, Nick Anthony, Nicky Barnes Jones,
Ozymandias Von Gimmiesome, Pamela Hosford, Pat Bryant,
Patricia Brower, Patrick Marshall, Philip Spencer,
Phillip Lawlor, Rachel Temple-Storm Watkins,
Randall E. Atha, Rebecca True Wilson, Renee Nene,
Rich Taylor, Rob Moffitt, Robin Mahaffey, Rogue Tomato,
Roz Stanley, Ryan Bilbo Colley Garland, Sandra Byrd,
Sandra Tufo, Sara Smolarek, Scott Stanley,
Scott Wehde, Sharon Berghorn, Shaun Thysse,
Sherry Ballentine Barton, Simon Tran, Spencer Richardson,
Stephanie Dagger, Steven Thornbrugh, Suzy Wegner,
Tammea Gaunce Tooley, Tanner Proctor, Tez Leaver,
Tim Kremin, Tina Hutchinson, Tina Mcleod, Tom Hall,
Tom Lambert, Tom Perry, Tony Devonshire, Tracy Carlson,
Tracy Carlson-King, Travis Jorgensen, Trey Smith,
Truls Fundingsrud, Veronica Costa Smith, Vikki Marsh,
Wayne Sanford, Wednesday Corey, Wendy Betancourt,
William Joe Roletter, Zac Dobney, Zach Rocha

Table of Contents
Prologue
Chapter 1 - Mike Journal Entry 1
Chapter 2 - Mike Journal Entry 2
Chapter 3 - Mrs. Deneaux
Chapter 4 - Mike Journal Entry 3
Chapter 5 - Mrs. Deneaux
Chapter 6 - Mike Journal Entry 4
Chapter 7 - Stephanie and Trip
Chapter 8 - Mike Journal Entry 5
Chapter 9 - Stephanie and Trip
Chapter 10 - Doc and Porkchop
Chapter 11 - Mrs. Deneaux and Dennis
Chapter 12 - Doc and Porkchop
Chapter 13 - Mike Journal Entry 6
Chapter 14 - Doc Baker
Chapter 15 - Mike Journal Entry 7
Chapter 16 - Stephanie and Trip
Chapter 17 - Mike Journal Entry 8
Chapter 18 - Dennis and Deneaux
Chapter 19 - Mike Journal Entry 9
Chapter 20 - Doc
Chapter 21 - Mike Journal Entry 10
Chapter 22 - Captain Najarian
Chapter 23 - Dennis and Deneaux
Chapter 24 - Mike Journal Entry 11
Chapter 25 - Lieutenant Barnes
Chapter 26 - Mike Journal Entry 12
Chapter 27 - Talbot Family
Chapter 28 - Mike Journal Entry 13
Talbot-Sode #1
Talbot-Sode #2
Epilogue 1 - Deneaux - Pre-Zombie Apocalypse
Epilogue 2
Epilogue 3

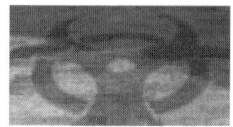

PROLOGUE

Fuck death, it's not the enemy, zombies are.

BT, Tracy, Travis, Justin and Tommy got in the truck. The rest of my family, new and old lined the roadway waving as we departed. When I was sure we were far enough away to avoid retribution but still within sight, I stopped the truck and got out.

"You should have let me have the gun," I yelled to Ron.

"Not a chance," he yelled back.

I drove off the road a ways, scraping the front fender against a large oak and leaving a large swath of white paint.

"You little fuck!" he yelled, looking to chamber some rounds into his gun. I floored the gas.

"You're such an asshole," Tracy said from the backseat.

"What? It was an accident. I'm innocent," I pled.

"You don't have an innocent bone in your body," BT added.

"Listen…if that's the worst that happens to this thing I'll consider it a victory," I said.

BT contemplated for a moment. "Agreed."

"See, hon, I was just getting the bad part out of the way." I turned to face her.

"Uh-huh." She answered warily. I don't think she was buying it.

"So what's the plan?" BT asked.

"Really?" Travis asked back.

I smiled wanly. I actually did have an idea. Odds were good that the doc was somewhere along the route Eliza had taken. Sure, that left a lot of land to cover; however, there was no alternative. BT and Justin needed help. I would not – I could not – dwell on the impossibility of this mission. Doc was alive; I was staking their lives on it.

We'd gone a few miles, the overall mood in the car was guarded excitement. Team Talbot had scored a major victory. Eliza was dead, and nothing short of a good old-fashioned resurrection was going to bring her back. Now, normally that would have been a laughable proposition, considering the last one had happened close to two thousand years ago – depending on your beliefs. But since the zombies had made 'coming back' commonplace, I'd had the wisdom to burn Eliza.

I thought I'd get more enjoyment out of the event. All I really felt was sorry. Her first years were marred with all manner of brutality inflicted upon her. She, in turn, had wrought that on the world in spades. It was all she knew. She looked so at peace as she laid upon that funeral pyre. Tommy had carefully combed her hair and placed her hands over her chest, nearly covering the twisting knife wound Tracy had inflicted. Nothing short of new clothes was going to hide the blood that had dried to a brown thickness across her upper half though.

Tommy kissed his sister lightly, struck the match, and lit her lighter fluid-doused body up. He watched for a second as the flame took hold before he walked away. We were all out there to witness the event. I stayed to the bitter end; I felt that I owed her that. The flame had burned hot enough to be felt over twenty-five feet away. The pyre collapsed in on itself after a while, sending plumes of sparks skyward. Eventually, after many hours, the flame had died out.

As if on cue, a light rain had started blotting out the final embers; soft smoke drifted up. *I almost can't believe that we won*, I thought as I approached the ashes. She had seemed so strong, cunning, and vicious. What chance did we have?

I kicked over a small, blackened log. A glint of gold caught my attention. It was what remained of the Blood Locket. I had been tempted to grab it as some sort of memento of the occasion – proof that we really had succeeded. After further reflection, I booted ash over it. It was hers; it always had been. And, in retrospect, I wanted nothing to do with it.

***

"It's always road trips," BT said, looking through the window.

I had been lost in thought. "What?"

"Who knew that the zombie apocalypse would be one road trip after another?"

I was still holding on to visions of a burning Eliza and her hand falling from her breast, her pointer finger extending out towards me. Possibly in accusation or as an invitation to join her.

I came up with the ever witty "Huh?"

"Shit, Talbot, how much room you got in that head of yours that you travel so far away?" BT chided me.

Travis laughed. "Sorry," he mumbled when I glared at him through the rear view mirror.

"It's not his fault you're a space cadet," Tracy told me.

And then BT's words hit. I think if I added up the days since the zombies came, we truly had spent the majority of them on the road. Defending a homestead definitely had its own share of dangers, but that was nothing in comparison to all manner of nasty and deadly things that could and most likely would be discovered on the roadway.

"He's left us again," BT turned to say to Tracy.

"Welcome to my world," she replied.

"Sorry, I was really just thinking on it. Being on the road sucks, and yet, here we find ourselves again," I said.

"It's got to be better without Eliza…right?" Justin asked without too much conviction.

"One would hope," was what I said. My thoughts didn't mirror the sentiment.

"Zombies!" Travis shouted. It was loud in the small confines of the truck.

My head was on a swivel as I looked around. "Where?" I was trying to pull a Regan from *The Exorcist*.

(The whole head pulling a three-sixty thing for those of you not brave enough to have watched it, like me.)
"Oh, God!" BT said.
I saw his Adam's apple bobbing wildly in his throat. I'd never seen him turn green; I wouldn't have thought his skin color would have allowed it. Granted, it was a dark green like Godzilla as opposed to a Kermit-like green, which I guess is more fitting anyway considering his size.
"I know that smell," he gulped. "Pickled weasel."
I slammed on the brakes, the truck coming to a skidding halt. I think Tracy bounced her forehead off BT's headrest. My throat was closing, tears were welling up in my eyes. I had no sooner shoved the truck in park when I opened the door and was outside gasping for air. Truth be told, I don't think I was the first one out; but since I was rapidly losing consciousness, it was difficult to tell.
When I had finally pulled in enough ragged breathes of air to stop my pupils from dilating, I turned back towards the truck, and I'd swear I saw a brown mist swirling around inside that cab. I noticed two things that almost blew my mind. The first was that Tommy had not vacated like the rest of us, and the second was the big bundle of fawn fur he had in his lap.
"What the fuck is Henry doing here?" I asked, pretty much to myself as everyone around me was still suffering the after-effects of what could only be described as the usage of a biological weapon.
I waited a few moments longer, letting the cloud dissipate; although I was figuring it could be sticky enough that it would adhere itself to the interior of the truck, thus further reducing its resale value. Tough to sell something that smelled like sewer gas, even with a clean CARFAX.
"Henry, what are you doing here?" I asked him as I approached.
I gingerly tested the air with my nose as I cautiously approached. His stub of a tail was banging rapidly back and

forth. He tilted his head up so I could scratch under his chin and chest where he liked it most.

"Did you get a hold of Lyndsey's cooking again?" I asked him as I grabbed his massive head.

I was referring to my sister, whose stabs at cooking had lined many the bottoms of trashcans. I'd once watched her, fascinated, as she made chocolate chip cookies from scratch. The resultant thing that emerged from the oven had looked like liver and tasted worse.

I was thrilled to see the dog…and worried. He was one more loved one I would need to be concerned for, but evidently he had decided to not be left behind again.

"Get him out of the truck," Tracy said, coming up slowly. When I gave her a confused look she elaborated. "Whatever made him make that smell is close to the surface. He needs to get rid of it before we start back out."

"Ooh." I nodded in understanding as I helped the big guy down.

Henry padded over to the soft shoulder of the roadway, did a quick once over to make sure no one was looking, and then went about his business. I think I saw a couple of crows die as they circled above and into the waft of air that came from his pile.

"Better?" I asked him.

He did seem relieved. I thought he knew better than to eat anything my sister dropped. She was getting better, though; the things she would pull off the stove were starting to resemble real food more and more. Not that they tasted any better, they just 'looked' more edible.

In a few more minutes, we were back on the road.

"Is it safe?" Tracy asked.

She could have been referring to any number of things. And I had not a single answer for any of them.

CHAPTER 2 – MIKE JOURNAL ENTRY 2

The ride had been somewhat muted after Henry's umm...outburst. I'm thinking most of us in the car were more or less holding our breath just in case. I know I was even driving about twenty miles per hour slower just so I could stop faster if the need arose. Luckily, we'd only had one false alarm; Justin had moved in his seat causing the material to squeak. I had the front end of the truck dipping down I was bringing it to a halt so quickly.

"What do you think the odds of this are?" BT had asked. "I mean it's pretty much like looking for a needle in a haystack."

"How big is the haystack?" I asked him in all seriousness.

"You know it's just an analogy, right?" he queried back.

"I mean, if the stack isn't too big and maybe we have a giant white tarp underneath when we separate the straw we could probably find the needle fairly easily. Maybe even get some magnets. That would be fucking genius."

"Just turn the damn truck around," he told me. "I'm not sure how long I can be in here with your crazy ass."

"We'll find him," I said.

"You're that sure?" he asked in all seriousness.

"Yes...there's no other alternative." What I left unsaid was that if we didn't, this trip would end with a bullet for Justin and himself. Eventually they both would succumb to the zombie virus they each housed inside themselves.

We were nearly to the New Hampshire border when our first—and I could only hope, last—spate of trouble reared its ugly head. I had to slow the truck as we were coming upon zombies. So far, only in the ones and occasional twos, and then they really started to thicken. A bunch were meandering along the shoulder; but most tended to stay in the roadway, making driving become more like a video game as I tried to avoid hitting them.

"Oh, *these* zombies you avoid," Tracy said sarcastically, referring to her Jeep Liberty I had totaled seemingly years ago on our quest to Walmart to get Justin and subsequently Tommy.

"You've got to let it go, woman," I said, not risking turning back towards her. One, because that would take my eyes off the road; and two, I didn't want to see how much I had angered her.

"This is Eliza's work," Tommy said as he placed his hands on the window and stared out. "She called them here, and now that she's gone…"

"They've lost purpose," I finished. Made sense. They had a new purpose now, though. As they saw us, they started to congeal on our space, which was somewhat funny. I mean, at least at first. It was hopeless for them, but that abruptly changed as we came upon the main part of the horde.

"My God, there must be hundreds," Tracy said in alarm.

Yeah there were hundreds…adding up to a thousand or more. Plus they looked hungry; and considering that we were the only items on the menu, well, you get the point.

"Now what?" BT asked me.

"Should have just taken the damn Gatlin gun," I told him.

I had the truck crawling at a measly ten mph. We were in imminent danger of becoming encircled. Going forward was not going to happen. Not without a tank. And back was rapidly losing its appeal as well.

"Everyone got a seatbelt?" I asked as I buckled myself in.

"You can't possibly go through them." BT's eyes were growing wide.

I smiled a sick grin at him. I felt like I had just eaten old, slimy, cheap, (you know the extra fatty kind), uncooked bacon, and maybe it had a coating of green with a few maggots thrown in just for effect. Yeah, it was *that* bad.

I heard belts buckling so quickly it almost sounded as if it had been choreographed.

"Dad?" Travis asked.

"It'll be alright," I lied.

I took out my first zombie as I hit him dead center with the grill of the truck. His head struck the hood with such force that it sent a spray of broken teeth and blood halfway up the windshield. I was glad for small favors when, instead of his whole body coming up the truck, we were just momentarily jostled around as I ran over him.

"Gross," Justin said. He had turned around to see the damage done. I'd seen enough of it in my rear view mirror to be happy I was only viewing a six-inch-by-two-inch rectangle. I couldn't be sure, but it looked like I had run over its midsection, pushing internal organs out through its mouth. Long ribbons of what looked like skinned animal parts lay on the road next to its head. The slimy bacon was sounding worlds better right now.

The nose of the truck dipped down as I drove off the road and into a culvert. My heart skipped a beat or seventeen as I dug the front end into the upslope. The wheels spun for a moment, I think it was zombies who actually saved us. A few slammed into the rear end and lent just enough force to allow my rear wheels to catch and make the truck start up the other side.

I rolled down my window. "Thanks for the push!" I yelled as I waved. It's quite possible I wasn't completely under control of my own emotions. (Lack of blood flow to the brain most likely being the cause—see earlier part about heart skipping beats).

"You *are* fucking nuts!" BT yelled, looking around I think for another seatbelt to strap over himself.

"Please tell me you haven't just figured that out?" Tracy asked. She had both hands wrapped around the back of his seat as the truck was bucking wildly back and forth and up and down.

We were off-road now, the high grass and weeds making it a particularly difficult chore to see the surrounding terrain. I saw the small barbed wire fence and heard the high-pitched twang as we snapped through the line. I exhaled hard as my chest was forced into the steering wheel. We were in danger of high centering over a large rock, the screech of metal was deafening. I could only hope I hadn't just taken out the oil pan.

A group of birds flew up as I was barreling down on them. "Pull!" I shouted enthusiastically. This only made BT dig his fingers harder into the dashboard.

"Damn you, Talbot," he muttered.

I was racing across the expansive open field, thankful to whoever had spent the time to clear it of trees. My hands were swinging back and forth on the steering wheel so rapidly from the uneven ground it really did appear like I was 'playing' at driving much like a child might.

"They're falling back," Justin said, probably in the hopes that I would slow down.

The rising of the oil pressure was a contributing factor in determining that I needed to go even faster to put as much distance between us and them as possible.

"I smell smoke," Tracy said.

"That'd be the engine," I told her, I could only hope it wasn't actually caused by the scummy pretend bacon sloshing around in my stomach.

"Not one fucking day, not one day could you make it with my truck!" Blared over the car speakers.

"What the hell?" I asked, looking around.

"I hooked up a two-way radio to the car sound

17

system," Ron's voice drifted out.

"Sorry about the truck," I told him.

"Screw the truck, how much trouble are you in?" he asked, concerned.

"No video camera?" I asked, quickly sweeping a hand across the front of the stereo.

"Mike," Ron said smoothly.

"Umm...enough," I said vaguely, not trying to alarm the rest of the occupants.

"Where are you at? I'll send help."

"This is kind of like On-Star," I told him.

"BT, where are you guys?" he asked, completely deciding to skip over me.

"Pretty close to the New Hampshire border, saw a sign saying something about toll booths," BT replied. I think he was happy to be doing anything else besides watching me drive.

"You guys must be close to Kittery," Ron said.

"Did he say something about kittens?" I almost shrieked.

"Kittery...he said Kittery." BT did his best to calm me down. "But right now Ron we're off...umph...off the map. Will you slow down so I can talk?" he roared.

"Sure, sure, I'll let them know what I'm doing," I told him as I pointed behind us. A legion of zombies blocked out the entire rear view.

"You've never listened to me before, don't start now."

"Oooh, fudge," I whistled.

"What's *oh fudge*?" Ron asked.

We had narrowly missed a metal hydrant sticking up from the ground. My guess was that once it had been used for agricultural purposes, it had almost become our demise. As if the ruts and valleys of this uneven land weren't enough, now I had to wonder how many of those 'meat sticks' were around. (Is further explanation necessary? See, if we got stuck it would be like 'meat on a stick' for the zombies.) Not the best analogy, but I was scared; we were on suspect turf with a failing vehicle, and no place to hole up. Oh yeah, and I almost forgot to add the part about the zombies chasing us. The *shitload* of zombies chasing us.

"Road!" Justin yelled so loudly I nearly lost control of the truck altogether.

I was going to thank Captain Obvious, but I was too relieved after our venture in the unchartered.

"Look out, man!" BT shouted.

It was not enough warning, the passenger side of the truck rose precariously high as I hit what looked like the rear axle of some large truck, lying in the road. The impact had either shifted the tire off the rim or blown it out completely; didn't matter which really. We now had a disabled wheel to go with the rest of the problems. Coolant was blowing all over the windshield, smearing the glass, making it that much more difficult. I felt rather than saw when we touched down onto pavement. Smoke and fluids were pouring from the hood; the truck was hobbling along like we had square tires.

"I'm not hearing anything. Is everyone alright?" Ron asked.

We took our turns letting him and each other know we had made it through to the other side nearly unscathed.

"How about the truck?" he asked.

"Umm…it's salvageable," I told him as the poor thing creaked and groaned its final death throes.

"He means it is *salvage*," Tracy clarified.

I glared at her.

"Son of a bitch. Find somewhere to stay I'll start getting things rounded up. This is on tape, so just let me know where you go and we'll find you. Mike…" He paused.

"You might want to hurry," I told him as I looked back. The speeders were doing what speeders do, haul ass. "Okay, baby, you're not quite dead yet, get us out of here," I begged the truck, caressing the dashboard.

"I heard that," Ron said.

"You're supposed to be hurrying," I snapped as the front fender sparked along the roadway. We were on the outskirts of Kittery, I guess, not that I really knew. The houses were much too close to the roadway and didn't look too particularly stalwartly to withstand any sustained zombie attack. By the time I hit the main drag, the engine was beginning to cough and sputter, the businesses here looked like they catered to tourists and the large front-facing picture windows looked like a large invitation to the zombies about to visit. This way they could see the food inside before they sampled the wares.

"Take a right," Tracy said as she slapped my arm. I don't think it was intentionally so hard, but one never knows what past transgression she was just now remembering.

"Shoe store?" I asked stupidly, rubbing my arm.

"Oh," I said appreciatively when I saw the building up ahead. It was the town library, made from brick and mortar; from this distance it looked somewhat like a castle. I could only hope its defenses were as formidable. The building was huge, and two stories high. The windows...the blessed first story windows were at least seven or eight feet off the ground. No zombies would be coming through those. There was, however, the wide staircase that led to the front double doors. That of course was a problem. But right now those doors were shut, and I hoped they stayed that way.

"Ron, you still there?" I asked. I waited for a moment before I remembered he said this was recording. "Okay we're going to the library...(I looked around)...on Wentworth. Big brick behemoth. Didn't think this many people read in Maine. See you soon, big brother." The last part he may or may not heard as the engine began to throw a rod, the loud metallic thumping making it difficult to think, much less talk. Time was running short; I pushed my foot heavily down and was rewarded with a spurt of speed followed immediately by the seizing of the engine. I was now coasting towards the library; thankfully, it was downhill.

"Talbot, the library," BT said.

"Yup." I told him.

"It's coming up."

"Yup," I replied.

"Fuck." He said resignedly, once again bracing himself.

The truck jolted as I jumped the curb, we crossed over the cement walkway and were now riding the brick pathway to the front. A handrail bisected the wide stairway, a fair amount of the truck's momentum was taken as I hit that rail, shearing it from its moorings. I had at least one of the gods on my side that day as the front end of the truck kissed the front doors and stopped with hardly a tap on the brakes on my part.

"Can I look yet?" BT asked.

"Um…sure," I told him, "but don't look back. Everyone out." More superfluous words had never been spoken; even Henry was halfway out by the time my words ceased.

Tracy looked at me questioningly. "The windows," I told her, pointing.

Travis, Justin, and Tommy were busy gathering all our supplies. I grabbed the shotgun, went down the stairwell and off to the left, blowing a hole in the closest window.

"BT!" I shouted. I was going to have him toss me in, and then I realized I could do it on my own. I may have lost my soul, but at least now I could play in the NBA. I got onto the ledge of the window and cleaned the broken glass with the butt of the gun. I hopped inside the building, taking a real quick glance around, making sure we weren't jumping into a mess worse than the one we were leaving.

I was pretty certain all was well when I turned back to the window. What I saw, I did not like. The truck had been losing speed for a long way, but I didn't think it was enough to allow the zombies to catch up. They were streaming onto the roadway.

"Tracy, get over here!" I shouted.

She must have seen them, because she didn't so much as tell me to 'hold one horse'. With her hand outstretched I pulled her up easily.

"Grab my gun and make sure nothing bites me in the ass, please," I told her as I put her down.

BT handed up Henry who apparently thought playing Superman was the coolest thing ever. His stubby tail was wagging rapidly. The boys were now tossing me up the ammo and food and whatever else was in the truck. Most of my attention was on the zombies coming our way.

"How much more shit is there?" I asked as I deposited another box on the floor.

"Last one." Travis jumped up to grab the ledge. I reached down under his arms and yanked him in.

Justin stuck his hand out, I was somewhat alarmed at how light he felt; it was as if the disease were eating him from the inside out. "Travis, Justin, carefully check out this building, make sure there's no zombies and no way for them to get in."

Travis nodded and then they were gone.

"Go," BT urged Tommy. I stepped aside as Tommy effortlessly jumped up and through the window.

"Show off," I told him. He smiled and turned back to help me with BT.

"Any time," I told BT who was watching the zombies. The fastest of them were now on the walkway.

"You going to be able to pull me up?" He was looking pretty scared, and who could blame him.

"Don't worry, fat is lighter than muscle," I told him. He glared at me as he stuck his hand out. Even with my added strength, he was heavy. Luckily, Tommy shouldered his way into the window frame and helped me—okay, more like did it himself. It got a little awkward when we had to turn him sideways to fit through the frame, but other than that, we were all in and at least safe for the moment.

"Couldn't you have just checked to see if the window was unlocked?" BT asked when the waft of zombies drifted through the opening. Even Henry seemed repulsed as he walked away to investigate his new digs.

I was still looking at the broken window when Travis came back. "There's a basement door and a fire escape on the second floor. Both open outwards, are steel, and definitely locked."

With the front doors blocked by the truck, we were in pretty good shape. I mean other than being surrounded by a thousand zombies. Yeah all was grand.

"Could be worse," I told Tracy. "We could have got stuck in the shoe store."

She laughed. "I don't know how you do it."

"Do what?" I asked.

"Make me laugh in these situations." She squeezed my hand.

I didn't ask her what the alternative was. "Want to go play librarian?" I asked huskily as I playfully swatted her butt.

"What does that even mean?" she asked.

"Who cares?" I told her.

"Wait, I really need to get all the facts in a row here. Okay, first we're in a library with two of our children, three including Tommy. We're surrounded by zombies waiting for your brother to rescue us somehow, and yet you have time to think about sex?"

"Well, duh," I told her. "The day I stop thinking about having sex with you, I hope I'm dead."

"Let's go see if we can find a quiet area."

"That worked?" I asked as she led the way.

BT was griping as he tried to find things to cover the broken window. He looked over as he watched us leaving.

"Umm, we're going to check to make sure the books are stacked properly," I told him.

"Holy crap, Talbot, you finally started shitting gold coins." He was smiling as he pulled the Maine state flag down and pinned it up over the opening.

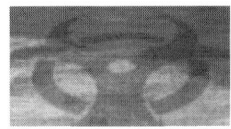

CHAPTER 3 – MRS. DENEAUX

"What the hell is this?" Mrs. Deneaux asked the empty cab of her eighteen-wheeler.

She had decided to forgo the main highway leading out of the state, preferring to drive the coastal Route 1. It was slower going, but she felt like she would be less likely to encounter trouble. And that had been the case right up until she saw the obvious trap set-up. A small SUV was parked perpendicular to the roadway straddling the median line and most of the two lanes. The driver's side door was open, and a man was on the roadway lying on his stomach with his face pointed towards her.

She had stopped the truck a good fifty yards from the ploy, the engine was idling as she surveyed the scene. She cackled, the truck hitched as she placed it into first gear. She was about to pop it into third when she blatted the horn loudly. The man in the roadway's eyes got large as he saw the huge truck barreling down on him.

"Feeling better?" she asked his retreating form as he ran to the side of the road.

She was laughing as she sent shards of the SUV hurtling into space. The truck barely slowed.

"Crazy bitch!" the man yelled at her.

She heard a shot ring out from the other side of her, and then nothing, as if whoever had shot had thought better about wasting bullets.

"Idiots."

She continued down the road. She was unsure of her future when she'd left Michael's brother's home. And she'd certainly never foreseen Eliza falling to that idiot; well, technically the idiot's wife. She would have never thrown her lot in with the vampire if she'd known that.

"Can't know everything, Vivian. Otherwise you would have cut your husband's balls off *before* he cheated and shut off the money." She cackled again. "It wouldn't have been too hard, they were just dried up little nuggets anyway, looked like prunes. That would have been so much more satisfying than killing him. I don't know what it is about men and their precious little packages. Looks like a worm carrying worn leather luggage."

She was thoroughly enjoying her wit when she saw her second human encounter of the day. Her shriveled heart accelerated a bit as the person had a slight resemblance to Paul, Mike's friend who she had pretty much killed by proxy, sending him away with no shoes and no weapon.

The momentary heart hiccup evened out when she realized the hitchhiking stranger was not him. Same color hair, but it was receding slightly, and this stranger had a thick beard with some reddish undertones. She looked around to see if this was again some sort of trap. She stopped the truck well ahead of the man, he started to run towards her. She beeped her horn, he looked up and she motioned for him to come over to her side.

"Thank you, thank you," he was saying over and over again.

"Don't go getting all excited just yet," she said down to him. "Turn around."

When he didn't immediately do as she requested she aimed her seven-inch barrel Colt .45 at him. A small hatchet was in the small of his back, held in place by his belt.

"You planning on burying that in my skull?" she asked.

"There's zombies, did you expect me to be unarmed?"

"What else you have on you?"

"That's it."

"Strip," she told him.

"I'll do no such thing."

"Bye," Mrs. Deneaux told him as the truck slid effortlessly into first gear.

"Wait, wait!" He started to unbutton his shirt. She brought the truck to a halt.

"Hurry up, I don't have all day," she told him as he sat on the pavement to pull his shoes off.

"Shit there's zombies!" he said in a panic. A small group was coming up on them. "Let me in," he pleaded grabbing his things.

"Not until I see everything."

"The zombies."

"Better get moving then, either with the clothes…or with your feet."

"Never heard of trust?" He scrambled to undo his belt.

"Oh, I've heard of it, never understood it much. The more people say 'trust me' the more likely they are to screw you over."

"Cynical bastard," she heard him mutter. "Here are you happy?" he asked in his briefs, doing a quick three-sixty to show he wasn't hiding anything more.

"Them too." She motioned with her gun.

"There's no time!" he shouted.

"I've got plenty."

"Listen! I do not have a shotgun shoved up my ass!"

"That would be a neat trick. Off with the underwear or I'll be on my merry little way."

He looked to the zombies and then his potential savior, trying to decide who was the biggest threat. "Fucking fine!" He whipped his underwear down.

"Definitely no weapon there," she cackled as she looked down upon his manhood. "I've seen Ken dolls packing more heat."

"Can I get in now?" he asked angrily.

"Oh, I suppose so."

The man quickly picked up his belongings and ran around the front of the truck. Mrs. Deneaux hit the lock and let him in. She leveled her gun upon him. "Hand over the axe," she said evenly as he stood on the running board.

"You going to shoot me?"

"If I'd wanted to do that, I would have. What kind of narcissistic, self-absorbed bitch do you think I am?"

"If you weren't pointing that gun at me, I'd probably tell you." He handed the axe over.

She laughed. "That's the funniest thing anyone's said to me all day."

"Can I put my clothes back on?"

She looked one more time over at him. "Please do, all that pale skin is burning my eyes." She got the truck rolling just as the first of the zombies impacted with her front end. The truck kept right on rolling as it flattened three of them into the pavement.

Mrs. Deneaux's new passenger braced himself as if the truck cared at all for the small speed bumps.

"What's your name?" Mrs. Deneaux asked, completely unconcerned with the zombies that had congregated in the roadway.

"You should look out," he said in alarm.

"For them? They don't care." She picked up speed. A plume of brackish blood spread from the impact, two different colored eyeballs smacked the windshield. "Don't see that every day."

"Dennis, my name is Dennis," the hitchhiker said, keeping an eye on the side-mounted rear view mirror.

"Well?"

"Well what?" Dennis asked, turning to her.

"Did I get a strike?" she asked, referring to the zombies that had been set up loosely like bowling pins.

"You're sick, but you left a seven-ten split."

"You keep that up and we'll get along fabulously. What's your last name?"

"Waggoner." Dennis shifted around to put his briefs and pants back on.

"What's your story?"

"I bet yours is more interesting, but I'll give you the short of it," he told her. "I was staying at my dad's."

Mrs. Deneaux looked over at him. "Little old to be a cellar dweller aren't you?" she asked haughtily.

"Right before the zombies had come, I was in the midst of a divorce from my wife. We lived out in Arizona…where she's from. When I caught her cheating with the garbage man I decided to move back to my home town of Walpole."

"The garbage man, was that a step up?"

"I see you've taken your show on the road."

"No kids?"

"Dodged a bullet there. Apparently God frowns upon demon spawn and human procreation."

"Where's Walpole?"

"Massachusetts, south of Boston," Dennis said, slightly muffled as he pulled his undershirt on.

"What are you doing here?" she asked. "You're a few hours from home."

"My father's place was great. He owned a townhome in the center of town. Place was like a fortress. Had a couple of skirmishes with zombies and some idiots that wanted in, but no one ever did. Get in, I mean. Once the zombies started retreating…"

"Hibernating," Mrs. Deneaux explained.

"That makes sense. Well, once they started doing that, it was pretty easy to go out on supply runs. Although, we were never really in too much danger. My dad lived in a retirement building. Most of the folks, well, they died in those first few days."

Mrs. Deneaux thought about. 'Sure; most of those people would have been first in line for the shots, and then first in line at the hospital when they started to get sick.'

"We just took what we needed and shared with the survivors that were in there."

"Did your father get bit?" she asked.

"No, good old fashioned flu did him in."

"Ironic," Mrs. Deneaux said.

"How so?"

"It was the flu inoculation that started all this."

"The flu shot?"

"You didn't know? I thought that to be common knowledge."

"No wonder there were so few residents left."

"The bulb burns brightly above your head," she said snidely.

"Now I can see why you were alone in this cab."

She laughed. "You still haven't answered why you're up here. Why not stay in your father's place?"

"After I buried him, I did stay for a while. I guess I just got lonely and I sure wasn't going to look for my ex, though. She probably was leading a group of the zombies around on her own sinister designs. I have, uh *had*, a couple of friends out in Colorado, but I couldn't even conceive of making that trip."

Mrs. Deneaux got a tingle up her spine. "Any chance your exes name was Eliza?"

"What? No. My friends out in Colorado…one of them has family up here in Maine, as close to being my family as can be possible without blood. It seemed like an easier trek up here, at least until my Monte Carlo broke down."

It can't be, Mrs. Deneaux thought. She had put the pistol back in its holster, but now she was reaching for it.

"Who is this second family?" she asked, already knowing the impossible answer.

"Talbot. My friend out in Colorado is Mike, but I know his whole family…Ron, Gary, Glenn, Lyndsey, and their dad Tony. All of them except for Glenn live up here, and who knows, maybe Mike came home too."

Her left hand wrapped around the grip. She squeezed it so tight it hurt her arthritic fingers. "They're all dead," she told him, uncharacteristically losing her cool.

"What? You can't possibly know that. And why would you even say such a thing?"

"It's the truth." She pulled the gun an inch or so from her holster. She was debating just putting a bullet in him right now. "I was with Michael when he left Colorado."

Dennis was looking at her. "You're lying. Why?"

"Is this the same Michael Talbot that lived at Little Turtle? Had a wife named Tracy, three kids, Nicole, Justin and Travis? And a smelly beast named Henry?"

Dennis was looking at her incredulously, his head nodding. He was thinking back on what he'd told her, it certainly wasn't all that. "You know Mike?"

"Knew," she corrected him. "I barely escaped with my life. His brother's house was overrun with zombies. I did my best to save them all, in the end it wasn't enough."

Dennis was just staring at her. She was having a hard time discerning how much he believed. In the end it was grief that saved Dennis' life. He turned away just as a torrent of tears sluiced down his face. "They're all I knew." He hitched. "I...I thought for sure they'd be alright."

"It's a hard world," Mrs. Deneaux said, taking a sidelong glance at him.

It was many miles before anyone spoke.

"Where are you going?" Dennis asked, wiping his face clean.

"Going to try and find somewhere safe. Somewhere with a community and a high wall. A real high wall."

"I was going to ask you for a ride to find a car, but now that seems useless. Do you mind if I stay with you?"

Mrs. Deneaux almost told him no; being this close to one of Michael's friends could not be good. For some reason, the fates had aligned to put him in her path. That was something she couldn't figure out. For good or bad, she would see this through, at least partly. As soon as it looked somewhat bad, she'd toss him or shoot him, whatever the case necessitated. "Just don't try to make any moves on me," she cackled.

She's nuts, Dennis thought, *and she's all I've got.* "I'll do my best," he told her.

CHAPTER 4 – MIKE JOURNAL ENTRY 3

"I can barely remember my name," I said to Tracy.
"What?" she asked .
"You f—"
"Talbot!"
"...my brains out," I finished.
"It's stuff like this that makes me think twice and sometimes three times about doing anything with you. Get your clothes on before people start looking for us."
"Oh, I don't know, all this nudity is very liberating," I told her, wishing I could just lie there a few years longer, even if we were in the horror book section.
"Yeah? Tell that to the zombies," she said, looking at my rapidly deflating manhood.
"You really know where to hit a person."
"I love you, Talbot. Now get your ass up. I'll meet you downstairs."
"Nice view," I told her as she walked away.
She flipped me the bird, but I could tell she was smiling.
"I might die tonight, but at least I'll go out happy." I stood and began donning my duds. I had just finished tying my boots when BT rounded the corner.
"Ever hear of your inside voice?" he asked.
"What?" I could feel fingers of heat traveling up my neck.
"Acoustics are pretty good in this place," he said, smiling. "The boys couldn't get down in the basement fast enough to go and check it out, been down there the entire time. Even Henry looked a little embarrassed."

"Shit. Does Tracy know? She'll kill me."

"Oh, from the sounds of it, I think she'll be fine for the time being." He was smiling ear-to-ear. "Always one for ambience I see," BT said, pointing to the column of scary tomes.

When I caught up to her, Tracy seemed completely unaware that none of her kids would look her—or me for that matter—in the eye. *Well this sucks*, I thought.

"Anything worth noting in the basement?" I asked them, trying to change what they were thinking about. Talk about uncomfortable.

Justin was conspicuously looking off to his left. "There's windows, but they're small and don't even open."

"Yeah and the door is steel," Travis added. "It's locked and we stacked a bunch of furniture against it."

"Big bunch," Tommy said. I swear his face was a couple of shades deeper red than I'd ever seen.

Henry was at least happy to see me. He came over, tail wagging. I was happy to lean over and pet behind his ears. It gave me the chance to not have to try and ignore the six hundred pound gorilla in the room.

Travis had gone over to the windows. "There's more coming. Should we start shooting them?"

"We'll hold off for now. Wait for the cavalry to come, I'd imagine we're going to need the rounds then." I was looking around. With the appropriate supplies, we could hold out here forever. I was sort of amazed that someone else hadn't thought of it. If books were edible we'd be set.

"When we get out of here, find Doc and get Justin and BT fixed, we should find a fort," I blurted out.

"That's a lot of whens and ifs," BT said.

"The last military installation we went to didn't work out so well," Tracy said, referring to Camp Custer.

"I'm talking like that fort we visited in Bucksport Maine, Fort Knox. That place has like two-foot thick walls. We could stay there forever."

"That place is about as comfortable as I suspect Mrs. Deneaux's place would be," she replied.

She was right; the fort was cold and dank, even in the middle of the summer, we'd freeze before winter ever set in. "I wonder what the battle axe is up to?"

We had searched for her body after the battle with no luck. I couldn't imagine a zombie eating her, more like the other way around would be my guess.

"She can't still be alive can she?" BT asked. "Eliza had to have killed her."

"My guess is she scared Eliza, too," I said.

"It would be just like that old bird to make it," BT said.

"She's a survivor for sure. Let's just hope we've seen the last of her," Tracy replied.

"More like a case of herpes, got a feeling she'll be revisiting," I said.

"Wonderful," BT and Tracy said.

CHAPTER 5 – MRS. DENEAUX

"Go check it out," Mrs. Deneaux said.

"Why me?" Dennis asked, looking at the store-front.

"You don't expect me to go dashing about do you? I'm a frail old woman."

"You're an older woman, granted. Frail though? I don't think so." Dennis exited the truck. "Can I have a gun?" he asked, coming up on her side of the big rig.

"I should think not." She handed his hand axe down.

"I've made my share of poor life decisions," he said, looking up at her. "I think I'm adding to the tally."

"Stop being overly dramatic and go get some supplies. If you take too long I won't wait."

"And here I thought we were making inroads with our friendship."

Dennis headed toward the front entrance. The reverberation of the engine bouncing off the storefront blocked out all other noises. He thought about asking her to shut it off, but he'd been with her long enough to know the answer. His boot crunched on mounds of broken glass, all from the windows, the door, however, was surprisingly intact.

A small bell placed strategically over the door heralded his entrance. The foreign sound almost sent him running. The inside stunk of bleach and the all too familiar stench of death, like there had been a hideous crime performed here and someone had tried valiantly to clean up after. The store was destroyed; there was little of any value still left inside. A gun battle had raged and, by the splatter, the ones wielding the weapons had used shotguns.

Dennis went in a little farther. He felt like he was

between a rock and a hard place. If he came out with nothing, she might leave; and if he stayed in too long, she'd leave. The more he thought about it, the better of an idea that sounded like. There was more to the Mike story and the flippant way she had dismissed their deaths. He'd stay with her if only to find out. A glint of glass caught his attention. He bent over, pushing away a half-destroyed box of Cheerios.

"Well shit, not my flavor, but I'll drink it."

He wrapped his hand around the neck of a bottle of bourbon somehow unscathed in the melee. He was still looking at the label as he stood. It took him one constriction of his heart to recognize that there was a zombie standing before him. The monster seemed almost as confused, but reacted quicker, its teeth trying to bite down on the bottle held out before it.

Dennis heard a resounding crack. He thought the bottle had been broken, and that had been proven when he felt sharp shards sprinkle onto his hand. He realized his mistake when he saw the broken bits of blood-stained teeth stuck to his hand.

"Gross, man!"

Dennis did his best to keep the bottle between him and the teeth. He brought up his axe-laden right hand, swinging it with all the force he could muster, his balance was pushed onto his back foot and he could not put as much into it as he hoped. Yet, the blade dug deeply into the soft tissue at the top of the zombie's shoulder. The skin split apart in a wide wedge as the sharp steel sliced through and struck the collar bone, shearing it in two. The zombie's left arm hung uselessly by its side as the connective muscles and tissues were hewn through. It cared little for the damage wrought.

With its right arm, it snagged hold of the bottle, trying to bring it and its wielder in closer to its dangerous teeth. Dennis most likely could have got away if he had merely let go of the bottle; the thought just never occurred to him. He pulled the blade free with a wet 'plopping' sound and reared back for another attempt. This time he caught the zombie on the side of the head, neatly bisecting the ear. He thought he was going to be sick when half of the zombie's ear fell to the floor, with an audible squishing sound. The zombie's head cracked like an over-boiled eggshell. Black ooze the consistency of bad Jell-O leaked out of the devastating wound. The zombie shook violently for the span of a few heartbeats and fell to the floor, nearly taking the fought-over bottle with it.

"That would have sucked," Dennis said as he fumbled with it before regaining control.

He had been so pre-occupied with his fight that he did not hear the tinkle of the bell, the explosion of the pistol round going off would have been hard to miss, though. The sound had not finished echoing throughout the store when he felt the vibrations of something falling behind him.

"Mike would never have turned his back on a zombie," Deneaux said around a cigarette.

"Damn." Dennis turned to see a zombie that had gotten to within handshaking distance behind him. He wasn't sure which was scarier; that, or the crazy old bat with the large caliber gun framed in the doorway. "Th-thank you," Dennis stammered.

"If you could have done the same, I'm sure you would have." She approached, deftly stepping over the fallen zombie.

"Aren't you afraid it could still be alive?" Dennis asked.

"Oh, sweetie, it was a head shot." She dragged her smoke-smelling left hand across the side of his face. "What do you have here? Twenty-year-old scotch. Fantastic," she said as she easily took it from him. With that, she walked back out of the store.

"Bitch is crazy," Dennis said, following soon after.

He could not, however, shake the feeling that he had somehow been safer in the store with the 'live' zombies than in the truck with Deneaux, who was chugging scotch like it was ice water. She would occasionally hand him the bottle, and he'd take sips; not because he enjoyed it, but because she was plowing down the highway at speeds in excess of eighty or so miles per hour and she was clearly lit. He figured if he were going to die, it might as well be with a buzz.

Deneaux started singing. Dennis thought it was Sinatra. He quickly started talking, because the sound she was making was about as grating as listening to squirrels have their nuts torn off.

"How did you meet Mike?" Dennis asked.

Deneaux's singing stopped immediately. She looked over at him warily, her eyes narrowing like a cat getting ready to pounce. When she figured there was no ulterior motive in his question, she began to talk.

"We lived in the same complex. Can you believe that? A commoner like him and me sharing the same residential area. Idiot was screwing his secretary."

"What? Mike was cheating on Tracy? I don't believe you," Dennis said incredulously.

"Michael? No, he's too high and mighty to stoop to that. High moral fiber and all."

Dennis thought that sounded more like a slight than a compliment, especially with the tone in which it was delivered.

"My husband, well, that's a different story. If he could have a got a watermelon to tell him what a fantastic lover he was, he would have fucked that as well. Oh right, you want to hear about Michael." Mrs. Deneaux smiled when she looked over at the shocked expression on Dennis' face. "Well, let's say that, due to circumstances that I should have controlled better, I found myself living at Little Turtle where Michael also resided. We held out for a while, but even with my best efforts, the zombies still were able to get in. I was able to get on a truck much like this one and barely escaped with my life. For some inexplicable reason, the driver, Alex, after being miles away, turned back around and rescued Mike and his family."

"How did he know to turn around? Radio?"

"Something about this kid Tommy in Michael's group being psychically linked to Alex' wife Marta. Personally, I think that's a pile of rubbish. Want to hear the good part?" she asked. She continued, not wanting or waiting for a reply from her passenger. "Tommy is...I mean, *was*, a vampire." She looked over quickly to see if her slip had been picked up. Dennis was busy wincing after his last nip of the caustic alcohol. His eyes flew open at the mention of vampire. "Oh, I can see you don't believe in vampires. Well, let me tell you, they exist...had one pursuing us across the whole damn country."

"Tommy, the vampire, was chasing you guys? I'm having a hard time believing you."

"It was his sister Eliza, the first woman I've met that's meaner than me. Although, now that I think about it, maybe that isn't the case, because that bitch is dead and I'm still going strong." She lit another cigarette. "Still having trouble with the vampire part?" she asked, almost tenderly. "You're going to have to trust me on this one. I made one of the biggest mistakes of my life when I threw my lot in with Alex and Paul and the rest of the twits when Mike and his family split from us. They were heading up to Maine. I just wrongly figured that with him gone we'd shake Eliza. I had no idea how inept at survival my group was going to be. That Paul couldn't shoot. His wife Erin, at least she knew which end to point."

"Wait, Paul and Erin? As in Ginson?" Dennis asked.

"Oh, right. I guess if they were good friends of Mike that you'd most likely know them as well. Makes sense."

"Oh, my God," Dennis said excitedly. "I can't believe this! How are they?"

"Dead," she said flatly.

His head dropped rapidly.

"Paul was eaten by cats and his lovely wife…well, she made her last stand with the Talbots."

"Cats?" Dennis asked through tear-glazed eyes.

"They weren't zombies if that's what you're asking, just garden variety starving cats."

"How is that possible?"

Deneaux ignored the question. "It was Mike that came to our rescue when Eliza had us pinned down. I might have been able to have gotten us out of there, but I'll give him credit when it's due."

"How?" Dennis asked, trying to pull himself out of his depths of mourning.

"Eliza was using Paul as a means to get to Mike, for some unfathomable reason she wanted him dead badly. He truly had a penchant for pissing people off—especially women—probably told her that her fangs weren't big enough." A sound much like a crypt opening emanated from her mouth. It was meant to be a laugh.

"Yeah, that's Mike. Always too much truth and too little tact. I loved him for that."

"He got us out of that much like he did every obstacle placed before him…sheer stupid luck. Why I hadn't seen that earlier I'm not sure. Perhaps I had, but the thought of being able to get out from under the gaze of Eliza had its own benefits. It started to all fall apart when Mike tried to put a stop to the whole thing. We launched an offensive without the proper weapons or personnel for that matter. Lost Brian, you don't know him, and Paul, on that ill-fated attack. Mike almost died as well, but like I said he has an uncanny ability to preserve life and limb. Gary—"

"Gary? As in Gary Talbot."

"One in the same. A little on the nuttier side of the Talbot tree, but he could shoot. He led us all back to Maine. It was good for a few days and then Mike came and death was close behind him. In the end, Eliza did Michael in. Tracy killed Eliza and then the zombies destroyed everything. Michael had gotten me up into this very truck to keep me safe before his showdown with Eliza. I stayed in here for three days until it was clear of enough zombies that I could leave. The devastation was immense, genetic debris was everywhere."

"Are you sure none of the Talbots survived?"

"Yes," she answered a little too quickly. "Ron's house was on fire and I could hear them screaming from the cab. It was quite shattering." She swiped away a non-existent tear. "How long have you known Mike?" she asked, diverting his attention away from the fact that she was not all that distraught.

"Seemingly forever." Deneaux noticed that her bad acting job had passed him by. Dennis was lost is a sea of nostalgic fog. I was new to the high school, heart of Red Sox country, and I was wearing a Yankees hat. He still befriended me."

"Is that important?"

"More than you know." He laughed slightly. "We became fast friends, Mike, Paul and me."

"That is devastating to realize you just lost two of your closest friends."

Dennis couldn't tell from her tone if she was really empathetic, or if she was just enjoying twisting the knife of realization. He continued on, not for her, but for himself. "I owe Mike my life. Paul got into a pretty bad car accident and Mike pulled us both from the wreckage."

"He was in the automobile with you as well?"

"He got ejected."

"There was enough force that he was ejected from a car and yet he was still able to get up and pull his friends free from a destroyed car?"

"Burning…the car was burning."

"Hmmm…seems that Michael has been doing his

death-defying acts for a lot longer than I'd realized."

"I always wanted to repay that debt. Now it appears I won't get that chance."

"You're not going to get all morose on me, are you? Are you one of those weeping winos? Give me the bottle back."

"You don't understand. He was all I had left."

"Now we have each other," she said after taking a large swig.

This time he hoped she was joking, but she was as tough to read as a snake. If they were all each other had, he figured he would have been better staying at his dad's. Still, if she was a means to an end and got him to other people, he'd deal with her crazy ass until then. It hurt to put Maine in the rearview mirror though.

CHAPTER 6 – MIKE JOURNAL ENTRY 4

We didn't do much as we sat there. I was beginning to think Ron wasn't coming, or he had taken some circuitous route that took him past Montreal first. Can't say I'd blame him; Montreal is a pretty sweet city. As long as he brought some Canadian beer back with him, everything would be fine. I picked up book after book, thinking that eventually I'd find one I could start to read, but anything that didn't have pop-up pictures and start with 'See' I couldn't concentrate on long enough. Even if I found something worth reading I was unsure as to when I'd have enough time to finish it. *Hold on, Mr. Zombie! I'm at this crucial part in the book!* He or she would understand.

Travis had found some emergency candles in his attempt to get as far away from the unthinkable, unimaginable things that his parents had been doing earlier. I smiled at that. I wasn't overly thrilled with an open flame this close to so many combustibles, but I liked the thought of being plunged into darkness far less. The zombies, for once, were being respectful of the library rules and being quiet. Even the smell was tolerable.

No that's a lie. It was putrid. We had just become accustomed to it, I suppose.

The boys had fallen asleep. Tracy was relaxing in a lounge chair, a book resting on her stomach, just where I wished my head was at this moment. It was Tommy that kept me away from that most desired of spots.

"You alright?" I asked him as I came up beside him and draped my arm over his shoulder. He was intently staring out the window, not at the zombies, but rather at the sky.

"I miss her," he said without turning to look at me.

I could have lied and told him that she was in a better place; but that would be a lie. Even in my semi-unconscious state, I heard that deep rumbling voice, and the malice that was interlaced within it, when *something* came to get her. Eliza deserved everything that was coming her way—and then some. Her soul was what I bled for. It was the innocent in all of this. I contemplated asking him if there was a way to retrieve her and then stomped the shit out of that thought. If the boy could get to the Gates of Heaven, odds were pretty decent he could do the same with Hell, and I'd be damned if I was going to do that. (Pretty good pun if I do say so myself...and since it's my journal and all).

"I'm sorry, Tommy. I'm sorry for you."

"But not for her?" he asked.

"No," I told him truthfully. I'd like to think he appreciated my honesty, but that's bullshit when most folks tell you that they want your honest opinion. That's all great and fine as long as your honest opinion of them is deeply flattering, otherwise, they want you to go fuck yourself. We are strange creatures.

"I hear her cry out from time to time," he told me.

I shuddered. Growing up a good Catholic boy I could only ponder the things she was going through...and then some. What could I possibly say that would make any difference? "We're your family now, Tommy."

"After everything I've helped my sister put you through?"

I nodded.

"There will come a time, Mr. T, when you'll curse me for what I've done," he said, turning to look into my eyes.

"Maybe," I told him honestly, "but not tonight."

That seemed to ease his heart a little, but he didn't move away from the window. I did though, before he could talk me into some asinine plan I had no business being involved in. As I was walking away, I thought for the briefest

45

of moments that the zombies had somehow broken through. And then I realized Henry had strategically placed himself in my path, and let loose a heavy butt grumble.

"You know they have medication for that," I told him as I got down to scratch behind his ears, his massive head shifting up so I could get a better angle. "Friggin' ham," I told him. "You still smell bad, though." He didn't care. His paw came up and smacked my arm when he thought I might be leaving. "Oh, not quite ready for your scratching session to end?"

"Get a room," Tracy said from a few feet away. I had not seen her move. She was now standing by the head librarian's desk.

I wouldn't swear it on a stack of Bibles, but I think I heard Travis closely echo his mother's words. Something to the effect of "I wish you guys had gotten a room." Pretty sure I turned beet red. I was exceedingly happy we were running on candlelight at the moment so no one else could see my embarrassment.

My suspicions were confirmed when I heard BT tell him, "That was a good one."

"I hear something!" Justin said excitedly.

He came bounding down the stairs. We were all quiet for long moments. It was getting to the point where I figured he had merely heard one of Henry's deep-seated gaseous fluctuations. Then it was unmistakable.

"Engine," Tommy said.

"More than one," BT said, readying his rifle.

"It had better not be more rednecks." I grabbed my rifle.

In under a minute we were all locked and loaded. God help those that stood against us. Actually, scratch that last sentence. 'Fuck 'em.' In terms of a fighting unit, I'd never been alongside so many people that had seen so much action. On one hand, I was happy they had the fighting experience; the flip side of that was dismay. Dismay that they had to have that much fighting experience.

My gut twisted a little with the thought of my loved ones potentially in danger again. *Just drive on by*, I thought. At first, I thought that was the case as the engine noise first grew louder and then began to dissipate with distance. I could literally feel the tension in the room begin to break, and then that quickly it rose again as the engines were once again approaching.

"Fuck, fuck, fuck," I muttered.

"How is it, that during the 'end of times' it's all zombies and rednecks?" I asked BT as I clutched my weapon.

"Oh I'm sure there are some good people left," BT stated.

"And?" I asked.

"And what?"

"Oh, I can tell by the way you left the end of that sentence that you have more to say."

He was smiling now.

"See? I knew it…out with it." I prodded.

"I think you're an asshole magnet."

"An asshole magnet? Well that's fucking new. Wasn't sure assholes were magnetic."

"Now you know."

"Well I feel better," I told him.

"I thought you would."

"Oh one more thing, BT," I said as I was going over to check the boys' positions.

"Yeah?" His face serious now.

"You were attracted to me." I didn't stick around long enough to see his response. A tossed book clipped my heel; that would have to suffice.

"No firing until we're sure," I told Justin.

"Do we let them in?" he asked.

"I can't imagine they'll want in. First off, they'd have to get through our perimeter security." Justin was looking at me strangely. "The zombies."

"Oh."

"And for what purpose? To check out some books? The risk is most definitely not worth the reward. It's just some folks foraging," I said hopefully.

For a few seconds, my bleaker imagination ran wild and I had visions of Eliza arisen from the dead to finish what she had started. I was fairly certain that wasn't the case, though. I'd convinced Tommy that the best send-off for his sister was cremation by funeral pyre. Trust me when I say that I made sure that fire burned hot enough to return her to her most basic of vestiges. What was left wouldn't have filled a pepper shaker. I checked that as well.

Engine noise began to echo off the small buildings that lined the road leading towards us. And then they were upon us. Two pick-up trucks sat side by side, their headlights illuminating the swirling mass of death and decay.

"It's Uncle Ronny!" Justin cried.

"Some things never change," Travis said to me, referring to his brother's flair for the obvious.

"And sometimes I like it like that," I told him. "Okay, everyone, he may pull that Gatlin gun out, so get ready to duck." I wasn't going to though. I loved that thing, and I wanted to watch it spit fire! "Alright…get ready," I said when we heard a door open.

Zombies were beginning to move rapidly towards the two trucks. For the life of me, I couldn't understand the delay in sending a savage lead curtain downrange.

"Any day!" I shouted.

"Oh! Hey, Mike!" Gary yelled, looking up in approximately my direction. The night was fairly well lit with a healthy half-moon rising, but it would have been difficult to see me recessed in a window even if it was full. He was lit up pretty good, though.

"Gary, you know there are zombies coming your way, right?" I asked, truly concerned.

He appeared to be muscling into some sort of backpack. I could hear other voices down there. I couldn't make out the dialog, though.

Gary hefted the package onto his back like a rucksack and then secured a strap across his midsection. Although, where a rucksack was made of a canvas-like material and soft, this looked solid. Roughly the size of a spare tire if you were to stick a spare tire in a box for shipping. Suffice it to say, it was big.

Gary took two steps towards the library then quickly went back to the truck to grab his rifle. I smacked my forehead with my palm. Zombie apocalypse and he leaves his rifle behind. Now my heart was hammering. Gary was holding his rifle to his chest.

"Covering fire!" I shouted. "And be fucking careful!"

We opened with a hail of lead. Zombies collapsed to the ground as we shattered skull plates, scattering brains all over the front walkway. Yup, then I got a sick memory of an old commercial 'a mind is a terrible thing to waste.' If I hadn't been so worried for my brother, I would have gladly enjoyed the dark humor.

"Gary, fucking shoot!" I yelled, watching in seemingly terrified slow motion as the zombies raced towards him. We couldn't shoot the closest ones. With our angle, any bullet would come dangerously near to him.

When I thought all was lost, the zombies just…stopped. Gary had a nearly perfect bubble of protection around him. It was terrifying to watch. I now knew what the box housed on Gary's back was, but to realize that your brother's life rested solely on the soldering skills of a man who had named himself Mad-Jack…that was fucking scary.

"Cease fire!" I shouted, although that already seemed to be the case once everyone saw what I was looking at.

"Is he singing?" BT asked. "He is. What is that shit…REO Speedwagon? Why are you crackers always bat-shit crazy? You'd never see a black man tip-toeing through

the zombies singing crappy 80's music."
"Hey, I like REO Speedwagon," I told him.
"I'm sure you do." He said it as an insult. I'm positive of it.
"And I'm not a cracker," I said weakly.
"Uh-huh," was his response. "Cracker ass cracker."
"What the hell is he wearing?" Tracy asked, coming up beside me.
"Looks like a jumpsuit. Where the hell did he get a jumpsuit, and why?"
Well, I got the answer to the second part of my question soon enough as Gary moved into the stream of light radiating out from the front of the truck. It was difficult to see at first, and to be honest, it took my mind a few seconds to piece it all together. Over the left side of his chest was a stitched tag like the military would use; the name 'Talbot' clearly marked in white thread. It stood out against the gray possibly brown material of the jumpsuit. It was the patch on his right arm that gave me the most difficult time trying to discern. When it did, I nearly fell on my ass laughing so hard.
"What is it?" Tracy asked, wondering how I could find any humor in the situation we found ourselves in.
"Gary…" I started trying to get my laughing under control. "He's…got…a zombie buster's patch on!" And then I was howling all over again.
"I told you crackers were crazy!" BT shouted.
Even Tommy, who was almost always dour-faced lately, was smiling.
"Nice outfit, Uncle Gary!" Travis shouted.
"Thanks," Gary replied, beaming.
"Any chance that's an old Halloween costume?" Tracy asked me.
"Doubtful," I told her.
"You know you really should have given me full disclosure about your family before I married you," she said.
"We would have never been hitched if that was a

prerequisite."

"I should have put it in a pre-nup," she said with all seriousness, never taking her eyes off of Gary.

"How's it working?" Mad-Jack asked. He had his window rolled down a quarter of the way.

Gary gave him the thumbs-up. To my way of thinking, if he wasn't getting eaten, then it was working.

"Mike, what did you do to my truck?" Ron asked with chagrin from the driver's seat of the first truck.

"That not obvious to him?" BT asked me.

"I know, right?" The destroyed remains of 'said' truck were pinned on the handrail, leading up the main steps into the library. And anybody including a casual observer would note that the thing was destroyed.

I led off with "Ummm," and then right into a smart-ass comment, "first prize at the demolition derby was a bucket of fried chicken...seemed like a fair trade."

"You suck, Mike," Ron intoned.

"I would have done it for that," BT replied.

"Yup...definitely a pre-nup. Next time, I suppose." Tracy shook her head.

"Next time?" But she was already heading away.

"Were there biscuits?" BT asked.

"What?" I didn't even know what he was referring to.

"The prize, Mike, the damn prize! Did it come with biscuits and gravy?" BT asked, clearly agitated.

I was shaking my head. "There was no..." BT's face began to contort to one of anger. "Err...I was saying there was no mashed potatoes, but tons of biscuits and gravy." He relaxed at that point, a smile creeping across his face, his eyes half-closed as he remembered some past meal. "And I'm the *crazy* one," I said, making sure that he couldn't hear me.

"Uncle Gary, you're going to have to go to your left. There's a fire escape and the doorway is on the second floor," Justin yelled to him.

Gary looked up. I could see the pained expression on his face.

"How heavy is that thing?" I asked him.

"I had to use two car batteries," Mad Jack replied. "And the case is three-quarter-inch plywood which Gary made me paint black. Although the weight added from the paint would be negligible. The components are heavy-duty because I wanted to make sure they would hold up in a battle scenario, then there's the—"

"Mad-Jack! Just pounds, man, that's all I need," I said to him.

"Well, I usually use the metric system like all scientists, but I'm sure you wouldn't understand kilograms."

"I'm going to kill him," I said under my breath.

"Okay, let me do the conversion…carry the five…add in the remainder…divide by pi." There was a pause. "Roughly a hundred thirty pounds and six ounces. Give or take an ounce or two."

"Shit, we didn't carry that much in the Marines," I said to anyone close. "You going to be alright, brother?"

His thumbs-up was much less enthusiastic, and his smile looked more like he had to take a shit and there wasn't a toilet for a mile. Oh don't go turning your nose up, we've all been there.

"Everyone grab your gear. BT, can you take over for Gary when he gets here?" I was referring to carrying the zombie repellant. I was going to be busy hefting my own cumbersome bundle. Henry did not like the indignity of being carried. He was fine with riding or being pulled along in a wagon, but carrying was somehow beyond his station.

BT nodded, slowly returning from the world of saliva-worthy meals.

"What's the plan, Mike?" Tracy asked nervously.

"You must be nervous if you even asked," I told her. "Here it is in a nutshell. Make sure you're always within reach of BT."

"Sounds easy enough," she said.

"One would think that." Although I knew from multiple personal experiences that any battle plan unraveled at first contact with the enemy.

We could hear Gary's labored breathing and heavy footfalls coming up the stairs. When he was about halfway up, I realized we were going to have a problem. The zombies already on the staircase, although being repelled by the machine, had nowhere to go. They were pressing up closer to the library wall. They didn't have the wherewithal to jump over the side; most likely it was a failsafe in them…or just stupidity.

"Gary, hold up!" I shouted, hoping he could hear me through his groans of protestations. His rendition of Queen's *We are the Champions* was suffering greatly from his distressed intakes of air. "And keep your head down!"

BT pressed his face up against the small window that overlooked the fire exit. "It's never easy."

"Where's the fun in that?" I asked him.

"Sick bastard. How is it that you make Deneaux look like a viable traveling companion?"

"That hurts, man."

The difficulty was going to be compounded because the door opened outward and a good ten or twelve zombies were huddled up against it. The person or persons pushing the door open was going to be exposed to the zombies while those behind him would be shooting. It was not an enviable position.

"Maybe we should have Gary go back down the stairs to ease the pressure," Tracy suggested.

"Good idea. I hope he can make it back up, though," I told her. I empathized with my brother. That thing was like strapping a human on your back, and not a little baby one.

I was about to tell him when his singing (dare I call it that) cut short and he shouted out, "MJ, this thing is blinking."

"What color? Because if it's a green, that's alright, just the box doing a self-diagnostic. Now if it's yellow that's still okay, it means the box has detected a problem, but it's fairly certain it can self-correct."

"Fairly fucking certain," I mumbled. "I'm going to kill him."

"But if it's red—" he was continuing.

"It's red!" Gary replied.

"Um...erm...I would suggest running," Mad-Jack shouted to him.

BT and I were already heading for the door. Our combined momentum drove some of the zombies clear off the small landing where I hoped they dashed their skulls against any hard object below. I had slammed into the door, shoulder first, thinking I wasn't going to get much movement, but when the freight train that is BT also crashed into it, the thing opened easily enough. I found myself falling, the steel grate of the landing rushing up to meet me. Just where I wanted to be—by the feet of zombies. That's sarcasm, although in hindsight, it beat the hell out of being by their mouths.

BT was screaming a war cry. I'd like to think my scream sounded fierce as well, but mine was more fear driven. I could hear rounds being fired above me. I was on eye level with a zombie that was in serious need of an anti-fungal medication. Mini brown cauliflower pustules were erupting from its toenails, and trust me when I tell you, I was fixated on that. I was deathly afraid it was going to shuffle those growths right up to my nose. If they touched me, odds were I'd go into shock. I felt hands wrap around my lower legs, and I kicked out thinking it was zombies.

"Talbot, if you kick me, you'll be sleeping alone for years," Tracy told me. She and Travis yanked me back into the sanctuary of the library.

BT had a good four or five zombies pinned behind the door and the railing. Justin and Tommy were clearing the few remaining ones away from him. MJ's machine had done more than just repel, now the zombies fixated their attention on it. They were in such a rush to get away from it that they weren't even bothering with the food literally a mouth's span away. Gary had just made the landing as Tommy put a knife I didn't know he was carrying straight through the eye socket of the last remaining zombie. Shooting anything alive is nightmare worthy, but there's something about a knife that just ratchets up that gross factor. It's a much more personal way to dispose of a life (such as a zombie's is). The knife easily slid into the soft tissue of the eyeball, cracking through the delicate orbital bones, and then finally coming to a rest in its brain. The zombie stilled as its headquarters were breeched. Tommy had a fierce grimace on his face as he pulled the knife free and kicked the zombie over the rail.

    The zombie sailed a good fifteen feet in the air—sometimes I forgot just how strong Tommy was—before the thing's forward progress was stopped by a strategically placed elm. If not for the tree, the zombie may have broken some flight records for his kind. Even Gary's panting couldn't drown out the sickening sounds of shattering bones.

    "You alright?" BT asked Gary, not stopping for a response as he physically picked him up and into the library. Travis grabbed the handle to the door and pulled it shut before a new wave of zombies heading up the stairs could get in.

    "Well that sucked," I said as I watched zombies smack into the now closed entryway.

    I didn't watch long enough to see if history would repeat itself. (The whole glass licking thing.) Tracy had grabbed a chair and dragged it over to Gary who looked like he was on the verge of collapsing. BT and I helped him out of MJ's contraption. I think the hundred and thirty pound estimate was a little light. Even with BT's strength and my enhancements, we struggled. I'd swear I saw the floor sag when we put it down.

"How the hell did you carry that thing?" BT asked Gary, looking at him with newfound amazement.

"Nice outfit," I told him.

He was too tired to grin.

There was a light on top of the unit that was now shining a steady red, but was dimming rapidly as I watched it.

I went back to the window that overlooked our 'saviors' and spoke into the radio we had salvaged from our now defunct ride. "The light was a steady red and then went out. How do we fix it?"

"Oh dear," I heard MJ say.

"Oh dear? Any chance you could be more specific?" I asked.

"Batteries are dead."

"Dead? It was barely on for five minutes," I told him.

"Forty-five."

"MJ, unless we were in some sort of time warp, that thing wasn't on for more than five minutes. Six, tops," I told him.

"I performed tests," he said. I could see his head sag from my vantage point.

I'm not the quickest thinking man on the planet, although considering there were way less men, I was probably gaining on that ladder. Sorry, errant thought. Then realization hit. "Really, MJ, you didn't think to change the batteries after your tests?"

"It never occurred to me," he said reluctantly.

"You have got to be shitting me." I moved away from the window.

"What's up?" BT asked, he kept muscling the heavy box up and looking over at Gary like he couldn't figure out how he had done it.

"Well you're now doing curls with the world's largest and most likely heaviest paperweight."

"It's broken?" he asked.

"Dead batteries." I would have kicked the thing, but I liked the configuration of my foot bones just the way they were.

"I carried that thing for nothing?" Gary moaned.

"Not for nothing, brother. You got to show off your new outfit." He smiled at that and immediately fell asleep, his legs twitching spasmodically from the stress they had been under.

"Mike," BT said, lifting the box again. "This thing is closer to two hundred and fifty pounds."

"I wonder. Let's see if we can get this thing open."

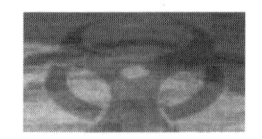

CHAPTER 7 – STEPHANIE AND TRIP

"Stephanie, we can't afford any dead weight," Curtez Riggs, the self-appointed leader of the group, said. "We're barely holding on here and he doesn't contribute at all."

Curtez didn't relish his role, but with his stint in the Army, he felt he was the best qualified to keep his work mates alive when they had become trapped in the hotel offices. It was his fast thinking that had kept the majority of them safe even when their supervisor had rushed headlong into the zombies in a panic to get back to his home.

Curtez had kept them alive and they had gone out on multiple successful foraging raids to get weapons and supplies. They'd made due in an increasingly hostile world. Everyone had a part to do in that success…save one.

"He's my husband, Curtez. What do you expect me to do?" When he didn't immediately respond, she continued, "I know he's a little eccentric."

Curtez' eyebrow arched at 'little'.

"Okay, a lot eccentric, but if nothing else, he brings a lot of entertainment value." Stephanie was trying to diffuse a topic that had been building the last week. Curtez did not take kindly to those that didn't assist directly in their survival.

"I'm done listening to how many times he dosed to the Grateful Dead, and that sometimes he thinks he has seven fingers on each hand, Stephanie. That's just not going to cut it anymore. He eats more than a man that skinny has a right to. It's like he's perpetually stoned."

That might not be so far from the truth, Stephanie thought. "Let's cut through the BS, Curtez. What are you suggesting?"

"Do I really need to say it?" he asked.

"I think maybe you do. I think maybe you need to tell me that you want to kick my husband out of our little corner of the world."

Curtez was struggling. He felt that he was being pushed to the brink of something he did not want to attempt to cross. His true hope was that Stephanie would talk to Trip and get some action from him, not this. "Fine, Stephanie, I want him gone."

She really didn't think he'd say those words and they hurt as much as if he had physically slapped her. "I can't, Curtez, I can't make him go out there alone."

When Curtez didn't say anything, she knew what his silence was implying.

"We'll umm...we'll leave in the morning. I hope you can sleep with your decision," she told him. "Hello, John." She walked over to her husband who was furiously working at something.

"Who?" he asked, looking up.

"Oh, Trip, I love you so much." She bent down to kiss the top of his head.

"I made you something." He beamed proudly. "Been working on my Origami." He handed over something that looked strikingly like a rolled up wad of paper used in an office basketball game.

"It's lovely," she said, turning it around and over, trying her best to see what hidden wonders it held, like her husband obviously did.

"You have it upside down," he told her.

"Oh, I see it now," she lied. "Tomorrow morning I thought you and I should go for a walk."

"Perfect, I think we're out of Genoa salami."

She cocked her head. Not once had they had salami since they'd been holed up—Genoa or otherwise—and for the life of her, she couldn't ever remember him eating it.

"Well then we should probably get some." She

smiled.

John the Tripper slept peacefully that night, dreaming of Pop-Tarts and some strange man he felt like he should know wearing a poncho that looked eerily familiar. His wife, on the other hand, paced throughout the night keeping a watchful eye on the street below them, looking for any signs of trouble.

Stephanie gently shook her husband awake the moment light began to seep into the office. Curtez was watching her, his dark eyes never wavering. She wondered if, and hoped that, he was rethinking his position from the night before. He came over as John arose and stretched.

"I'm starving," John said as he scratched his nether regions. "Hey, Diggs."

"It's Riggs. Here Stephanie, I packed you some supplies." He handed her a backpack.

"I hope there's a deli slicer in there," Trip said, taking the bag and putting it on.

"Trip, you're in your underwear. Don't you think you should dress first?" his wife asked.

"We going to be gone that long?" he asked. "These underwear are very comfortable. I bought them in Spokane back in '88 when the Dead were in town."

Curtez knew he had to stay strong; he had just handed down a death sentence to these two. It was for the betterment of the entire group though. The sacrifice of the few for the good of the many was the Army way.

The group gathered around the trio when they began to figure out what was going on. Stephanie was pelted with questions and pleas not to go. She knew if she told the group why she was leaving that enough of them might rally to her side, but she wasn't overly confident. Quite a few of them had surrendered all of their decision making to Curtez. She couldn't take it if her friends turned on her as well. Even if they did, she would make an enemy of Curtez and it was very likely that he would find her more and more difficult missions to undertake until finally one day she wouldn't come back, and at that point, her beautiful, wonderful Trip would be completely at his mercy.

Although, better than Curtez had tried, yet somehow her husband had always come out on top. She smiled at that. She could see Trip getting to Riggs so badly he would just walk out, but that wasn't fair to the rest of the group. Riggs had made some hard choices for the group. Ultimately, he had kept them alive. What was the point, though? They were marking time here and nothing more. This wasn't *life*; life was meant to be lived. As Stephanie said her tearful goodbyes, Trip promised them hard roll salami sandwiches when he returned.

Steph's heart dropped as she heard the latch from the fire door close behind her. She and Trip were descending the stairs while three people from their group where coming up, bags of supplies in all of their hands.

"Where you guys heading?" Hal asked. "We got plenty of stuff, medication, bandages, food, even found some beer," he said beaming.

"Any salami?" Trip asked.

"Huh?" Hal asked.

"We're going to try and find other survivors," Steph told him solemnly.

"Stephanie, you can't leave," Melissa, her closest friend even before the zombies came, said. She had since hooked up with Hal, even though they had made fun of his constant advances, when the world of man ruled.

"I need someone," Melissa had confided with her one night…after.

"I understand completely," Stephanie had answered her back.

"We ran into a nest on our last foraging mission," the third, Lisa Evans, said.

Easily the second toughest survivor in the group after Curtez, Lisa and Curtez often butted heads. Stephanie thought for a moment about dropping to her knees and pleading with Lisa to be her champion, to save them from the insanity of this adventure.

"They're not too far behind, if you're going...you need to do it quickly. Are you sure?" Lisa asked, resting her hand gently on Steph's forearm and looking deep into her eyes for the truth the woman was hiding from her.

"We have to, I already promised everyone salami," Trip responded.

"Steph?" Lisa asked, not letting go.

"Salami for everyone," she nearly sobbed.

"Okay. Then go west down River Street, stay away from Pohl's. Good luck," Lisa told her as she ascended the rest of the way up the stairs.

"Why Steph?" Melissa asked.

Stephanie thought about telling her; but that would only create dissension in the group, and they were already on the brink. No, she would leave with her head high and with no parting shots for Curtez, even if he deserved it. *Damn him.*

"There's more out there, Melissa. And I...we...we want to find it." She thought a moment about asking Melissa to join her, but she couldn't bear the thought of watching her friend fall into harm's way.

Melissa left a small puddle of tears on Stephanie's shoulder before she ran sobbing up the stairs. Hal gave Stephanie a stiff hug and then stuck out his hand for Trip. Trip gazed upon the hand as if it had sprouted wings.

"You should become a hand model," Trip told him, grabbing Hal's proffered extremity and pulling it closer to his face to examine it.

Hal pulled his hand away in embarrassment. "Um...yeah, you two be careful," he said, following his girlfriend.

"It's just salami, why is everyone so concerned?" Trip asked his wife.

"It's just been a while since anyone has had any and

they're very grateful."

"Oh...that I get," Trip said, whistling loudly as they pushed open the door that led outside.

Steph wished he'd lower his pitch, but by the time she explained to him why he needed to they could have walked a block. Steph could feel the many eyes of her previous group looking down on them. She would not give Curtez or his followers the satisfaction of the sheer terror that had to be etched on her features. She didn't buckle even when she heard whom could only be Melissa tapping on the glass.

"Where are you going?" Steph asked, struggling to keep up with her husband who seemed to be a man on a mission.

"Bus station," he told her between tunes. "We need to get to Pagliaro's. They have the best meats."

"Trip, Pagliaro's is in Chicago. We're in Philly."

"That's why we need the bus, Steph. Sometimes you're such an airhead," he playfully admonished her.

"Do you hear that?" Steph asked in a lull between Trips *sets*.

"Sounds like it's raining fish." Trip cupped an ear, listening.

The funny thing is that it does, Steph thought. But it wasn't fish; it was the footfalls of many, many zombies. Some wearing boots, some shoes, some stilettos, and flip-flops. Others would be barefoot, and for some reason she couldn't discern, some of them would have on mismatched footwear as if they had been in midstream putting their shoes on when they'd changed over. The pounding of feet on pavement echoed throughout the narrow city streets, the sound building up as it echoed off the myriad of storefronts and office buildings.

"Come on, Steph. The buses run on tight schedules and we don't want to miss it," Trip told her, his gait noticeably longer.

"Nobody is here. We're either real early or real late,"

Trip said as they walked inside the terminal. "Come on, let's see if we can find any of the drivers." He pulled her out into the back. Six city buses stood parked perfectly in their allotted spots, a seventh had crashed through the twelve foot razor wire tipped fence and somehow completely flipped onto its back like a giant turtle.

The driver had obviously tried desperately to get back to the terminal as his passengers warred with one another. It was easy enough to see who had won the battle, blood and bits of bodies covered most of the remaining windows that had not been broken out.

"I think that one is out of service," Trip told her when he saw she was looking at it.

A hand shot through a window near the middle, oblivious to the fact that its arm was being neatly carved up against a jagged piece of glass. Black liquid, oozed down the spike of solidified sand. Hands began to beat against the thin aluminum frame like children caught in a car that had slid off a road and into a lake and was quickly sinking below the surface, furious that they would be forever trapped in a watery death.

Trip had already moved on, Steph hurried to be with him. He had moved to the bus furthest away from the crashed disaster. "What are you doing?" she asked as he pushed a small black button located to the left of the bus door. The answer became readily available as the door popped open.

"Your chariot awaits," he told her.

"Trip, I don't think the buses are running anymore."

"Good thing I was a bus driver once then." He climbed aboard, quickly making himself comfortable in the driver's seat, donning a cap and shirt that the previous driver had left behind.

"Glad I have this." Trip said happily as he pulled out a folded up square of tin foil. He proceeded to encase his new hat with the thin metal. "Can never be too safe."

Steph was about to ask him at least ten well-founded

questions; the least of them being how he was going to get the bus started, when it roared to life. A plume of black diesel smoke drifted past the windshield.

"Sounds good. I should do a quick mechanics check on it, though," Trip said as he arose from his seat.

Steph looked to their right, zombies from the crashed bus or the ones that had been running in the streets were now heading their way. "Maybe later, Trip, we should get going."

"Nonsense, the best bus trip is the uneventful one." He quickly sat down when he saw the same sight as his wife. "Although, with more fares coming, we really shouldn't mess with their schedules."

It took Stephanie a moment to realize that he meant to let them aboard.

"I chartered this bus for myself!" she blurted out. "No other passengers!"

Trip turned towards her slowly. She could almost hear the gears in his head spinning.

"Oh yeah, you were going to pick up some friends before the show! I remember now. Party bus here we go! Right on, man." He pulled the doors closed just as the nearest zombie slammed into it. "Sorry, fella! The lady bought this ride for herself!" he yelled to the zombie.

Steph let her heartbeat slow down a bit before she realized they weren't moving. Trip was looking at her.

"We're going to be late, we need to leave."

Trip pointed to a sign at the front of the bus: *State Law – The operator may not move this vehicle until all passengers are below the yellow line.* Stephanie noticed her right foot was halfway across. She quickly moved it. Trip nodded in approval and turned back around. The bus pushed up against the fence before Trip realized he needed to be in reverse. "It's been a while."

If ever, she thought.

Trip was hooting and hollering as if he were the one that had chartered the party bus as opposed to driving it. The bus rocked back and forth as he pulled out of the depot and off the sidewalk.

"Curb check!" he yelled as if he needed to be heard above the music only he could hear. "Are any of these people in your party?" he asked her as a wave of zombies headed their way.

Stephanie emphatically shook her head in the negative and said the words aloud lest he mistake her actions; it wouldn't be the first time. A few months before the zombies came, Stephanie had returned home from an extended business trip and had been all kinds of desiring to be with her husband. She had dressed in her sheerest negligee, lit a bunch of candles in their bedroom, and when he'd come back from taking a walk, she had cooed to him that she was 'so hot', she'd also used the 'come hither' finger movement. Trip had walked into their bedroom blew out every candle and had immediately left. He came back an hour later with seven different types of ice cream.

"This should help with the heat," he told her enthusiastically.

After they ate to their hearts' content, they made love. She smiled at the remembrance but decided there and then she needed to be as clear as possible when dealing with him. The ice cream had been great, but it had cost her hours on the treadmill to get rid of it.

Trip 'blatted' the horn as they passed by the hotel. He was waving happily upwards at the people looking down.

"Son of a bitch," Curtez said, smiling that they were safe. His conscience eased.

"Zombies in the stairwell!" Melissa shouted.

"How is that possible?" Curtez asked, running over towards her. "You guys were the last through! Did you shut it?"

"Of course we did." Hal came to Melissa's defense. "And besides, we weren't the last ones to use it."

"Bitch," Curtez hissed. Grabbing his rifle and heading

back towards the windows he was determined to take some shots at the retreating bus.

"What are you doing?" Lisa asked.

"Bitch left the door open because I kicked her and her doltish husband out!" he shouted, lifting the gun to his shoulder. He knew it was a futile effort; any decent firing angle had long since passed.

"You did what?" Lisa and Melissa asked at nearly the same time.

Curtez turned to face them. "He was useless, he needed to go," he said, defending his position.

"You're a jerk." Melissa turned her face into Hal's shoulder.

"Really, Curtez, that's how you decided to handle the situation? So if I get hurt and can't do anything, you going to kick me out too?" Lisa asked. "Is that the society you're trying to create? Fuck the weak and infirm?"

"It's not like that, we're trying to survive. Resources are scarce."

"So you took it upon yourself to be judge, jury, and executioner? Don't you think we maybe should have talked about it first at least? This isn't your little fucking Tinker Toy group to do with as you please. And I've known Stephanie almost as long as Melissa. She'd no more put any of us in danger than she would Trip. You, on the other hand, are just an asshole. Had I known that decision had been made, I would have left with them."

"Me too," Melissa cried.

Hal turned when he heard noise in the stairwell. His eyes grew wide as he watched the unthinkable happen. "The knob! The fucking knob is turning!" Hal pushed Melissa to the side and dove for the door, grabbing the bar that was used to open it from their side. His fingers turned white as he gripped it hard, attempting to hold it from opening.

"Well there's your answer, Sherlock," Lisa said to Curtez. "Looks like our friends are getting smarter. I told you she wouldn't betray us, she's not you." She got into position a few feet away from the door. "Okay, Hal, let go and move away from the door."

"They'll get in," he said in a panic.

"How long are you planning on holding that door?" she asked.

"Melissa, get my rifle," Hal told her. He waited until she was a few feet away before letting go and grabbing his rifle. The zombies had the door open before he could spin and shoot his first round.

Lisa drilled the first one in the forehead, blood sprayed back into the stairwell covering the next zombie to come through. He did not seem to mind the blood bath in the least. He quickly met the same fate as his friend.

"We need to move those bodies!" Lisa shouted. She had effectively created a doorstop.

Nobody made a move. Lisa's words had stung Curtez. He truly felt that he was doing what was best for the group and now he felt the need to atone for his actions. He yelled as he ran towards the door, his gun firing bullets into the zombies that hurried to get over the fallen. His steps faltered as he was drilled in the side with a ricochet; the bullet piercing his side, going in and out. He did not stop to assess the damage until he was over the zombies in the doorframe.

He was still yelling when his rifle's bolt stood open, his magazine empty. "What the hell?" he asked.

Six zombies were dead, there were no more in the stairwell. He saw the sunlight diminish as the door below him closed.

"Where did they go?"

His answer came quickly in the form of a woman screaming. He watched through the open door as zombies flooded into their location, having come up the stairwell on the opposite side of the building. It was not difficult to see that all had been lost. Lisa, Melissa, and Hal were rallying those not yet fallen into a defensive posture. Curtez could see the writing on the wall. He'd seen positions overrun, and that was what was happening here. He quickly pulled the zombies stuck in the doorway and flung their bodies down the stairs.

He thought to call to Lisa but knew she would want to stay and try to save as many of the people as possible. He closed the door quietly and watched. Somehow, through all the noise and confusion, Lisa realized what he was doing. She turned and looked at him through the small window set high in the door.

He opened the door. "I have no bullets, what do you want me to do? It's over Lisa, come on!" he told her. She shook her head, but begrudgingly she tapped Melissa and Hal and motioned to the door.

The four of them crowded around the small, wire-encased glass window and watched their friends and co-workers fall quickly to the zombies. Three or four zombies would descend on a fallen human, tearing into them even as they thrashed about. Screams were cut short as throats were ripped out. Eviscerated and de-limbed people lined the floor, rapidly firing nerve endings making their bodies twitch violently.

"I can't watch anymore." Melissa headed down the stairs. Hal was next to pull away to comfort Melissa. Lisa's breaths hitched as she watched.

Curtez was distraught that all he had managed to save was lost in a matter of moments. *How though? How had they learned to open the doors?* It had seemed a task light years beyond their skill set.

"We've got to go," Curtez said to Lisa when it looked as if the zombies were finishing up with the warm bodies still available to them. If they could turn a handle, pressing an arm bar would be a piece of cake.

"Where to?" Lisa asked, all hope seemingly burned out of her.

"I wonder if we can catch a bus."

"Hello?" Melissa asked as the door on the first floor

opened up.

"Do you think it's Stephanie?" Lisa asked Curtez.

He knew they were long gone. Right now seeing Trip come up those stairs would be the most welcome sight he could imagine. He knew better. They had walked into an ambush.

"Melissa, Hal, come back up here," he told them.

"Wh—" Melissa started.

She began to scream when she saw a trio of zombies running towards her. She hadn't completely turned around when they dragged her down. Chewing quickly through her clothes and into the soft tissue of her buttocks and hips. Hal grabbed her right arm as she fell. He was pulling her back towards him when one of the zombies peeled off from Melissa and lunged at him; he put his rifle wielding arm up reflexively. The zombie bit down hard on his elbow joint, shattering it into three shards.

Melissa was forgotten as he pulled his right hand free to swing at the zombie. He caught it on the side of its head, shattering one of his knuckles—the pain not even registering in comparison to his elbow. The zombie had not let go and was shaking its head back and forth, trying to rip a piece of him free. Curtez went down a few steps and slammed the butt of his gun into the zombie's nose, rupturing the cartilage and most of the bones in its face. Melissa was mewling as the two zombies on her were ripping strips of meat from her legs. Bone was exposed on her left leg as she still tried to push away with her right.

Lisa was frozen, trying desperately to take her gaze from the scene below her. She wanted to run, but there was nowhere to go. She still had rounds in her rifle, but the engaged fighting was too close to use them. The zombie that had bit Hal was falling away as Curtez slammed it twice more in the head. He had pushed the face almost halfway into its skull. A zombie with a long thin strip of muscle meat in its mouth hissed at Curtez before it chugged the morsel down its throat.

"FUCK YOU!!!!" Curtez screamed as he rammed the rifle into its head as well.

Hal had fallen to the stairs, a glaze of shock sinking down on his features. His mouth was becoming slack, his eyes were losing focus. Curtez figured it was partly from the pain, but the majority was most likely from watching his girlfriend get eaten less than two feet away. Blood was sluicing down the stairs from Melissa's torn legs. She was still alive but had long since retreated into herself. She was not cognizant of the events unfolding around her and was on the verge of passing out from blood loss.

Curtez had blood and gore all over him as he dispatched of the second zombie. He raised his weapon to take down the third. The zombie stood and backed down the stairs, warily keeping its eyes on Curtez.

"That's right, motherfucker!" Curtez yelled at it, taking a step to meet it. "I'm the biggest, baddest mofo around!" he screamed, slamming a blood encrusted hand against his chest.

Lisa was nearly flung against the far wall as zombies began to push against the door she was standing next to. "Curtez!" She had turned and braced her legs against the wall and leaned her upper half against the door. The forearm of a man and a woman zombie were sticking through the small opening their initial push had afforded them.

Curtez looked down the stairs. The way was clear, he could leave. With more difficulty than he felt he should have, he turned the thought away. He ran up the stairs, bringing his rifle back, he moved it forward and pulverized the two arms until they hung limply, nothing much more than tendon holding them to their masters. Lisa was nearly able to shut the door completely.

She bumped violently when more zombies pushed from the other side. Curtez joined her in repelling the attack. They stood there for a moment, shoulder-to-shoulder.

"Now what?" Lisa asked him as if she thought he had the answer.

"Well, I suppose I should count to three and we'll both head down these stairs as fast as we can and pray we can stay one step ahead of the zombies behind us," he told her earnestly. "Move to my other side."

"Why?"

"You're slower."

"Isn't that better for you?" she asked.

"I'm sick of leaving people behind," he said with a deep sadness.

"What about Hal?"

"Zombie broke skin."

Lisa's mouth became tight-lipped as she slid past Curtez. He moved further down the door so she would have room.

"Ready?" he asked.

She licked her lips.

"I'll take that as a yes. One…two…three!"

Lisa pushed off from the door and was halfway down the flight of stairs before Curtez followed. Curtez was no more than three stairs down when he heard the door behind him crash open. He didn't bother to hazard a look, he knew what was coming. Lisa was standing in the open doorway leading outside.

"Go, go, go!" he urged her, catching up.

He stopped short when he saw what was blocking her way. A dozen zombies were standing in a semi-circle looking at them. He was barely able to register how complete of a trap it was when he felt a spike of pain and heat in his neck as a zombie tore into him. *I should have gone with Trip*, was his final thought.

Lisa bolted, nearly breaking free of the ring; it was a bite to the back of her skull that brought her down. The zombie's teeth had cracked through the thick plate and skimmed against her cerebellum. With her motor skills misfiring, she could not get her left leg to bend properly. Stiff-legged, she still tried. It was a short-lived attempt as a zombie dove onto her back and drove her into the ground. Her front teeth shattered as she hit the pavement. She couldn't think why she thought it, but a bus ride sounded like the best thing in the world right now…and then her eyes shut.

CHAPTER 8 – MIKE JOURNAL ENTRY 5

"Mike!" Ron yelled through the heavily crackling radio while BT and I stared at hex-head screws and wondered how we were going to get them out. The library housed all sorts of 'How To' home improvement books. But in all of them, one needed tools.

"How about we just smash the damn thing against the ground until it opens?" he had asked at one point. I was inclined to agree.

I ran over to the window, figuring Ron was getting ready to give me tongue-lashing number two for destroying another truck. I knew something was wrong the moment I looked out. Zombies were surrounding the truck, and not just milling about, they looked aggressive. We'd found that, throughout most of the invasion, if the zombies had a choice between a car and a building, they invariably stayed around the building. I can't really attest to why this is. Maybe they felt that the odds of more people being in the building were higher. As good a theory as any I suppose.

But that was changing right now. Zombies that had been perfectly content to wander around our stronghold were now peeling off and heading towards Ron's truck, and what was more unsettling was that they were trying the door handles.

"Holy shit," I said aloud.

"Are they trying to get in?" Tracy asked me.

I thought about going with 'You think?' Luckily, from time to time, an inspiration of wisdom hits. "Yup," was my answer. "Looks like our friends slept at a Holiday Inn."

"What the fuck are you talking about, Talbot?" BT

asked, coming up next to me.

"You know, because they're getting all smart and shit," I said defensively. "Want me to shoot some of them?" I yelled down to Ron. I was ignoring BT's shaking head.

"Don't you fucking dare!" I heard him somewhat through the failing radio and the span of distance; although that latter voice was muffled from the closed windows.

From his angle, it would look like I was shooting right at him. I mean, I wouldn't be, but there was a chance I'd send rounds into his engine…and that wouldn't be good. Zombies or not, he'd get out of that truck and come up here and kick my ass for wrecking another one.

"I was afraid this might happen," Tommy said from the next window over.

We all stopped to look at him. "Any chance you would like to elaborate?" BT finally asked.

"Eliza sort of kept the zombies at bay. With her giving them commands, they never had to think much past what she told them to do. With her influence gone, they are free to learn, or relearn, or just plain remember, I'm not sure."

"How much of any of that can they do?" I asked, fearful.

"Well…none of them are ever going to write great novels. But opening doors and figuring out basic tactics shouldn't pose too many problems."

"How do you know all this?" Tracy asked.

"When I was linked to Eliza I could feel what she felt when she reached out to them. She suppressed them to keep them under her rule."

"Who would have figured having Eliza around would be a good thing?" BT asked as a statement.

"This is worse than pissed-off flying monkeys," I said off-handedly; a thought I probably should have kept to myself.

Tracy stopped her thoughts to look over at me.

"Huh?"

"Heavy medication day?" BT asked her.

"Forget it," I said, feeling fingers of embarrassment flick up my neck.

"We gotta go!" Ron shouted as the zombies began beating on the hood and glass of his truck.

"I didn't think the cavalry was supposed to retreat." Travis said, beating me to the punch.

"We'll be back!" Ron yelled over squealing tires.

"Seems the cavalry is re-grouping. Boys, this changes things a bit. Stay together. I want you to check out every weak area this place has, no matter how small the chance you think a zombie can use it. I want you to either fortify it or let me know about it. Tracy, Tommy, if you two could keep an eye on the zombies, me and BT are going to get this box open."

"What about Gary?" BT asked.

"Let him sleep," I answered. I went over to the librarian's desk and began to rifle through it until I found something I thought we could use on the screws. "Hope this works," I said, holding up a pair of toenail cutters.

"Damn, did she cut horse hooves with those?" BT exclaimed.

I hadn't noticed how big they were until he had said something. I was just happy to have a tool. Then thoughts of what those had been touching began to dominate my mind. *What if she had toe fungus like the zombie?*

"Here, you should probably use these." I thrust them out to BT and quickly rubbed my hand on the side of my pants.

BT figured out my unease and the source of it quick enough. "This little thing grossing you out a bit?" BT asked, holding them dangerously close to my face.

"I'll hit you, man."

"I can almost see the germs wriggling around on it." BT held it up to his eyes. "Looks like some of them have horns."

"Why? We have zombies running around outside trying to get in and you feel like you have the time to give me shit?"

"Because it's fun, man," he said, sticking his tongue out and nearly licking the apparatus.

Heaving was not out of the realm of possibilities. As difficult as it was, I had to man up. My man-card was already in jeopardy of being revoked. As soon as this shit was over I was going to have a metal one made. Then I rethought my strategy; metal rusts.

"Just get the screws, will you," I said to him, peeling my eyes from the horror he was trying to inflict on me.

BT slowly removed half the screws, the soft metal on the clippers was beginning to twist. We could only hope it would last. Justin came up behind me. I hadn't even heard him approach as I was concentrating so hard on the process in front of me.

"Hey, Dad."

I hoped the small jump my heart took went unnoticed.

"Hey," I said back.

"Everything's secure, but they're trying all the doors."

"Fuck...that's creepy," I said. "Whatever happened to the good old days?"

BT stopped. "Good old days?"

"Yeah, stupid slow shufflers," I told him.

"Yeah, those were the good days," he said, getting back to the box.

"There's more...they're really starting to congregate around the small basement windows," Justin reported. "Trav's keeping an eye on them. We don't really think they can get in that way, but they seem real interested."

"BT, you good?" I asked.

"No. Without you watching, I'm not sure how I'll ever get this done."

"Funny. I'm going downstairs."

"Alas, what will I ever do without your micro-management?"

"Come on, Justin," I said.

The basement was darker than I remembered; then I realized it was because the zombies were crowding out the ambient light. Mostly we were staring at legs, but more than a couple of the windows had the faces of the living dead staring back at us. Talk about a nightmare. Think about that the next time you have an opportunity to go down into your basement and get supplies. We were fish in a fishbowl and the cats were trying to figure out how to get their paws in. Did I mention I fucking hate cats?

"Shit!" I heard BT bellow upstairs.

"You alright?" I yelled.

"Broke a nail," was his terse reply.

I was about to say something when a zombie hand slammed against the thick-paned glass, followed quickly by another. And then, as if they had synchronized their attack, pounding was going on all around us. I did a quick three-sixty to watch. Travis pulled back from where he was to be in the relative comfort and safety of us.

We were all holding our breath, so it was pretty easy to hear first one window crack and then another.

"Well, this just got interesting," I said more as a way to calm my skipping heart.

"Shoot?" Travis asked nervously.

Tracy and Tommy had come down from the top floor to see what was causing so much noise. Large pieces of glass shattered on the cement floor. Hands shot through, trying their best to seek purchase on something that was WELL out of reach. On a few of the windows, hands and arms were replaced with heads as zombies tried to wriggle their way in. Fortunately, they were getting hung up on their shoulders. A smaller woman zombie was able to flop most of the way in; her gratuitous, child-bearing hips became her sticking point.

"Shoot the ones that are stuck," I said, hoping that we would create a logjam and prevent any further attempts.

If they were gaining smarts, they would realize that they could use small sizes to their advantage; that meant women and children zombies. The woman zombie was flailing about, trying her best to get in. Between her movements and my nervousness, it took me three shots to still her. The first had slammed into her shoulder, the second, went wide right and into a framed reproduction of a Picasso painting. At least I hoped it was a reproduction. I'd never liked his *art*, but I was not into indiscriminately destroying invaluable pieces.

The third caught her in the top of her head. She fell against the wall, her head leaving a bloody stain where she struck. Similar shots rang out around me, with the desired affect being achieved. I was breathing heavy like I'd just run a marathon. Okay, that's a lie. I'd never be able to run a marathon. Let's go with 'I was breathing as heavy as if it was the fourth quarter in the Super Bowl, tie game and a commercial break came on, and not only did I need to take a world-class piss, I also needed to get a few beers for my guests and reheat the nacho cheese before the ads were over. Yeah, that's better…that's how heavy I was breathing.

"Seems to have worked," Tommy said. He was still on the stairs with Tracy.

"Trace, could you see how BT is doing?" I asked. She was all too happy to oblige.

Then what previously would have been the unthinkable began to happen; the zombie woman began to move…and not of her own volition. She was being dragged from the opening.

"Well that sucks," Travis said.

I couldn't have put it any more eloquently. She left a bloody smear as her head dragged against the wall. Then, the rest of the zombies we had used as an informal barricade were slowly moved out. In one case, I think the zombies were going for psychological warfare. They battered and rammed one of their own into the basement, breaking every substantial bone in its body to do so, the snaps and cracks echoing throughout the room as we watched. When the heap of zombie remains plopped wetly to the floor, all of our eyes were riveted to it.

At this point, I would have yielded the basement to the zombies and closed it off, but we didn't have that luxury. To give up this room meant we would lose the library. There was no way to close this section off. It was a wide staircase that led down to it and no door at the top.

"Shit! Should have thought of this sooner. Look for tools…hammer, pry bar, any strong piece of steel." The boys weren't moving. "Now!" I shouted to get them going. "Upstairs!" I told them when they started to go deeper into the basement.

"What are you thinking?" Tommy asked.

"I'm thinking that beautiful staircase has to go," I told him. "It worked for a while in Little Turtle, it should buy us some time here."

"We don't need tools," he said to me.

I looked at him like he was a vampire. Which I guess he is, so that makes sense. Tommy came down to the first step and gripped the lip of the first stair. I saw his fingers whiten and an intense look on his face, and then I heard the groans of ten penny nails as they began to yield their prize. The wooden step shot up and flipped over a few times before coming to rest halfway up the stairs.

"That'll work," I told him.

The next wave of zombies began to try and find an entrance. It was not lost on me that most of them were women and a slight man. It was the five-year-old that fell to the floor that really got my attention though.

"Faster, Tommy," I said as he looked over his shoulder, horror clearly evident on his face. The zombie child came closer. Its teeth were not bared; he had almost a sad expression on his face as if he were asking for my help.

I raised my rifle up—the child's small head directly in front of my steel sights. That got him going. His arms came out and hatred squeezed out any semblance of a child in trouble from his face. I pulled the trigger, the top of his head vaporized in a spray of blood and skull plate. He skidded to a stop no more than ten feet from me. I heard three more steps clatter away. That was followed by more bodies hitting the floor. Two were women and one was a man that I think was the previous world record holder for oldest living human being. That he was able to stand and start running at me should have been a sight to behold. Instead, it was just fucking scary as hell. He looked like a Halloween prop brought to life. Something that shouldn't be…was.

The rifle jumped in my shoulder as I drew a breath, exhaled, and blew him back to the hell he had come from. I had a trio of zombie women running towards me and reacquired a target. The round caught her in the neck, shattering her spinal column, her head falling forward to her chest and still she came.

"Tommy!" I shouted, to make him aware we were about to become overrun as more bodies hit the floor. I moved quickly away from the 'one shot one kill' philosophy. I sent the rest of my magazine into the two remaining women. Their bodies danced until I found the 'kill' zones, dropping them hard.

I'd bought enough time to reload. I pressed the magazine release, going old-school. When I'd first joined the Marines we'd been taught to just press the release and let the magazine fall where it may and then jam a full one back into the well. By the time I was getting out, they had realized in a combat situation they were losing tens of thousands of dollars in 'lost' magazines. We were then being shown how to salvage the spent bullet holder before putting a full one in. It cost us precious seconds while people were trying to kill us, but hey, anything to save the government a buck or two.

The magazine clacked to the floor, I slammed another home, pulled the charging handle back and was in business once again.

"Few more seconds," Tommy told me.

"That's all we have," I told him back.

Tommy was straddling the risers, pulling on the wood. I was left to wonder if our new and improved zombies would be able to do this as well. In fact, when I turned to see the advancing horde, I realized that more than one was staring intently at Tommy as if they were learning some new skill.

"Up, Tommy!" I yelled.

The way in which I commanded it gave him no doubt that I did not want to be questioned or second-guessed. He turned to me once before bounding up the stairs. The six or so that he'd removed would have to be enough. I destroyed the zombie that had been so intent on him.

"I could have gotten more," Tommy said with chagrin as he looked down at the stairs and his handiwork.

"Most likely, but they were watching you. And not watching you like they wanted to eat you. Well…that too I suppose, but they were watching you like you were a teacher and they were rapt students."

"That's not good."

"No, not at all." I told him.

"Talbot, nice of you to join us," BT said as he was working on one of the last screws.

"Sorry, I was getting a pedicure."

He looked up. "Wouldn't doubt it."

"Travis, Justin." I motioned to the stairs. "Shoot only if they start making headway." We had a fair amount of rounds, but I didn't know when we were *really* going to need them.

Gary at some point had moved from his chair to a reading couch, he and Henry were snuggled up tight and somehow still fast asleep. BT shrugged his shoulders when he saw me looking at them. Tracy was at my side as we watched BT pull the cover off the box.

"I'll be damned," BT said. "How in the hell did your brother carry this?"

"Well, he *is* Gambo," Tracy said.

In addition to the two dead batteries, there were what we hoped were two 'fresh' ones.

"Extras, he put friggin' extras in here," BT said, shaking his head. "I knew it weighed more than a buck thirty. How does he forget something like that?"

"Just because you're brilliant doesn't mean you're smart," I said.

BT nodded in agreement.

"Oh bullshit," Tracy said. "That doesn't even make sense and BT's over there agreeing with you."

I gave her a cheesy smile. It had seemed like genius when I said it, upon reflection it began to lose luster.

"At least the crazy bastard used wing nuts to attach the leads," BT said as he quickly went to work on replacing the batteries.

"Dad, what about now?" Travis asked. He had his rifle in his shoulder and pointed down the stairs.

"Yeah, definitely," I said, not prepared for the explosion of his rifle near to me. Two zombies had stepped onto the first riser, looking like toddlers attempting their first steps. The old adage 'practice makes perfect' popped in my head. I was not going to give the remaining one the opportunity. I blew off the bottom of her leg. My thinking was that, if the zombies could learn, maybe they would know that climbing meant maiming which in turn meant death. It was a bit much for me to hope, but I did it anyway.

"Dad, you didn't hit it in the head," Justin said. "I know, I know, Captain Obvious. Is there a reason I should know about though?"

"Just testing a theory," I told him.

The zombie turned herself around on the floor and

was now looking up at me. Hatred burned through her eyes. And hatred implied intelligence. Then she began to pull herself back towards the stairs. Her hands gripped the riser and she started to pull herself forward.

"So much for that," I said as I put a round in her forehead, snapping her head back violently. A group of zombies was milling about at the bottom. Occasionally one would get divine inspiration and give the balancing act a go.

"How long before they figure out they can climb?" Travis asked with some trepidation.

"I was thinking the same thing," I told him.

Where the stairs continued on was about chest to head level high, depending on the zombie. Not an overly hard climb for someone with dexterity and the know-how. The speeders had all the dexterity they needed; it was just a matter of getting all their parts to move in the correct unison.

"BT?"

"I've got the new batteries in, but it's not doing anything and I'm afraid to just start flipping switches. Looks like a high-tech server room inside this thing."

"I hate to be Deputy Downer, but I think we're going to need that thing before the night is done," I told him.

"Really?" Tracy asked. I nodded to her.

"These fuckers are going to start pole-vaulting this chasm soon." On further reflection I should have maybe kept that thought to myself. Always one to comment first and recant later, it's a pretty good thing I never got on Twitter; inserting a hundred and forty characters into my mouth instantaneously would be bad for my dental work.

"Alright, boys, time to take back the night," I said.

"Huh?" Travis asked.

"I think it was a line from a movie, sounded good before I said it. We're going to take back the basement. I'm sick of waiting for them to figure out a way up here. Ready?"

Travis shrugged. Justin nodded.

I opened fire, immediately followed by my boys. At

this close range, the effects of the bullets were devastating. Bodies bounced around as they caught our rounds. Books exploded in a cloud of confetti from errant shots and ricochets. We'd descend a step or riser every time we dropped a line of zombies. We didn't give them much of an opportunity to fill their ranks as we decimated their force.

Within a couple of minutes, we had taken out the twenty or so zombies who had made it in. It would have been impossible to accurately count the dead given the amount of body parts that littered the floor. Okay, so impossible might be an over-exaggeration. How about fucking disturbingly gross? The basement was ours once again, but she was much like Helen of Troy, now that we had her back we didn't want her. It smelled like an old octopus with diarrhea. Stop for a moment and let that sink in. Yeah it was *that* bad.

We still didn't have a way to keep them from coming in. All I'd really bought us was a moral victory. Those do have their own importance. I was at the bottom step when I heard the familiar plop of a zombie dropping in.

"Seems these old buildings have leaky windows," I said to Tommy.

He had come down to survey the damage after I'd sent the boys back up. Why I still felt the need to protect them from these sights eluded me. They'd seen this and worse ten times over.

"I can pop off a few more steps," he said to me.

"I'll watch your back."

Tommy jumped down and quickly pried three more steps off. I'd only had to shoot two approaching zombies. Either they were running out of little ones, or they'd figured out the futility of this avenue of attack. I reached down and helped Tommy back up, although I'm certain he didn't need it.

"Wish I had a flamethrower," I told him as we sat, our legs dangling into the library basement, almost without a care in the world like we were "sitting on a dock by the bay".

(I know, it's a great song.) "I'd torch these bastards."

I looked upon the fallen zombies. It was not out of malice I said that, but rather, it would be easier to see them as they enemy if they were molten shapes as opposed to the expectant mother to my right, the teenager with braces in front of me, the business woman in her tattered power suit. They had just been people, not even combatants. A flamethrower would have been nice.

"Not sure if that'd be a good idea in a library," Tommy said to me.

"Sure it would. We could pretend we were in Georgia and this was a good old fashioned book burning."

"I'm going to talk to Mrs. T. I think it's time for your meds. For your information there are no records of book burnings in Georgia." He rose. "You staying?"

"For a little bit." I was having a hard time taking my eyes off the young woman who couldn't have been much older than my daughter, her stomach was protruding slightly from a baby bump. She had probably been out shopping for baby stuff when she turned or was bitten.

"Two for the price of one." I sighed.

Her size and shape reminded me of my daughter. It was only fine lines of fate that separated the dead woman's lot in life from my Coley's. I wanted to cry for the woman and her lost child. Yeah, fire and dehumanization would have been great just about then. I stood and walked away from the stairs—or more correctly, what was left of them, I may have heard something fall into the basement over my sniffling.

"You alright?" BT asked, never looking up at me. He was busy concentrating on the box innards.

"How can you tell?" I asked.

"We've been hanging around long enough now for me to get a bead on you, plus I saw you wiping your nose." He smiled, looking up. "They're zombies, Mike," he said seriously.

"They weren't always."

"And Nazi soldiers were once small children playing just like American kids You can't go down that road."

"I get it, BT, I get it. I'm not going soft on the zombies, just a momentary twang for the lost humans."

"Let me know when your period bleeds out."

I don't think I said anything for a full minute. First, I was in shock at his words, then I wanted to laugh uncontrollably, and then—most importantly—I wanted to make sure Tracy had absolutely not heard a word. When I cycled through all of those thoughts and emotions, I merely made a fist and thrust it out to BT who again, without even looking, raised his own fist and bumped mine.

"Good one, man, good one," I said, walking away. "Get the box working."

"I think Uncle Ronnie is coming back," Travis said from the mezzanine level above me.

I went up to him. He was right. I could see the truck swinging onto the road that led to us and it looked like he had a stadium worth of admirers following.

"MIKE!" he shouted as he approached.

I waved and shouted back. "Up here!"

"This isn't working so well. I think we've awoken every hibernating cell this side of Portland. You're going to have to try an escape soon."

"Ask MJ how to turn the box on, we found batteries," I added, not wanting to waste the time and explain.

Ron had the truck rolling slowly. I could see him talking to MJ in the cab. He was running out of real estate in which to drive on, soon he would be out of earshot and he would have to loop around again.

"He says behind a group of small wires there is a switch labeled in Russian. It looks like an H and an A. He said it's very important that you make sure to—" And then he was around a bend.

"Why doesn't he use the radio?" Tracy asked.

"It's just static," Travis told her.

"MJ probably fixed it," BT threw in.

"What do you think that last part was?" Travis asked.

"Oh, I'm sure it was nothing or incredibly imperative."

"Not helpful, Dad," Travis said.

"We'll just wait until they come back around. Knowing MJ, if we do something wrong, the box probably has a self-destruct on it."

"Do you think?" Travis asked.

I really wanted to tell him that I was just kidding, but now I wasn't so sure.

"Hey, BT, Mad Jack says that there is a button behind a bunch of cables labeled with—"

"HA," he finished for me. "I thought it was some sort of nerd joke."

"Apparently it's Russian."

"Why would he label something in Russian?"

"Maybe the part came that way?" I tried to explain.

"It's done with a sharpie," BT said. "Damn nerds. Should I push it?"

"Umm…"

"What the hell does 'umm' mean? Is there more to it?"

"Yeah, but then we couldn't hear them. Plus, I'm not sure if there is an off button."

"I could always pull the battery lead."

"There was more to it. I think we should just wait…no sense in possibly damaging it."

"You doubting my tech skills?" he asked.

"No. I'm doubting the way in which MJ engineered this thing. For all we know, he has it booby-trapped."

"Booby trapped?" BT stepped away from the box. "I've been inside that thing for an hour!" he said hotly.

"Relax, I'm sure the yield couldn't be much more than a megaton or two."

"I've never liked you." He went to sit down.

I went back to the window, waiting for the return of MJ and his additional instructions.

"You hear that?" Justin asked. He was on the far side of the mezzanine.

I looked to Tommy who, besides a bat, had the best hearing among us. "No," he said.

"Maybe the library is haunted," Travis said.

"Oh, that would be wonderful," Tracy replied.

"I'd rather have zombies than ghosts," I said to no one in particular.

"Let's hear it," BT said.

"You can shoot zombies," was my more than common-sense reply.

"That's really your argument?" BT asked, sitting up. "Never had a damn ghost bite me. Afraid of a little 'boo' in the night?"

"Who the hell isn't? Ghosts freak me out."

"Ghosts don't have germs," Tracy added.

I had to think about that for a second; she did have a valid point. "That's not a proven," I told her. "Who knows what nasty things they have on the other side."

"Oh, Talbot, sometimes I feel sorry for you," Tracy said.

"You should be feeling sorrier for yourself," BT said to her.

"Alright…there's no reason to get personal." I tried to diffuse the line of conversation.

"Zombies!" Justin screamed. At first I thought he was just weighing in, right up until his rifle fired.

Zombies were coming up out of the basement. *What the hell?* I thought, my mind trying to reconcile the impossible.

Travis joined his brother in the firing. They were spilling onto the first floor, getting dangerously close to where Henry and Gary had been slumbering, both of them now missing from the couch.

"Gary!" I yelled.

"Above you, Mike! I've got Henry, was trying to see if they had the new Koontz book. I'm really enjoying his *Frankenstein* series."

That was one less thing to worry about. Now there was only the zombie repeller to think about. The territory it was in was quickly falling to the advancing army of undead. Tommy came out from a stack of books. I want to say it was the Self-Help section, but I wasn't positive. He took two incredibly long strides to the table and, with one arm, scooped the heavy box up. He turned, took another two strides, and then was air-borne. He made Air Jordan's famous leap look like something kids did on a sidewalk when they were playing hop-scotch.

"Holy shit," was all I could manage to get out.

BT had taken the more traditional approach of running up the stairs. "How are they getting up here?" he asked as he got his rifle to his shoulder.

"Maybe they have a carpenter," I said as I took my first shot. I caught the zombie high in the neck. The arterial spray lasted only a few moments as the thick fluid that arced out either congealed or dried around the wound.

"Ghosts are more scary, huh?" BT taunted as he fired rounds.

"Kiss my ass," I said as I finished off what I had started with the first zombie. This round caught it on the side of the skull, and then the bullet exited and scraped down the front of the face to remove a fair amount of features along with it. "Who needs ghosts? That will haunt me for a long while," I said as the zombie fell to the ground; the charge immediately brought forward by the next one. We held them at bay for a little bit, but more and more began to die on the stairs leading up to our level.

"This can't be happening," I said softly even as I kept shooting them.

They'd obviously found another way inside. We were

no longer shooting at the small and malnourished. Full-grown speeders were coming our way.

"Ammo check!" I yelled as I sat down to start stuffing 5.56 rounds into my saved magazine.

I had a little over a hundred. When everyone checked in, I figured we had somewhere in the neighborhood of five hundred. At one shot one kill, I thought we might make it. In a traditional combat scenario, it's probably a hundred rounds per kill. With zombies, that number dropped significantly because they just didn't give a shit. With good shooters and close quarters, the number probably went down to four or five bullets per kill. Maybe even as good as three; beyond that was pushing it. These zombies were fast, and nerves would always play a factor. Add in more than one rifle trained on a target and you start to see the problem. We'd be able to stop a hundred to a hundred and fifty of them. Then what? We still needed to get to the truck.

"Tommy, hit the switch!" I told him from the other side of the atrium.

"What about MJ's warning?" he asked.

"Running out of options…we need to make it to Gary's truck. Everyone get to Tommy."

We were a tight ball of humanity within moments. The problem was, none of us were all that confident in MJ's box, and zombies were streaming towards us. This was the ultimate game of chicken. This was harrowing; the twenty feet of distance we had to wait for the zombies to traverse was among some of the longest in my entire life. It's one thing to fight the enemy to the end; it's a completely different feeling to just let them come on in. I had a rough estimate of where ten feet was, and if the first zombie crossed it, I was ready to give the order to start shooting again. Of course it would be entirely too late, but I wanted to go out with a swirl of smoke around my head. I'd been born into a warrior's family and I wanted to die with one.

I had my rifle up (as did we all). The zombie in the

lead was snarling, blood and drool dripped from his mouth. Jagged teeth were exposed as his lips were pulled back in a snarl. Its arms were extended halfway. If this was the Revolutionary War and the battle for Bunker Hill, I'd never have been able to fire given the now famous orders to shoot only when you can see the whites of their eyes. The zombie's eyes blazed a bright red as if he'd burnt them gazing at the sun too long. His footfall came down a good seven or eight inches closer than I figured it should have. His left eye blew out in a viscous spray of material as I neatly punched a hole into its skull.

"Dad?" Travis asked nervously.

"Not yet. Itchy trigger finger," I told him.

We had to wait a bit longer. There was one more zombie that must have been faster than the group, after him…it was a horde. He was going to be our test dummy. How close could he get, though? This wasn't a force field; nothing was physically going to push him back. He was running full tilt at us. Even if he absolutely could not stand what the box was emanating, he'd cover that distance to us easily before he could shift gears and get away from us.

"Tommy, grab the box! Everyone to the stairs!"

We had to bring it to them. They would be moving slower as a mass on the stairs, thereby giving them more time to be repelled. I shot our test subject. The zombies were three-quarters up the stairs by the time we reached the edge. We were now in 'supposed' effective range and they had not yet stopped, although strange looks began to crease some of their features. Three stairs became two, their mouths were gnashing wildly, looking for something with which to sink their teeth into.

It wasn't until they were in hugging range that they faltered. They were scrabbling trying to get away from us. The issue was the press from behind. The zombies closest to us were being forced towards us. This was too close for comfort.

"Fire!"

I had to use the barrel of my weapon to push the zombie away that I wanted to kill. Fifty or sixty rounds later, we had created the bridge in distance we had been seeking. The downed zombies had sufficiently slowed up the ones following enough so that they had time to feel the effects of the box and give us our full ten feet. I would have been much happier with a hundred yards, but I'd take what was given. We'd asked for and received a reprieve. Now we just needed to use it to our advantage. We descended the stairs slowly—agonizingly slow to be honest. It wasn't that the box was not working, it was just the press of zombies was so dense as we moved, that it took longer for the ripple effect to reach them. At some points during our escape, our protective radius was reduced to half because the zombies nearest us just couldn't push back hard enough.

If you thought the stench of a zombie was bad, you haven't yet had the wonder of experiencing its breath. Maggot-infused meat, bursting with pustules of pungent pus, capped off with crusty skin growth was preferable. We'd mostly kept the zombies in a hundred and eighty degree arc around us, always keeping a wall to our backs. That was about to change as we filed out of a side entrance. The zombies outside who had as of yet not discovered the secret entrance couldn't believe their luck when they thought lunch was being delivered. We weren't more than fifteen feet down the sidewalk when we found ourselves completely surrounded by snarling, swiping, biting zombies. I'd been in some torturous situations since this crap had started, and I'll tell you right now, this one was right up there with the best of them.

"You smell something?" BT asked.

"You're kidding right?" I asked back.

Anything less than a fully stocked Yankee Candle store was not going to break through what the zombies had to offer. Who hasn't been to a mall with one of those stores?

You can smell the damn thing from the food court on the other side of the building. I'd been dragged in a few times only to have my head begin to pound from the sickeningly sweet cloying smell of sandstone and petunia. I think in order to work there you have to have your olfactory senses removed.

"Smells like plastic," BT pressed on.

And yeah, there it was. Subtle, compared to our surroundings, but it was there, that sharp smell of plastic heating up. And there was only one thing capable of doing that right now.

"Gonna have to move a little faster," I told everyone, trying my damnedest not to instill any more panic than we had going on at that moment.

Tracy glanced over at me and thought better of asking 'Why?' when she saw my face.

"Umm, Mike?" Gary asked as we got closer to the truck.

"Yeah, brother," I said, tight-lipped as the stink of heating and frying wires began to become more prevalent.

"The truck is locked."

"Okay, unlock it then." I wanted to ask him who he thought was going to steal it here. The zombies seemed like a pretty good theft-deterrent, but I let it go. When he didn't immediately respond I was figuring there was something more going on. "Did you lock them in the truck?" We'd have to break the glass and that gave the zombies a way in, but if we took off fast enough, that shouldn't be an issue. Again there was that silence. "What, Gary? What's going on?"

"The box is on fire!" BT said. I could see the glow of it shining off his face and eyes.

"Gary!" I demanded an answer. If we had to make a stand, the library was still our best chance, and we'd need to just about sprint there to make it.

"IgavethekeystoRon!" He said it so fast that it sounded like one word.

"Why, man? In what fucking universe did that seem like a good idea?!" I was pissed. He was going to get all of us killed.

"Talbot!" Tracy shouted at me; whether for giving Gary a ration of shit or to get me focused on what we should do next, I don't know.

Gary was near to tears. "I was afraid that I might lose them, or if I died you wouldn't be able to get them. And I locked the doors because I'd seen zombies messing with handles and I didn't want any of them to get in." His voice was near to hitching.

Now I felt like an asshole. Everything he had said was a valid reason. He'd even thought of the contingency if he had fallen while trying to save us. Fuck, I'm an asshole. Well, I guess that's already been established. Why I felt the need to keep reiterating the point still eluded me. Tommy had placed the box down. I would imagine because it was becoming too hot to hold. That it was still keeping the zombies at bay was a slight miracle.

I caught a glimmer of light on the side of my face; I was thinking that the box was finally flaring up, and then it dawned on me that it was from the wrong direction. Ron was coming! I wouldn't have been surprised if he had a wide-brimmed hat and a sword. The cavalry was coming, and the throaty roar of his engine let me know he was being quick about it.

"You ready, Mike?" he yelled.

He was holding up something shiny. At first I thought it was a bullet or bullets and I couldn't figure out what he meant. As he got closer, I realized it was the key. With the press of zombies around us, he would not be able to get close enough to just hand them off; the truck would not be able to take that kind of damage. I played center field for a few years in high school, but back then, a dropped ball only meant derision from your teammates, a potentially lost game, and not getting into Suzie's skirt because of an error. I guess the stakes *were* just as high now.

He never waited for my response as he sent it spinning out into the night. I didn't think they were going to have the distance needed to get to me. BT had watched Ron's toss and was moving away from the limited protection of our frying box and into the fray of zombies. I was on the move as well. I was quickly placing targets in front of my peep scope. Firing and moving, firing and moving. BT's gaze was not wavering from the key ring. Justin turned when he heard the first of my reports.

I don't think he knew about the keys, but it was impossible to miss BT and him heading away and me cutting a path for him to move. It was his additional shots that helped keep BT safe.

"Got it!" he said excitedly. For a wild moment I thought he might spike them like a wide receiver will once they reach the end zone. Then I remembered he wasn't me.

"Hurry up!" I shouted.

I think the only thing keeping the zombies back now was the flame from the box. At this point, it couldn't still be broadcasting a signal. Luckily, it was only one key. BT's hands were shaking violently, and if he had to fumble for the right one, things would have gotten a lot hairier. With the door open, I started flinging family members inside, bouncing them off the steering wheel, headrests, dome lights, I didn't give a shit; a contusion or a concussion was better than what was being offered outside.

"GO!" BT shouted at me. I was going to argue, you know the whole hero complex thing. "I need this one, man, I think I'm two behind," BT added.

If I stayed any longer we would have both died trying to one up the other. And as long as I was still in the lead, I would yield this one. I slid quickly into the driver's seat. BT handed me the key as he slammed the door shut and jumped into the bed of the truck. There was some grousing from the back as people rubbed their heads or checked for various scrapes and bruises from their rough ushering in. Ron was already speeding off, a bunch of zombies in tow.

Unfortunately, we weren't rid of our entourage; they were banging on all sides of the truck, the glass was next. I took off, noticing that a zombie had actually attached himself to my driver's side rear view mirror. I don't know if he thought he could eat the image or that the image was actually a person, but that sucker had latched on tight, it was a good block before he fell away. One lone tooth had been imbedded in the hard plastic shell that housed the mirror. No way was I going to touch that thing.

"I didn't really have that much fun, Mike," Gary said from the rear seat.

"You don't say?" I asked him. Now I just needed to catch up to Ron, but it was easy enough to follow the trail he'd left behind. Zombies that had stopped following him, and that had begun to mill around like they do, once again started running when they saw us.

"They're like those little fucking lap dogs that yip when anything comes close," BT said in complete disgust. Travis had opened the small window that divided the cab from the bed.

I didn't agree. My aunt had one of the little bastards; all you had to do was give it a slight kick in the head and it would go away. No such luck with the zombies. We were a couple of miles out from the library when the smell hit. I thought for sure we had a zombie straggler, maybe hidden in the bed of the truck with BT, although I'm sure he would have said something by now. I wasn't the only one to notice the stench either. Heads began whipping around, looking for the offender, then we all began to settle on Henry. He was the only living being capable of producing that kind of odor.

"IT fwas meef," Tommy said sheepishly.

"What?" I asked him.

He held up a foil packet.

"Foiled froccoli," he said as small pieces of the pastry

fell from his mouth.

"Did he just say he's eating a boiled broccoli Pop-Tart?" BT asked.

"Wiff femon glaze," he managed after finally swallowing what he had.

"Out the window," I told him.

"I eat when I'm nervous," Tommy begged.

"Come on, man, who eats a boiled broccoli Pop-Tart with lemon glaze? Mike, man, tell him again to get rid of it!" BT pleaded. We'd stopped a few miles back so that he could get in the truck. Now I think he wished he'd stayed where he was.

"Can I have a bite?" Gary asked. "Sounds delicious."

It ended up being another five miles until we caught up to Ron. He was being overly safe and I thanked him for it. We'd had enough close calls, and I'm just talking the last half hour.

I hugged him tight. There would always be time to give him shit. But right now, he'd saved my family's life and I expressed my gratitude the only way I saw fit.

"Thank you," I told him as I let go of the embrace.

"We're family, Mike. I didn't have a choice."

"Interesting way of putting it, brother." I smiled.

"Everyone's okay?"

I nodded. I was suddenly exhausted. You sometimes forget how much the high stress situations take out of you. The body can only produce so much adrenaline, and when it's done, it's worse than coming down off of a caffeine-laced eight ball. (Not that I know what that would entail.)

"You still going forward with this?" He phrased it as a question, but he already knew the answer. I had to; there were no choices in the matter.

"Where's the box?" MJ asked, looking inside our truck.

"You mean the kindling?" I asked him back. He had a blank expression on his face. "It caught fire," I explained.

"What! How? Why? You didn't discharge the R2 capacitor before you started it, did you!"

"Missed that step," BT said.

"We were a little rushed, but for the sake of argument, let's say we knew about this D2 resistor."

"Capacitor," he clarified. "R2."

I think he was going into shock. "How long would it have taken to discharge?" I asked.

"You have to go slow or there's the risk of fire."

"Risk," I repeated.

"Six minutes should be sufficient."

"BT, how much time you figure we had to get that box on before the zombies ate us?"

"Not six minutes, Mike."

"Listen, MJ, I can't thank you enough for the zombie repeller, it saved our lives, it truly did. And you're a friggin' genius for inventing it. Couple of things, though…it's far from a portable device, especially when you start tossing spare car batteries in it. And you may want to work on that discharge thingy. Other than that, man, thank you." I hugged him as well. MJ stiffened. He wasn't one for too much human contact. I made sure to stay in longer than was socially acceptable.

"Okay, Mike, now I know you're fucking with the man, but now you're starting to make me feel uncomfortable," BT said.

"Your hair smells good," I told him before I finally let him go. 'Call me.' I mouthed, making a mock phone with my pinkie and thumb. He skittered away pretty fast, mission accomplished.

"Mean, man, that's just mean," BT said.

"Listen, you know as well as I do, he was either going to give me shit for the next ten minutes about how I should have saved the box…or worse, fifteen minutes telling me how it worked."

"True, now what?"

"Same as it ever was, I suppose."

We'd all had a few minutes to reflect on what had happened. I was proud that, as a whole, we were able to get past it fairly easily. Some better than others, Henry didn't even seem to care. He had immediately gotten out of the truck, went to the side of the road, took care of a little business and then waited patiently until someone put him back in so he could lie down. *Must be nice*, I thought. Not the shitting in front of everyone, that part would be awkward, I'm more referring to the part about just curling up and going to sleep. Oh and someone picking me up and putting me in the truck would be nice as well.

"We've got to get going, Mike," Ron said. "I know Lyndsey's son Jessie and husband Steve, and the women for that matter are more than capable, but I don't feel right being away this long."

"I understand completely. Again...thanks, Ron. I swear I'll be better to this truck."

He didn't even acknowledge that last part, we both knew better.

He got into his truck.

"Um...you forgot one," I said after he shut his door.

"He wanted to go with you," Ron said as he pulled away.

"Glad to have you aboard," I said to Gary.

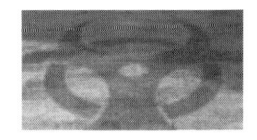

CHAPTER 9 – STEPHANIE AND TRIP

"Honey, it would be better if you stayed in the middle of the road," a clearly nervous and agitated Stephanie said to her husband. He'd miraculously not hit anything yet, but even blind luck has to find its target eventually.

Trip dutifully slowed down. "I've been thinking about this for a while now."

Stephanie waited patiently for him to continue. "Well, apparently, you're still thinking about it." She almost put her fingernails through the seat cushion as he came within a fly's wingspan of clipping a parked cop car.

"About what?" he asked, turning almost completely around to look at her.

"Oh, my God, Trip! I swear you're going to give me a heart attack. How about you stop the bus for a moment and we talk."

"Fair enough," he told her, slamming on the brakes and nearly sending her flying into his seat. When the bus was completely stopped, he smiled and looked at her. "Okay, you first. Do you have any spare tickets?" he blurted out before she could say a word.

"What?"

"The show, it sounds like you and your friends are going to have a great time and I just wanted to know if you have any spares. I mean, I can make it worth your while. I have all sorts of party materials and I'll even throw in the bus ride for free," he said excitedly.

"Trip I…"

"That's cool." He bowed his head. "I know how hard it can be to get them sometimes. If I give you money, can you get me a shirt at least? Three xl."

Stephanie laughed. "Oh, Trip, what would you do with a triple xl shirt?" She rubbed the side of his grizzled face.

"Blanket for me and you," he told her.

"You know there's no show right?"

"You hired this bus under false pretenses? Are you smuggling weed?" He looked around for any hints of trouble. "I'll help you, but I don't like the illegal stuff."

"Just about your entire life is one illegality."

"Should we go look for Ponch?"

She'd thought a lot about the man her husband called Ponch. He had a haunted look about him that she was not able to explain, that and the speed and strength he had displayed when he had launched her husband off the truck and onto the fire escape defied explanation. She sat somewhere in between wishing to seek him out and avoid him at all costs.

"Would you even know where to go?" Stephanie asked, hoping that her husband's break into lucidity would be short lived.

Trip pulled out a carefully folded piece of paper from his back pocket. He unfolded it before handing it to his wife. It was an address, and she didn't need to see the name on top to realize whose. Although it was funny to see that John had scratched out 'Mike' and wrote 'Ponch'.

"Why not?" she asked. It wasn't like they had a plethora of other options to explore, and just maybe she would find out what Mike was hiding.

"Do you think you can find an extra ticket for him as well?" Trip asked as he turned around and started the bus up again.

"Probably."

"Oh great, he'll be so excited. Now, I just got to get on the highway and to his house before the show starts."

CHAPTER 10 – DOC AND PORKCHOP

His head was pounding. He couldn't remember the last time he'd slept, or eaten for that matter. His life had been a whirlwind of pain and loss after his wife was savagely killed in front of him. Eliza had opened his beloved's throat and then let her psycho brother drain her dry. It had been a horror that had fundamentally changed who he was as a man. Doctor Baker had been reduced.

He reasoned that, if he still had a soul, it had been diminished as well. The world he lived in was dimmer—muted might be the appropriate word. He still had enough about him to realize he might be going insane, but not enough to care. A sliver of light as thick as a pencil and as bright as a laser blazed across the cell. Doc Baker scurried into the corner lest some new horror be unleashed upon him. He couldn't fathom anything worse than what had already happened, but Eliza was imaginative if nothing else.

"Doc, are you in there?" a familiar voice asked softly.

Baker didn't fall for the bait. Eliza had been breaking him down mentally for weeks. He didn't yet know what this new angle was, but he wasn't sure how much more he could bear.

"Doc, it's me…Porkchop," the rotund little boy said.

"Pork…" he croaked. "Porkchop?" His throat was so dry that he almost choked on the words.

"It's me, Mr. Baker…Dad!" Porkchop said as he threw the door wide open, letting the full intensity of the sun sear across the small cell.

Doc tried as best he could to sink into the walls to be free of the light. The light that hid nothing, the light that revealed all. He wanted nothing to do with it. There were things out there he never wanted to see.

Doctor Baker had taken Porkchop in after the boy had been forced to dispatch of his abusive father with a videogame guitar controller after the man had eaten his wife, Porkchop's mother, and had next set his sights on the boy.

"Where's...where's..." he wanted to say Eliza but couldn't bring himself to actually verbalize the words; to do so might bring her presence.

"I think she's dead," Porkchop said, coming in another step, his nose wrinkling at the stench in the cell.

Doc knew those words should bring some warmth and lightness to his heart, but the shroud it was enveloped in would not yield its Boa-like constriction.

"They're gone, everyone is gone," Porkchop said. "Even the zombies."

"Close the door," Doc said. He was ready to curl up and die.

"We can leave, Mr. Baker."

Doc stared at Porkchop's form until he began to take definition, the blurring image fading into that of a scared boy.

"For what, Porkchop? I've lost everything."

Porkchop didn't seem hurt by the words. He knew Doc's wife and kids had been mercilessly slaughtered while the man had been forced to watch. He would have been next had not everyone merely left.

"I'm still here." He thrust his chin up.

"Porkchop, I just want to die." Doc turned his back to the light.

"If you want the door shut, do it yourself." Porkchop was crying as he walked out.

Doc cried the moment he was alone. His body rocked with the sobs, tears fell in sheets. His face puffed up and his sinuses threatened to swell closed, and yet he still kept going. On some level, he wondered if he could die from the dehydration effect of so much water leaving his system. His face was a mask of agony as he wailed; primitive guttural sounds ebbed and flowed to a high keening and everything in between. The sense of loss was so acute he did not know if he could go on. Even as he stood, he could not figure out why.

He shielded his eyes as he stepped through the doorway. Birds sang off in the distance, light streamed through the long narrow corridor he found himself standing in. Chipped paint hung in sheets. He wondered if it was lead-based and laughed at the absurdity of worrying about that. He leaned against the wall, the force of reality threatening to crush him. His face pulsed with pain.

He tenderly reached up and touched it. The angularity of it was unfamiliar; a coarse beard covered most of it, something he had been meticulous in maintaining when he had a wife and kids. He nearly slid down the wall.

"For Porkchop," he said, taking a step rather than faltering. It took him close to a half hour to make it down that corridor. When he pushed through a door he found himself in a cafeteria. A lone boy sat at a table crying, an industrial-sized can of baked beans open before him.

Porkchop was self-salting the beans as he ate, large tears falling into the container. A spoonful of the caramelized side dish was halfway to his mouth when he saw Doc enter. He was out of his seat and halfway to the doc before the spoon stopped rattling on the floor.

"You look like shit!" Porkchop said, almost knocking the doc over as he slammed into his legs.

Porkchop's arms encircled the man. Doc reciprocated. Somehow, Doc managed to tap untouched reserves; more tears flowed, striking the boy on the top of his head. He didn't notice as he was making his own puddle on the floor. After a few moments, it was difficult to tell who was supporting whom.

"There's…there's food," Porkchop said. "Lots of it." He pulled away. "You need some." He grabbed the man's hand and led him over to the table he had been sitting at.

Porkchop helped the man to sit; he pushed the beans under his nose. At first, the smell of them had turned Doc's stomach, making him want to heave the snot and bile that was beginning to coagulate in his system. Then the survival switch kicked in. He didn't wait for Porkchop to return with a spoon, he stuck his dirt-encrusted hands into the slop and pulled out heaping handfuls, shoving them in his mouth, not even bothering to chew.

"My mom said it was rude to eat with your hands," Porkchop said, thrusting the spoon between Doc's mouth and the can.

Doc looked up at him. A bean-stained grin formed on his lips. He took the spoon and started using it like a steam shovel. "Bigger spoon," the doc said around mouthfuls.

Porkchop came back with a ladle and a can of beer. That seemed to appease the doc who was now drinking the beans like one would a tall cool glass of water. Doc popped the top of the beer, and in one long pull, emptied the contents.

"Another, please," Doc said after a heavy belch.

Three beers and another can of beans later, Porkchop was finally able to sit and eat his own meal. The only sounds for the next hour were that of the contented slurping and subsequent masticating of food.

"Excuse me," Porkchop said.

"For what?" Doc asked a moment before the blast hit him. Doc fell over in an attempt to extradite himself from his spot as quickly as possible. He was scurrying on the floor pushing away.

Porkchop was laughing so hard, beans were dripping from his nose. That laugh was something they desperately needed. At times it was almost manic, but it flooded their bodies with endorphins. When the air had cleared to acceptable levels, Doc grabbed his food and moved to an adjacent table. A grinning Porkchop quickly joined him.

They moved from table to table as one or the other, and often times both, would foul the air. It was one of the best days either of them had had in what felt like a century.

When they were finished, Doc led Porkchop outside. A large asphalt parking lot dominated their surroundings. They were in a factory that looked as if it had fallen into disrepair long before the zombies came. They stood on a small concrete stoop leaning up against a rusted out handrail.

"How did you get free, Porkchop?" Doc asked after taking a moment to look around.

"They just left," Porkchop told him. "I was in an office room with a guard and then we heard guns going off right outside. He told me not to move or he was going to break my kneecaps. I believed him. He went out and never came back. There were more gunshots, and then when it stopped, I heard some of the men arguing. One even mentioned that Eliza must be dead because the vials weren't working anymore. There was more fighting and more shooting, I don't think it was at zombies this time. And then there was nothing. No shooting, no fighting, nothing. I didn't want to move, though, because he said he was going to break my kneecaps. I don't think you can walk with broken kneecaps. But I was soooo hungry…I couldn't sit there anymore. So I tried to figure out what was worse, having broken kneecaps or starving to death. I thought that I might not mind the broken kneecaps so much if I was full, so I went looking for food."

Doc let him ramble, the kid was in almost as bad shape as he was, and the talking seemed to be having a therapeutic effect on him even if the doc couldn't keep up.

"Found the kitchen pretty easy. Mostly canned stuff, I was smashing them on the ground trying to open them before I found a can opener, but once I found the can opener, I was able to get them open. I was so hungry I didn't even bother to check the labels. The first one I got was a whole chicken. Who cans a whole chicken, Mr. Baker? It was horrible…all shriveled up and white, had this thick coating of grease on the top of the water. I almost wasn't hungry after that. I hid it under a big bag of rice so that I wouldn't have to look at it again. Then I started making sure I saw stuff I wanted. Found a huge can of peaches, and I ate them all in maybe five minutes, then my stomach really started to hurt. I probably ruined one of the toilets, I couldn't get it to flush when I was done."

"Fruit can do that to you," Doc said, smiling softly, stroking the boy's head.

"I probably should have come looking for you sooner, but…but I didn't even know if you were still…." He moved on, not willing to voice it. "Then I saw the baked beans and I LOVE baked beans, they're so sweet and squishy. When I started to open them, the smell reminded me of home somehow, and then I needed to go looking. I needed to know if you were still around." Porkchop looked down at his feet.

"I'm glad you found me," Doc said. "How did you get my door open?"

"It was unlocked."

"How long have the men been gone?" Doc asked, silently berating himself for giving up.

"Two days."

"And you heard them say Eliza was dead." When the Doc heard no response, he looked down to see that Porkchop was nodding. "That would explain why the zombies attacked and the men fled. Without her, they had no reason to stay together. I wonder how Mike killed her and I wish I had been there to watch. Did they say anything about Tomas?"

Porkchop shook his head.

"Good, I hope he's still alive. I want to be the one that puts a stake through his heart."

"What now, Mr. Baker?" Porkchop asked, obviously afraid.

"We get away from here in case any of them decide to come back, we get a car, and then I guess we head to

Maine and try to find Mike."

He had absolutely no clue how he was going to do that, though. He knew that Mike had gone to the Pine Tree State, but he didn't know which pine tree he might be hiding behind. He was fresh out of options. The alternative was just to sit down and die, though. That wasn't necessarily a bad idea, but he had two things he wanted to take care of first. Number one was getting Porkchop to safety; he had let his entire family down including his dog, he would not fail Porkchop. And secondly, he would kill Tommy—of that he was sure. Love and hate burned hotly and in equal parts within him, they would be enough to sustain him until the end. There was one other thing as well, and he would make sure to pack it up before they left.

Within a half an hour, they were ready to go. Doc had found a gun he was completely petrified to hold. He stuffed some supplies and food into a backpack. In his left hand he carried a worn suitcase, in his right a Smith and Wesson .38. Porkchop was carrying as many containers of baked beans as his arms would allow. Doc stared longingly at a few of the big rigs around the complex. He'd climbed into one of them, the keys still in the ignition. After a few false starts and a bucking to make a rodeo performer proud, he exited the vehicle. The thing was beyond his skill set.

"Porkchop, do you want to wait here?" Doc asked the struggling boy. "Get in the cab. I'll be right back with something that doesn't have a clutch."

Porkchop shook his head emphatically 'no'.

As of yet they had not encountered any zombies. Doc was hesitant to stay walking down the center of the roadway; it kept them entirely too visible. He was also not big on lurking close to houses where zombies may or may not be hiding. He knew his hesitancy and indecision were going to get them killed. Non-action was just as bad as a rash one. The sidewalk seemed the safest bet. He constantly scanned the area, looking for any signs of trouble. Porkchop was too busy readjusting his stockpile to do much more than follow along. They had gone perhaps a quarter mile when Doc saw a group of people coming towards them—four or possibly five, he couldn't tell from this distance. He knew he needed to get his glasses prescription renewed, but he hadn't seen an optometrist in a while. And it wasn't looking like he'd be able to make an appointment any time soon.

Doc stopped Porkchop's forward progress by blocking him with his suitcase. Two of the cans clattered to the ground.

"Hey!" Porkchop said, chasing after one of the rolling tins. When he stood, he looked where Doc was looking, the can all but forgotten as he raced to get behind the man.

The group coming was less than a hundred yards away. Doc looked to the left; there was a yard with a fence. He had no doubts they'd been spotted. Rifles were raised and trained on him. He thought that perhaps he could give enough of a distraction for Porkchop to get away. But once they were done with him, they would surely go after the boy.

"Stop right there!" Doc said in his most authoritative voice.

"Or what?" The man in front asked.

"I have a gun!"

"So do we…and more of them than you. Bigger calibers and greater range. You got anything else that might dissuade us?" the same man asked. They were still approaching, but slower and with more caution. They fanned out as they did so. There were definitely five of them, and two of them looked to be female.

"We don't want any trouble," Doc said.

"Have the boy come out from behind you. Hiders make me nervous," one of the women said.

"Yeah, you don't want to make Hildie nervous, she's the best shot here," the man said.

Porkchop came out from behind Doc's legs. Inspiration hit him. "Stop right there, he's carrying bombs!"

Doc shouted.

There was some scoffing at that, but stop they did.

"Let's say I believe you. Why are you making the kid carry them?" the man who Doc thought was the leader asked.

"Shit," Doc muttered.

"Hildie." The man nodded.

Hildie raised her rifle up, a wisp of smoke drifted off her rifle. Doc waited for the crash of bullet into sternum. When a sufficient amount of time passed he opened his eyes. *Not such a great shot*, he thought.

"NO!!!" Porkchop wailed.

Doc watched in horror as Porkchop was falling to the ground. Doc dropped his gun and suitcase to get to the boy. He didn't hold out much hope, someone shot with a high-powered rifle without a chance to get to a hospital was as good as dead.

Doc's left hand came down in slick pile of sticky wetness. Porkchop was sobbing, Doc rolled the boy over and cradled him in his arms. He was crying himself, he'd already faltered on one of his promises.

"How could you?" Doc wailed.

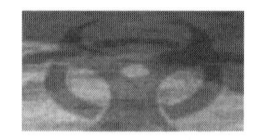

CHAPTER 11 – MRS. DENEAUX & DENNIS

"How are your sucking skills?" Mrs. Deneaux asked. "Oh, relax," she said when she saw the horrified look on Dennis' face. "This beast is going to need gas soon and I was wondering if you knew how to siphon gas."

"I've done it a few times…not my favorite thing in the world," he replied.

"Better than walking?" she cackled.

"Better than walking," he agreed reluctantly.

"We're going to need a hose." She stopped the truck where she was.

"What are you doing? There's no hardware store here."

"There's a house, haven't met a homeowner yet who doesn't have one. Fetch."

"Oh, you're a peach." He said as he got out.

She reached over and locked the door. "No hose…no entry!" she shouted before she lit another cigarette.

"Hope you stick the cherry in your eye," he told her as he retreated up the lawn.

Dennis was still muttering about his misfortune of hooking up with Deneaux when he rounded the corner of the Victorian style house. It had been beautiful once, but a mast-laden ship captain had probably lived in it when that was the case. Most of the paint had peeled off, and the wooden clapboards were twisted and appeared in agony as they tempted time and fate while clinging precariously to the sides of the house.

He had not been prepared for the sight that awaited him as he strode into the backyard. A pile of zombies was stacked up against the house, hidden from the elements by a large overhang used in previous years for firewood, Dennis assumed. Directly in front of him, and a few feet away from the beginning of the zombies was the spigot to the house, and attached to it was a gray-green hose coiled around a hose hanger. Dennis licked his lips. Was Deneaux serious? Would she really not let him in? He knew she was a few donuts shy of a dozen. How far did he want to push her?

There was another house a couple of hundred yards away, there was, however, no guarantee he wouldn't run into another zombie pig-pile. If he'd been thinking properly, he would have just cut off a length of hose with his knife. Instead, he moved closer to the deadly mass, gripped the end of the hose and began to twist. A milky eye opened, fluid dripped and fell to the ground. Dennis was struggling to get a good tight grip from the angle he was at.

"Did they use a damn impact wrench to put this on?" he asked the gods quietly.

He moved his body closer to the spigot so he could get better leverage. As the pile next to him stirred slightly, he looked over for any signs of trouble. When he was fairly confident it was probably just settling, he went back and tried to twist the hose off.

"Rightie-tightie, leftie-loosie, right? Or is it leftie...locking, rightie...relaxing? What am I saying? That doesn't even make sense. Which one doesn't make sense?" The zombies being so close had triggered a fear deep within and he was having difficulty thinking beyond anything more basic than RUN!

The pile shifted again. He almost cut and ran, not the hose, though, no, that would have made too much sense. His hands were sweating profusely, he was losing any sort of grip he had. He rubbed them vigorously against the front of his pants trying to dry them off. A zombie arm stuck out from the pile. He hoped it was merely a matter of an adjustment, and he held onto that thought all the way up until the fingers began to open and close.

His fingers slammed shut almost as tight as his sphincter. He twisted until he thought his hand was going to break. Rust broke loose from the connection just as a zombie rolled off the top. No matter how much he kept trying to rationalize, it wasn't going to work. The zombies were moving. The hose twisted agonizingly slow.

Dennis was frozen with indecision, turn and run while he could still safely make it, or cut it entirely too close and finally get the stupid spigot to give up its prize. He kept turning, although he was certain he'd entered into some sort of time warp as the zombies were beginning to move entirely too fast, and he was crawling.

"This is like a bad dream."

He kept his gaze steadily on the zombies. He made two more full turns before he realized the hose was free.

"No time to unwind."

He grabbed the entire hanging apparatus; thankful it was only held in with two screws and into wood that had long ago seen its best days. He pulled so hard that he almost toppled over. He had not been expecting it to give so easily considering how the hose had been frozen. He righted his balance, gave a quick glance over to the zombie pile, and was shocked that at least two of the zombies were now getting to their feet.

Foot race, he thought. Dennis knew in his youth he'd been pretty fast, not world class mind you, but fast enough to make more than one opponent on the football field have to pick up their jock strap after he'd juked by them. He'd stolen more bases in his career on the baseball field, second only to Talbot and *that* lucky bastard usually went on an errant pitch and subsequent passed ball by the catcher. They'd joked about it for many years,

"You should have an asterisk by your record," Dennis would complain.

"Don't be a hater, man. It's not like I was using performance- enhancing drugs when we played. Drugs, *yes…but certainly not of the performance enhancing variety. You should get me a beer. I'd do it myself, but my legs hurt from all the miles I stole on the base paths."*

"Kiss my ass," Dennis would tell him.

That had been MANY long years ago. Dennis hadn't let himself go like some of his friends, but he wasn't working out five times a week either. His job laying floors kept him fit, but the punishment to his knees had taken a lot of time off any sprint he'd be able to muster.

He was halfway across the front yard, fairly secure in the fact that he had enough of a lead to make it with relative comfort to the truck. He could hear the first of the zombies just making it around the side of the house. He looked up to the truck, and at first thought his eyes were playing tricks on him. Deneaux with one arm was sucking passionately on a cigarette and with the other she was beating furiously on an air drum to a beat he could just make out. She had the music in the cab cranked and was having a grand old time. She was staring straight ahead paying him absolutely no mind.

He was doing the mental calculations of knocking on the door and having her reach over with how close the pursuing zombies were. His comfortable lead was beginning to diminish rapidly. He could keep running; but to where? And his left knee that continually filled with fluid from his occupation was already beginning to throb. They'd be on him before he had a chance to get to the next house.

That was going to be the least of his problems, he realized soon enough. He was dragging a good twenty to twenty-five feet of hose behind him and the zombies were stepping on it, not intentionally, he hoped; but it kept jerking in his arms and threatening to pull away from him. He got to within fifty feet of the truck when he found himself airborne…and not in the correct direction. The hose was pressed tightly to his chest, and when two zombies simultaneously came down on his tailing's, he was pulled from his footing. His ass thudded to the ground and he let out a loud grunt as he made contact. With his right hand, he pushed up and was moving again. How much ground he had given up, he didn't care to check.

He could hear the footfalls behind him. He didn't have a chance.

"LEFT!" bellowed out from the truck.

He didn't know if she meant his left or hers and then he figured she was a pretty self-serving individual and it would ALWAYS be her left. He moved to his right, as a bullet blazed by his head, the trail of it leaving a finger of heat along the side of his face. The zombie behind him fell, dragging its fingers on the back of his leg. That was enough to spur him on.

"Better hurry," she prodded, as if he needed the extra incentive.

More bullets flew, none as close as the first, but he was running directly towards the hand-held cannon she was wielding. It was a truly unsettling experience.

"On your own," she told him, sitting back down on her seat.

Dennis' knees were screaming in protest with the speed he was forcing upon them. He figured he'd be lucky if his meniscus didn't just snap from the stress. He timed his steps to make sure his stronger right leg was the first to hit the running board on the side of the truck. He launched himself so hard he nearly missed the door handle. He jammed his finger so bad that he was positive he'd broken it. The handle engaged and the door swung open; he shifted his body to allow it to open freely. He tossed the hose assembly into the back sleeper portion of the cab. Mrs. Deneaux was calmly loading more shells into her gun.

"I think you should hurry," she told him without looking over.

Dennis slammed the door shut, not having enough time to pull in the rest of the straggling nylon.

"That'll get your blood pumping," Mrs. Deneaux said

as she snapped her cylinder shut.

Does a reptile's blood actually pump? Dennis thought.

The truck began to rock gently back and forth as zombies began to run into it. It became more frequent, louder, and caused the big rig to move even more.

"Like a hail storm." Mrs. Deneaux started the truck back up.

"In what fucking world is this like a hail storm?" Dennis asked, trying to catch his breath. There wasn't too much on him that wasn't throbbing in intense discomfort or outright pain.

"I see you've been letting your cardio slip." She grinned as she lit another cigarette.

They had just started down the street, when Dennis' door flew open. He thought for a moment that the hose trapped in the bottom had done it. Then, when he saw the zombie hand reaching in, he knew that wasn't the case. Mrs. Deneaux reached into her lap and in one fluid motion, pulled the gun up, and drilled the zombie flush in the forehead. He fell away, rolling into his comrades who were struggling to keep up.

"Might want to shut that," she told him. "Maybe lock it this time as well."

Dennis was hesitant to reach out. He did it quickly before another zombie that was hanging on could get in position to reach the door. He slammed his hand down on the lock just as a zombie appeared in his window. Even over the roar of the truck's cylinders, and the slow crooning of Conway Twitty, they could hear as the zombie attempted to open the door by repeatedly lifting up and letting go of the handle.

"They've never done that before," Mrs. Deneaux said, not yet putting her still-smoking revolver down.

"Now what?" Dennis asked.

"Ask him what he wants." She stopped for a

heartbeat...then she cackled.

"This shit funny to you? I almost died!" Dennis said angrily.

"Did you?" she asked calmly.

"Did I what?"

"Did you die? Because if you didn't, you should just quit your bitching."

Dennis didn't know how to respond. He'd never met anyone quite like her, and for that he was thankful. They went a little further, most of the zombies became distant memories; a heroic few were still trying to keep up. Then there was the one right next to Dennis. The zombie had finally stopped attempting the handle and was now smacking his hand against the glass. The glass and Dennis jumped with every contact made.

"Roll down the window," Mrs. Deneaux said.

"I'd rather not," he replied even as he grasped the handle. "How far?"

"Far enough so he can stick his head in and take a bite out of your ass."

"That'd be pretty far."

She stopped to look at him. "Now I see why Michael may have enjoyed your company." Her voice was a little softer when she spoke again. "Far enough where I can blow his ugly head off and not break the glass."

Dennis unrolled the window half an inch. "I've seen you shoot, that should be plenty."

She motioned with her gun-holding hand to go further. He was not happy that, with every down turn of her hand motion, the missile launcher was pointed at his crotch. He complied, quickly, knowing that nothing she did was without purpose. The window was about a quarter of the way down. The zombie gripped the lip of the glass and was trying to pull his head in.

"This is going to get messy," she said as she pulled the trigger. An explosion of gelatinous zombie material sprayed Dennis across his face and chest. He rolled the window back up with his eyes closed.

"Use this." She handed him some sort of cloth.

Mrs. Deneaux might not be his favorite person in the world, but she'd scored points with that small gesture.

"You did well. Now let's go find some gas."

Dennis could only hope that would be easier than getting the hose, but he doubted it.

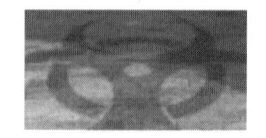

CHAPTER 12 – DOC AND PORKCHOP

"Bomb huh?" the leader asked as he came up next to the duo on the ground. He lightly kicked the burst can, sugared beans spilled out.

"What?" Doc asked, trying to clear his eyes so he could get a better look at the 'shot' boy.

"He's fine." The man laughed. "My name is Captain Najarian. Most of what's left of my platoon just call me Cap." He extended a hand to help Doc up. "The shooter is Corporal Hildie. Her illegal fraternizing partner next to her is Lieutenant Butz. Just call him 'Buzz' or he gets mad. This is my wife Dina," he said, introducing the woman to his right. "And then there's Chaplin. We think he might be prior military, but since he hasn't said a word in the two months we've known him, we don't have a clue."

"I'm Doctor Baker and this here is Porkchop," Doc said, still shaking from his earlier encounter.

"Doctor as in physician? Or one of those PhD types with an advanced degree in like astronomy?" Lt. Butz asked.

"While I do like astronomy, I am a practicing physician. Or at least I was."

"You're a pretty valuable commodity, Doc. What are you doing out here?" Cap asked.

"Oh, you poor thing," Dina said, trying to comfort Porkchop over his fallen comrade.

"It's a long story and we really must be going," Doc said curtly. He did not want to become another hostage for his services.

"That way?" Buzz asked. "Nothing but zombies up there."

"This is Hildie…bring the ride," the corporal said into

a radio handset. He had not noticed she was carrying a pack that housed the piece of electronic equipment.

"We can't go with you," Doc said, trying to find a way to extract himself. "I need to find a safe place for Porkchop, and then I have some personal business to take care of."

"Doc, just come back with us. Look around…decide if it's somewhere you'd like to stay. You do a few things for us and then decide it's not someplace you want to be, I'll outfit you with a ride and something better than a .38 snub-nose."

Docs eyes grew wide. Dina was shushing Porkchop.

"Do it for him, Doc. It's a safe place."

"Camp Custer was a safe place," Doc said.

"Whooooee! You were at Camp Custer? We were getting ready to rendezvous there, by the time we showed up, there wasn't much left," Buzz said. "Thing looked like it had been plowed under, dead people and zombies everywhere. Shit was still burning, thousands of birds were circling for meals."

"Buzz! Dammit! I think he has a fair idea of what happened there," The captain said heatedly.

"Oh…sorry."

"Buzz here is a Marine, they're not known for their smarts," Captain Najarian said. Buzz smiled wanly. "At least let us get a better meal in you and your boy and pay him back for that dead can of explosive beans."

Doc nodded reluctantly. They weren't going to let him go quite so easily anyway. The 'ride' was not a tank, half-track, or any other type of military truck for that matter. A white mini-van pulled up. The driver, who did not look much older than Porkchop, stepped out.

"Who are the newbies?" he asked.

"Doctor and his kid," Hildie said.

"Sweet, get in. Your shot woke up a few of our dead friends, and I'm thinking they're going to want to crash this party."

It was a tight fit. Porkchop seemed the happiest with the arrangement. He ended up on Dina's lap, which the doc found sort of amusing considering that the 'boy' was bigger than her.

The captain turned from his seat in front. "Can you tell us what happened at the Camp, Doc? We saw the trucks, but we can't figure out who would attack and for what reason."

"Do you have a psychiatrist wherever you're taking me?" Doc asked.

"Got a school counselor," Hildie replied. "Why?"

"Oh, you're probably going to want to have me committed after I tell you the story is all."

The ride was shorter than Doc would have imagined. He was still relating his story about the Camp, Eliza, the zombie-laden trucks, and then his subsequent capture and torment when they arrived. Everyone was so enthralled they didn't leave the small confines until he was done.

"So you're confident this Eliza was a true blood-sucking, soulless vampire?" Captain Najarian asked.

"You don't seem so surprised," Doc said.

"We've heard about her, even captured a few truck drivers who seemed to be reluctant to talk with us. And you think she's dead now?"

Doc nodded. "Porkchop heard some of the men talking about it before they left. That was, of course, after the zombies they were shipping around turned on them."

"This is some weird shit. You believe him, Cap?" Buzz asked.

"I can assure you, if I was going to make something up, it would be far more believable," Doc said in his defense.

"I'm not a hundred percent sure I believe in who Eliza was, but those men did. We have some people studying the vials she had them wearing to see if we can replicate the effects they say they did," The captain said.

"Oh…they worked. But without Eliza alive, I think they're useless now," Doc said.

"Convenient." Buzz extradited himself from the minivan.

"Don't mind him," Hildie said. "Strong as an ox, loyal as a dog, dumb as a grape. But I love him," she said as she also got out.

"Come on, sweetie," Dina said to Porkchop. "The mess hall makes the best peanut butter and jelly sandwiches."

Porkchop looked to Doc. Doc nodded. Porkchop's face lit up. "I'm really kind of hungry, the beans are great, but I always need to fart after I eat them and then sometimes I fart so hard I'm afraid I'm going to crap my pants and I don't have any other pants to wear and I don't want to walk around all day in crappy pants."

"Yeah that *would* be crappy." Dina laughed, Porkchop joined her. "Maybe I can find you some new pants too…just in case."

"I'd like that, as long as I don't have to go into the dressing room. There's always girls in the ones around me and they laugh and giggle a lot, talking about this boy and how that one kissed her and did these shoes make her look fat. How can shoes make anyone look fat? Fat makes you look fat," Porkchop entreated.

"No dressing rooms or shoe talk, I promise." And then they were gone.

"Let's get you cleaned up as well, Doc. You look like you've had a rough go off it. I'm sorry about your family, I truly am," He said. "One more thing, though, who is Michael Talbot?"

CHAPTER 13 – MIKE JOURNAL ENTRY 6

"What about a snow plow?" Gary asked.

"What about it?" I asked, looking back at him in the mirror.

"Why aren't we riding in one of those?"

I didn't have a valid response. It made sense. A ton of sense. A few tons of sense.

"That's actually an awesome idea," Travis said.

"Will we all fit?" BT asked.

That also was a valid point. The truck was beyond its limit with the eight of us. I wasn't sure about a plow, but it was basically a dump truck retrofitted with a plow. Really wouldn't be room for more than three or possibly four. And I was not keen on splitting up.

"What about two dump trucks?" Tracy chimed in. I think she liked the idea of the bigger, much safer, vehicle.

"That'll call for way more gas," I said, although that idea was not completely out of the realm.

"What if some of us got in the back?" Travis threw in.

"Naw, that's not safe. It's all steel, and you'll get tossed around like bowling balls," I said. Travis was still thinking that sounded fun as hell. Youth is its own folly.

"Wait, wait! What if we built something we could anchor seats to back there?" Gary said, the light clearly shining above his head. "Hear me out before you say anything else. We could build a two-by-four framework inside the dump part; maybe even put plywood up on the sides for added protection. And it wouldn't be all that difficult to mount a couple of bench car seats to that. It'd be perfect."

"And what about inclement weather?" I asked.

"Can't you just say 'rain'?" BT asked. "Inclement weather," he mocked, shaking his head. "It's rain, Mike."

"Well, it could be hail too." I tried to defend myself.

"Tarps," Gary chimed in, "we could have tarps pulled over the whole thing. Maybe even mount a couple of battery lamps inside so we can see."

"Sounds like an RV on steroids." I had meant it in jest, but the more I thought about it, the better it sounded. "Who gets to tell Ron we left his truck by the side of the road?"

"NOT IT!" Gary shouted.

I don't know if they planned it that way, but just about all occupants in the truck save myself responded simultaneously with 'Not it'. Even Henry punctuated this with a well-timed burp that, if listened to slowly, could have the potential to have sounded like 'not it.'

"What's one more truck in the grand scheme of things?" BT asked, shrugging his shoulders at me. "It's not like he's not already expecting it."

"Okay, first off we have a lot of things going on. We have to find a plow and then the appropriate supplies to retrofit it."

"Talbot, we're in the Northeast. How hard do you think it's going to be to find a plow?" Tracy asked.

"Is that sarcasm? Because everyone needs a smart-ass. It's my ass that's on the line here. Gary, assuming…" I stopped to look at my wife. "Assuming we find this plow, how long are you thinking it will take to modify?"

"We'll need tools, and some torches for welding, but I think with some help I could have something pretty good to go in two days, tops."

"Man, I don't like the idea of having to hole up for two days, but the idea of that rolling tank…I'm not going to lie, that sounds pretty enticing. And that two-day deadline is pretty firm? It's not like that time you promised your friends you would build them a pagoda for their wedding?"

"It was short notice," he intoned.

"How short?" BT asked.

"Six months," I told him.

"Have you ever seen all the angles on those things? It's as bad as doing geometry," Gary said, trying to diffuse the stares being directed at him.

"That's kind of funny, Uncle Gary, because it's exactly like doing geometry," Travis said.

"Yeah, well…no one told me that."

"Yet you promised your friends this?" Tracy asked.

"Hey, their wedding was just as beautiful in the tent," he said in his defense.

"Okay, we'll try this. Two days, Gary, that's it. We'll find a DPW in the next town, I'm sure they have a garage with plenty of tools. You figure out what we're going to need, and a few of us will go out and grab it."

"Mike you know how I feel about this splitting up stuff," Tracy said nervously.

"It'll just be a few hours, in and out, I promise," I told her.

"You know nothing's easy any more, right? It's not like shooting over to Starbuck's for a latte."

"Iced Caramel Macchiato," I said.

"What?" she asked, exasperated.

"I don't like lattes I like Iced—"

"Yeah, Talbot, I get it. That's not what's really important here."

I was going to argue with her that it MOST assuredly was important. I'd had an addiction to the damned macchiato. But perhaps it wasn't the appropriate time. "Hon, for the foreseeable future, this is how it's always going to be. Just taking a crap is a dangerous proposition right now."

"Eloquent," BT chimed in.

"You mind if we have a moment?" I asked him.

"We're crammed in here like sardines, and you want

me to ignore the only thing going on? You must be crazy." BT said.

"Thanks, man." I told him.

He grinned.

I continued after I directed a nasty glare at BT; he cared little. "These are the chances we are going to have to take. There just isn't a way around it. I'm not thrilled this is the way it is, but maybe finding Doc will change it. This reward is worth the risk."

"I know, I know. I'm just always afraid that when you walk out that door, some or possibly all of you won't be coming back."

"Honey, you know that isn't going to happen. How many times have I tried to leave BT behind, and he keeps coming back?"

"Fuck you, Talbot," he said, reaching over to try and sideswipe my head.

"I'll put this thing in a tree if you keep swinging at me," I told him as I ducked away.

"And that's different from your normal driving how?"

"Hilarious. Alright here's our next town."

"You couldn't pick a different place?" Tracy asked.

"What's wrong with Salem?" I asked her. "There were witches here not zombies."

"If we were battling aliens, I still wouldn't want to go to a haunted house," she said.

What kind of argument can you make against that? I took the off-ramp leading in any way. We stopped at the town hall. BT and Gary had gone up and into the building while the rest of us set up a defensive perimeter.

"Five Jefferson Avenue," Gary said happily from atop the steps.

"Yeah, because I know where Jefferson Ave is," I mumbled.

"Be nice, Talbot," Tracy said out of the side of her mouth.

"We follow this road for like a couple of hundred yards, take a right, and we'll be on Jefferson, and then it's just about right there," BT said, looking at a map that had been ripped from a phone book. "It's quiet here." BT looked around.

"The witches cast spells to keep it that way," I told him.

"Makes sense," he said, coming down the stairs.

"You can kiss my ass, Talbot," Tracy told me.

"I don't know why you say that to me as if I'm going to take offense," I told her. "I'd do it gladly."

Salem really did look as if it had been relatively untouched. That did little to make me feel good though. The last place I thought had been untouched by the zombie invasion had merely been a time bomb waiting for an unsuspecting food supply to walk by, and Cash had paid the penalty with his manhood. I cringed just thinking about it. That's it, next chance I got, I was going to get a metal male chastity belt. Yeah, right now Bennett, Colorado and Salem, Massachusetts had just about that same feel. Although, I'm pretty sure Bennett didn't have any witches, but I could be wrong.

The DPW building was much like the rest of this place—undisturbed. And it was creeping me the fuck out. Battles, mayhem, and destruction I understood. Where was everyone? The gate was open, which was a good thing, because the chain that was wrapped around the left side of the sliding fence looked like it could keep King Kong penned up.

"What do you think, Mike?" BT asked.

"I was thinking I'd maybe like an ice cold beer while I'm sitting on a recliner in some ski chalet. Maybe a good football game on, and I've never had a pedicure in my life, but that sounds like a good idea as well."

"How long have you known him?" Gary asked.

BT just shook his head. "I mean about this place,

Mike."

"Then you really should be more specific," I told him. We were still sitting in the truck staring at the small building that was DPW headquarters. "Gary shut the gate," I told him as I pulled all the way in. "Wrap the chain, too."

I did not take my eyes off the building. It only took us a couple of minutes to do a complete sweep. We couldn't even find so much as a trace that something bad had happened. Besides a bunch of dust and cobwebs, the place looked like it was waiting to open up. Salem had three plows, one of which was in the garage in more pieces than a jigsaw puzzle. The other two were all geared up with large plows and a full dump of sand.

"Pick one, brother," I said, handing him the keys that I had found on a pegboard next to the receptionist's desk. A large plume of black smoke shot from the exhaust pipe, the diesel engine was incredibly loud in the still of the day.

"Dump the sand and shut that thing down," I told Gary as I jumped up onto the runner.

If whoever was still in the town hadn't yet known of our visit, they sure did by now. It took Gary a few minutes to figure out how to work the lift, and he damn near died for it. He'd—hell all of us really—forgot to unlatch the tailgate to the truck. So, as the dump portion began to raise up, the sand couldn't escape. Gary's front wheels were six inches off the ground and threatening to hurtle him and the truck into the air and onto its back before I shouted at him to let it back down. Luckily, the learning curve had already been traveled and he knew how to do it quickly. But it was more time that the loud engine was thrumming. I undid the tailgate, Gary raised the truck back up and, when all the sand was out, he popped the truck into gear. When he stopped a short ten feet away, the tailgate slammed into the rear of the truck with enough force to sound like a Howitzer had been fired. And then he did it again.

"What the fuck are you doing?" I screamed at him. It

wasn't a quarter of the volume of the still echoing cannon-shot.

"Getting any sand that was stuck in the truck bed loose."

"It's loose! Drop the damn thing!" I told him.

"He's your brother," BT said to me.

"Yeah, but we're in this together," I retorted.

"We're alright," Tommy replied. He was off in the far side of the yard and had one hand cupped to his ear. He seemed to be listening for something none of the rest of us could hear.

The resuming quiet once the truck was off had a calming effect. If man was ever able to scrape himself up off the sidewalk, it was going to be difficult getting used to our noise pollution again.

I went back into the office and rooted around until I found what I was looking for.

"Gary, give me a list of what you need," I told him.

"I'd rather go with you in case I see things I could use."

"You need to make sure that thing is mechanically sound. BT and I will go grab supplies."

"Wonderful, do I get a say?" BT asked.

"No," I told him forthrightly.

Gary was furiously working on his list like it was a timed event.

Tracy was giving me a decent version of stink eye.

"You can almost see the hardware store from here," I told her. "It's less than a mile."

"Talbot, we've been over this before, I hate separating."

I knew she was right. I'd been breaking the damn unwritten horror rule for pretty much the entire invasion. *Never Split the Group!* Eventually, it was going to bite me in the ass. The town was quiet; there was no denying that. I didn't think it was because all of the zombies had gone on vacation though. My guess was stasis, and as of yet, we had not discovered the giant lair. I felt like a blind man walking down a street full of sinkholes; eventually I'd fall in.

"Fuck it, you know what? You're right. I probably should take Gary so he can get exactly what he needs. We can fit everything and everybody in the back of the truck."

"Really? You're really agreeing with me? Are you alright? Is the disease you have terminal?" she asked in mock horror.

"I'm flexible," I told her.

"Yeah, just like wrought iron," BT said.

"Or ceramic," Tracy added.

"Oh, that's a good one," BT said. "Because it's brittle."

"Kiss my ass. Gary, you think you can drive this thing without tossing the people in the back all around?"

"I'll give it a shot," he said with a smile.

"Wow that is *so* not comforting." I said.

Gary was driving, and of course Henry got to ride up in the cab. I put him up there before I could get any objection from Tracy. Tracy went up there as well because, after the big dog took up his space, she was really the only other one that could fit. That left me and the boy's club to hold on for dear life in the back of the truck. I made sure we were all holding onto the edge of the bed as Gary pulled out. Even completely expecting it, I almost did extensive damage to my dental work as my head bobbed and almost slammed into the steel.

"He drives as good as you," BT said, holding on for dear life.

Tommy was actually perched on the roof like an antenna; the swaying and jerking of the truck having completely no effect on him as if he had his own internal gyroscope. I noticed that his rifle was in his hands, and he was scanning the buildings as we passed. It was not a comforting feeling. If he knew something, though, he wasn't sharing. Justin and Travis seemed to be enjoying the improvised carnival ride.

"What's up with Tommy?" BT asked, nodding his head to where the boy was sitting.

I shrugged. I didn't know. "He's feeling a disturbance in the force."

BT looked at me for a few seconds, a questioning furrow developing in his eyebrows. "Is that a *Star Wars* reference? I told you, I'm not into that geek shit."

"Geek shit? *Star Wars* changed my life."

"Did it get you laid?"

"I was twelve when I saw it."

"I'm talking later in life. Did you ever tell a woman you were a huge *Star Wars* nut and she just wanted to jump your bones?"

"Well, no, nothing quite like that."

"Point made." He smiled.

"So you equate life altering with getting laid?" I asked.

"Don't you?"

I paused. For the second time that day, I'd been presented with an argument I could not dispute. "Well, it was still a great movie," I blustered, doing my best to save face.

"Friggin' nerds," I thought I heard him mumble.

Unlike the rest of the town, the hardware store had been hit. The front windows were smashed out and what looked like long ago dried blood was pooled up all over the front sidewalk. From who or what was impossible to tell. The brown stains on the cement were the only remnant left from what had happened.

"Tommy?" I asked.

He shrugged. Gary was idling in front, the sound echoing off the store and making everything that much louder. Without any prompting from me, he shut the truck down. The resulting quiet wasn't any better.

I climbed up and over, placing my feet carefully as I

descended down the side of the truck, finally finding the tire. When I was confident I was not at an ankle turning height, I jumped down. I immediately had my rifle at the ready. "We should have walked." I said taking stock of my bumps and bruises.

"Isn't there another hardware store we can try?" Tracy asked as I came up alongside her window.

"Probably, but I heard these guys were having a sale," I told her as I advanced cautiously.

"I've got the coupons." BT rushed to catch up.

"You guys should take your show on the road," she replied.

Tommy slid down the roof and hood and silently landed next to us.

"Impressive," I told him.

"I've been practicing."

"For what, a *Starsky and Hutch* remake?" BT asked.

"You're giving me shit about *Star Wars* and you like *Starsky and Hutch*?" I chided him.

"Now a 1975 souped-up Ford Gran Torino will get you laid," he said, referring to the car in the popular TV series. Again the bastard was right. "Can't really drive an Artoo unit around, now can you? And if you could, you sure couldn't find room for a date."

"I liked it better when you didn't like me," I told him as I advanced on the store.

"What makes you think I like you now?"

"There are machetes in there," Tommy said, brushing by us both.

"So?" I asked, following him. I wasn't planning on visiting the rain forest anytime soon.

Tommy had already entered the store. BT and I were hard-pressed to keep up.

"Take the sheath off," Tommy said as he tossed me a large bladed machete. He didn't say it loud, but there was definitely a sense of urgency implied. He did the same to BT.

BT looked over at me. I shrugged, but he was also ripping off the wrapping that protected curious little kids from being able to wield a dangerous weapon. As all of you know, 'child-proof' applies to adults as well. I was struggling with the damn thing.

"Put your gun up," Tommy said, rubbing his thumb along his now exposed blade and nodding in satisfaction.

My first thought was to tell him to 'fuck off'. Then I shouldered my rifle. Tommy spun away from me.

"Oh fuck!" I said, hurriedly working on my blade as I peered down the aisle. A zombie was peering at us, his head cocking from side to side like it was assessing something—or more likely us.

"No shots," Tommy said, getting into a defensive posture.

"What?" BT asked, finally looking up with a look of victory on his face for being able to conquer the damned wrapping.

"How'd you do that so fast?" I asked, sweat breaking out on my brow.

"Because I'm not a…" And then he stopped. He must have caught a glimpse of the thing looking at us. "Shit."

I smacked the blade hard against a shelf, the force shattering the plastic wrap It also had the un-added benefit of getting the zombie to move.

"Leave it to you, Talbot," BT said, getting his blade up.

"I didn't make him materialize."

Tommy was swinging, and if not for the speed he possessed, I think the zombie would have sideswiped the blade; as it was, it was pretty close. The blade clipped the top of its head about an inch from the edge. The speed and the torque with which Tommy delivered the blow sheared off the left side of its face. It fell away like a sliced piece of bologna from a dropped package. Had I seen it in a movie I would have thought the effect was as cool as hell. Live and personal, it was horrifically disturbing. For the briefest of seconds the zombie just stood there, his brain, eye and teeth all exposed on that side. Then he fell away, the weird part was he landed almost perfect in conjunction with his sectioned face like he was trying to reattach it by proximity.

"Behind you," Tommy breathed without actually looking.

I came up with the standard "Huh?" Luckily, BT had taken his morning coffee.

"Mike," came his reply.

By the time I was turning, his blade was already in motion. He lodged his midway through the zombie's neck, the head lolling to the side. I wasn't having the easiest time with these disturbing images. There was a reason I didn't like melee weapons.

Upset stomach or not, I needed to get into the mix, because I could guarantee I'd be more sick if I became a meal. BT almost killed me when he wrenched the blade free—the flat of it striking me in the top of the forehead. I staggered back, blood pouring into my eyes, probably split my skin open like an overripe peach.

"Sorry!" he shouted, his blade once again moving forward.

Another fucking reason to hate close combat. I quickly wiped my sleeve across my face, mopping up the worst of it. A zombie had closed to within a couple of feet. I didn't have enough time to swing so I jabbed the thing like a spear, catching him directly in his open mouth. I cringed as the blade struck and, at points, stuck against his teeth. Fingernails on a chalkboard had nothing on this. I drove the point through the back of his neck, and yet he still kept coming forward. I brought my right leg up and kicked against its belly, driving him backwards enough to extract my weapon. This time I took a solid swing square on the top of its skull. The bones held out as long as they could before they caved, sending splinters into its fucking diseased brain bucket.

I didn't have time to revel, nor did I want to. Zombies were coming in from both sides of the aisle. Tommy was like a ninja behind us, I could hear his blade whistling through the air. He was practically a food processor. 'For all your zombie mixing needs!'

BT could have been swinging a fly swatter and still would have probably stopped the zombies; he was putting that much force behind each blow. The three B's were constantly arcing up and around us each time he would remove his blade from whatever he had hit. I'm talking blood, brains, and bone bits. Is that four B's? I was going to tell him he should use a little more finesse, but the moments could not be spared, and I don't think he would have appreciated it.

The battle was mostly silent. I don't think anybody outside even knew what was going on. Besides the occasional grunt and resulting thud of a fallen zombie, we were all too busy concentrating on the task at hand to talk. I wanted to call out for some reinforcements. The boys would certainly come in guns blazing, but for some reason, Tommy was against it and I'd have to defer to his judgment for now. However, if we started to lose more ground, I'd have to suffer with whatever those consequences entailed. Dying was dying anyway you sliced it.

"The shelves," Tommy said. I won't swear on it, but the boy sounded a little winded, and if he was winded, then odds were that BT and I were exhausted. How long could the adrenaline hold out? And what about the damned shelves?

"Oh." I mouthed when I had a spare millionth of a second to check. Zombies were peering over at us; some of them were even in various states of climbing. "What in the hell is going on?" I swung, taking off an arm right above its elbow.

"Mike, fight is up front," BT said with a slight edge of panic lacing his words. "Is there a sale on lawn ornaments or something?"

"Party crashers." I told him, slicing Lefty across the face from his cheek through one of his eyes.

BT was backing up, and I was getting caught in the middle between him and Tommy. Maybe, if they pressed hard enough, I'd shoot up in the air like a burst pimple. It'd be safer up there. Unless of course an industrial-sized fan was spinning and then all bets were off. Tommy pushed by me and was now side-by-side with BT as I sliced up Lefty who had finally made enough headway that I could get a kill shot. It wasn't long before another took his place. I'd been so focused on the one in front of me that I'd almost failed to see that the entire twenty feet of shelving had climbers.

"BT, help me!" I yelled as I pushed up on it.

I'd love to be able to write and say that I was able to push it over on my own, but it was definitely BT's bulk and strength that sent the thing toppling with a loud and resounding crash. Most of the zombies that had been coming up where pinned under the bulk of the metal. Of the ones that weren't, they were strewn around trying to regain their footing. We pounced on them. I could see the boys out of the corner of my eye racing in; the crashing noise had gotten their attention.

"NO GUNS!" I yelled. I had swung with a sideways twist of my arm. Again I caught a zombie in the mouth, this time no teeth as the blade cut through his lips, into and through the muscles of its jaw and then finally the jawbone itself. I tore through, coming out below its ears. The top of the head flopped onto my boots; of course, brain side down. There was another set of footwear I'd never wear again.

BT was hacking away at the zombies pinned to the ground before they could get away. Two zombies had gotten up and were heading towards my boys.

"I don't fucking think so," I said angrily as I tore into a zombie, the blade catching it in the hollow of its neck and slicing all the way down her back. The glistening of her spine was going to be another thing I added to the nightmare catalog of the day. She fell over as her head canted to the side. She wasn't dead, but her lack of locomotion meant I could deal with her later. The next one I caught up to in a few strides. I launched from the ground, machete raised high and brought it down just as I landed, opening its head like a butterfly from hell.

"Talbot!" Tracy cried, exiting the truck quickly. I spun, thinking there were more zombies coming. I was confused when I didn't see any. Tommy and BT were also coming out.

"What's the matter?" I asked, searching to find the threat she was so concerned about. Blood whipped away from my head with the centrifugal force of it. I'd forgotten completely about my head wound.

"Sorry…my fault." BT came up beside me. His hands were on his knees as he leaned over, catching his breath.

"Are you hurt?" Tracy asked as she came up to me.

"BT tried to kill me," I told her.

BT almost fell over as Tracy shoved him. "If anyone is going to kill him, it'll be me!" she told him.

"Sure, sure," BT said, ambling away.

Gary was directing the outflow of materials from the hardware store into the truck. Tracy was working on my head which had finally stopped bleeding. She had me wrapped up like you see in those old Revolutionary posters, all I needed was a fife and I'd be all set. At least BT had given me a valid excuse from doing any heavy lifting. He'd come over every once in a while to apologize to me. I had a sneaking suspicion he was doing it more to appease the missus.

"Will there be any problem with the blood?" Tracy asked.

I knew what she meant. BT had just pulled the blade out of an infected skull and then thwapped the crap out of my forehead.

"I should be fine. The transmission seems to be

through saliva."

"And what about Justin's scratch?"

"Maybe whatever that zombie had eaten was finger-lickin' good." Horrible pun and I wished I could take it back. Tracy gladly didn't respond at all. Although I think I saw her face pale a little.

"Mike, we're still going to need to get some lumber," Gary said once he was satisfied they had everything of use they could get out of the hardware store.

"I'd love to be able to help, I'm still a bit woozy, though." I was actually doing much better, the splitting headache was merely a memory of itself, but there was no way I was going to not malinger, especially since I now had a valid excuse. No one save me and probably Tommy knew how fast my body could heal itself, and he wasn't saying anything. The kid was nearly silent as he went about his work. Looked like he was figuring out algorithms he was so lost in thought.

"Why no guns?" I asked when we got back on the road.

"We were surrounded by three zombie dens and they were huge," Tommy told me. "They're honing in on sounds that only humans make. Rifles and engines being at the top."

"They're distinguishing?"

"Resources are low."

"So then the truck brought those zombies?"

"I guess. I think that was a patrol."

"A zombie patrol? Tommy, I'm not liking this at all. Did they send a runner back for reinforcements?" I asked. The implications of zombies with tactics was fucking scary. I can't think of a better way to describe it. An idea flashed in my head like a strobe. "So somehow you knew the dens were there. Could you find them?"

"No, Mike, it's too dangerous," Tommy said, alarmed.

"So you can."

"Mike, what are you doing?" BT asked.

"Be vwery, vwery quiet, I'm hunting," I said in my best Elmer Fudd voice.

"You're certifiable and somehow I'm stuck with you." BT moved to the far side of the truck bed. "Lord, I haven't asked you for much, and I'm pretty sure I've never done anything in my life heinous enough to deserve this." He was quiet for a moment. "Is this a test? Is that what this is? Am I promised a spot in Heaven if I can get through this? Probably a Sainthood. I could deal with that, Saint BT. Patron saint of dipshits."

"I can hear you," I told him.

"I'm not talking to you," BT said.

"Alright, first we get Gary's wood, then me and you are going to reduce the zombie population," I said.

Tommy did not look nearly as happy as I felt. Normally, I'd let sleeping zombies lie, and maybe this was as bad as the Japanese waking the US into World War II, but they'd come out the other side an economic power house. *It's all well that ends well*, I kept telling myself. I refused to remember anything about the atom bombs and the shit-storm Japan had been for a while.

The lumber store went worlds better than the hardware store, and I was still able to milk my injury. I grabbed a couple of ten-foot long two-by-fours and then rammed them into everything around me. BT felt so bad, he had snagged them out of my hands and insisted I sit down. So I did.

"You're a horrible actor," Tracy told me. She was standing guard.

"Good thing then that BT's not a critic," I told her.

We were halfway back to the DPW shop when I shouted at Gary to stop for a second. He'd almost sent the lot of us hurtling into the front of the truck.

"What's up?" he asked, looking out and up as I struggled to regain my feet. I told him to wait.

"You need help, Mike?" BT asked.

"I'll be right back." I jumped out of the truck. I thought I heard him tell Tommy that 'I looked fine now once all the hard work was done.'

I was breaking all my rules today as I walked into Anne's Bike Shop. Number one was having to fight zombies with a bladed weapon; and second was using a mode of transportation that was unprotected. I grabbed a couple of bikes and then handed them out to the boys. I went in and grabbed a couple of more. Plus a few flat repair kits and some spare tires.

"What are you doing, Mike?" Tracy asked.

"Going green," I told her as I hopped back up.

"What's with the bikes, Mike?" BT asked, not at all pleased with the wheeled machinery by his feet. "You know I don't know how to ride, right?"

"It'd be interesting to watch for sure...almost like a circus act."

"I'm sure I could wrap one of these things around you, though."

"Zombies like the sound of engines. I'm removing that from the equation. Tommy and I are going to wipe out a few dens." I told him.

"This your idea?" he asked, looking at Tommy. "No, of course not," he answered before the boy could say anything.

"Listen, I'm not doing it because I'm looking for any more trouble than we already have. Just hear me out. It doesn't look like zombies will die on their own. Neither time or starvation seem to play a part in their physiology. Fuck, they're like Styrofoam coffee cups, they're never going anywhere." BT nodded. "And now it looks like they are starting to tap deeper into the brains they infest. Day by day they're getting smarter. I mean, I don't know if it'll come down to it, but what if they start to figure out how to wield weapons or shoot guns. What then, man? We're already swimming in a pool of shit and now they want to try and drown us in it."

"Fairly graphic analogy…but probably fitting," Tommy said.

"The stasis time is going to be our best chance to take out as many of them as possible," I told him.

"On one level, Mike, I'm completely with you. On the other…what are the odds your wife is going to let you do this?"

"I'm not telling her," I said without skipping a beat. "And neither are any of you." I pointed to Travis, Justin, and BT.

"Tommy and I are going to head out tonight and see if we can make some Z'mores."

"That's fucking gross," BT said. "If you're not telling her, then we never had this conversation." He pointed back and forth between us.

Gary had us all doing things while he welded different supports and brackets to the truck. Most of it I really didn't have a clue what they were going to end up doing, but when he started cutting out gun wells with the acetylene torch, that I knew. It was brilliant! He was making a homemade tank. And then I had to revert back to 'What the hell took so long?' There were two ports on every side including the front. He also cut out a large window that let the folks in the cab see into the back and vice versa. He welded a couple of runners and then slotted through a good-sized piece of Plexiglas so that we could slide it back and forth.

I'd argued with Gary for a bit as the sun began to set. He wanted to throw on the generator to run some lights so he could see and also use some of the power tools that would have made the building process quicker and easier.

"Are you thinking this through?" I asked him. "You want to be the only place in the entire city lit up and making noise? Might as well throw on an 'open' sign."

"I could just about finish tonight," he begged.

"It's looking great, man, it really is. We'll work on it tomorrow. Plus we won't have a hostile audience watching us."

"We've got the fence to keep them out."

"Zombies are starting to climb. Do you want to spend the next two days trying to defend this area and not be able to? Or do you just want to do what you need to do tomorrow and we can get out of here?"

"Well…option two sounds better, but option one gives me lights."

"Funny guy, do what you can tonight." And then I walked away to find Justin who was patrolling the perimeter. "I'm going to need you and your brother to have a late night tonight standing watch. You alright with that?"

"Whatever it takes," he told me. "Unless mom comes looking for you…and then I'm throwing you under the bus as fast as I can."

"That's not being a team player."

"I am a team player, just *her* team."

"Fair enough, she always wins anyway. Seriously though, I want the both of you out here tonight. This isn't just a matter of watching the gate anymore."

"Do you know what's going on?" he asked in seriousness.

"Yeah, the zombies are using the resources available to them and I don't like it one bit."

I don't know how the woman does it, either I'm pretty readable like a damn open book or a switched on e-reader, or she's just plain psychic. I acted as casually as I could all night. Never checked my weapons or my ammo, never talked with anyone in hushed tones. I just went about my business, but I could feel her eyes on me constantly. She was looking for something. This was why, early on in our relationship, I'd learned to never lie to her. I just couldn't get away with it. Now that's not to say there weren't times I didn't use subterfuge, but never with the spoken word. All of my stuff was done with plausible deniability.

Like the time when the kids were young and she had to go to California for corporate training or some crap. I was supposed to be watching the kids, but Paul was having this party over at his house, with a band and everything. Now most guys would figure out this elaborate lie about why they had to drop the kids off at the in-laws. See, that involves too many questions. I just brought them with. Paul gave them a room with a TV and I brought some toys. And I would drunkenly check on them from time to time. Responsible parenting? I think not. But it sure saved me from trying to remember what I told her or didn't. I almost got caught when she asked about the kids' new toys, things I had bought for their silence. We all have skeletons. At least mine don't have as much meat on them as some folks. Shitty rationalization tactic, but it's how I cope.

This night of all nights, though, the woman would just not go to bed. If I could have found some sleeping pills I would have gladly slipped them in her drink. As much as I wanted to press her on the subject of how tired I was and that we should go to bed, I knew that this tactic would immediately send up a red flag for her. Once that was raised, I'd never get out without a proper grilling. I think it was somewhere in the neighborhood of one or two o'clock, not really sure, I didn't have a watch. On a side thought—it's amazing how quickly the man-created concept of time becomes significantly less important in an apocalyptic setting. At least, the preciseness of it. I mean, we were still using things like tomorrow or tonight which were generalizations that I have to believe all animals use. But as for 6:32 in the morning, well, that particular time can go fuck itself. (That was what I used to set my alarm for when I had to go to work.)

She fought it. She did…but when she pulled the third shift for guard duty, she figured she had to get some sleep. It was brutal acting this nonchalant. I was revved up like an ADD sufferer at a kaleidoscope convention. I just wrote that and I'm not sure if it makes sense. How about a six-year-old mainlining espresso? Yeah, that's better. I waited until her breathing deepened before I moved. I wanted to kiss her forehead, but she'd know; not sure how she would, but she'd know. We were connected like only soul mates can be. And how was that still possible if I was a little light in that department? Concepts for a later time I suppose. Tommy was standing at the door to the office Tracy and I were staying in. He was quieter than a cat.

'You ready?' He asked in my head. I was about to tell him to be quiet when it dawned he hadn't spoken aloud. I was not a fan of that mode of communication. I patted his shoulder as I moved past him, he followed.

"Heading out for some bread?" Came out of the shadows.

"Hey, BT," Tommy said.

"Now where would you two be going at this hour of the night?" he asked, stepping out of the shadow of the building, the thin sliver of moon barely illuminating any of us.

"Don't you have some busses to bench press or something?" I asked him.

"We're off to destroy the hives," Tommy told him.

"And I wasn't invited? I feel like I've been left behind on the night of the prom."

"I'm sure that wasn't the case," I told him. "You were probably the Belle of the Ball."

"Careful, Talbot, how fast do you think I can get upstairs and tell your wonderful wife?"

"It's not your size that repels friends, it's your mean streak," I told him.

"So what's the plan?" he asked.

"Plan?" Tommy asked as well.

"Not cool, Tommy," I told him. He shrugged his

shoulders in response. I'd been getting that a lot lately. "We're going on bike, BT."

He got the implication; his leg was not a hundred percent and might never be. The bullet he caught should have sheered his leg off, and my field surgery was anything but expert-like. Doc had undone a lot of the damage I'd done, but a bullet is a bullet. Our bodies aren't designed to deal with the trauma they inflict. They do the best they can to repair the damage but it's not a perfect science.

I saw it in his face, he was warring within himself. His pride was hurting. No one wants to hear there's something they can't do. He was also thinking about giving me a healthy ration of shit. How'd I know this? Because I know BT. Plus I would have done the same thing if the roles were reversed. I thought about adding that Tommy and I were faster than him, but then thought better of it, that would be more like rubbing salt into the wound while we were pouring alcohol on it.

"BT, I am concerned with how these zombies are behaving, I'd feel worlds better if you patrolled with the boys," I told him.

"So I'm basically on guard duty while you two play hero commandos."

"BT, I'm asking you to watch out for the things I hold dearest to me. I can't think of a more important job. Plus you said it yourself, you can't ride a bike."

He looked long and hard at me to see if I was trying to appease him. Sure, a piece of me was, but the vast majority was sincere and he saw that.

"I'll watch them, Mike, and I swear nothing will happen to them, but I really do want to blow some shit up." He walked away.

"I didn't think he'd go so quietly," Tommy confided in me.

"Oh, I'm sure at some point this will come back around. I'll have to deal with it at that point, I suppose. Let's get out of here before Tracy figures out I'm gone.

Tommy didn't even say a word, he knew better.

I felt like a damned ninja when I jumped up onto the fence. I'd almost cleared it not realizing my newfound strength. I think I sub-consciously tried to force down what part of me was. I very rarely used my new skills and just tried to march on as if all was as it was supposed to be. I truly hoped that the boys had not witnessed this feat. I launched myself up and over the rest of the way, landing softly on the other side. I paused for a moment, waiting for my body to react to the forces of gravity; for the bottoms of my feet, my ankles, knees, hips and back to scream their protests at jumping that distance and the more pain-inducing landing.

I gingerly took a step, when I realized I was going to be spared all those pops, groans and potential breaks. For that, at least, I was happy.

"What about the bikes?" Tommy asked.

"I just said that to throw BT off."

There was that constant underlying funk of the dead as we roamed the streets. None were around us but the smell hung like a low covering of ground fog.

"You know where we're going?" I asked Tommy softly.

"You do know we can communicate without speech right?" he asked.

"Yeah, I know, it just weirds me out."

"Weirder than getting eaten?"

'Fine, have it your way,' I said through our silent communication.

'Another mile or so.'

'How do you know?'

'The smell is most of it, and if you stopped closing your mind off to it, there's still a connection there.'

'You're giving me crap because I don't want to talk with zombies?'

'Good point.'

We turned a corner and realized too late we weren't alone.

'Miss that one?' I asked Tommy sarcastically.

"No guns." He pushed my muzzle down.

"Dammit." I grabbed the machete from its sheath behind my back.

"Hear that?" Tommy asked, putting a hand up to his head.

On some level I did, there was this low grating buzz that I just figured was a brain aneurysm. I told Tommy I didn't hear anything.

"He's communicating."

"With us?" I asked, genuinely concerned. The last thing I wanted was a heart-to-heart with Larry the Lurcher.

"Other zombies," Tommy said in a tone that left no room for doubt that he thought I was nuts to think such a thing.

The zombie was actually wavering between running at us and waiting for his buddies to come. For a moment it looked like he was going to flee as I came at him with the large blade. Now that would have been something to see. A zombie running from me, I would have paid good money for that. Instead, I was witness to the slicing open of his head. Blood blew out in a halo. That incessantly irritating sound he was making stopped before he hit the ground.

"Did it work?" I asked Tommy, wiping my blade off on the zombie's shirt. At this point I wasn't sure if I was making the blade dirtier or cleaner, all sorts of disgusting things were ingrained on the material. Shit, I think I even saw mushrooms growing (and they weren't of the psilocybin variety either).

"Yeah, cutting his skull worked just fine," Tommy answered, not understanding my question.

"I meant the SOS; did he get it out in time?" Now there was very little chance I was going to be able to get away with this without Tracy finding out. I was covered in all manner of disgusting little tidbits.

"I think the range is pretty limited, but I'm no zombie expert. Still, I think it'd be for the best if we left this general area."

"You sound a lot like my other son…Captain."

The observation may have been obvious, but that didn't mean we shouldn't heed it. We moved over to the next side street, hoping that if any zombies were coming, they would be on a different approach.

We stayed in silence the rest of the way. I could sense Tommy's agitation as we got nearer to the town's gas station.

"Getting close," he hissed, not even heeding his own earlier advice.

"What's with the gas stations?" I asked. "Seems like they wouldn't want to be around something so volatile."

"The smell, the gas masks them."

"I don't know about that." My own eyes were watering. "That sure does make them a lot smarter than I would like to give them credit for. Let's get this done," I said to Tommy.

I almost popped my knees out of their sockets when I attempted to thrust up from our hidden vantage point and didn't move. Tommy had a firm grasp on my shoulder harness and I couldn't budge.

"Guards." He pointed to a small group of zombies milling about over towards our far left.

"Guards?" I asked. It just looked like a gaggle of the slimy fucks. "They just look like they're hanging out." And then I answered my own question. They were hanging out watching over their brood. "You have got to be shitting me. How can we possibly kill that many without one of them sending off a message?" There were eight of them that we could see from our vantage point and I had to believe they had more behind the station. "Will they go for bait and not call for others?" I asked.

"Mr. T, I have a tenuous link, I'm not the zombie

whisperer."

"I looked over to him. "That's funny, you know. I just thought you should know that. Alright, let's give this a shot. I'm going to move over to their side and when they notice me I'm going to run towards here and hopefully we can kill them all."

"Hopefully?"

"Hey, don't give me shit. At least I made a plan this time."

"Not really much of one," I heard him mutter. I backed up so I could move around quietly.

Zombies were predators plain and simple. Why would they call for help if a meal was on the line? I mean, why share all this delicious meat with forty or fifty of their closest friends when eight should be sufficient to get the job done? At least that was my hope. If we got the whole den in on the action, we were going to have to leave in a hurry.

I was perpendicular to the front of the station. I had been so intent on being quiet that they had not noticed me yet. When I got within thirty or so yards, I started whistling *All My Love* by Led Zeppelin. I have no idea why that song sprang into my head, but it sure as hell got their attention.

All nine heads swiveled in my direction. Nine? I looked quickly in the direction I needed to go; it was about a football field away—maybe a Canadian Football field. I licked my lips, hoping that my flight would trigger their instinctual need to pursue. No worries on that front, they were already coming.

"I did this voluntarily?" I asked as I started to run.

If I didn't have some of Tommy's blood in me, I wouldn't have made it, plain and simple. The zombies weren't running to a spot where I was, like they had been, but rather where I was going. They were on an intercept course and they had a better angle. Getting a touchdown was going to be difficult.

"Coming in hot!" I shouted to Tommy when I was

within a few feet.

"Like I can't see you."

Tommy stuck out his hands, absorbing my speed and helping me to slow so I could turn and help him fight the enemy. Nine, even for Tommy would be pushing it. The zombies fanned out once they saw that I had stopped and was standing my ground with another. Their hasty approach became one of slow and steady caution as they began to stalk us.

"This is unreal," I said referring to their being able to adapt to the situation and act accordingly. I honestly didn't think the use of basic weapons was too far out of their grasp, so to speak. "I'm thinking we should attack before we're completely surrounded."

Tommy barely waited for the reverberations of the words to stop before he moved to his side, his blade whistling through the wind. I was mid-swing when I heard a head strike the underbrush. We moved in a fluid dance of death, spinning clockwise to our center. The black steel of the blades quickly becoming covered in all manner of what was once human detritus. I'd killed three on my trip around the merry-go-round while Tommy doled out the ultimate punishment to five. The ferocity with which he dispatched his impartial judgment was awe-inspiring and quite frightening at the same time. He had more of his sister in him than either of us would have liked to admit.

I did the math quickly in my head, three plus five is eight, we were light a zombie. Then I noticed one was hauling ass back towards the building.

"This sucks. I like stupid zombies just fine," I said as I hurtled over two dead ones.

I caught him just as I felt that niggling feeling in my skull. The tip of my blade sliced straight down his neck and back, parting the skin and giving me a perfect view of his spine. I watched the compression of his disks as he kept running before blood began to well up in the one inch wide opening. He quickly side-stepped, my next slice catching him low in the neck, more towards the collar bone. The blade was lodged deep into bone, so much so that I completely stopped his forward momentum. We both nearly went down with my wrist attached to the machete by a heavy hemp cord.

The blade popped loose as he struck the ground. He was staring straight up at me as I brought the heel of my boot down on the middle of his face. I turned my face as gore shot up and around my contact point. The next time, I stomped my whole foot down. I'd done it so hard that it sent shock waves throughout my entire body. I twisted my leg like I was putting a cigarette out, or maybe doing the funky chicken dance, you decide which analogy fits better.

I was breathing heavy; not so much from the exertion, but from the fight itself. I was disgusted by what I had just done; yet, in one sense, exhilarated. I'd defeated my enemy on the field of battle. It was them or me, and it *always* had to be them. This wasn't dominoes; there was no margin for error. As Tommy walked up, we both watched the zombie's legs twitching like the death throes of a cockroach. Now *that* was fucking disgusting.

"Did he get his message off?" Tommy asked.

"I was hoping you could tell me."

We waited there a few moments longer. Restless-Leg-Syndrome Rex had finally stopped his movements when we dared to move again. I had just opened the door to the station and taken my first step in when Tommy spoke.

"It could be a trap."

"You don't think you could have brought this up before I walked in?"

"Sorry." He shrugged his shoulders.

It was possible the entire pile of zombies in here were waiting for us, but I didn't think it probable, mainly because the zombie I was chasing had to have been calling for help. They would have come streaming out to aid, not lie in wait. At least that was my thought process going in. The stench was a physical presence pushing on all of my senses. I swear it was so thick it was like a translucent wall that I could reach out and touch.

"Is there any need to go further in?" I asked Tommy. That we had found a clutch of them could not be denied.

He shook his head. I think he had been smart enough to hold his breath. Why I didn't think of that was beyond me. We had a little bit of luck on our side; the store section had three gas containers. Two were on the smallish side, maybe a gallon, and the third was two-and-a-half. I snagged them and went through the door that Tommy was thankfully holding open. I took a big breath when I got outside like I'd been underwater for three minutes. Tommy drove a tire iron through a gas tank and we were in business. A fair amount got on the ground, but enough got in the cans that we were going to be able to go forward with our pyrotechnics show.

"You cool with your end of this?" I asked Tommy once I laid my plan out.

"Seems like you're getting better with the 'thinking out' process." He told me.

"Yeah, I'm pretty fond of my skin and of those around me. You ready?"

Personally, I was petrified. The last time I'd messed with fire, I'd nearly died. Sure, I got to meet Trip, but the odds that another kindred spirit like that lived in this area was slim—or any area for that matter. *I wonder how he's doing?* I thought as Tommy headed back in. I was right behind him, the murky light offered from outside barely penetrating the garage bay, but what little did shine in was more than enough to see the nightmare bedded down.

'How are they not crushing the ones below?' I thought-asked Tommy.

They had to be ten deep. They were stacked more in a pyramid structure rather than the traditional cordwood fashion we'd grown accustomed to. Another new development. Tommy was almost as silent as a ghost as he ran around the zombies, letting gas from the two cans spill around them. He almost made it undetected; right up until his hip struck the corner of a workbox sending a lone wrench spiraling to the ground. I watched the glint of it as it circled downwards. The noise it made in the silence of that tomb was deafening. I caught the milky eye-shine of more than a few zombies as they heard the solitude of their domain being shattered. That they were awake and alert that quickly was another something new. Tommy started tip-toeing back to me.

"Too late," I told him. "They know we're here. Let's go!"

I pulled a grenade from my belt. The truckers at Ron's had left a lot of little goodies, this being one of them. The pile shifted as zombies began to come down.

"Go, GO!" I told Tommy as I pulled the pin.

I released the handgrip and dropped the grenade into the gas can. I'd cut off the nozzle of the can just for this particular effect. I truly wished that I could stay and watch the show, or at least have a camera set up so I could play it back later. I tossed the grenade-laden can, hoping that I had timed it to go off just as it reached the apex of the rapidly diminishing pyramid.

Tommy was once again holding the door for me. As I reached it, he grabbed my shoulder and launched us both as a plume of flame pummeled us at nearly the same time the percussion from the explosion hit.

"Holy fuck!" I said as we came to a stop from our roll. I had to shield my eyes from the brightness that blazed before us.

"We should move further away," Tommy said, grabbing me to help me up.

I don't know what it is about watching large plumes of fire and ash that fascinate men so much, but I was so transfixed I didn't even notice the stream of zombies pouring out of the station. A fair number were on fire or had some serious bodily damage as the explosion had ripped through them. But for every three or four burning or damaged ones, there was one that was in pretty decent shape and they all looked like they had revenge on the mind. Or steak…one or the other.

"Oh boy, they look pissed," I said as we started running.

Tommy was heading back the way we had come.

"Tommy, not that way," I said, steering him away. He immediately understood why. "Next time I think we need a bigger explosion."

I saw him nod. I took a quick glance over my shoulder, actually happy that I only saw about twenty or so zombies. An accurate count was beyond my capabilities at the moment, but once we found a place that was semi-defendable we should be able to dispatch of them relatively quickly before another hive could get in on the action.

"Do you think Tracy heard that?" I asked Tommy as we ran. "Because you realize that, if she did, she's going to know exactly who did it."

"You sure do pick strange things to be concerned about at strange times," Tommy said, not slowing down.

"Yeah, it's no joke being trapped in this head."

"It's got to be easier on you than those around you." He may have muttered or it could have just been the sound of his footfalls echoing off the houses as we ran.

He slowed half a step and smacked my shoulder lightly with his hand. When he got my attention, he pointed to a small apartment building. It looked more like a giant house segmented into ten or twelve units, seemed as good a place as any. We'd put some distance between us and our potential eaters, but we hadn't shaken them. In hindsight, I guess we could have, but we'd wound them up. They wouldn't be going back to sleep anytime soon, and I sure as hell didn't want them stumbling across our DPW spot. That fence wouldn't hold them back, and I didn't want to be rolling around in the back of the dump truck like a super ball for the next hundred miles.

I ran up the stairs on the closest unit. I reached a small landing. I put my machete away and moved my rifle to my shoulder.

"Hold on, I've got an idea," Tommy said as he pointed to another landing that was across a narrow gap. He stepped up onto the railing and with little effort he bridged the gap. He broke through the lock on the apartment and a few moments later he came back out the door. "All clear." Then he came back to join me while getting his rifle ready.

The zombies that had been tailing us the closest knew we had deviated from the path, but they weren't entirely sure where we'd gone. They stopped in front of the apartment and started looking around, raising their noses to the air in an attempt to pick up our scent.

"I'll give them something to smell." I felt the familiar push against my shoulder as I sent them a high velocity projectile. The lead zombie's head disintegrated into a plume of blood. He hadn't hit the ground before his posse advanced on our location. Tommy's rifle joined in and we destroyed the front ranks of the zombies.

"Shit…how many made it out?" I dropped the empty magazine into my hand and switched out. The zombies made the foot of the stairway while I was reloading. "No sense in saving any bullets," I told Tommy.

"Is that what you really think I'm doing?"

I shrugged.

"Reloading," he said, warning me. This was my cue to maintain a controlled but sustained rate of fire so I could keep the zombies at bay until he was back in the firefight. I was halfway-ish through my magazine, the zombies were close to midway up the stairs. We were going to have to employ our escape plan soon. Then my throat closed shut. I thought I was going to pass out from lack of air. I saw as the muzzle of Tommy's rifle came back up and the tell-tale click as he released his charging handle.

I pushed the barrel down just as he fired, the bullet slamming into the cement landing right next to my foot sending fragments flying.

"Mike?" Tommy asked in alarm.

"It's Melanie," I said, my heart sinking.

"We have to go!" he shouted, getting up on the handrail.

My niece was less than five steps away.

"Oh, sweet Jesus," I said as I joined Tommy. He launched and I was right behind him. She was snarling and hissing at me over the gap. I could see her debating about making the move. Tommy was firing again as some of the slower zombies saw our new location and began coming up the new staircase.

"Mike?" Tommy asked. "You alright?" He would fire and then look over at me.

I was staring over at Ron's daughter, wondering how I was ever going to tell him and Nancy. Except for the blue tinge to her skin, she looked very much like my niece. Her blonde locks were matted to her head and her cute pug nose was wrinkled up in a snarl, but other than that, yes, she still looked like family.

I held up the rifle. She was leaning over so far that I was literally pressing the muzzle up against her forehead. "Do it! Do IT! DO IT!!!!!" I realized I was screaming this; trying to ramp myself up to do the unspeakable. My firing pin clicked, nothing. I tried to pull the trigger again and nothing happened. I turned the ejection port towards me, a casing was stuck between the bolt and the port door. "FUCK!" I cried in frustration and grief.

Melanie growled at me. She was alternating her gaze between me and the staircase she was on. The zombies were coming up the one we were on now. I noticed she wasn't budging, she was waiting. Probably figuring we'd eventually have to hop back onto her side and into her mouth. She was a particularly clever man-eater, always had been I suppose.

"Mike, I could sure use your help," Tommy said, trying to shake me out of my reverie.

I pulled the charging handle back and dug the jammed brass out. I released the handle and pushed the forward assist sending the bolt home. I blew through my thirty-round magazine as fast as I could pull the trigger. They weren't all kill shots, but it definitely clogged up the main artery.

"Let's go!" Tommy grabbed my shoulder.

He pulled me into the apartment. I watched Melanie's eyebrows furrow in anger and frustration as her dinner got away. Tommy was busy leveraging a couch and a dresser against the door. He had them sufficiently pinned against a support wall that would make getting through that door some doing from the zombies. I was too busy sobbing to take much notice of his engineering feat, although I would later wonder why there was a dresser in the apartment's living room.

"Mike?" Tommy asked, placing his hand on my back. I was sitting on a chair leaned over, my head in my hands, tears free falling from my face.

"My niece is out there, Tommy. I held her when she was first born. I babysat for her. I may have even traumatized her when I made her watch *Dawn of The Dead* one of those times."

"How old was she?"

"I think she was seven."

"You let a seven-year-old watch *Dawn of the Dead*?"

"She was very adamant. God I love that kid. What am I going to do?" I asked, looking up at him.

"The Christian thing," he said, surprising me.

"And what the hell would that be? Exorcise her demons?"

"Put her out of her misery. And then tell her parents so they can begin the mourning process."

"Is there another decision tree we can pull solutions

from?" I asked, trying and failing miserably to lift my sinking spirits.

"She deserves at least that," Tommy said.

"A bullet from her uncle...yeah, that seems fucking fair," I said softly, anguish crushing out my anger.

Tommy said nothing more. What could he say? Zombies were at the door to the apartment, luckily, his makeshift defenses were holding.

"I'll be right back," I said.

"I'll come with you."

He knew where I was going and what I was going to do, and ultimately, it was our only avenue of escape. I went into the back bedroom, my boots pressing down on the soft pile of the rug, the sheer drapes billowing softly in a slight breeze. The bed was made and a couple of books were on the nightstand. At a time when I wanted my senses dulled, I was hyper-aware. Had I looked a bit longer I probably could have figured out the thread count on the neatly turned down sheet. I opened the window further, pulled the screen in and tossed it on the bed. I stuck my head out and reached up, grabbing hold of the gutter. The building looked new enough that I hoped the screws that held it in place would support my weight for the second or two that I would need.

I pulled my body out of the window and then swung my legs up and onto the roof. So far, so good. If it gave out now, I'd be heading to the ground head first. I pushed up with my right arm and then found myself atop the roof. Tommy looked much more graceful as he gripped the gutter with both hands and pulled himself up high enough that he was able to land on the roof in a standing position.

"Show off," I told him.

Tommy had moved ten feet to my one as he headed towards the apartment front door and our ultimate destination. I was in no rush. This wasn't like pulling off a Band-Aid. I wasn't going to feel better once this was over. No, in contrast, I was going to feel infinitely worse. I was going to kill this girl and then tell her father I'd done so—deeper into the depths of hell I plunged. If getting my soul back had been hanging precariously on a ledge, I'd just sprayed lighter fluid all over it, lit it on fire, then decided to piss the flames out and kick it over the precipice.

I came up beside Tommy. He was staring over the edge and straight down at Melanie. "Do you want me to do it?" he asked.

I shook my head and thanked him silently. "She's my niece." I brought the rifle up and switched the safety off.

Her gaze shot skyward towards me. Above the din of the zombies banging on the door, she heard that small metallic sound. Of-fucking-course she did. Her once deep blue eyes were looking up at me; for a moment I almost saw the girl I knew. If I just stayed focused on them, I would have not been able to shoot. It was the rage contorting the rest of her features that made me realize she was gone and would under no circumstances be coming back. I never heard or felt the shot as my body rocked back slightly. I would, however, never forget the look of confusion on Melanie's face as the bullet dug into her head and destroyed her brain. I'll swear to the day I die, if that ever happens, that for the briefest of moments, she was lucid and knew that her uncle had betrayed her.

"Come on," Tommy said. "We have to go before the rest of them figure out where that came from."

"I'm so sorry, sweetie." I turned to follow.

Tommy ran to the far side of the building and then just leaped. I was kind of in shock, and now I had to try and figure out what he was doing. I quickly got to the edge to see if he was alright. He was looking around and then up.

'Come on,' he was mouthing, moving his arm for me to follow.

"No fucking way. That's got to be like thirty feet." My body at this stage in my life could barely handle the shock of a five-foot drop.

"You can't be this dense, you're half a vampire you'll be fine." *Shit*, I thought as I steeled my courage to jump. I was in the air when he added. "And if you break something I'll carry you."

I hit the ground and rolled like I'd been taught in paratrooper school. It was probably a superfluous action, but I didn't see the reason to take any unnecessary risks.

"I don't think any of them saw us," Tommy said as we headed out.

Tomorrow, when the zombies cleared out, I was going to go back and give her a proper burial.

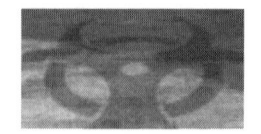

CHAPTER 14– DOC BAKER

They had pulled into a large warehouse through fences that looked as if they had been erected post-zombie. Two large mechanically run gates patrolled by a platoon of men let them in after doing a thorough check of them all, looking for any signs of infection. Machine gun nests were strategically placed on the top of the building, allowing those up there to rain hell-fire down on any and all invaders.

"I thought it would be bigger," Doc said.

Captain Najarian laughed. "I've heard that before. Come on, Doc," The captain said as he led Doc to a hydraulically operated manhole cover.

"Down there?" Doc asked.

"Most of our base is actually down here. This warehouse merely houses the way in. Any problems with claustrophobia?" the captain asked as he descended.

"No more than the average person. I feel apprehension at tight spots."

"The way in is a bit tight. After that, it opens up."

Doc was happy that he had only to walk bent over for a few hundred yards. He had been under the mistaken impression that at some point the conduit was going to squeeze down and they would be forced to crawl. When they came to the end, a large blast door stood open. A Marine armed with a sub-machinegun saluted as the captain entered. When it finally opened up, he was amazed. The initial room was, for lack of a better term, cavernous. Man-made, but cavernous. A group of ten to twelve personnel sat hunched over computer monitors in the center. A large screen dominated the far wall; although nothing was projected on it at the moment.

"We're attached to the grid, such as it is. We've found other holdouts, and we either try to retrieve them or send them supplies if they're already in a stable environment. We've been able to uplink with satellites and have a decent communications grid going."

"Impressive," Doc said.

"We're trying to mount a comeback, Doc. If it's going to happen, this is where it will start. I'm hopeful, but I'm also realistic. Man is barely holding on. Even without the threat of zombies, man is turning on each other. We're trying to restore some order of normalcy before we completely do ourselves in."

For the first time in a long while, the doc found some hope. "Weapons?" he asked.

"Some, we've got a few attack choppers and a few jets with more pilots to fly them than machines to be manned. What we're running low on is mechanics to keep them serviced. However, this war is not going to be won with bombs and bullets, it's going to be won with these." The captain pulled out a vial. "Or something like it. Come on." He led him across the room and through another corridor.

"What is this place? It certainly isn't a sewer."

"Back in the 60s, when the Cold War was in full swing and we thought the Ruskies were going to send nukes at any moment, the US built these havens all across the States in case the president was visiting somewhere and couldn't get back to a safer place. Supposedly this can withstand a direct nuclear strike."

The doc was looking around. "I'd just be happy if it would keep zombies out."

"In that, we are in agreement," the captain said to him. "Welcome to the hospital wing." Captain Najarian swept his hand for the Doc to enter before him.

"What kind of equipment do you have here?" Doc asked in wonder. The room was easily fifty-by-fifty and had thirty hospital beds, each with heart monitors. Most of the beds were unoccupied.

"Just about everything a major metropolitan hospital would have. X-ray, MRI, diagnostic machines up the wazoo. I'll be honest, I don't know what most of the stuff is, but I'm told it's top notch."

"Medicine?"

"Everything from Aspirin to Zinc."

"This is incredible."

"I thought you'd think that."

"You have doctors on staff?"

"We have more mechanics than docs. Hospitals were hit the hardest when the outbreak occurred. We have Doc MacAvie, but I think he's like a hundred and eight and retired before this place was built. There are some technicians, a few nurses, a coroner and then the head of staff, Doctor Fenling. She's about as prickly as a dried out cactus, but she's proficient at what she does. She's a top-notch surgeon, has a harder time with the smaller cases like broken bones and such. She also has the bedside manner of a pissed off chimpanzee."

"Sounds charming."

"Oh, you have no idea."

"What do you have the techs working on?" Doc asked.

"A cure."

Doc paused. "And?"

"Most of these guys were drug analysts. You know, making sure Joe Job-Seeker wasn't puffing a few magic dragons before he started stocking shelves. I think we have everything they need. A pressurized, sealed lab, culture growing ability, all the machinery they could ever dream of, but it's still like first graders trying to comprehend advanced physics. They're fumbling in the dark here."

Doc clutched his suitcase to his chest. This place was the key, he knew it, but that didn't diminish his personal vendetta. There was most likely no safer place in the nation for Porkchop. Could he leave him, though, and strike out on a fool's quest? Tommy needed to pay for what he had done to him and his family. It mattered little that Tommy had been forced to partake in the destruction. He was the only semi-living thing still out there that could slake the hatred that burned in Doc Baker.

"I might be able to help, Captain, but I'm going to need a couple of things in return."

"Name it. If I can get it authorized, I'll do it."

Doc nodded and then licked his lips nervously. "I want Porkchop to be allowed to stay here."

"That's an easy one, Doc. I've got a feeling the next request is going to be a lot bigger."

"Eliza had a brother."

"Tomas?" the captain asked, surprising him.

The Doc had a hard time swallowing as acid from his stomach shot up through his esophagus at the mere mention of the name. "Yes…him. I want him destroyed and I want to be the one that does it."

The captain rubbed his face. "Well, I was right. That one is a doozy. If this Tomas exists…"

"I can assure you he does. The blood of my family runs strong through his veins."

"Okay, so he does exist. And if I am to believe that his sister was indeed a vampire that controlled the zombies, then almost by implied relation, Tomas' blood might have the same effect on them as his sister's. I can't destroy what could potentially be a remedy for what ails us. I am truly sorry for your losses, Doc, I am. But you've got to see this on a broader scale."

"I'll look at it on any damn scale I want to!" the doc said, nearly yelling. "You and your fancy little get up weren't there while Eliza was ripping up my family, while her little lap dog Tomas drained them dry. I was! They begged me to help them, they were screaming for me at the end. And I couldn't do anything." He was sobbing. "She made me watch, she was even laughing at my torment. I have to…I have to kill him. It's the only thing that will bring me peace."

The captain put his arm around the doctor. "I've been through some difficult losses myself," he said, his eyes getting a momentary distant glaze to them. "I can assure you that killing him will not bring you any solace. In fact, it will only make matters worse."

The doc wanted to shrug the man off, but the racking sobs were making that impossible.

"If we can catch him and we can get what we need from him then I promise, Doc, I'll let you do whatever you feel like you need to. Fair enough?"

Doc finally got himself down to some sniffling. "I have some paper work, vaccines and some other samples I was working on. I'd like to get them replicated."

The captain stepped back. "Vaccines, Doc? Vaccines for what?"

"The start of what you're looking for."

The captain's entire body fleshed out in goose pimples. Hope, which had seemed such a small elusive bastard, had just doubled in size for the captain.

He made sure Doc's suitcase was treated like the gold it was and had personally made sure that the contents in its entirety were safe. The doc rested for a few hours before he came looking for the captain.

"You ready for the rest of the tour?" the captain asked.

"There's more?"

The captain led the way. The corridor was dark and narrow as they stepped in. The captain hit a light switch, illuminating the hallway. It was not more than a couple of feet across. On the left was smooth concrete, and on the right were large glass panes that went nearly floor to ceiling.

The doc gasped when he saw what was in the first room.

"We're safe," the captain said, indicating to the

housed zombie.

"Are you sure? I've yet to see a horror movie where holding the monster was ever a good idea."

"We've got to know our enemy to better destroy them."

"Sounds very *Art of War*-ish."

"In a manner of speaking, it is. We've been doing tests on them to discover ways to stop the viral takeover. Also, we've been doing extensive testing on their abilities to learn and adapt. They're not exactly the mindless brain eaters we thought they were. In fact, just recently they've begun to exhibit intelligence of a sort we didn't think they were capable of."

"How so?" the doc asked, not willing to step too close to the glass.

"They can't see you, and that glass would stop a bullet."

"How big a bullet?" The doc took a halting step further in.

The captain laughed. "Big enough. When we brought in Zippo here, he couldn't so much as open a door, no matter what kind of handle it had on it."

"Zippo?"

"Yeah we give all of our zombies names that start with 'Z'. Zippo, Zedrick, Zeus…"

"You named a zombie after a god of old? I'm not so sure I agree with that. How many of them do you have?"

"Fifteen."

"Fifteen? *That* I definitely don't agree with."

"You're not the only one, I can assure you, but the research it could provide would be invaluable."

"Alright, I am attempting to move past the fact that a zombie is no more than a few feet from me. What advances are they exhibiting?"

"Well, for instance, our buddy here has figured out doors. I'm talking regular doorknobs, handles, push-bars, everything...even being able to pull them open, which before recently was something completely out of their skill set. It's almost a geometric progression. In a few more months, they'll probably be able to do their own research on how to stop us," the captain quipped.

"That's not really amusing."

"I didn't really mean it that way. They're beginning to scare the hell out of me."

"You mean they weren't beforehand?"

"I had gotten used to the enemy. Now they're rewriting the rules and I'm not a fan. Doc, I want to tell you something, and I hope you don't get mad."

"I'm listening."

"We weren't out on some routine patrol when we came across you. We were looking for you. We had drones in the sky for just that purpose."

"Looking for me? How could you possibly know I was out there?" He paused. "The truckers you captured. That makes sense. So then this wasn't really a choice coming here?"

"Not really," the captain said, taking a particular interest in the flooring. "You weren't safe out there, Doc. You've got to realize that, and there just aren't many of you guys with your expertise around. It's you and skilled people like you that are going to get this country...shit, the world...back on its feet. Anyone can shoot a damn gun."

"Not me," the doc said.

"Okay, maybe not you. But you shouldn't be. I brought you here hoping that the innate curiosity I've seen in all doctors would take over and you'd want to stay."

Doc turned to look directly at the captain. "And what if right now I told you I wasn't interested in this place and I wanted to go on my own."

"I won't keep you. Although, I did see your eyes light up when I told you about the lab and patients that could use your help. You stay, Doc, and my word is my promise. I will do all I can to bring this Tomas to justice."

"The only justice for that animal is a bullet in the brain."

"Then that's what we'll do...eventually."

"Ever broken your word?" Doc asked.

"Once," He answered. "I was seven and I told my mom I would stop climbing the tree in our backyard. I climbed it anyway, fell out of it, and broke my arm in two places. I vowed there and then I'd never break another. Karma works entirely too fast in my case to go against it."

"I'll stay. I'll see to your personnel and, God willing, I'll find something to stop the zombies. I was wondering why in the hell you guys were walking with a perfectly good ride."

"Actually, a couple of reasons on that. We figured you might hide if you heard a motor and secondly the sound of the engine bouncing off buildings really seems to get the zombies going. We left him sitting in a clearing so he wouldn't attract any unwanted attention."

"Now that we've cleared the air, when have the zombies begun to exhibit this steep learning curve?" Doc asked.

"It's really been within the last week. The last few days, I suppose."

"Roughly the same time Eliza was supposed to have died," Doc was pondering.

"Coincidence."

"Doubtful, I don't believe in them and there's too much history to disregard the correlation. Eliza had control over the zombies, possibly even suppressing their natural ability to adapt and to learn."

"And now the yoke is off," the captain finished.

"Quite."

"Well...how far could they go?" Cap asked.

"They have the entire human brain at their disposal," Doc said, letting those words sink in for a few moments for the both of them.

"Are you saying we have the potential for super-soldiers here?" the captain asked.

"If you mean a killing machine that can move indefinitely, kill indiscriminately, and not fear death…and even begin to avoid it, then I think we're already there. As a virus, it is only concerned with one thing, the perpetuation and replication of itself."

"Doc, the only advantage we hold against them is their single-mindedness, their oblivion to gun fire. If they start to develop tactics and can even begin to wield weapons then that makes your work here that much more important. We cannot survive Zombies 2.0 with the numbers stacked so greatly against us."

"I think we've moved past 2.0," Doc said. "Help me get set up and I'll get to work."

Neither noticed that the zombie was peering out in their direction, hands pressed up against the glass. Its tongue flicking in and out rapidly like a snake.

CHAPTER 15 – MIKE JOURNAL ENTRY 7

Our walk back to the DPW compound was slow and quiet. Zombies were afoot and pissed off. I hoped they'd stay at the apartment complex for a while, but I was pretty sure that eventually they'd realize we'd departed and then they'd be on the prowl. The sun was just beginning to rise when we got to the front gate. I know I shouldn't have been surprised, but I was when I saw Tracy waiting for us—for me, more specifically. Everyone was up and looked as if they had been most of the night. How could they not be? We'd rocked a major explosion and then had some ground warfare. As soon as she did her quick head count, she'd known the cause of it all.

I knew she was pissed, I could see it in her features, and she had a right to be. I'd snuck out in the middle of night to dance with another. That it was Death only made it worse. I'll give her this, she showed restraint. She had to have seen something in the set of my jaw or the lilt in my eyes. I was not the same man as I had been the previous evening.

"Mike?" Tracy asked as she began to undo the chain.

I stuck my hand through the gap and grabbed hers, tears began to flow from my eyes.

"Mike, are you bit?" BT asked, coming up quickly. "Help him, Tommy!" BT said as he physically removed Tracy from her spot so he could undo the chain quicker.

"I'm not bit, BT," I told him as he started turning me around, looking for a wound.

"Well, you're not bit, your family is here, and you still have your rifle, I'm stumped. What could possibly make you cry?" he asked.

Tracy was standing next to me. "Mike?" She saw that BT's efforts were going for naught.

"I saw Melanie," I told her.

It didn't take her long to put all the pieces together. If I'd seen Melanie and all was well, the girl would be here with us. "What are you going to tell Ron and Nancy?"

"The truth, I suppose." I took in a sobbing breath and then exhaled just as loudly. "Although, I don't know how I'm going to do it."

"Should you?" BT asked. "What good will it do?"

"At least they'll know…they'll be able to move on," I told him.

I know he didn't mean his question; he was just trying to give me an out. I'd thought about lying, not that she was dead, but maybe rather in the manner in which she had died. Would it make the blow any easier if I said I came across her body in her car? No, there was no good way to deal with this.

I walked into the shop where Gary was busy at work.

"Man, did you hear all the fireworks last night?" he asked when he saw me come in.

"Front row seats," I told him.

"That was you? Are you alright?" He stopped and actually looked at me.

"Not sure if I'll ever be alright." I decided to let him know now before he had to ask another ten questions. "I saw Melanie…she was a zombie," I added quickly, making sure his hope meter wouldn't rise too high before I smashed it against a rock.

He didn't say anything. He turned and went back to work. He didn't want to know the particulars, and who could blame him.

"Where's the radio?"

He pointed with a wrench-laden hand. Tracy was at the doorway watching. She came over to me and grabbed my hand once I picked up the microphone.

"Ron, you there?" I barely managed.

"Hey, little brother, everything alright?" my sister Lyndsey asked.

"Is Ron around?"

"What? No cracks about my cooking?" she quipped.

"Not this time."

"Is Justin there? I've got someone here that would love to talk to him."

"Sis, could you please just get Ron and Nancy?" There was a pause; I knew she had questions. They were going to have to wait. "Now, please," was what I said. *Before I lose my courage*, was what I thought.

It was an indeterminable amount of time later when he finally picked up. "You fuck up another truck?" was the first thing he asked.

"If only. Is Nancy with you?"

He picked up on the tone even through the electronics.

"Yes," I heard him dry gulp.

"I found Melanie."

I could hear them both gasp, this wasn't the 'I FOUND MELANIE!' let's celebrate and pop tops off champagne, maybe dance wildly around a small fire sound.

"And?" Ron prodded cautiously.

I was sobbing. "Ron…Nancy…I'm so sorry…I…I…" I had to stop. I couldn't collect myself for long moments. Tracy was alternating between squeezing my hand and stroking my head. "She was a zombie."

Now I could hear their cries to match my own.

"NO, MIKE, NO!" Ron shouted through the mic, the power of his loss bleeding through.

"I killed her," I said so softly I wasn't sure I'd even made sound.

I must have, though, because Tracy brought both of her hands to her face.

"Damn you, Mike, just fucking damn you," Ron said through his haze of tears.

"Too late," I said, letting the mic swing free as I stood and walked away.

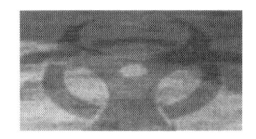

CHAPTER 16 – STEPHANIE AND TRIP

"Do you have any change?" Trip asked, taking his hands off the oversized steering wheel to check his pockets. The bus started to veer off the highway. "There's a toll booth coming up."

"I'll find some!" Stephanie said, her nerves fairly frazzled.

Life with John was an adventure, something she'd always considered a positive. His free spirit and kind nature attracted some of the nicest people she'd ever had the pleasure to meet. However, in the midst of an extinction event, she found the constant monitoring of his erratic, eclectic, idiosyncratic behavior to be exhausting. It appeared to her that he looked for ways to get them into trouble only to somehow through divine intervention find his way out again.

She'd had her suspicions since before they got married that Trip had an army of Guardian Angels that watched out for him. Why he had garnered such a legion she wasn't sure, but she was intrigued enough to stay and find out. Her only fear was that at some point they would go on a group vacation and leave Trip to his own devices. For God's sake, the man had somehow parlayed selling water at the tailgating parties for his beloved Grateful Dead into millions. This from the same man that sometimes forgot how to flush a toilet. She'd once caught him with the tank to the toilet off and a plastic cup; he had been getting ready to scoop the waste water out of the bowl and into said tank.

Just this morning he'd pulled into a gas station after he told Stephanie that they'd been on 0.0 gallons for a little past fifty miles. She hadn't known. He'd found a hand pump, something she was certain he'd never used before in his life, and then proceeded to top off the bus. All the while waving away her concerns as he sparked up a joint.

"Good for the soul," he'd told her between inhalations.

"Not if you're on fire," she'd told him.

"It's a small joint; I'm not going to catch fire from this." He stopped to take a look at the cherry at the end of the homemade cigarette. "Now, back in '76, Pinty made a huge one." Trip extended his hands. "Now *that* one caught my hair on fire. Almost joined the army because of that."

"What?" Steph asked. Looking around for zombies she knew had to be around. Trip couldn't have cared less about his surroundings as he would take a drag and then make a few pumps to keep the liquid flowing.

"Yeah, I burned a patch of my hair down so low that Pinty said I was starting to look like an army man. I guess they give you these short haircuts." Trip loosed an involuntary shiver thinking about it. "At the time, I figured I'd join and they could even my hair out to match the burnt part."

"Wait," Steph said. "You were going to join the Army for the haircut?"

"I didn't have any money for a barber," Trip said as if that explained everything perfectly.

"What stopped you?"

"From what?" he asked, looking at her blankly.

"Joining the Army." She smiled, thinking of a drill instructor trying to get Trip to do anything military-like. Although, knowing him, she figured he'd be an officer before boot camp was over, some sort of promoting from within the enlisted ranks test.

"The Army was closed."

"They were closed?"

"Yeah, it was Sunday. Even Army guys get to take a day off and partake of some Mother Earth." He grinned once again, holding up his rapidly depleting joint.

"Why the Army and not the Marines?" Stephanie asked, trying to distract herself from everything else, if she was being completely honest.

"I wanted a little off the top," Trip told her. "I'm not crazy."

"Give me some of that," she said, reaching. She didn't normally smoke weed, but he seemed to be enjoying himself, and if she could take in just a small measure of that, then it would be worth it. She took two puffs, on the second she began to feel the effects. Only, instead of it relaxing her, it made her even more paranoid than she had been. "We should get back in the bus."

"I'd like to see if they have any munchies. I could really go for a tuna fish and bacon sandwich."

She'd never heard of the combination before, but it did have its merits.

"I'll be right back," Trip said as he finished gassing up. He put the hand pump in the luggage carrier under the bus.

Stephanie was frozen in a haze. She couldn't decide if she should wait right there, go in with her husband or get in the bus and start it up. She didn't know if it was messages from her own drug befuddled mind or one of Trip's invisible entourage, but she thought starting the bus seemed the wisest course to take.

Trip came out a few moments later, his hands full of items he had picked up inside. The door had no sooner closed behind him when Stephanie saw the zombie peering through the glass at him.

"Trip, run!" she had shouted from the steps of the bus.

"Geez, I know you're hungry, but I'll drop stuff if I do that. I'll be there in a second."

Steph watched in agonizing detail as the door opened a crack, the zombie taking this point in time to figure out the machinations of the door. Trip was halfway to the bus when the zombie stepped through the opening.

"I want the food now!" Stephanie screamed. Looking over her husband's shoulder at the rapidly approaching zombie, who, if he could have vocalized it, would have used the exact same words.

Trip started jogging. "Never seen someone get violent over the munchies," Trip stated as he ran.

Stephanie ran back to her seat and grabbed her pistol, quickly getting back to the step, she pointed.

"Holy cow, Steph, I said I'm coming." Trip added an extra gear to his pace. He was within ten feet of her, the zombie within grasping distance of her husband. She didn't have a shot from this angle. Trip's confused mug dominated her field of vision. "Is this because they didn't have bread?"

"Get in here!" she shouted, grabbing his shoulder and physically yanking him into the vehicle with her free hand. Her right hand bucked as she fired the gun. The zombie's knees buckled, his head slamming off the bottom step.

"Did he not have a ticket?" Trip asked, looking down upon the body. "Do I have a ticket?" he asked, dropping all the food on the floor so he could check his pockets.

Steph gingerly pushed the leaking head off the step. "Shut the door, Trip." She could see dozens of zombies running across the parking lot towards them.

"I'm sorry!" he shouted before he closed the door. "I don't have enough food for all of you!" And with that he pulled away.

Stephanie fell back into the seat behind Trip. The ordeal had only lasted half a minute and she was exhausted. She was mad at herself that she still held so much anger towards Curtez for throwing them out. He'd killed them plain and simple. Sure, not yet, but eventually Trip's angels would be looking in the wrong direction and it would come swiftly and painfully. Life in the hotel wasn't easy, and it was still dangerous, but nothing like life on the road. The odds they were going to find this Michael/Ponch guy were slim.

Maybe she could tell Trip to turn around. She was sure that if she pleaded with Curtez, he'd take them back. She'd do double the work if that's what it took. She was about to tell Trip her thoughts when he abruptly stopped the bus in the middle of the road.

"Ready for some lunch?" he asked as if nothing had just happened.

"Sure," she said with resignation.

"It's okay, honey, I got some great crackers. You'll never notice that there's no bread."

"You still think I'm concerned about the bread?" she asked with an edge to her voice.

"Well, who wouldn't be?"

He gathered up some of the items that were on the ground and went out the door. She followed after a few minutes. He was busy mixing up a couple of cans of tuna with some mayonnaise. He had scooped out some mayo and then proceeded to dump the fish into the jar. Stephanie's stomach roiled a bit at the thought of that much of the condiment. He popped open some Ritz crackers, doused it in spray cheese, put on a thick layer of his tuna mixture, followed by some turkey jerky and then topped it off with another cracker.

"They didn't have any bacon," he said abashedly as he handed her the makeshift sandwich.

Mayo dripped around her fingers as she took the mini-meal from him.

"Eat it, eat it," he goaded, smiling as he watched her.

"Trip, I don't think I'm hungry," she said as some yellowish-white, paste-like substance began to congeal around her fingers.

"Put it in your mouth, you'll feel better," he told her as he made his own.

She tentatively nibbled around the edges. Her stomach wanted what her eyes didn't. She relented and bit halfway through.

"Oh, my gawd, this is delicious." She made sure to wipe off the stuff that was oozing down her face.

"Told you." He popped a whole one in himself. They were sitting on the roadway, leaning against the bus when they had finally exhausted their supply of crackers. Trip reached his fingers deep into the mayo jar and pulled out a small amount of mixture. "Split it with you."

"I'm stuffed," she told him right before she took two of his fingers in her mouth. He looked slightly saddened. "Relax, tilt your head back." Trip did as he was told and Steph proceeded to fill his mouth with spray cheese.

"Ewuff!" he said, trying to tell her that he had enough. Yet he didn't move his head to get away. She started to spray the cheese onto his face and beard. He swallowed hard and started rubbing his face all over hers.

"You're a mess!" Steph told him as she stood and ran to get away.

Trip stayed where he was, entirely too busy eating the food off his face to move. "This is too good to waste."

"Thank you, Trip." Stephanie came back and kissed him passionately. "I needed that."

"I didn't know I needed that until just now. You know what would go good with this right now?"

"What?" she asked him, her hand trailing down his shirt.

"Some wine. Some wine would go great with this cheese."

"How about after?"

Trip touched the tips of his fingers. "Cheese, wine...more cheese?" He asked when he got to his third finger.

"I'm not talking cheese, Trip."

"Later, honey. I think right now we really should get that wine."

She was about to protest when she heard the sounds of man. Engines to be specific...and more than one. "So just now you thought getting wine would be a good idea? Who told you that?"

"It wasn't right now, it was in the past…just a little while ago. And all the ritzy people drink wine with cheese, everyone knows that." As he was talking, he was ushering her into the bus. He had no sooner shut the door and started the bus back up when they saw the source of the noise. A gang of bikers was coming up behind them.

"Are they bad people, Trip, do you know that?" she asked, looking from him to the approaching motorcycles.

"They're not funky, that I know. The funkies mostly walk and run…always trying to cut in lines."

"The wine, though, it would be bad not getting it?"

"Sure it would. You can't effectively cleanse the palate without a proper chardonnay."

"Well then, let's go." She sat down to make sure her firearm was loaded and ready to go. Stephanie got up to walk a few seats away from Trip so that if they started shooting at her, they wouldn't be as likely to hit Trip.

"Hey, lady, no walking in the aisles while the bus is moving," he told her, and he wasn't kidding.

"Sorry. I'll be more careful next time."

"Darn tootin'."

Stephanie kept her gaze tied to the approaching motorbikes. She was having a difficult time getting an accurate number; after twenty they all started to blend together. That is when she noticed that the scenery was blurring by quickly.

"How fast are we going, Trip?"

"Speed is all relative to how fast the earth is moving."

"Okay, let's say the earth wasn't moving at all."

"Ninety-six."

Stephanie's stomach lurched thinking that the giant tin can was hurtling down the highway that fast. "How fast are they going if they're catching up?" she said aloud, not meaning to.

"Most of them look like Harley's, a couple of Japanese models as well, all of them capable of doing a hundred and thirty to a hundred and forty. My guess is that they're somewhere in the hundred and twenty range."

"How can you know that?" Steph asked, looking over to her husband.

"Know what?"

"Are we going to make it?"

"One doesn't 'make' wine, one savors it," he said, and then she watched as Trip actually stood on the gas pedal.

The bus was a missile. And still the motorcycles gained. She could start to make out individual figures riding them. Most were clad in varying amounts of leather, some had guns mounted on their handlebars or were tucked away in side saddlebags.

"I'm in a scene from *Mad Max*," she said, referring to a movie from the early eighties, one in which, as a much younger woman, she had walked out of due to all the violence. Her date at the time had stayed in for the remainder. Probably the most fortuitous time in her life. She had met Trip in the lobby; he had two tickets for the re-release of Disney's *Cinderella*.

He'd walked up to her like he'd known her for years. "Want to go to a movie, I have two tickets?"

"Excuse me? No thank you," Stephanie had replied.

"I was passing by the movie theater actually going to meet up with some friends. We were going to jam a little and then I saw the sign for the new releases and I figured I'd come in."

"You came in alone but bought two tickets?"

"Of course, who goes to the movies by themselves?"

"I just walked out of *Mad Max*. I have no desire to walk back in."

Trip had looked at her strangely. "*Mad Max*? The world's already crazy enough, why would I want to go see an angry man?"

"What then, what did you get tickets for?"

"*Cinderella,* of course. It's the re-release. Disney only opens their vaults every so often and when they do you have to snatch up the opportunity."

"So you came in here alone and bought two tickets to *Cinderella*?"

Trip was beaming. "That and Jujubes," he said, shaking the box in front of her face.

"Well then, Teddy can kiss my ass." She grabbed Trip's arm and they went into the theater.

"Was Teddy in the angry movie?" Trip asked after their first date.

She'd kissed him softly on the lips when he'd brought her home. "I'll tell you next time we see each other."

Trip waited until she went in and closed the door before going up onto the porch and knocking on the side window. Stephanie peeked out with a confused smile. "This is the next time I'm seeing you," he told her.

Stephanie knew at that moment she was falling in love with the quirky man. It had only grown as time had gone on—even now as they blazed down the roadway—she just hoped the scene unfolding around them was not somehow their entire relationship come full circle. She wasn't ready for the loop to close just yet.

"Did you ever find that change?" Trip asked.

"We'll be fine, they'll just take a picture of the license plate and send us a bill in the mail," she told him to keep his mind from wandering away from what he was doing.

Her hands were shaking as she went to the back of the bus. The bikers were within a hundred yards; if there was any chance that their actions were anything but nefarious that threshold was crossed when she saw a wisp of smoke rise from one of them and felt the impact as the slug slammed into the rear of the bus. On the aisle across from her, it took three seats to stop the bullet. Small fibers of stuffing were suspended in the air, swirling about lazily in the maelstrom that was happening around them.

Stephanie moved back four rows and rested the barrel of her gun on the seat behind her. She thought about warning Trip, but he'd have questions she didn't have time to answer. The shot was deafening in the closed area. She barely heard the explosion as the rear window blew out. She had to give Trip some serious kudos; the bus did not so much as shimmy in either direction. Although, in fairness, he probably hadn't heard it, lost in one of his alternate realities such as he was from time to time. She had aimed high, the shot merely meant as a warning to those who followed that maybe there was an easier mark out there. Instead of dissuading them, it seemed to spur them on. More shots began to pepper the back of the bus. The high 'tinging' as lead met aluminum reverberated throughout the structure.

"That's some horrible feedback!" Trip yelled over the rush of air. "They should get their sound system checked out!" he added. "Want me to have a look at it? I was a roadie once."

"NO!" Stephanie screamed. He most likely would have walked away from his steering wheel if she hadn't answered quickly enough.

One of the bikers who had been struggling with his rifle tweaked his front wheel just enough to send the rear of his bike up and over the front end, colliding with the pavement in a devastatingly spectacular destruction of metal and flesh. His helmet or his head had exploded on contact; she wasn't sure which as he was passed by quickly. She was saddened the accident had only taken out one other rider. The bikes were sent ripping through the underbrush on the side of the roadway. The drivers were merely stains left on the highway like a leaky old Chevy. After that incident, though, the bikers did spread out, making tougher targets of themselves.

Stephanie tried to get off more shots, but every time

she poked her head up, the bikers were near enough to see what she was doing and would take some dangerously close shots at her. She remained ducked down by the side and was just able to see as the bikes began to move alongside. She wondered if they would try to board like a pirate ship.

A gaping hole blew in the side panel right next to her thigh. They knew exactly where she was. She looked quickly out her window to see a large, barrel-chested, keg-bellied man attempting to reload his revolver at a hundred miles an hour, his long beard whipping around his face, making the task just that much more difficult. Stephanie felt herself thrust to the floor of the bus as Trip pulled it hard to the left, the rear of the bus catching the surprised biker broadside. The much larger bus barely noticed the contact. The biker was sent spinning down the roadway at first leaving a trail of sparks and then leather, followed quickly by skin, blood, muscle and finally bone scraping against the ground before he was done moving.

She looked up to Trip to gauge if he had any sort of reaction. She couldn't tell, he was singing *Fire on the Mountain* at the top of his lungs, his hands beating rhythmically against the steering wheel. The bikers pulled back slightly. Stephanie hoped that they were going to give up. What she didn't realize was that they were just attempting to get better firing angles on the tires. The bus rocked slightly as a tire on the other side was blown out in a hail of bullets.

"That's going to be a pain in the ass to change," Trip yelled. "Hold on!" Trip was laughing now. "Probably shouldn't have taken that second dose!" Tears from laughter were streaming down his face.

'Second dose of what?' She wanted to ask, but she was finding herself pinned against the floor and the bottom of the seat as Trip lay heavily on the brakes. A couple of the bikers were halfway up the sides before they realized what was going on. One of the bikers was unfortunate to not have been paying attention. Steph could see his screaming face illuminated in the bright red of the brake lights. Caustic black smoke ripped up from his tires as he tried to brake in time, the front of his bike went under the bus, his face collided with the rear, his chin catching the metal right below the blown out window. Bloody stumps of teeth were launched into the bus almost hitting Stephanie's stunned features. His bike had fallen away, but somehow the man was momentarily stuck on the edge. His jaw had been pushed back so far that his overbite was what was keeping him attached. His eyes were glazed over in shock, blood was pouring out of his nose and the top of his mouth. He lingered a few dreadful seconds longer before he fell away as well.

Trip juked the bus back towards the right, narrowly missing one of the bikers who was scrambling to slow down and get out of the path of the behemoth. He swerved into the soft shoulder of the roadway, his arms rippling against the forces that wanted to upend him. When he got to a complete stop, he took a moment to compose himself before he rejoined the chase. He hoped that his pants would dry before this was all over. His friend 'Lucky' was not quite his namesake as Trip clipped him. The bus lurched into the air as Lucky's bike went underneath. Stephanie smacked her head on the seat above her hard enough that she felt like a cartoon character replete with stars and everything.

Trip had taken out another biker, but at the sacrifice of another tire. These were not numbers he could easily sustain; the city bus was equipped originally with six tires and he was down to four. The bikers stayed a good fifty yards back, wary that their adversary might do something else erratic. If they had known he was a burned out hippy, they may not have been quite as easily spooked.

Stephanie stayed low on the floor and crawled back up to the front. Trip looked down at her.

"Crawling counts as leaving your seat, ma'am."

Steph pulled herself up into the seat behind him. She

looked over his shoulder. He was doing a slightly slower speed of eighty-five. She noticed the gas gauge was sitting at half. She knew they had not traveled far enough that it should be that low. In addition to losing two tires, the gas tank had been compromised. And right now there were more bikers than she had bullets.

"I love you," she told Trip.

"I love you too, honey, but that's not going to get you out of your fare," he said, reaching behind and grasping her shoulder.

Steph turned back to the bikers who had dropped off a little further and she knew why. The bus was leaving a steady stream of gas along the roadway like a cow pissing on a flat rock. It was only a waiting game now until the bus was drained dry, and like hyenas to a dying elephant, they would leap when the time was right.

"Want to drive for a minute? I've really got to take a leak," he told Stephanie.

He started to stand before she could even comment. She reached through his legs to grab the wheel, he stepped over and she quickly slid in to his spot; the seat was roasting. Trip stumbled down the aisle as he fumbled with his pants. Stephanie watched his progress in the over-sized mirror.

"What are you doing?" she asked in alarm as she watched him brace himself against the rear frame of the bus, his pants down by his ankles. She imagined his penis flapping in the wind as he sent sprays of urine towards the unsuspecting bikers. "Well shit, if that doesn't make them think he's nuts, then nothing will."

Trip was laughing like a loon.

"Is that guy pissing at us?" Blaze, the leader of the biker gang, asked. None of his people could hear him over the roar of their engines, but they had to have been thinking the same thing as they looked back and forth at each other. *How crazy is this guy?* He shuddered. He wouldn't stray from their raid, because now it would look like a sign of weakness, but he would make sure to hang back a bit and wait for mop up duty.

"That was fantastic," Trip said, coming up to his wife, his private parts at about eye level with her.

"You know you should really pull your pants up now," she said, glancing over at him.

"Oh!" he exclaimed, looking down. "I was wondering why it was so difficult to walk. When'd we get a bus?" He looked around.

"You do know you've been driving for a couple of hundred miles right?"

"Fantastic!" he said, not elaborating. "How'd I do?" he asked in all seriousness.

"Not bad considering you don't have a license."

"Any problems with the boys in blue?"

"Haven't seen one all day. Although for once, I wish they were out." She glanced over to her mirror. "Trip, we're running out of gas."

"When you get to the first major route going north and south, take it," he told her.

"Which way?"

"Which way is Maine?" Trip asked.

"North."

"Then we go north."

"Do you want to drive?"

"That's crazy, how would we ever switch while you were driving? Stephanie, sometimes I just don't know what you're thinking." He sat down and was still shaking his head a few seconds later.

By the time she saw the signs for 495 Northbound ahead two miles, her gauge was reading a quarter of a tank. Unless Mike's house was in the next fifty miles, she didn't know how they were ever going to get there. The bikers had kept their distance and maybe even a bit more so after Trip's display, but they were close enough to strike at will. She apparently was doing enough worrying for the both of them.

Trip was asleep on the small seat, his head completely bent back over the headrest so that his Adam's apple was the highest point on his body. More than once she thought about driving the bus into a giant sign column or perhaps a bridge abutment.

And she may have if she could have been convinced that the maneuver would kill them both instantly. Her biggest fear was that they might only be incapacitated with a broken leg or arm and then they would still have to suffer the wrath of the bikers. She had a feeling the men behind would not be swift in their dealings with them.

"Why am I so willing to give up hope?" she asked quietly.

"Because it's a fucked up world," Trip said. He was watching her closely. She had not realized he had awoken and certainly was not expecting that he would have heard her.

She'd once made him take a hearing test because of some of his inane responses to the most basic of questions. He'd lost somewhere in the neighborhood of fifty percent of his hearing from concerts, but certainly not enough to explain all of his answers. She was certain she had asked her question soft enough that he should have not been able to hear it in a quiet living room if they were next to each other. The fact that wind was ripping through the bus, plus the flapping of destroyed tires striking the pavement, and add to that he was two seats away, should have made it impossible.

"I'm so sorry," she said to him.

"We're still alive and we're still together. Plus, I have some killer weed. Want a hit? Want me to drive?" he asked as he nearly began to sit on her lap.

"Let me get out of the way, will you. The highway is coming up in about a mile." She pointed to a large sign with the familiar blue and white logo.

"Want to see something cool?" Trip asked he strapped on his seatbelt.

"Not really," she told him in all honesty.

The bus began to pick up speed just as they were approaching the off-ramp.

"Trip, what are you doing?" she asked, dread rising up fast within her.

She was convinced it would be impossible for him to take the turn at this speed. She checked back towards the bikers and saw that they had fallen back even a little more. *How much time will we have to escape from an overturned bus before they're on us?*

She felt her body get thrust against the bus wall, she was nearly pinned from the centrifugal force. Trip seemed to grow in his seat. She realized it wasn't that he was getting bigger, but rather, he was rising up in the air as the tires on the left side of the bus lost their contact with the ground.

"Are you kidding me?" she shrieked.

The bus was halfway through the clover, and the wheels had not yet struck down. Trip was laughing and would occasionally look over at his wife, at the contortions to her body, and face.

"This isn't even the good part," he told her.

She didn't even have time to respond before the magnet that was sticking her to the right was now pulling her to the seat back in front of her. The bus slammed back down to the ground as Trip lay down heavily on the brake. The smell of melting brake pads dominated the interior of the bus. Stephanie felt like a rag doll as she was pushed back into her seat. The bus was picking up speed as Trip drove it backwards.

"Look, ma, no hands!" Trip yelled as he drove with his knees.

"I'm going to kill you!" Stephanie screamed, holding on to anything that looked like it might save her life.

Blaze sped up when he saw the bus take the exit. He wasn't overly concerned about losing the much slower vehicle, but he liked it better when it was within view. The rest of his posse followed suit. He was looking forward to the catching and the subsequent beatings of the occupants of the bus for what they'd done to some of his men. That he'd started the whole affair was of no consequence to him.

He hit the ramp at a modest seventy-five and was just starting to lean into the turn when he saw the massive white of the buses rear end looming up in front of him. He had at first mistakenly assumed that the driver had stopped and decided to make a last stand here or they were already making a run for the tree line. It was the bright white of the back-ups lights that made him realize his mistake, and not a moment too soon as he veered sharply off the road and into the long grass on his right. His handlebars were bucking wildly, and it took all of his balance and experience to keep the bike from spilling him.

The closest two riders behind him were not quite fortunate enough to realize that the bus was coming full speed at them. He was swearing loudly, wrestling his bike when the collision of metal on metal hit. The impact broke, glass, metal, plastic, and the easiest of all…bones. Out of the corner of his eye, he was able to see as the bus rode up and over his brother-in-law. Blaze was infuriated; it was the first man his sister had ever hooked up with that he actually got along with. And now his brains were dripping off the guardrail.

The second biker to collide with the back had not been as fortunate. His bike, with him attached, got caught underneath the bus. The rear wheel was slowly eroding his left leg away and his screams could be clearly heard over the destruction of his bike. When the rear wheel of the bus had finally caught a significant enough portion of his bike to pull it through, it ran over what remained of his leg and up and over his pelvic bones, crushing them into dust. The front wheel missed his head by scant inches; Blaze wished it had hit him if only to shut up his wailing. The rest of the bikers had enough time to see what was happening and avoid the bus.

Trip stopped quickly and slammed the transmission into Drive. He waved at Blaze as he drove past, a huge grin plastered on his face.

"He's fucking crazy," Blaze said, not for the first time. When he stopped shaking, he got his bike back up onto the roadway.

"What a fucking mess," Armand said. He was Blaze's second-in-command. A big burly man with a long flowing goatee and bald head, he was nearly twice the size of Blaze, and most folks that came across the 'Double D' or 'Dying Days' bike gang, wrongly assumed him to be in command.

"What do you want to do with TW?" Armand asked referring to the man whose shrieks were giving him a headache.

"Bandage him up, get him on a bike, and we'll find him some help," Blaze said.

Armand looked at his leader.

"I'm just fucking with you, let's get out of here," Blaze told him.

Armand waited until everyone mounted up and was ready to start the pursuit anew before he walked over to TW.

"Help me, man," TW said, his bloodied arms outstretched towards Armand.

"I don't know what the fuck you think I could do for you, man. How you missed a bus that big is beyond me, though." Armand pulled his Colt 1911 from his holster.

"Wa-wait, m-man! I can ride. I can ride!" TW stuttered through a face full of broken teeth.

"I'd love to see that, I would. Gonna be a bitch changing the clutch with that leg though," Armand said, referring to TW's left leg that was only being held together by the stitching of his leather pants.

"Y-you can't leave me here, man."

"Why the fuck can't I?"

"You…you're my brother."

"Not anymore." Armand drilled a bullet in TW's skull.

***

"What was that?" Stephanie asked as Trip got the bus back up to speed on the highway.

"Huh?" he asked her. "Oh look at that, there's a rest stop ten miles ahead with a Burger King. You think, like, maybe a skeleton crew stayed on? I could really go for a smoothie."

Stephanie looked to the rear and saw the bikers were back. They were short a couple, but still had enough to do what they had set out to do. "Trip, they're still coming."

"I just needed to buy us a little more time."

"What do you know that I don't?"

"There's no secret, sweetie, every extra second I spend with you I treasure."

"I…I think that's the sweetest thing anyone has ever said to me."

"Plus there's always the chance you'll make the soufflé I'm so fond of."

"And there's the Trip I know and love." She smiled and hoped that there truly was a heaven, because she couldn't imagine spending an eternity without him.

CHAPTER 17 – MIKE JOURNAL ENTRY 8

After talking with Ron I didn't want to talk to anyone else—maybe ever. I walked the perimeter of the fence probably a dozen times before I reneged on my communication blackout. Gary had almost everybody doing something on the truck retrofitting.

"How much longer?" I asked him through a shower of sparks as he cut through the side of the truck with a torch.

"Couple of hours at the most," he replied, not stopping what he was doing.

I walked out.

"Where you going, Talbot?" BT asked, catching up to me.

"I'm going to bury my niece," I told him.

"You said there were zombies all over the place."

"I know."

"It'll be dangerous and foolhardy."

"I know that, too."

"You're still going to do it, aren't you." He said as a statement and not a question.

"I have to, man. I don't have a choice," I told him, my voice quavering a bit.

"Don't give me any shit; I'm coming with you this time."

I didn't say anything; his company was welcome. He came back a couple of minutes later with some spades he had dug out of a maintenance shed.

"Yeah, that'd probably help," I told him, grabbing one.

"Mike?" Tracy asked, coming out from the garage.

"I have to, Tracy."

"Hurry back," she said, giving me a small kiss that gave me the strength I needed to do what had to be done.

I saw Tommy watching us as we left. I was wondering if he had any thoughts or visions of what lay before us. I'd been thinking a lot about the kid and the first time we'd met. I didn't know if he actually had a spirit guide that showed him signs or omens, or if it was his own self and he had developed that guise. I guess in the end, it didn't matter. He'd saved us many times with his prophecies, the only thing was, he hadn't had any in a long while. I wasn't sure if it was because whatever well he had been dipping in had run dry or the future was so bleak he didn't want to share it.

Travis locked up the gate after we walked out. "Tell her I said goodbye," Travis said before turning away.

He'd only just gotten his man-card and didn't want to damage it too much so soon. It's perfectly acceptable to cry when no one can see you. He hadn't been overly close with his cousin, but they were family and they'd shared enough laughs that he would miss her shining face.

So there we were, two men walking down a street in a zombie infested town, carrying shovels, heads bowed.

"You gonna be alright?" BT asked me.

"Oh, I would imagine eventually," I said, finally gazing at something besides the pavement in front of my feet. "She was Ron's firstborn, apple of his damn eye. Daddy's little princess and all that. I'm trying to wrap my head around all of this. What if it was Ron telling me he had to kill Nicole because she was a zombie? I don't think I could take it, man." And BT watching or not, tears were flowing.

"You know I'm not good at this, right?" BT asked as he wrapped me in a hug.

"Still appreciated," I mumbled into his chest.

"We really should get going," he told me.

"I know." I slowly pulled myself away. "Thank you."

We didn't say anything else until we began to approach the apartment building. Maybe he was embarrassed or maybe he was pissed at the snot I'd left on his shirt.

"We're here," I said, ducking behind a small hedgerow.

"There are definitely zombies around." He wrinkled his nose.

"I'm just hoping it's the dead ones," I said as I poked my head up to look at the staircases. They were littered with zombies, some still moving, albeit not in a vertical position. Severed spines and broken necks or blown off legs were making any true form of locomotion difficult. The problem was that they would be able to communicate with their brethren if they caught wind of us.

"That's gross," BT said, pointing to a zombie that was pulling itself along the ground with its chin,. Glass and stone were embedded on the bottom of its face, blood was pouring from the wound as it shredded the soft skin. Leaving something akin to a giant red snail-trail

"I wonder what pulled zombie tastes like?" I asked. "I can't help it, the meat strips hanging off its chin remind me of barbecue. No one ever said I was right in the head."

"I'm going to pretend I didn't just hear that."

"I'd appreciate it."

"What are we waiting for?" BT asked as he watched my concern. "None of them here can catch us."

"The zombies can talk to each other," I told him as I got back down behind cover.

He looked at me for a bit. He didn't question my statement in the least. "I really hate zombies."

"That makes two of us. We need to finish off the survivors as quickly as possible."

BT grabbed his rifle.

"Nope." I pulled my machete from its scabbard.

"Oh come on, man, I'm clean. I've got on new shoes. You've gotta know how much brothers value new shoes."

"Take them off then."

"That's cold, man. That's just cold."

He might have thought it was 'cold' but he was serious about the shoes. He took them off, tied the laces together, hung them around his neck, and then put them down his shirt.

"You're kidding, right?"

"Do I look like I'm kidding?"

"How the fuck do I always get accused of having the issues?"

"You tell anybody about this and we're through."

"Nice socks." He was wearing argyle.

"Just because it's the end of the world doesn't mean I should dress that way."

"I'd love to debate high-fashion with you, but I want to get this shit over with."

"Don't let me stop you."

"Damn, are there zombies close by?" I asked, looking around quickly.

BT was on high alert.

"False alarm," I said, looking at his socks.

"My feet do not stink!"

"Says you," I told him as I stood. I wanted to come up on the side of the zombies and give them as little time to shout a warning or a dinner bell. BT was right behind. I won't even go into the litany of curses he expressed when his sock-clad foot came down in what we both hoped was dog crap.

"Don't say a fucking word." He bent and gingerly pulled off his sock.

"Damn, your toes look like sausages. And I'm not talking those little cocktail wieners either. Those are like full grilling sausages. Get a bun and some sautéed onions, someone could have a feast."

"Shut the fuck up, Talbot."

"Spicy mustard."

He glared at me. I did the wise thing and went silent…for a second or two.

"And not that I like it, but maybe that German coleslaw looking stuff.

"It's sauerkraut and shut the fuck up."

"Well, I know who I'm eating first if I go cannibal."

"Done?"

"I wonder how they'd grill up? Alright, alright, I'm sorry…it's my coping mechanism. Do you use ketchup on brats?"

"As soon as I'm done with the zombies me and you are going to have a talk."

We were about ten feet away when the first zombie caught sight or wind of us—probably smelled BT. I drove my machete through the relatively soft part of its skull where its nose was. I wrenched it free just as BT was bludgeoning another. I hoped he wasn't noticing the gore that had sprayed all over his chest and was even now most likely soaking through to the shoes he was so adamant about protecting. We moved quickly, putting the zombies down, I caught some 'chatter' in the back of my head but it was weak and not sustained. I felt fairly confident that, by the time we finished off the five or six that were still alive, they had not successfully gotten off a distress beacon. Not that they were all that altruistic to begin with or they wouldn't have left their fallen here. If they started to care about their own, we'd be over. Dying for others was a uniquely human trait and signified a higher order of thought, one of the few things that separated us from other animals.

Now, that is in no way implying that I think all humans are better than all animals, far from it. I'd had enough examples even before the zombies to prove that. I'm just saying that if zombies started looking out for their own, any odds of man making a comeback would be greatly reduced.

I put my hand on BT's arm, halting his progress as I

went up the stairs. Each step seemed harder than the one before it. By the time I got to the top, I didn't think I was going to be able to move my feet; it was not 'like' a nightmare, it was one. My niece still lay where I had shot her. She looked almost peaceful. I had to hope I had put her out of some misery. I placed one hand under her neck and the other under her knees. She was so light. My throat closed in pain as I picked her up. I just wanted her to wrap her arms around my neck and tell me she was alright and that I had saved her. Instead, her arms hung limply from her body. The deep purplish color on her features destroyed any fantasy I could possibly have that she yet lived.

"Some fucking hero I am," I said as I descended the stairs.

"I'm so sorry, man." BT said as he watched me carry her down.

I couldn't say anything more. To speak would have opened up the floodgates. There was a park in the center of town I remembered seeing when we had come in; that seemed as fitting a place as any to lay her to rest, and it would be easy enough for Ron and his family to find and visit when and if they would someday get a chance.

The wise and prudent thing to do would have been to dig a few feet down and lay her in peace. We went down six. How could I ever explain it to my brother if hungry dogs dug her up? We were almost at completion when I realized nothing would touch her, she was contaminated. Odds were, even the worms would steer clear. This was doing little to help my mood, which was already as sour as old lemonade.

I was putting the last few shovelfuls on top. BT sat down at a bench and was putting his shoes back on, grumbling about some stains or something. But I knew he was really trying to focus on anything other than what was going on. Hell, if I cared enough about my shoes I would have been right next to him.

"You going to say a prayer?" he asked as I tossed the

shovel aside.

"Why? God already failed."

"Take that back." BT stood.

Well, now I was going to deal with the wrath of God *and* the wrath of BT, and BT was closer near as I could tell.

"He doesn't mean that," BT said, looking up, I guess trying to cover for my blasphemy.

Honestly, I don't know if I meant it or not. I'd had my issues with faith since I'd turned thirteen and, as a teenager, decided I knew it all. Thus far, my immediate family was safe, but at what cost? I'd lost a son-in-law, my best friend and his wife, my niece, my father, and my soul. God charged more interest than a mafia don. Still, it could be worse…infinitely worse.

"I'm sorry," I said as I bowed my head. "Sometimes the burden gets too great." I didn't get an actual response, but I swear I got the sensation of 'I'll let it slide this time'.

BT stepped up, and for that I was appreciative. "God, please let this girl lie in peace, and let her family find solace in the fact that she is out of pain," BT said, wringing his hands together. I did make the sign of the trinity upon my chest and we left.

"What the fuck is wrong with you?" BT asked when we were far enough away from the gravesite--as if at this distance the big guy wouldn't hear him. "Pissing me off is one thing, pissing your wife off is another more stupid thing. But *Him*?" He pointed up. "What is wrong with you?"

"He understands," I told him.

"You say that like you met."

I didn't say anything.

"Wait? Did you? Forget it I really don't want to know."

"He doesn't like Jar Jar Binks…He told me so," I said.

"That doesn't prove you met God, but if you did, I guess that does make Him wise. Forget it. I don't even want to know how the conversation went. Knowing you, I can't believe He didn't just strike you down where you were."

"That's kind of funny, because that's what I said to him."

"You're kidding right? Forget it, man. You're fucking nuttier than trail mix."

We walked a little further, an uneasy silence building between us.

Finally BT spoke again in hushed tones, "Did He say anything about me?"

"He did say something about maybe picking my friends better, but most of the conversation revolved around *Star Wars*."

"I'm done with you, man. My momma always said crackers were crazy, something about their white skin not being able to stop the sun from cooking their brains." He widened his stride to pull away from me.

I smiled, with no idea why I thought poking the giant was a good idea, but just being around him lightened my heart. He was as true a friend as I had ever walked in life with, and the sooner we could find Doc and get him fixed up, the better. Just as the first rays of brightness cut through the fog that had enshrouded me, I watched as BT's steps faltered. He went down quickly to one knee, his right hand shot out and grabbed a hold of the chain link fence next to him. That kept him from falling over. I rushed up to his side. His face was twisted in agony.

"BT?" I asked in alarm.

"I'm alright," he hissed through his clenched jaw.

"Doubtful. Is it your leg?"

"Worse."

Fuck. I knew what *that* meant. "Don't hate me for this," I told him. I didn't give him a chance to respond. I picked him up much like I had Melanie earlier and honestly it wasn't even that much more strain. I would imagine it would have looked pretty funny to an outsider; it would have looked like Beauty carrying the Beast. Of course I'm the beauty, I'm sure you can figure out who the beast was in this statement. He had to have been in a crap-load of pain, because he didn't so much as grunt at me as I started running back to the DPW yard.

The extra strength I possessed made him feel like I was carrying a kid around ten-ish—so, not a great burden—but after a while, even that will begin to weigh in on your reserves. I was pondering how long I thought I could keep this pace up with him in my arms when I caught sight of movement through my peripheral vision.

"Zombies, always zombies. Couldn't be a fucking ice cream truck or maybe a herd of cute little deer. Nope has to be fucking zombies."

"Ice cream would be nice," BT wheezed.

I took a quick glance to my side. I had about a half mile to get to where I needed to be, and if I was doing my head-math right, I was going to come up short in this equation. The half dozen or so zombies had taken an angle on us and would catch up in the next couple of street poles.

"I've got something for you to eat!" I shouted.

I was pissed off at the world right now. I put BT down as gently as I could, my arms felt not quite like rubber, but they were throbbing a bit. I grabbed my machete at first.

"Screw that."

I let it fall back into its sheath. I pulled my rifle off my shoulder, pulled back the charging handle a couple of inches to make sure I had a round in the chamber, flipped off the safety, and sprayed the closest zombie with three quick rounds.

"How's that feel, fucker!?" I shouted as his head mushroomed and he fell backwards smashing his already shattered skull. "That's so damn good I bet you want some too, you ugly fucker!" I said to the second approaching zombie.

The first round caught him in the chest, the second in

the head. It snapped back and then fell face forward. Nothing stopping his torque as he plummeted, the crack of skull on pavement made a satisfying 'thwack'.

"Good shit, right?" I asked his still form.

Then the damn zombies did something I wasn't expecting. The remaining five stopped running towards me. I lowered my rifle a little bit.

"What's the matter, you guys not hungry enough? Am I not tasty looking enough for you? What about my friend over here, he could feed a fucking village!"

BT feebly put up his hand in protestation. "Leave me out of this."

The zombies had just plain stopped their forward progress. Don't get me wrong, they were eyeing us hungrily, but I could also see they were assessing the risk and reward of this venture.

"Not a damn fan of smart zombies!" I shouted, blasting a third into whatever hell it belonged.

They had to have been talking, because they turned and ran at the same time; not far though. Just far enough to watch, but not close enough that they figured I would shoot at them.

I stood there a few moments longer, trying to figure out what the hell was going on. When it became clear that the ones left were not going to charge, I guessed it was time to leave. I released my magazine, quickly jammed in some new rounds, and then put it back in the magazine well. When I looked back up, one of the zombies had vanished, my guess was to go and get his whole damn village. BT was pulling himself up.

"You alright?" I asked, grabbing him under the arm.

"Better, it's passed."

He said it like he was familiar with it. "This has happened before?"

"Ever since I've been bit, been getting more frequent since Eliza died, though, and more painful."

"It's progressing."

"At least we know where Justin gets it from," he said as he stood up completely. "You tell anybody you were carrying me and I'll sneeze on everything you own."

"That hurts, man, but we have a deal."

BT pretty much kept his gaze forward as if every step was a chore. I, however, stopped every few paces to do a three-sixty and see if we were yet being pursued. Our small tailing contingent stayed back about fifty yards and on the other side of the street. It was not a welcome feeling to have them stalking us like that. Herding came into my head on more than one occasion.

"We need to step it up, bud," I told BT.

He grunted but did as I asked. I had the distinct impression we were being led to the slaughter. The zombies behind followed diligently, never pressing the attack, just like the good little sheepherders they were. And then I saw two things almost simultaneously; one was rejoice worthy, the other…not so much. As we rounded a bend on Chestnut Drive, I saw the front gate to the public works yard…and also a shitload of zombies sprinting headlong towards us. They would pass by the gate coming towards us before we would have a chance to get there.

"I see them," BT said. He pulled his gun up, his hands visibly shaking. I knew it was from the pain and not the sight of the zombies.

Tommy and Travis were at the gate. They had heard my earlier shots and were looking for any signs of trouble when they saw the zombie horde.

"Going to need some help!" I yelled, getting Travis' attention.

"Justin! Gary! Mom!" he yelled behind him as I watched him get his rifle up.

Tommy was already cycling rounds through his weapon. Travis was soon behind him, adding his lead to the fight. BT and I were firing as we moved. Within short seconds, Tracy and Justin joined the mix. The zombies paid them absolutely no heed as they passed by even as scores of them were being rendered dead. If my magazine had not run dry at just that moment, I would have missed the zombies from the rear. They had started coming for us once they saw that we were distracted. I had been fumbling in my pocket for my loaded magazine when I caught sight of them.

"Son of a bitch," I said as I slammed the magazine home and spun, firing with less than three feet between me and the nearest one. I'd only had enough time to get the barrel up about chest high before he tried to impale himself on it. I shot two rounds center mass into him attempting to create some distance between us. The second round must have caught him in the spine. It was enough to push him back off my muzzle and allow me to raise the rifle up. His forehead sizzled as he made contact with the hot metal.

"Nice brand, bitch," I said as I double-tapped his skull.

He fell away just as his girlfriend came up to get in on the action. An anemic, crack addict with an eating disorder couldn't have looked worse than the thing that begged me to kill her. I happily obliged. The first round caught her in her brown, cracked teeth. The second blew the top of her patchy haired scalp clean off. The third and final zombie from the back stopped in mid-street and was looking to pull his iron out of the fire. I didn't give him the chance.

"You're like those little fucking yippy dogs that always wait for the person to turn around before they nip at people's heels," I was screaming as I advanced. "Well no more ankles for you to bite, fucker!" Two rounds later and he became a stain on the roadway.

I turned back to the front. We were screwed. The zombies had made it past the Talbot family gauntlet. There was nowhere to run.

"It's been a pleasure, my friend," I said to BT as I started firing.

"See, Talbot? This is what pissing off God does for you! Crazy-ass cracker."

BT was in the midst of reloading and I had a pretty good count on my rounds. I would take as much time as I could between shots so that we would not both be empty at the same time. BT's hands were shaking so bad that he fumbled and dropped his magazine.

Frustration welled up in me and threatened to come out in an anguished scream. Not sure what that would accomplish, and there really wasn't any sense in my last dying words being a dick to my friend. It was then that I heard—well I guess we, I saw BT's head pop up and realized he'd heard it too—the deep throaty roar of a powerful engine revving. This was going to be one of those few times when the zombies being smarter actually worked out in our favor. Not all, but at least some stopped to see what was going on. This gave me enough time to pop another magazine in. Two more after this one and then it was machete time. Oh boy, couldn't wait for that! Nothing quite like being covered in hot entrails.

I popped off a few rounds, reached down and grabbed BT's lost magazine. He thanked me with his eyes as I placed his magazine in. We were both up and shooting. The distraction was giving us a little breathing room. Damn near jumped out of my socks when I heard the large 'blat' of the truck horn. Knowing Gary, he'd super-charged it so that it sounded more like something a five hundred ton train would be making. I saw a giant shower of sparks as the truck hit a small dip in the parking lot. The plow dug into the soft pavement and sent a plume of pebbles into the air.

The truck smashed into the now Talbot-vacated gate. The chain held, the fence did not. At least a thirty-foot of section folded down like a paper airplane. Scores of smelly bastards were getting the Play-Doh treatment as their bodies were being shoved through four-inch squares. Zombie spaghetti sounded like about the worst thing ever. Meatballs would forever take on a new meaning. The plow was bouncing around like Gary had outfitted it with hydraulics; which wasn't out of the realm of possibilities. Some zombies began to scatter, others were a little slower on the uptake as the giant steel blade bore down on them, and then there were still the ones that were coming towards BT and me.

It wouldn't do any good to get rescued if we were dead. Gary was like that mechanical arm that comes down to clean out the pins while you're bowling. Zombies were being hurtled into space, dragged under the blade or run over, any of which caused instantaneous visual horrors. I wasn't sure how the timing of this was going to work. Gary at his present speed and direction was just as likely to hit us as the zombies he was saving us from. We were pinned down and there were not a whole bunch of avenues for us to escape.

Then I saw the ladder attached to the side of the truck. I started to do the damned salvation-math. It had all sorts of awesome variables like, Gary's speed, amount of zombies between us and the rungs, plus BT's ability to be able to hold onto a moving ladder. Fun shit like that.

There was a layer of only four or five deep of zombies between Gary and us when I felt BT's rifle graze the top of my head at top speed. If I had an inch more of height, or his massive arms had dipped just a fraction, he would have sent the top of my head into the cheap seats. I turned just in time to see a zombie in the midst of a heels-over-head situation; its face caved in. BT had struck it so hard that it literally left its feet. Well, that answered the 'strong enough to hold the ladder' factor.

"Holy shit. Thanks, man," I told him.

It was one of the earlier zombies taking one last final shot in the pursuit of food. And it had almost worked. How BT had seen it I didn't know. Maybe he had thought of something I'd done to him previously and was actually gunning for me but had gone high and I'd just been fortuitous. Highly coincidental, granted, but still possible.

Gary was creating a clearing big enough for a truck to drive through (see how I did that?). Although he had zombies to both sides and the rear, we only needed to be concerned with the side he was planning on driving by us.

I pointed to the approaching ladder.

"I've got damn eyes," BT told me.

"And an attitude apparently."

"You say something?" he asked gruffly.

"Just get on the stupid ladder."

Gary was fast approaching, and we'd done a decent job of clearing a path, although it was much like digging sand. Every time we took some out, more would fill in from the sides. I made a move towards BT, my hand extended, I was going to give him a little extra assistance up.

"You touch me and I'll scream rape," BT said.

"Well at least you're feeling better."

Gary was going about ten miles an hour, which sounds slow enough, but when you're standing still and have to hop on, it's fairly intimidating. BT flipped his rifle over his shoulder and reached out with his right hand. I turned and started running in the direction the plow was going. I couldn't get on until BT had moved his bulk up far enough to give me room to join him.

"Mike!" BT yelled.

It was a tone I'd never heard from him before. I was about even with the plow blade when I turned. BT's face had taken on an ashen quality. I was wondering if he was being hit again with the zombie cramp. It was then I noticed his right leg was off the ladder. A zombie had grabbed hold, which normally wouldn't have been an issue for BT, but two other zombies had also played piggy back with the first one. He literally had three zombies dragging on him and more trying to get in position to add their own anchorage. BT had wrapped his arm around the ladder step so that his armpit was firmly lodged, but I could see the strain in his face as he tried to shake his leg free of the huge parasites.

"Speed up, Gary!" I shouted. He was looking in the side-view mirror at BT.

A billow of diesel exhaust blossomed out of the stack behind the cab. I ran a little further ahead while I had the chance, swung the rifle onto my back and grabbed my machete.

"Again with the damn machete," I said as I turned back around. "Do not move!" I yelled to BT.

It would not have done any good if he started kicking out his leg and I slammed my blade into his thigh. The first zombie that had latched onto him was being dragged on his knees. It hurt me to even think about his kneecaps being sanded down on the ground like they were, especially with the other two hangers-on.

The timing had to be almost perfect. I took a step, already the cab was past, I was mid-stride with my next step and had pulled my arm back as far as I could. I was in full swing as my second stride hit the ground. The machete caught the zombie midway in the back. I heard its back break as the blade cut deep. The knife was ripped from my hand, but I'd gone deep enough, the added weight on the back of that zombie pulled him neatly in two. Okay, neatly might be a bit of a gross exaggeration. I guess as neatly as a human body can be severed. Every internal organ spilled to the ground, it looked like a dog food processing truck had rolled over.

BT was able to pull his leg up as the two other zombies rolled away when their ride ditched them. It was two more strides before I could stop my forward momentum. Now I was the one that had a problem. I was running headlong into the zombies and my ride was taking off the other way, plus I had lost the knife I hated using so much. I sure would have loved to use it now. I didn't have the room or the time to turn back around, and getting to my rifle was out of the question.

It was time to play unpadded football. I tucked my

head in and lowered my shoulder. I caught the first one in the chin with the point of my shoulder. I heard his teeth shatter right after he severed his tongue off. The flap of meat smacked wetly against my forearm.

I somewhat had the element of surprise as they weren't expecting me to be where I was, but I sure wouldn't have minded a big blocker to lead the way. They take all the big hits, and I take all the glory getting the touchdown. It was a working formula in high school. Why not now?

I was through my second or third row of zombies, each hit beginning to take just a little more of my forward thrust away. I could hear the back-up warning coming from the truck. Gary had thrown the rig in reverse and was thankfully coming back. I was beginning to see the light at the end of the zunnel (zombie tunnel) when Gary crashed the truck into a street pole. The truck didn't give so much of a shit as the pole toppled noisily to the ground. I hazarded a glance behind me as I finally broke free from the zombies. The truck was weaving all over the roadway, I think it would have been better if he had just ghost-driven the thing. No one at the helm would have been better than his maneuvers. I started timing when I should dodge to the side, getting eaten by a zombie all of a sudden seemed like the better alternative than being run over.

BT was off the ladder. For a moment, I panicked that maybe he'd fallen off, but he was waving at me from a hole cut into the side of the dump.

"Glad to see you're alright. Now get me the fuck out of here!" I yelled.

Rifles pointed out of two other slots and bullets began to take down zombies that had turned and were beginning their pursuit of me. Gary was pulling even with me, which was a good thing, because a bend in the road was coming up and I was certain he'd never be able to navigate it. I jumped, grabbing the ladder in flight, my head striking the side of the truck as Gary had given the wheel a quick twist. He'd rung my bell. I had to hold onto where I was for a moment until my brain stopped sliding around inside my skull. The wheels started squealing and jittering along the pavement as Gary hit the brakes. I swung against the side of the truck. What the zombies had started Gary was going to try and finish. I swung back the other way as we were once again going forward. BT reached his arm out of the firing hole and grabbed my shoulder. Unlike him, I was thankful for the help. I'd been a human piñata for the last few seconds and my body hurt.

Gary drove another half mile with me like that until he once again stopped short. If not for BT holding me in place I would have gone through the same cycle.

"Nice driving," I said to Gary. I added 'asshole' at the end, but quietly. He had saved me after all, even if he wanted to crack me open and see if I housed any internal goodies.

"You're welcome," he said, beaming.

We didn't have much time; I could already see the zombies coming. I climbed up the rest of the ladder and onto the top, which was made of tarp-covered plywood. There was a small hatch up there, which I climbed through and into the dump truck equivalent of an RV.

A dark red industrial carpet was glued to the bottom of the bed; two rows of bench seats were bolted or welded there as well. The entire area was framed out with two-by-fours, which held up the 'roof', that was covered with a tarp in case of inclement weather. Gun wells had been cut out of the metal body on the two sides and the rear. He'd even gone so far as to weld on small channels so that the murder holes could be covered up by sliding a thick piece of metal back into place. In the front, he'd cut out an actual window, put his channels back in and fitted it with Plexiglas. This way, the folks in the back could see up front and, if need be, we could move back and forth from the cab of the truck to the dump part. Now, if this thing had a wet bar, we'd be all set. My earlier irkdom to my brother was completely forgotten. He'd created something pretty unique and fucking awesome.

"Good job, man!" I said, smacking the glass.

I could see his grinning face in the rearview mirror.

"Thanks, guys," I told my boys and BT.

"We're even now," BT said. "For today."

"Fair enough. How you doing?" I asked. "Come on, man, sit down."

"Better now."

He looked like shit. Finding Doc was of paramount importance, but there were still a bunch of huge problems with that. Odds he was alive and well were slim, and even if he was, would he have a 'cure'? Would he succeed where others failed? He had to. There was no other answer. I would not watch BT die and after that, Justin's steady decline. That was NOT an acceptable outcome. This mission was as much about them as it was about me. I know I'm flawed, I was doing this in part because I didn't want to be put through the suffering. Is there such a thing as reverse altruism? Would God make the distinction that I was doing good for others for my own good? Same fucking thing, right?

Stop looking at me like that. You think Mother Teresa was a completely selfless person? I don't think so. Now I'm not saying she wasn't worthy of Sainthood, but don't you think she took great pleasure in helping others? Helping others made her feel good, absolutely nothing wrong with that. In a nutshell, that's exactly what I was doing. Getting Justin and BT cured would make me feel great--two big birds one huge stone. Bullet-proof argument once I needed to present it to the Big Man.

We had been driving for a while. BT was strapped in to his seat, sleeping contentedly. I smiled when I noticed Henry's head was parked in the big man's lap a decent sized puddle of drool leaking from the dog's muzzle. I was pacing a bit, it was slightly claustrophobic in the back, and the roof was maybe an inch from the top of my head. I was going to see if anyone wanted to come back here so I could go up to the front. I pulled the Plexiglas back and knocked on the back window of the cab. Tommy looked back at me, his smile laced in the red of what looked like strawberry. He shrugged.

"Wanf fwon?" he asked, holding up the familiar foil packet.

"Yeah actually," I told him when he slid the glass back. I was thankful when he handed me the entire packet. My hands were encrusted in filth so much so that I thought the crap might be able to find its way through the protective packaging.

"You want up here?" Tracy asked as I was enjoying my pastry treat.

"I'm busy," I told her, sticking my hand up.

"I'd kick your ass, Talbot, if I wasn't so tired," Tracy told me. "Gary can you pull over? I would like to get in the back."

Gary looked at her quickly and then at the window I was at.

"Oh I don't think so," she told him. "I'm not crawling through two windows on a moving truck no matter how much fun you think it would be."

"It actually does look like fun," I said.

I stuck my head out of my side and was looking down at the pavement blazing by. I thought about maybe Gary hitting a bump and me losing my footing and then I'd find myself stuck upside down in the hydraulic cabling as my head started to wear away on the ground.

"Yeah, maybe you should just stop," I told him, getting a little sick to my stomach just thinking about it.

Gary almost tossed me out the damn window he laid on the brakes so hard. "What is your problem with the pedals, man?" I asked him once I realized my heart wasn't going to burst.

I went back to where the hatch was, stepped up on the small ladder welded to the side and then down the other side. Gary had gotten out and was stretching.

Tracy came around and gave me a hug. "How you doing, hon?" She looked up at me.

"I've been better. At least she's at rest now. I can at least tell Ron that much." She got up on her toes and kissed me. "Thank you for that," I told her.

"Maybe we'll have to find a stack of books soon."

"Works for me."

I'd never before equated literary tomes with sex, but I was open-minded. The constant danger we were in had some inherent benefits, one being that it made you want to be more in contact with those you loved. There is comfort in intimacy.

"Next stop is Barnes and Noble," I told her before I helped her on the ladder, not that she needed it, but it gave me the chance to cop a feel or two.

I'd never once considered Tracy anything other than beautiful, but the hardness of the apocalypse had sculpted her into something almost otherworldly. Any chance I had to grab onto that, I was going to take it.

"Want me to drive a bit?" I asked Gary once my favorable view was gone.

"It's not as easy as it looks," he told me.

"I know, man, I just know you pulled some long hours and worked your ass off to get this done. Great job by the way."

"Thank you...and you're right, I could use a little shut eye."

Gary went up the ladder as well. I didn't help him, if he fell off and bruised himself up a bit, I would consider it a fair measure of payback. Gary had stopped at the interchange exit for 495, which was basically a route that skirted Boston and went down through Connecticut and picked back up with its parent route. So I could stay on 95 Southbound or take 495. It wasn't like Boston was going to be a hotbed of traffic, so that wasn't really a factor. And in terms of distance, I think it was about the same mileage. Route 95 stayed closer to the coast, so one way bowed to the east, the other the west.

"Any reason to take one over the other?" I asked Tommy. He shrugged. "I liked it a whole lot better when Ryan would at least give you some vague clues."

I hopped up into the cab. I was driving somewhere in the neighborhood of five miles an hour, looking back and forth at the route signs. I could not figure out why this was such a big deal, they led to exactly the same place. I cut the wheel at the very last moment, taking 495. My final reason was that if I was that close to Boston on 95 and saw a zombified Dustin Pedroia it would make this day just that much worse.

I'd been on 495 for fifteen minutes or so and nothing untold was happening. There was a build-up of more abandoned cars as we got closer to the outskirts of Boston, but nothing that we wouldn't be able to navigate through quite yet. And unless we started seeing tanks, I didn't think there were too many things this truck couldn't get through anyway. For about the fortieth time, I asked myself why no one had thought of this sooner, least of all me.

"You see that?" Tommy asked.

But unless he was talking about the small pile of crumbs he was creating in his lap, I didn't know how he could see anything else. He had not looked up from his parade of junk food the whole time I'd been in there. I wasn't complaining; he'd given me a Mallo Cup and a Devil Dog. From where? I didn't care. Sometimes it's way better to allow the mysteries of the universe to remain just that. What good has it been for science to remove all the mystery in life? Isn't it cooler to think that the Northern Lights are the gateway to the Spirit world and that the crackling sound it sometimes makes is that of the spirits talking? Or would you rather 'know' that its charged particles from the sun reacting with the earth's magnetic field?

"See what?" I asked, realizing that Tommy had even spoken.

"The smoke." He pointed through the windshield.

I could see a small funnel of it. It didn't look like much more than a small campfire throwing it off. Campfire meant people, though. I took a small glance through the back windshield. It seemed my driving had been relaxing enough for all of them to get a little much needed sleep. We weren't yet under attack; I was going to see how this rode out before I awoke them.

"Buckle your seatbelt in preparation for a bumpy ride," I told Tommy.

"Had it on since Gary started driving," he told me.

"Okay so it wasn't just me."

"Nope." He shook his head. "I thought he was trying to kill a snake on the floorboard every time he hit the brakes."

It was the further I drove that I realized this wasn't just a marshmallow roasting fire. Something was going on. Now I'd wished I'd taken 95. I was slowing down looking for the best place to turn my truck around when I saw it.

"Oh shit," I said as I saw the bus heading our way. "He's gotta be doing seventy."

That was fairly miraculous considering all the vehicles on the roadway. Smoke was billowing out of the front, luckily, the driver was going so fast that the smoke was traveling down the sides and to the back.

"Where's he in such a rush to get to?"

"I think it's what he is in a rush to get away from," Tommy said.

A bevy of bikers came into view. I did not want to get involved. First off, because I didn't want to expose anyone to the danger; and secondly, how did I know who the good guys were. Just because bikers were chasing a bus didn't necessarily make them the evil ones, now if it was a school bus that might change the equation. Sure…it cast them in a worse light, but by no means was it a definitive answer. No matter what I decided, I couldn't stay where I was; the path through the cars was too narrow for us and a bus. The ear-irritating sound of metal squealing on metal pretty much woke everyone up as I pushed against some cars in an effort to make room.

The herking and jerking of Gary's braking had nothing over what I was doing. Professional rodeo riders would have been complaining. I had created a sort of dugout through the cars and at the same time made myself vulnerable. There was always the chance the bus would race on by and the bikers would stop to check us out.

"Shit," I said just as I decided this was a horrible plan.

The bus was within a quarter mile or so when I threw the truck in reverse. I was pinging the back of the truck off of more than a few cars.

"See? I told you it wasn't easy!" Gary shouted through the glass.

"What's going on?" BT asked, sticking his head through. It was good to see him looking better.

"Company." Tommy pointed to the rapidly approaching bus and motorcycles.

"Shit," BT said.

"Couldn't agree more," I told him.

"Any idea who's who?" he asked.

"Your guess is as good as mine," I told him, my head jerking as we ripped off the front fender of a Toyota.

"That bus is coming up fast!" BT's eyes were growing big.

"You been talking to Captain Obvious lately?" I asked him, trying my best to avoid the parked cars that seemed to be jumping into my path of their own volition.

The bus was less than a football field away, within seconds he would be abreast and then past. Then the bikers, then probably a couple of thousand zombies behind them, a yeti, and a pack of werewolves…why not?

I had run out of time. I could hear the bus honking its horn. Where the hell did he think I could go? His front end was inches from my plow blade, billowing smoke was obscuring the driver. It was another quarter mile or so before the cars cleared up enough that the bus could attempt to pull past me, which he did. I was still driving backwards somewhere in the neighborhood of fifty miles an hour. I was too scared to actually look down and check though, figuring I'd lose control if I did so. My full attention was riveted to the small four-by-eight inches of reflective glass to my side.

I heard, "Ponch!!!" It was yelled out from the bus as it pulled alongside.

I spared a quick glance. "John?" I asked, not believing what I was seeing.

"Who?" he shouted back.

"What's going on?" I asked, trying to figure out the biker situation.

"My wife rented a party bus! We're going to a concert…she got a ticket for you, too!"

"Hey, Mike!" Stephanie yelled out. She was on the other side of her husband holding onto a handrail for all her life was worth. I could see the white of her bones shining through she was clutching so hard.

"Good or bad?" I asked, hoping she would catch the meaning of my abbreviated question.

"Bad." In reality, I didn't even need her verbal response, it was in her panicked

expression.

"BT."

"On it," he said, getting the boys at their firing stations.

I started to slow down and so did Trip.

"It's really good to see you, man. Stephanie wanted to know if you still had her sneakers," Trip rambled.

Stephanie was shaking her head back and forth.

"Don't slow up, man, you'll be late for the show. I'll be right behind you!" I told him. There was no traditional rationalizing with Trip, you just had to speak the correct language.

"Oh…right, right. I'll get the sneakers from you there!" He was all smiles.

I gave him the thumbs-up.

"You hitching, man? I can give you a ride, we've got plenty of room," Trip said.

"GO! I'll see you there!" I yelled over to him.

Steph must have said something, because he gave me the thumbs-up and pulled past. The bikers were almost on me by the time I had stopped the truck and got it back into drive.

"Well, fuckers, it's time to learn a thing or two about size differential. I feel like BT around us regular folk," I said to Tommy.

I started to see the wisps of smoke as many of the bikers started shooting at us.

"Well, I guess that answers that question," I said as I began to build up some steam.

I was going somewhere around twenty miles an hour when I cut the wheel, catching a biker head on. The truck bucked, and even with my seat belt on I left my seat, but that was nothing compared to the biker. I launched him. I'd sheered the bike nearly in half on contact. The rider was sent spiraling into the air to land in a death pirouette.

"Should have worn a helmet."

"I don't think it would have helped," Tommy replied.

I drilled two more bikers—both of these head on—before the others tried to get around me. Most started drifting over to the shoulder so they could do just that. I could hear bullets smacking into the body, a few even broke through the windshield.

"Shit! I just got shot," I said, looking at the blood running down my shoulder. "Don't let any of those fuckers past!"

The truck quickly became a rolling gun blind. Bikers who were slowly picking a path through the snarl of traffic became relatively easy targets. We dropped at least five or six of them before they decided whatever prize they were seeking from Trip and his wife just wasn't worth it. I saw a smallish guy, raise his hand up in the air and whirl it around in the traditional 'rally here' gesture. He turned and gunned his bike, leaving a trail of rubber as he did so, the rest quickly followed suit.

I followed for a mile or so just to make sure it wasn't a ruse on their part and maybe they were doubling back. It wasn't long before I lost sight of the much faster bikes, and still I thought about pursuing them. I immensely disliked leaving an enemy out there.

"We going back?" Tommy asked.

Of that I wasn't so sure. What Trip was doing here was beyond my comprehension. There was a pretty good chance he had already forgot about our encounter and would just keep going to whatever destination he had originally set out for. His wife was with him, though. I'm sure at some point she'd get him to pull over. Or, more likely, the bus would just quit. The smoke pouring from the thing indicated it had suffered a fatal wound.

"Douche bags always regroup, it's like a genetic thing," I said to Tommy.

"We can't catch them."

"You're right," I said, close-lipped. I did a beautiful three-point turn in the center of the highway, only smashing four or five cars as I did so.

"What the hell was all that about?" BT asked as we started heading North on 495.

"You're about to find out."

It was about five miles by the time I finally saw the bus. It was parked on the side of the road; smoke was still coming out of it as if it were on its last legs. Trip had his back to me, and as I drew closer, I noticed he was pissing on the tire.

"Nothing to see here!" he said as I pulled up alongside. He was waving his hand for me to pass.

"You know you can get a ticket for public urination right?" I told him.

"See, that's just the man trying to regulate everything. Pissing is one of the most basic human functions, and you and your oppressors are going to tell me where and when I can do it!" Trip said. I could tell he was getting pissed off (pun intended). He was halfway turned around to look at me, dick still in hand.

"Come on, man," I told him, shielding my eyes. "Some things can't be unseen."

"She's a thing of beauty," he said happily.

I hoped he was talking about the plow.

"Ponch!" he yelled excitedly. "When'd you get here?"

"Where's your wife?" I asked him.

"Where?" he asked, stuffing himself back in his pants. "She gets mad when I piss outside."

"So you hate when the man tells you where and when to piss, but you're afraid of your wife telling you the same thing?" I asked.

"I don't live with 'the man.'" He looked around.

"Who's Chong?" BT asked, coming down off the truck.

"Ponch, you in the circus now?" Trip asked, looking up at BT.

"BT, this is Trip. Trip, this is BT." I stepped aside. They were going to need to feel each other out in the ways that best suited them, and I personally wanted nothing to do with it. Trip caused me great mental headaches and BT could cause me great physical ones.

"You're funny, little man. How about I spin your head off?" BT asked as he moved a couple of paces closer to Trip.

"Threats aren't really going to work," I said aloud. BT shushed me.

"Like a top? That would be fantastic, because then I'd

be able to see my butt. I've always wanted to. Stephanie says I have a nice one, but I really have to take her word for it," Trip said, trying his best to look over his shoulder and down his backside.

"How about I just plant you in the ground instead?" BT asked.

"I've always wanted to know what it was like to be a cannabis plant, so still and serene, swaying in the breeze and drinking rainwater. Just let me get a few things." Trip went back into the bus.

"What's wrong with him?" BT asked me as Trip walked away.

"Oh… it gets worse," I answered.

"This is the guy that saved your ass?" BT asked, pointing up to the bus.

"At least three times."

By now, everyone had come out of the truck and gathered around.

"Whoa," Trip said as he stepped out of the bus. "Where'd everybody come from? Were you guys in the bus?"

We all heard some rustling in the woods and then Trip's wife Stephanie emerged. "I'm so sorry. I had some…um…pressing needs to attend to."

"She had to pee," Trip stage whispered.

"Trip!" she said, flustered.

"What?" he asked innocently.

"Stephanie, it's nice to see you again." I stepped forward. "Did the hotel fall?" I asked. Other than that, I could think of no reason why they would be this far east, certainly not a foraging expedition.

"I…umm had a disagreement with the person in charge," she said hesitantly as she looked sidelong at her husband.

I got the implication. Someone where they were staying didn't like Trip and had forced them out. "So what are you guys doing here?"

"Looking for you," she told me.

"Are you kidding? I told Trip in passing where I lived while we were riding in his crazy little helicopter. I never figured he'd remember. I was just trying to say something so I wouldn't bite my tongue off in fear." Maybe I slipped him my address, I couldn't remember, it was a pretty trying time.

"I have a helicopter?" Trip asked.

"Come on, man. I'm here and I'm not believing this," BT said. "How is this possible?"

"Divine intervention?" I said as an explanation. Stephanie nodded, having had that same thought not too long ago.

"Is it that implausible? Look at all the variables that were in place for us to meet on that section of 495. What if Gary had taken an hour longer or finished an hour sooner? What about my decision to even take 495? That's three just within the last two hours. What about everything else? Not to mention on Trip and Stephanie's side. I mean, one more rolled bone from Trip and we would have missed them."

"Coincidence," BT said.

"I'm not so sure," Tommy said.

"Listen, we all know I'm no theologian," I said.

Tracy snorted. "Sorry, involuntary reaction." She was still trying to stifle a laugh.

"You done?" I asked.

"I'll be fine."

"Maybe God is helping just a bit. What if this whole cluster-fuck of an apocalypse wasn't his doing? Let me finish," I said when I saw BT about to protest how an omnipotent being missed something so big. "Listen, we all know my half-assed thoughts on God and the devil. I personally think they're great friends, but what if there's another. Something that is the epitome of evil."

"That's not the devil?" Travis asked.

"Not in your dad's world," BT answered.

"The devil is God's justice, plain and simple. Don't cross God, never meet the devil. Sounds like a plan to me. But this," I said, sweeping my arms, "this I don't think was either of their doings. Something else is in the mix."

"What is it?" Tracy asked, her earlier smile gone.

"Man," Trip said.

At first I thought he was referencing back to 'the man' but this made sense. "You might be on to something."

"Mike, come on. Where are you going with this?" BT asked.

"Hell if I know, but it could be man. God is reward for a life lived well and the devil is punishment for being an asshole, the whole karma thing."

"Tell Beelzebub hi for me," BT said.

"Nice," I told him. "Okay, let's go with the free will thing. We are all able to do as we want without any outside influence."

"So the devil-made-me-do-it defense can't be used anymore?" Trip asked.

"In Mike's world, yes," Tracy told him.

"I'm moving off planet then," Trip said.

"I think he's already there," Travis said to Justin.

"Good one," Justin told his brother.

"What if we went too far? What if God wants to try and set things right?" I asked.

"Why doesn't he just come down here and do it then?" BT asked. "Or send us laser guns that don't need reloading or not let our loved ones die!" Now he was shouting.

"I don't think he can," I said, hoping that wasn't blasphemy.

"An all-powerful being that can't…that doesn't sound right," Tracy said.

I noticed Tommy nodding, but I didn't know if it was in agreement with me or Tracy.

"I think maybe he set it up that way." I was flying by

the seat of my pants now, not an unusual position for me to be in.

"His game, his rules," Gary chimed in.

"Oh, not you too?" BT said. "When did Talbot become synonymous with crazy?"

"It's been a long time," Tommy said, reflecting back on some of the Talbots he'd encountered along the way, more than one making him smile.

"I think Gary's on to something," I said. "Maybe he knew that once he created this world that he wouldn't be able to stop himself from tinkering with it from time to time, so he created a way to keep himself out."

"How, Mike?" BT asked. "How could anything stop him?"

"Same way you could build a wall that you couldn't get over," I told him. I don't know if I was swaying him yet, but it was giving him pause to consider. "I'm just saying that there seems to be a LOT of times that his presence seems to shine through more so than others. Like there are holes in his wall or net."

"Or a back door where he can come in quickly and leave," Gary said.

"Sure. Listen maybe I'm completely wrong, but come on, how the hell did we find Paul? Or how did Trip find us? And I'm going to use that same logic in the hopes that he finds a way to guide us to Doc. That's the hope I'm holding on to, BT. My son's and your life hang in the balance. I can't think of a better person to lay my faith on."

"Can't argue with that." BT turned slightly away. "Fucking pollen," he said, going towards the truck.

"Stephanie, I can take you two to get another car and I'll give you directions to get to my brother's house. He'll take you in no questions asked. Okay, he might have a few questions, but you'll be welcome there," I told her.

"I'm a little done with being alone on the open road," she said.

"I can't say I blame you. You're welcome to come with us, we have the room." She looked dubiously over at the plow. "Gary did some great things in the back. I'm not sure how long we're going to be traveling, and I have no idea what we're in for, and I'm pretty sure your bikers will come back once they pull their tails out from between their legs. It's that damn free will again, makes some people do the stupidest shit."

"I'd still rather we stay with you," Stephanie said with relief.

"Man, I hate to bring this up," Trip said, "but do you have Stephanie's sneakers?"

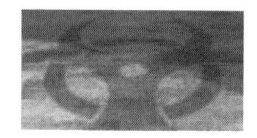

CHAPTER 18 – DENNIS AND DENEAUX

Getting the gas had been infinitely easier than getting the hose with which to siphon it. Dennis was happy he'd only had to swallow a little of the caustic liquid before it flowed freely into the rig's tank. Mrs. Deneaux kept a lazy lookout for trouble as she lit another cigarette.

"Do you mind?" Dennis asked. He was looking at the wavy lines caused by the gas vapors that were less than two feet from where Mrs. Deneaux was smoking.

"You've known me long enough now, sonny boy, to realize I don't."

He'd officially made up his mind at this point that, as soon as he had an opportunity, he was leaving her crazy ass behind. He just couldn't get past the crushing feeling of loneliness when he did think about striking out alone. Everyone he knew and loved was gone or missing. He'd never felt so helpless or hopeless in his entire life. A traveler in a land without stops.

"You ever butcher animals?" Mrs. Deneaux asked after a particularly long drag.

"What?"

"Do you hunt?"

"No. Why?" Dennis asked.

"I was just wondering, because a piece of prime rib sounds about the most delicious thing in the world right now, and if I come across a cow, I'm going to shoot it and eat it. Maybe right where it lays, lord knows I've had rare enough cuts that they were still flopping around on my plate."

"That's gross," Dennis told her.

"Weak stomach? This ride is going to be more fun than I had originally thought. You just about done?" She flipped her butt. It somersaulted less than three inches from the outer edge of the vapors.

"Crazy bitch with a death sentence. Unfortunately, it's me she's trying to kill," Dennis muttered as Deneaux walked away.

He put the gas cap back on and grabbed a bottle of water to help wash the bitter after-taste of fuel from his mouth. He was leaning against the front bumper when his heart about stopped. Deneaux had given the horn a sharp long blast.

"Bitch, what is your problem!?" he said hotly.

"You might want to get a move on." She pointed off to her side.

Dennis took a couple of steps so that he could see. It looked like a whole hideout of zombies were coming their way.

"Shit," he said as he spun to get back to his side of the truck and in. When he was safely in, the door locked and the window completely rolled up, he turned to Deneaux. "How long have you seen them?"

"Oh, at least a quarter mile." She smiled at him.

"No chance you could have given me a little more heads up?"

"I was wondering if you had any sixth sense in you and would maybe be able to tell. When I realized that wasn't going to happen, I honked the horn. What more do you want?"

"Sixth sense, what are you talking about?"

"Well, I'd swear your friend Michael was prescient. He could smell trouble a mile away. Of course it didn't stop him from going in that direction, but at least he knew something was there."

"I just can't believe he and Paul are dead. We shared so much. I feel like I should know in my gut. You know?" Dennis asked, looking intently at her profile.

Tears were in his eyes, because that was the emotion

he was feeling, but he was also studying his driver. Something just did not sit right with her reckoning of events. She was staring straight out the window, seemingly lost deep in thought; then a zombie whacked the side of the truck, bringing her back from that distant land.

"And yet he is," she answered as she started the truck.

It was not lost on Dennis that she used the singular while he was referring to the plural. He would dwell on the words later, but the zombies that had grabbed on to the truck were a big enough distraction for now.

"A little more warning and we wouldn't have any hitchhikers," Dennis told her.

"Oh, you've got to live a little dangerously."

"Call me crazy, but just being alive these days would qualify."

She looked over to Dennis. "Very good. I'll keep that in mind."

"I seriously doubt it, but thank you. What do we do if we don't come across a settlement of some sort?"

"I've got enough cigarettes to get through this lifetime. Oh, don't worry" she said when she saw Dennis' features fall in resignation. "Man has this innate desire to be surrounded by his or her peers."

"I just can't believe that there's so few people left now." Dennis watched as a zombie fell from his side of the truck. It struck the ground hard and spun a half dozen times before it came to a rest in the roadway. He was glad they were pulling far enough away that he could not see the damage the tumble had taken on it.

"The world's better off," she said callously. "Too many poor people looking for a handout. This weeds the weak ones out."

"This isn't a 'weeding' this is a genocide."

"Toe-may-to, toe-mah-to. There were too many people. The zombies were merely a balancing act on the scales of life. Some have to die to get back to equilibrium.

You can't have any significant change without it."

"How very New World Order of you."

"My philandering husband was in all those hush-hush groups. They were constantly looking for ways to cull people so that dominion would be easier. Looks like they figured out half of the equation."

"You're saying the zombie plague was purposefully created by man to control other men?" Dennis asked incredulously.

"What? You didn't know? Well then I have a whopper to tell you about Santa Claus."

"Hilarious."

"It probably was my asshole ex. If not for me, he'd be waiting out this whole thing in a secure bunker somewhere. Looking for the opportune time to come out and lead the survivors to salvation."

"What do you mean if it wasn't for you? Did you turn him in?"

"In a matter of speaking. Are you a cop?" she asked, cackling.

"No." His eyebrows furrowing while trying to figure out what she was talking about.

"I killed the cheating bastard. Who knows, maybe if I'd done it a few days sooner, I could have prevented all of this. But where would the fun be in that? I would have missed out on all this," she said, taking her hands off the steering wheel spreading her arms wide.

"This is a good time for you? Are you kidding me?"

"I haven't been this alive in decades," she said, finally putting her hands back on the wheel.

"Billions of people are either dead or zombies."

"Most of them, I'm sure, were assholes."

"These men that are hiding, do they have a cure?"

"I can't imagine a cure, but they'll have inoculation. They have to offer something to get the survivors to become subservient to them. Probably something that needs a booster shot as well."

"So instead of a true vaccination, it will be something like a tetanus shot?"

"You're getting it now. Otherwise it would be like making a light bulb that never burns out."

"Your husband was in on this?"

"He always was ambitious…at least with me pushing him," Mrs. Deneaux said.

"I'm sorry, this isn't ambition this is murder. Do you have any idea where these men are?"

"I have an idea. Why?" she asked suspiciously.

"We need to get what they have."

"Yes, we'll just waltz right in to their heavily fortified bunker, grab what we need, and be on our merry little way."

"Exactly," Dennis said, finally feeling better. Maybe there was a chance of something more in this life than just making it to the next day.

"You're serious?"

Dennis nodded.

"Why not? It would be nice to have some servants afoot."

"Where to, then?" Dennis asked.

"Why, the cradle of civilization," Deneaux said matter-of-factly. Dennis wore another look of confusion. "Athens of course."

"How are we going to get to Greece?" Dennis groaned.

"Georgia," Mrs. Deneaux once again cackled.

Dennis didn't know if he was getting used to her, or if it was that they had some hope, but the grating noise that issued forth from the fissure in her face wasn't quite as irritating now as it had been.

CHAPTER 19 – MIKE JOURNAL ENTRY 9

Once everyone got settled and I convinced Trip I did not have Stephanie's sneakers anymore, we left. This time I decided 95 South was the better of the choices. I backtracked on the Mass Pike towards Boston and went on our alternate road. The bikers may have had enough and maybe they hadn't. If we however stumbled across them, they might be so inclined as to start the fight anew, and I was still sore from my last go around. I had a small pucker mark to remember our last exchange.

I had told Justin to come up front with me as I drove so we could have some privacy. BT was having some symptoms creep up on him, and I wanted—no, I needed—to know how my son was feeling.

"How you doing?" I asked him.

"I'm not as bad as BT," he answered, quickly getting where this conversation was going. "I've been getting these bad cramps in my gut every couple of days for about the last week. At first I thought it might be Aunt Lyndsey's cooking."

We both laughed at that. "What changed your mind?"

"I'd still get the pains even when she didn't cook. And then I started watching BT when I knew he thought he was alone. We're kind of on the same time line."

"Huh?"

"When I hurt, he hurts. And unless he's the world's biggest baby, I'm thinking he's in a lot more pain."

This was killing me to ask, and I knew I didn't even want the answer. "How long?"

"Dad, BT might be days away. I figure I've got a

week or two at the tops."

And there it was, my heart was wrenching in my chest. It felt like my rib cage was crushing in on itself like I had a working garbage disposal in there. We were coming full circle to that time in my office the night he had been scratched going on the fool's trip to save Paul. And for what? My fucking friend and his wife were dead. Maybe they would have been able to ride the damn thing out in their attic. Couldn't be worse, that's for sure. So we had potentially only forestalled my son's death and theirs.

You know when you're watching a movie, and the hero or heroine says 'I'd give anything for just one more second with…(insert loved one here)' that's bullshit. I'm fucking greedy, I don't want the blink of an eye, I want years. I want barbecues, grandkids, weddings. I want all the shit that goes with a full life lived. I don't want one beat of a heart, can't even say a proper goodbye in that time frame. I had seventy-two hours or so to save my friend—not much more than that to save my son—and I truly didn't have a clue where to start.

Well, if my theory about God had even a shred of validity, the big man was going to have to pull out all the stops on this adventure. Just the same, I was trying to put the gas pedal to the floor on the plow. We were heading south at a respectable seventy-five miles per hour. I was lost in no small amount of worry when Travis knocked on the Plexiglas divider. Justin turned and slid the glass back.

"They're back," he said.

"What the fuck did Trip do to these guys?" I asked no one.

"I don't know, maybe they paid him for some origami," Travis replied.

"What? Have you been around him too long? It's probably a contact high. You want to sit up front with us?" I asked Travis.

"I'm fine," he laughed. "He just keeps wadding up

pieces of paper and then he displays them as works of art to us."

"Yeah, that pretty much sounds like him. How far are the bikers?"

"Half mile."

"What are you going to do about those pansies?" BT asked, nearly crowding Travis out of the window. More quietly, he spoke this part. "Mike, let me sit up there with you. This Trip guy has pudding for brains. He keeps calling me TP, and then stops himself and asks if I'm Native American."

"What? *Oh*...tepee, I get it," I said.

"Yeah, so do I, but I don't want to sit near him anymore. I thought your form of crazy might be catchy, but it oozes off of him."

"I'd love to help you, man, I would," I smiled, "but with the bikers so close behind us, I don't want to stop the truck. Maybe you should help him fold up some paper."

"Oh, and that's another thing. He hands me this thing that looks like a paper meatball and he asked me what I thought of his rendition of the Eiffel Tower. I mean, this shit can't be for real can it?"

"You get used to him."

"Mike, I don't want to. He kind of scares me, man."

"A biker gang is pursuing us and you're more worried about a guy that torched his last brain cell back in 1979?"

"Exactly," BT replied.

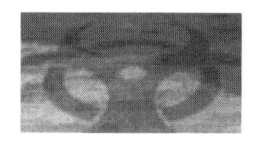

CHAPTER 20 – DOC

"So, Captain Najarian, is it true what the captured truckers said?" Dixon Hawes, former Senator of Texas and one of the richest men in the world, asked.

"I rarely trust the word of a prisoner being tortured, but it does seem that they were telling the truth," The captain answered.

"So the mythical Dr. Hugh Mann's suitcase is real. I never thought I'd see the day when that would be discovered. How is Doctor Baker doing?"

"His research is going well. I don't believe that he has caught up to our team yet, though."

"Should we bring him into the fold, Captain?"

"I don't think so, sir. From what I can tell, he's approaching the problem from a different angle. I don't know who's right and who isn't, but to have him see our progress may alter his way of solving the problem."

"Agreed. Have you got copies of the contents of the case?"

"It took two valiums in the good Doctor's dinner to do it. He never leaves the suitcase. It has all been copied and brought to the main research facility."

"He has no idea the true purpose of this place?"

"No, sir, he believes it to be what I told him."

"Would he come on board if he did know?"

"Doubtful, sir."

"What about using this Porkchop as leverage?"

"I would prefer it didn't come to that, sir, but possibly."

"Just a few more months, Captain, and we would already be in power. That's how close we were to a vaccine. I don't know what that idiot Deneaux was thinking."

Winston Deneaux owned the facilities that had housed the viral agent. It had been his sole job in the whole process to safeguard it and then distribute the weapon when he was told to.

"He lost focus when he started screwing his secretary," Dixon said, his large jowls turning a shade of angry red.

Captain Najarian had heard this rant before and stayed quiet. He did not remind Hawes that it had been the senator's idea to send Lori Stanton to spy on Winston. The captain was impressed that the old geezer could even get it up to do her. *Had to be pills*, he mused. Even with Deneaux's screw up, the captain had been sent to retrieve Winston once the zombies came. When he got to the house, someone had beaten him there. The old man was sitting in his armchair with a neat bullet hole drilled through his head. Looked like a professional hit. The poor bastard hadn't even seen it coming.

"What about this Michael Talbot? Has there been any luck in finding him?" Dixon asked.

"Sir, it's a little difficult to spare the resources looking for this man right now."

"I want him found, Captain. The man and his family were in possession of the suitcase for over seventy years, we need to know if they've discovered any secrets to the doctor's research. We cannot afford any loose ends, do you understand me?"

"Loud and clear, sir."

"Then I want you to make this your first priority. Send up those drones and have those little video game players find him!" Spittle was now coming down the senator's chin.

"Sir, if he's out there, the pilots will find him. If not, I can assemble a team and we'll go up to his brother's house in Maine."

"No more loose ends, Captain. We're so close I can taste it. We will run this world the way it was intended. With an iron fist!" he shouted as he brought his hand down on the table they were seated at.

Absolute power corrupts absolutely, the captain thought. But he was not complaining, he had been promised complete control of the military, and once the zombies were eradicated, he would rebuild an army that the world would quake at. *Looks like I caught a little of the fever*. In theory, he liked everything the Triumvirate stood for. It was an equality of all those below the ruling class.

Crime would be wiped from the planet, because to commit one was tantamount to suicide. Justice would be swift and final. Man would be free to practice whatever faith they desired so long as it started with a solemn prayer to the Triumvirate. People would earn their keep or they would be denied the protection and vaccination they offered. As quickly as the senator and his party could give, they could take away. Even if a person had received the vaccination there was a way to override the produced antibodies and reintroduce the zombie virus. All those that did as the ruling class dictated were safe. A populace that had to capitulate or die, that would ensure their complicity.

The Captain had always considered himself a patriot and now he was on the side for Socialism. 'Wouldn't the world be better off with one leader, one direction. All striving for the betterment...of what.' He paused. 'Dixon.' Was the only answer he could come up with. Dixon had approached him with such lofty ideals when the plan was in its infancy. A world without wars, hate, drugs, crime, the worst of humanity wiped clean from the planet.

'We'll be the new Noah's Ark.' Dixon had promised.

On some level the Captain knew the fallacy, less people meant less war, hate, drugs and crime but certainly not the eradication of them. It was the power Dixon offered that truly intrigued him, no matter what Dixon's words said, it was the implied meaning that spurred them both on.

"Sir, we are having problems with the zombies."

"Don't get bitten, seems like a safe enough problem to avoid," the senator said peevishly.

Easy enough for you to say, you haven't left this place since the outbreak, the captain thought. "It's more than that, sir. It appears that the zombies are getting smarter."

"How smart can a brain eating zombie get? I don't care, Captain. Once we can secure the vaccine, none of that will matter."

The captain saw it differently, but it was useless to argue with Dixon. The man was so fixated on being Supreme Commander as to be blind to everything else. He wondered how long it would take until he got the command to take out the only remaining member of the Triumvirate. With Deneaux's death, there was only Dixon and Harry Wendelson, the largest land baron in the United States, the man who owned the land they were now residing on. Captain Najarian would do it because he knew which side his bread was buttered on, and then there'd be nothing between Dixon and the asshole he was sure to become.

"Leaders always die," the captain said as he walked away from the senator. "And then who knows how high a lowly captain can climb."

His first stop was to the pilot's room, which, in retrospect, did look a lot like a basement filled with PlayStation playing gamers. Then off to see Doctor Baker. The drones had proved an invaluable tool in finding him, there was no reason to think they couldn't do the same for this Talbot guy.

CHAPTER 21 – MIKE JOURNAL ENTRY 10

The bikers never got any closer that day; they also didn't get any further. And gas was beginning to become an issue (even with the fifty gallon fuel-filled drum Gary had put in the back, attached by a hose to the fuel tank) as we traveled out of Massachusetts, Rhode Island, Connecticut and into New York. By the time we were midway through Virginia, it was evident we were going to need more.

"Must be a low crime day," I said aloud.

BT had enough impetus to get away from Trip that he crawled through a hole I didn't think was going to allow him through by half. He almost got stuck once and then Trip had started talking about patting his thighs down with lard and BT had pulled himself the rest of the way through. The talk of being buttered up made me remember my time in the cave. I nearly had a breakdown just thinking about it. As it was, when I slept, I dreamt about it almost every night. I'd wake up in a cold sweat and every part of my body felt like I was in the grip of a vise, barely able to move my fingers. I wouldn't wish that on Mrs. Deneaux…wait, I just might, but only if I could watch.

"Why I rise to the bait I have no idea," BT said sadly. "Okay, Mike, I'm listening."

"I mean, why else are they following us? What do they hope to gain?" I asked, truly wanting to know.

"They're a gang, Mike, they're seeking payback. Doesn't matter to them at all if they started it. What matters to them is that they end it. Their leader will look weak if he doesn't."

"What if we kill him?"

"Chances are they'll scatter at that point, but it's tough to tell which one it is."

"We need to get off the highway."

"Oh shit, man, you've got that 'I've got a plan' look on your face. Or you need to take a crap, they're both pretty much the same."

I ignored his barb. "We need to either draw them in closer or find a place to lay down an ambush. If you're right and they're going to keep following us, I want to get rid of them now. Plus, it gives us a chance to get some fuel.

"So let me get this right. You want to lose them or set up a place to waylay them, both pretty much requiring stealth."

"Yeah that sounds about right."

"You do know you have your blinker on, right?"

"Son of a bitch." I turned it off. "Habit, man. Stop looking at me like that."

"Being Nicole's wet nurse would be more fun than this."

"No it wouldn't," I responded.

"Probably right."

"No shit."

The bikers did indeed close the distance as I took the off-ramp. Maybe three hundred yards or so, far enough away that getting a decent shot off was nearly out of the question, but close enough that they'd be able to see me turn off. My gas gauge had just passed down below a quarter. One way or the other, we were coming to a head.

"How much longer?" Trip asked, sticking his head through the window.

"Doesn't that window have a lock?" BT asked.

"How much longer until what, Trip?" I asked, giving BT a cross look.

"Oh! Hey, Ponch!" he said happily.

"He hurts my head," BT said.

"It should be soon enough," I gave him an answer to

his mythical question.

"Oh great," he said, pulling his head out.

"Hey, Mike, some of the bikers are leaving the main group," Gary said, coming up to the window next.

"Maybe they're getting sick of chasing us," Justin said with hope.

"Or more likely they're setting up their own ambush." BT said it as I was thinking it.

"How many in the main group still after us?" I asked him.

"Dozen or so."

"Still too many. Alright, I saw signs for gas a mile up. Get Travis, Tommy, and Tracy up with some guns. Justin, I want you to go back there, too. Well this ought to be an interesting ten minutes," I told BT, referring to how long it was going to take to refuel.

"What do you want me to do?"

"What you do best," I told him, "look mean."

The bikers stopped as we did, one or two dared to get in closer, then thought better of it when one of them had the lens of his headlight blown out.

"Come on, come on, come on." I quickly pumped the hand crank, too nervous to look around much.

"I wonder how they're doing for gas?" BT asked, standing next to me.

"I would think they've got to be getting low as well."

"I say we torch the station," BT said.

"It's not a horrible idea, but it's not really going to slow them down. There are probably ten stations in a mile radius from here."

"I know that man, but how often are we going to have the chance to do it."

"It would be a hell of an explosion," I said with a gleam in my eye, thinking about the resultant mushroom cloud. I don't know what it is that is built into a man that causes him to love when things explode.

"Plus, it might give them pause to reconsider chasing us," BT hastily added.

"Dude, I'm already convinced. You don't need to keep rationalizing with me. You got any ideas how to get this done?"

"I was a cop, of course I do."

"Wait, you were a cop? How come I didn't know about that?"

"I didn't tell you?"

"No, I think I would have remembered that coming up in a conversation. I knew there was a reason I didn't like you."

"Likewise," BT answered.

"So, did you have much reason to blow up gas stations on your patrols? Was it retribution for the owners not giving you enough of those cheap donut wannabe's?"

"Come on, Mike, those things are gross. It's like eating chocolate chalk."

"You must have never smoked weed, because those damn things are heavenly. I mean not that I smoked pot, I've just heard some people talking about it."

"I said I *was* a cop."

"What's the matter, was internal affairs closing in on your corruption?"

"You watched too much television."

"That's it, isn't it!" I said as BT moved to the side of the truck to talk up through one of the openings.

"Gary! Going to need a couple of flares," BT said. "And no it was a girl named Callis."

He said that last part so softly and with such sadness, I do not think he meant for me to hear him.

"Behind the seat up front," Gary responded.

"Dad they're just sitting there," Travis said. "Most of them don't even have their guns out."

"Well that's a good thing," I responded.

"All these engines idling are bound to attract some

unwanted attention," BT said as he peeked around the truck. "What are they doing? They follow us halfway down the East Coast and then don't do shit when we stop. Makes no damn sense."

"Agreed." I tapped the side of the tank, trying to get an idea of how full it was.

"How much more on that thing?" BT asked, looking back at me.

I could see strain on his features. I couldn't tell if he was about to have another attack or something had him concerned. "What's the matter, man?"

"This doesn't feel right." BT's nose wrinkled up. "You smell weed?"

"Well...now that you mention it."

Trip came around the front of the truck, a large plume of smoke preceding him. "Hey, man, what are you guys doing here?" he asked with a big smile.

"BT's a cop," I said to him.

"The Indian is the fuzz?" He quickly put his joint-laden hand behind his back, a small swirl of smoke arising behind him.

"Indian?" BT asked.

"Native American?" Trip answered.

"You're not following the thread correctly," I said to BT's confused countenance.

"Enlighten me then to drug-speak."

"He's calling you TP, remember?"

"You have *got* to be kidding me! I thought we were past that. Fill the damn tanks so we can get out of here. Guy can barely remember his own name, but this he'll never forget," BT was grumbling.

"Hey, man, aren't Indians supposed to be all mellow and one with the earth?" Trip asked, already forgetting that BT was a cop. He had brought his joint back up to his lips and was taking a drag.

"You don't shut up, I'm going to scalp your ass," BT

said, pointing a giant finger at Trip's head.

"Dude is harshing my high, Ponch."

I shrugged my shoulders. "He harshes mine all the time."

"You should tell him you can't scalp an ass either," Trip said in a conspiratorial tone.

"Not a chance, the Chief already looks pissed off."

Trip got next to me and we were both staring at BT. "Yeah, I think you're right, man. Look at that vein on his forehead, looks like a speed bump." Trip moved closer to BT and had his finger out as if to feel it.

"You touch me and I'll cut your ponytail off!" BT roared.

Trip's eyes got huge and his mouth opened into a perfect oval. "No wonder your tribe kicked you out," he said, before retreating the way he had come.

"Dude, I didn't know," I said to BT.

"You let *that* guy pilot a helicopter you got into?" BT asked, shaking his head.

"There wasn't much of a choice."

I was luckily excused from explaining myself further when the bikers as one began to throttle their engines. Even though they were a couple of hundred yards away, the buildings channeled the sound effectively. It was deafening.

"Are they coming?" I shouted as I pumped furiously.

"No!" Travis shouted back.

"Pack up, Mike!" BT said, coming over.

"What's the matter?"

"They're hiding something. Come on, man, the extra gallon or so isn't going to make a difference."

My OCD said differently. When I filled a tank I was compelled to top it off--just my nature. So I almost ignored BT, I'm glad I didn't.

"Here, let me see that," he said, taking the hose. He splashed a fair amount of gas around the access hole. "I hope this truck goes fast enough."

"Hope? How fucking big is this explosion going to be?" I asked.

BT smiled.

"Oh shit, is that what my smiles look like? Because you look slightly insane," I told him.

"Get in the truck, Mike."

I did. After a quick headcount I yelled at everyone in the back to get down.

"Pull up some," BT told me. He jumped up onto the running board on his side.

"They're coming!" I heard from multiple voices in the back.

BT lit the flare just as I caught movement from a side street. My stomach lurched to my throat as I saw the huge cement truck squealing its tires while making the turn. It was heading straight for us.

"Get in!" I shouted to BT.

I hit the gas just as BT launched the flare up over the back of the truck. More things were happening than I could even begin to process, it was unfolding so fast. Our truck, although a powerful beast, had all the get up and go of a snail crawling through frozen molasses. The cement truck had taken its turn somewhere in the thirty-five mile an hour range and was gaining fast.

For a moment, I thought that BT had missed with the flare. I saw sparks dance from the end as it struck the ground…and then…nothing. The blue flame was nearly invisible as the vapor caught, a rippling ribbon of flame snaked from the ground and down the rabbit hole. The truck was still picking up momentum when I felt rather than saw the concussion hit. The truck went from forty to fifty as the blast forced us along. We were rocking around like a ship in a hurricane. Our back end may have left the ground momentarily, but I'll be damned if I knew for sure.

The cement truck was easy enough to spot, though, it was engulfed in flames. Fuckers probably saved our lives as they blocked a path of propellant from hitting us. I had no clue about the bikers, I'm sure at least a few of them became deep-fat fried fuckers. The resultant fireball took up my entire rear view mirror. I would have stopped to admire the view, but I was scared shitless.

"Had no idea it would be that big," BT said, gripping tight onto the dashboard.

"Comforting," I told him, my foot still securely wedged down to the floor on the gas pedal.

By this time the cement truck was riding our ass. Most of the gas that had dropped onto their exterior was now burning out. The tires still had a lick of flame to them, but that looked like it would be extinguished soon as well. My hope that the explosion was going to take them out was dashed as the driver slammed into our rear end.

"What the hell was that?" Gary shouted from the back.

"Bikers traded up!" BT responded.

I could hear bullets pinging off the heavy steel of the backend. I was confident it wouldn't break through, but it had to be loud as hell in there.

"You guys ready for some payback?" I asked. "Hold on!"

I waited while everyone braced themselves, or I at least hoped they did, before I slammed on the brakes. The truck lurched as the cement truck was now battering us. When I finally got the plow to stop, I threw it in park and jumped down.

"What the fuck are you doing, Talbot?!" BT screamed. I was already firing before the words got out of his mouth.

"RUN INTO ME WILL YOU?" I was screaming as I came around the side of my truck.

I'm not sure who was firing from the rear of the dump truck, but the glass windshield on the cement truck had shattered and caved inwards towards the cab. The driver and passenger had both ducked down under the dash. That did them little good as I blew dime-sized holes through the door.

"FUCK YOU!!!!!!" I was shredding my throat as I dropped a magazine's worth of ammunition into that small compartment. "How's that feel?" My body was as tense as taut metal; cords on my neck were threatening to snap.

"Mike, let's go!" BT yelled.

He grabbed my shoulder and was pulling me back to the truck. The bikers were hauling ass to come up on to us. We made two nice targets, all ripe for the picking.

"COME ON!" I shouted, beating one fist against my chest.

Bullets began to whizz by, one catching the material of my jeans down by my thigh, the heat in its passing giving off a sweet savory scent of smoked bacon. The bullet that caught me in the shoulder was the one that got me moving. Twice in one day, new record for me.

"You alright?" BT asked once we were back in the truck and again moving.

We had pulled away from the wreckage of the cement truck. The boys once again had clear firing lanes on the bikers who pulled back quickly or accelerated past as they again started to take fire. I watched at least one biker go down with what looked like a gut shot. Horrible way to go, and I couldn't think of it happening to a nicer person.

"Just a scratch," I told BT.

"Just a scratch? I saw the exit wound in your back."

I had a fair amount of blood pooling in my lap, and with my heart beating somewhere in the vicinity of two hundred beats a minute, the flood was pumping out rapidly.

"Tracy! Mike needs some medical attention!" BT yelled as my head slumped forward.

I struggled to keep it up. It was becoming difficult to focus, and for a moment, I had the sensation that my vision was tunneling. I felt myself being physically removed from my seat. After that…it was a fade to dark. *Th-th-that's all folks!* Why I had images of Porky Pig in my head is beyond me. I'd always been a big fan of Bugs Bunny.

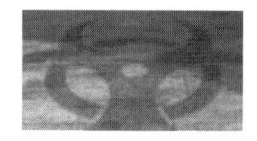

CHAPTER 22 – CAPTAIN NAJARIAN

"Captain Najarian, sir, I thought you might want to see this," Corporal Graham said as he handed a stack of high-resolution images to his commanding officer.

"Well that's certainly an explosion. Where's this from?" Captain Najarian asked.

"Virginia, sir. Richmond. It used to be a gas station, Mobil, I believe."

"Now it's a parking lot. Someone blowing up a hive?" the captain asked, referring to the zombies propensity to go into a stacked stasis when food stores became low.

"I figured the same thing, sir, so I looked at some of the satellite images before the explosion and this is what I came up with." The corporal handed over another stack.

"That a snow plow?" the captain asked.

"Yes, sir, and there appears to be twenty or so bikers and a cement truck chasing them."

"They're not together?"

"Some of the images catch muzzle flashes." The corporal pointed to some of the places where he had circled a small point of light on the images.

"I'll take your word for it."

"Sir, there's more."

"I'm listening."

"I went back and looked at the imagery for hours. The motorcycles have been chasing this truck down a fair portion of the East Coast."

"They either really pissed them off, or there's something in there they really want. Either way, it's worth checking out. Get a drone up and send it out. Program the satellite to stay on that cement truck. Let's see what the fuss

is all about."
"Right away, sir."

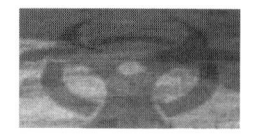

CHAPTER 23 – DENNIS AND DENEAUX

"Home stretch," Mrs. Deneaux announced as they passed through Columbia, South Carolina. "I need to get some sleep; you stand guard," she told him before she removed herself from her seat and climbed back into the rear of the cab and into the sleeper.

"Yeah sure," Dennis replied.

Her breathing became the steady rhythm of one asleep almost immediately. He had a hard time believing that she had just moments before been awake and barreling the truck down the highway.

"That's some scary shit," he said softly. He was contemplating getting out of the truck to stretch his legs and get fresh air when Deneaux spoke.

"I don't care what you think," she said evenly.

"What are you talking about?" He turned around. She didn't respond and he couldn't see her face.

"He was a zombie! Of course I shot him!" she shouted.

Dennis' heart leapt. *What is she talking about?* he thought. He reached over and turned the dome light on. Deneaux's eyes were wide open yet unfocused. *Like a fucking snake*, Dennis thought. *She's so paranoid, she sleeps with her eyes open.* He quickly shut the small light off.

"Screw this, I'm going outside. The dark and zombies are less scary." He would have done so, but Deneaux's next words riveted him to his seat.

"Michael has no proof."

Mike as in Talbot? Dennis thought.

"I didn't kill Brian or his precious friend Paul."

What the fuck are you talking about, you old bat?

"They died because they were stupid!" she screamed. "It's alright though, even if he had something, he'll never find me now."

There was a pause. "What the hell are you looking at?" Mrs. Deneaux asked Dennis. "You never seen an old woman sleep? Or are you one of those perverts that likes to watch women sleep and then do all sorts of nasty things to them. I bet that's what it is, isn't it? Are you playing with your little pecker even now? Here let me see it, I still know a trick or two."

Dennis nearly spilled out of the truck in his haste to retreat to safer ground. He was twenty feet away before he stopped hearing Deneaux's cackles.

"Don't pay any attention to her," he told his scared penis.

When he calmed down a bit, he began to go over the words Deneaux had said in her sleep. She'd implied two things: that she had complicity in Paul's and this guy Brian's deaths; and that Mike was still alive. If she had done something to Paul, it would make sense that she was trying to put as much distance between herself and Mike as was possible.

"What now, Dennis?" he asked aloud. "This lady is nuts and dangerous…two very scary adjectives. The smart move would be to go find a ride and get the fuck as far away from her as possible. Go back to Maine and see if she was lying to me all along."

He'd always spoken his problems verbally. He would tell Mike and Paul that it gave his brain a chance to reason the issue out as it had to take the time to circle back around and into his ear canals. By that time, he'd usually have a solution, but not this time. *Is she full of shit about the New World Order stuff as well?*

"One more day, man. I'll spend one more day with her. If there is a chance of getting a vaccination or a cure, I owe it to Mike and his family to find it. One more day. If it doesn't pan out, I'm leaving her."

He thought about going back into the truck, but he wasn't ready for anymore revelations just yet, and if she hadn't fallen back asleep, she'd start shrieking about his manhood, and it had JUST crawled out from his belly. He wouldn't put it through that abuse again so soon.

When Dennis was certain the crone was asleep, and he was nearly sleeping on his feet, he cautiously made his way back into the cab. He awoke a few hours later as the truck started up. Mrs. Deneaux was back in her familiar seat.

"Sleep good, lover boy?" She placed her hand on his thigh and cackled when she saw the expression on his face. "I'd be the best you ever had," she said as she put the truck in gear.

Dennis squashed down the taste of bile that had risen in his throat. "I'll keep that in mind."

"I'm sure you will." She was smiling at him, her tobacco stained teeth gleamed dully.

Mrs. Deneaux hopped on Route 26, which brought them mostly in a northwestern direction before she hopped on Route 85, then 441 which brought them straight into Athens, Georgia.

"Coming up to the lion's den," she told Dennis, her earlier smile not even tracing the corners of her mouth. To Dennis, it seemed to be the first time she showed any outward sign of stress.

Mrs. Deneaux pulled her rig up to a non-descript building.

"Here?" Dennis asked. "It looks abandoned."

"I'm going to do all of the talking. If they ask you anything, you let me handle it."

"You're not bringing your gun?"

"We're already under surveillance. If I show any sign of aggression, they'll just shoot us."

"You seem to be taking all of this in stride," Dennis said, wanting to jump out of his seat and away from the madness they were about to descend in to.

Mrs. Deneaux stepped away from the truck and towards the fenced building. She began to wave her hands at a camera that Dennis thought couldn't be operational due to the askew angle in which it hung.

"There's nobody there," Dennis said, coming out of the truck. He was thinking that he should have just left her last night when he heard footsteps approaching.

"What do you want?" a man asked, coming out of the shadows of the building.

Dennis wondered about the caliber of the hunting rifle the man held in his hands. "Enough to kill me, I'd imagine," he muttered.

"Why, Sergeant Decker, you don't recognize me?" Mrs. Deneaux said almost sweetly.

The man's scowl was quickly replaced with a look of bewilderment.

"Mrs. Deneaux? You're alive?" he asked.

"In the flesh."

"And bones," Dennis added quietly.

"Who's he?" The sergeant pointed over to Dennis.

"Boy toy."

The funny thing, Dennis thought, was that the Sergeant didn't scoff at that remark.

"Stay here. I've got to run this up the flagpole. I'm only a lowly enlisted man."

"I told you to apply for that commission. I would have had Winston endorse you."

"I'm sorry about your husband," the sergeant said solemnly.

"I'm not, he was a cheating asshole," Mrs. Deneaux said effortlessly.

Mr. Deneaux's philandering was well known. The sergeant had always been amazed that Mrs. Deneaux had stayed with him. Although who could blame her, with all the power the man wielded, she was almost royalty—at least in the clandestine circles in which they traveled. The general public didn't know her, but she was a legend, most crediting her husband's rise to power on her brains and tact.

"Can we at least come inside the gate?" Mrs. Deneaux asked before he retreated.

"Sure, sure," he said, opening a hidden panel and pressing a button. The gate, that looked chained shut slid effortlessly open. "Come on." She waved to Dennis.

"Definitely should have left last night," Dennis mumbled.

"Come on, sweetheart," Deneaux said as she blew him a kiss.

The sergeant spoke to someone inside the shadows of the building. The duo could not hear his words, although Dennis was sure it revolved around. 'Shoot them if they move.' They heard the tell-tale sign of a door clicking in to place.

"Got a light?" Deneaux asked the shadows. "That's very rude," she answered when no one came forward. She produced a light and lit a cigarette.

"Captain Najarian, you're not going to believe this," Sergeant Decker said when he got his superior officer on the radio.

"Oh, I might. What is it, Sergeant?" the captain asked.

"You got a minute to go to the surveillance room sir?" the sergeant asked.

A few moments later, the Captain was blowing air out from his puffed up cheeks. "You're right, I'm looking at her right now and I don't believe it." When the Captain had found Winston Deneaux dead, word had come down to find down the real brains behind the operation. When a team had finally got to her last known address at Little Turtle, it had been reduced to ashes and everyone including himself believed the old lady to be dead.

"What should I do?" the sergeant asked.

"Shooting her would be the safest course of action. Hold on, I'll come up to you."

It was not lost on the captain that Mrs. Deneaux had, at one time, resided in the same location as Michael Talbot. She could possibly have some information regarding his whereabouts and then maybe he'd shoot her. Sergeant Decker came out through the door, followed immediately by a man dressed in full battle-dress utilities.

Mrs. Deneaux smiled when the man came into view. "Captain Najarian, I thought you'd be a general by now."

"It really hasn't been that long since we've seen each other," he told her.

"I just figured you'd have a star waiting for you on the other side of the apocalypse," she said.

Captain Najarian stopped for a moment. It shouldn't have but it surprised him for a moment that she most likely knew about everything. The bunker was common enough knowledge in the upper echelons; the plan for why it was going to be used was not.

"Oh, you didn't realize that I knew about that? Very rich." She smiled.

"Why shouldn't I shoot you?" he asked in all seriousness.

"Do you really believe I would come here completely exposed without some sort of opt-out plan?" she asked, taking a large drag on her cigarette.

"No, no you wouldn't. What do you want here?"

"I want what's rightfully mine."

"Which is?"

"The seat next to those two old crones that want to rule the world. I can't believe that, in all this madness, they have yet to replace my dearly departed." Deneaux watched the captain like a hawk. "Oh, I see now. I dare say you want that seat for yourself, maybe all three seats by the looks of the way you've clenched your jaw. Planning a little coup during the reorganization of power? How quaint."

"Sergeant," the captain said with some strain, "Please escort our esteemed guest inside."

"And her…umm…kept man?" the sergeant asked.

"Oh, you should probably arrest him," Mrs. Deneaux said as she strolled towards the door.

"What are you doing?" Dennis asked.

"Well, I'm going to start a new life. You're a loose end I need to tidy up."

"What are you talking about?"

"Captain, this man is a subversive that has come here to relieve you of your antidote and give it to the masses. Sort of like Robin Hood, only without the tights. I don't think you'd fill out tights well," she said to Dennis.

"You heard the lady. Sergeant, arrest this man."

"You're a fucking bitch," Dennis said.

"Like that's the first time I've heard that. Captain, could you please show me to the quarters my husband would have housed in?" she asked as she took his arm.

"Hands behind your back," Sergeant Decker told Dennis.

***

"It's good to see you, Vivian," Dixon said. He'd carried a torch for his friend's wife since he'd met her back in the early seventies when Winston was just starting down his political career path. "I was truly sorry to hear about your husband. He was so close to achieving what we've been working on for so long."

"Dixon, you've never been much of a liar. It's a wonder you've made it this far in life, not being able to hide your true intentions." Mrs. Deneaux stretched out on her bed.

Dixon laughed. "You're right, he may have been my best friend, but he was a prickly old thorn. Still, it will be difficult to rule without his even hand."

"That's why I'm here," Mrs. Deneaux replied.

Dixon's eyebrows shot up.

"Oh come now, Dixon. I'm more qualified than my husband ever was…or that oaf Wendelson. We could rule together, like modern day monarchs."

She looked casually over at him. Her outward appearance was one of utter calmness, but inside she was a bundle of nerves. She hoped he wouldn't notice her imperceptible shake as she brought the cigarette to her lips. She knew he loved her, but would that be enough for him not to imprison her at the least and kill her at the extreme. Dixon was not known for his ability to share his toys, and this would be the biggest and shiniest he had ever owned.

"And what of the oaf?" Dixon asked.

"Well, certainly I'm not advocating his hasty departure from this earth, but maybe we could find a station more suitable for his talents. Like perhaps leader of the military. We would have a trusted and pliable man in that department."

"And Captain Najarian?"

"He's planning to take over as soon as everything is in place."

"You're quite sure of this?" Dixon asked.

"If you're not, then perhaps you're losing your ability to read people and I am backing the wrong horse in this race."

"He has been loyal to me for ten years. Why should I believe you?"

"He's been loyal for ten years because your goals served his."

"Ahh, Vivian, I've missed your council. When they told me you were dead I mourned."

"That must have been the worst six minutes of your life," Deneaux said with a laugh.

"What has taken you so long to get here?"

"I've been a little busy. In case you haven't noticed, there's a war going on out there. I sure would have appreciated a little forewarning."

"Alas…even we didn't know. It was your husband that jumped the gun."

"My husband? He wouldn't take a shit without someone showing him where the toilet was."

"As you know, it was his warehouses that held the flu shots. When the vice-president died from the flu, and the directive came down to fast track the vaccinations, someone at his plant had taken the bold initiative to ship them en masse, probably believing that he was doing the world some great good. Your husband found out about the mistake, but before he could send the stop order, someone put a bullet in his head."

Mrs. Deneaux's hand trembled more. She had just found out that she singularly had been responsible for the death of billions. Then she calmed a bit when she rationalized that it was going to happen anyway, she had merely sped up the process.

"Any idea who?" she asked evenly.

"It had to be someone that knew and would benefit from the early dispersal," Dixon said.

"That could be Wendelson or even Captain Najarian," Mrs. Deneaux reasoned.

"I don't see the reasoning for Harry."

"Captain Najarian perhaps. In the confusion of the world flushing itself down the toilet, he takes out one more potential adversary and no one is the wiser."

"Perhaps," Dixon said. "And then perhaps it was you. You had as much reason to kill the man as anyone."

"That's rich, Dixon. How would I get access to the millions he took from me if he were dead?"

"That's true, he was worth more to you alive than dead. It is so good to see you. Will you join me later for dinner and perhaps a drink?"

"I could think of no better way to spend my evening," she told him as he bowed slightly and headed for the door.

"What do you wish for me to do with the man you brought in with you?"

"Keep him fed for a bit, I have a feeling he will be a beneficial bargaining chip later on down the road."

"To whom?"

"Nobody you know, just personal business," Mrs. Deneaux replied. "I will see you tonight."

"Until tonight, Vivian. It is so good to see you," Dixon said as he quietly shut the door behind him.

Vivian waited until she heard him walk down the tiled hallway before she got up and threw the lock. She was in a nest of pit vipers, and just because she herself was one did not mean that someone wouldn't turn and strike at her.

"Who would have thought dealing with the zombies would be easier?" she asked before laying her head down onto her pillow. She slept restfully, her dreams not encumbered with the screams of the multitudes she'd had a hand in murdering.

***

"Mike, man, what have I got myself into?" Dennis asked, resting his head against the cool steel bars of his prison cell.

For the first day he was there, he truly kept expecting the old hag to come down and tell him that the whole thing was merely a ploy for her to gain his captors' trust. Then she would help him escape and they would do what they had talked about.

"She seemed so sincere," he berated himself for being such a patsy in her plan. "What good am I to her, though? Why bother even dragging my ass into this? Is it just to see me suffer?"

CHAPTER 24 – MIKE JOURNAL ENTRY 11

"Hey, Mr. T, how you doing?" Tommy asked, leaning over entirely too close. All I could make out with any detail was his nose.

"You smell like Pop-Tarts." I pushed him away slightly. "Help me up." I was in the back of the truck and we were still moving. That was a good thing. "What happened?" My head was still reeling. I felt like my brain was sliding along a grease-slicked track.

"Bullet severed an artery, even with your ramped up powers, you still nearly bled out," he said softly.

"Why does my mouth taste funny?" I asked him.

"We had to, Mike, there was no choice." Tracy came up to stroke the side of my head.

"Had to what? That had better not fucking be what I think it is," I said, attempting to stand, but the movement of the truck and my brain made that a difficult prospect.

"Relax, it's not black blood," BT laughed. "Is there such a thing as a racist vampire?" he asked Tommy.

"That's not fucking funny," I told BT. "You'd probably taste bad anyway, too much mean."

"I wanted to, Mike, I did," BT said seriously. "Tommy thought it would be a bad idea."

That made sense. I had already been dying; introducing zombie-tainted blood would have sent me over the edge.

"Who then?" I was looking around. "No…please," I said when I looked over to Tracy.

"We had to," she pleaded.

"Oh, Hon, this is not how I wanted things to go down.

I'm so sorry," I told her.

"I'm fine, you're fine. I've given more blood to the Red Cross, and I even got a juice box from Tommy." She smiled.

"We have juice boxes?" Travis asked, peering over the back of his seat.

Tommy stood up and went over to his pack to get one for him.

"Did…did I bite you?" I asked. I had to know. Did I now repulse her?

"We'll be together forever now," she said sweetly.

"No!" I cried.

"Hey! I'm not that high-maintenance of a woman," she said, visibly hurt.

"It's not that, it's not that at all. This is a hell I would not wish on BT, much less you."

"Nice, man, real nice." BT got up.

"I'm sorry, I was playing," Tracy said quickly when she realized it was physically hurting me to think she was like me now. "Tommy made a small cut." She held up her arm, a white gauze bandage wrapped around it.

"If it ever comes down to that again, just let me go," I told her, burying my head in her chest.

"Not a chance," she said, wrapping her arms around my head.

"I really kind of like it in here," I told her as my face was mashed against her breasts.

"You're ridiculous." She pushed my head away.

"I'd never leave the house if I had breasts. I'd probably just stare in the mirror all day and play with them," I told her.

"You almost died less than an hour ago and now you're talking about having breasts?" she asked.

"I'm alive, I plan on reveling in it and if that involves make-believe breasts, who am I to deny that thought?" I asked her.

"I know I did not just hear what I thought I heard," BT said as he walked past, taking a big sip off his juice box straw.

"You know those are for kids, right?" I asked him.

He slurped louder. "And it's delicious."

I sat there a while longer, left to my own thoughts--usually not a great idea during the best of times. It was then that I began to notice a grinding sound and a slight hitching in the truck that was getting progressively worse.

"Dad awake?" Justin asked his brother from the front of the truck.

"I am," I said, standing. I felt world's better than I had just a couple of minutes previous.

"Uncle Gary wants to see you," Justin said.

Got a feeling I know why, I thought, my mind racing to figure out what we were going to do once the truck broke down.

"Hey, Mike," Gary said. "How you feeling?"

"Better than the truck," I responded. "What's going on?"

"I think the transmission took a bullet or two, or it was on the skids anyway. But either way, we're going to be in some real trouble soon."

Too late, man, we're already in trouble, I thought. "How much longer do we have?" I asked.

"Few miles, I guess, before the wheels lock up or the transmission falls onto the highway or the gears inside just break and we start free-wheeling or possibly—"

"I get it, brother, I get it. Pull off the highway."

"Again?"

"I'm not going to sit in this steel box while those idiots figure out a way to get in. All they'd need to do would be find one RPG," I said. Gary looked horrified.

I thought the odds of them really being able to come across a rocket-propelled grenade were slim. I mean, it's not like you can go to an Arms Я Us and snag one, but that still didn't change the fact that I didn't want to be stuck in a box. The next exit was two miles up the road, and the truck was starting to vibrate something fierce.

"Dad? Smells like something is burning back here, and it's nothing of Trip's," Travis said.

"Well that's not good," Gary said.

By the time we were pulling off the highway, our speed had reduced by half and we were leaving a black cloud in our wake. The ride had gotten so rough that the truck felt like we were running on flats.

"Grab whatever stuff, you need," I told everyone. "We're going to be evacuating soon." I wasn't seeing any buildings that gave me the 'castle' type feeling. We were in a mostly industrial area. Warehouses and bars were in the majority.

I didn't like the idea of the large metal buildings. The wide open design would leave few areas to hide and plenty of ways in for a hostile force. The bars were looking better, but I couldn't get *Shaun of the* Damned *Dead* out of my head. Sure, he'd survived, but at some serious cost of life.

"Can you make it there?" I asked, pointing to where I wanted to go.

"I'm not sure if I'm going to make it to the next painted line in the roadway, Mike," Gary had to say loudly over the battering of the transmission's internal components as they ripped each other apart.

"Do your best," I told him before turning my attention back to the rear of the truck. "Okay, there is a stucco white apartment building. It will be on the passenger side of the truck when we stop. That's where we're heading." I announced to everyone.

"You and me, Henry," I said, reaching down to tuck him under an arm. His little stub tail was wagging wildly. He apparently was not picking up on how anxious I was, because he was all smiles and slobber. "You getting lighter, big dog?" I asked as I kissed his face.

"Get a room," BT said.

"I plan on it," I told him.

His confused look passed over quickly. "Shit, man, that was pretty good."

"I've been working on my timing and delivery."

This was followed by a loud clanging noise that sounded suspiciously like a vault door slamming shut or possibly a transmission hitting the roadway. The good money was on option two.

"Mike, we're coasting!" I heard Gary shout after he revved the engine and there was no response from the vehicle's transfer box.

"How far to the apartments?"

"Couple of hundred yards."

"We going to make it?" I asked.

"Yeah, but we'll probably be going slower than if we got out and walked."

As it was, I didn't know if we were much over ten miles per hour at the moment. Still, two hundred yards was a long way to run with motorcycles on your ass.

"BT, can you take Henry?" I asked.

"Why, Talbot?" Tracy asked.

"We need covering fire, Hon, and I can't do that with his beautiful mug in my face," I said, squishing his shortened muzzle with my right hand. Henry proceeded to sneeze on me. "Me and Tommy are going to give you guys the rest of the time to make it to that building."

Tracy saw the reasoning; now that's not to say she agreed with it, I'm just saying she saw the validity of the reason. There's not a woman alive that will let the facts get in the way of them winning an argument.

"Fine, just don't get shot again," she told me as she grabbed her backpack.

Really? I thought. *Wouldn't that kind of be the first thing I would avoid? That's like saying, 'Don't let that train hit you'. Or, 'don't let the chainsaw-wielding madman disembowel you'. Or better yet 'Contents of Coffee Cup are extremely hot, do not pour in lap'.*

A turtle hopped up on a double espresso would beat the plow's pace in a race at this point. "Everyone ready?" I asked as I gripped the release to open the tailgate. I got a bunch of nods. "Okay, everyone remember the drill."

"Yeah, dad, you said it like five times. When we drop down, we take two shots and then haul ass," Travis said.

And then the automatic response of 'no swearing' came out of mine and Tracy's mouth. I'm not even sure we knew we were saying it anymore. Maybe I'd dwell on that at a later point…if given the opportunity.

The truck was grinding to a halt as I pulled the lever. The tailgate opened slightly and I held it open with the bar Gary had put there expressly for this purpose. It kept the heavy door a good two or so feet open, plenty of room for a normal human to get through. BT damn near got stuck.

I was the first down. The bikers weren't quite so prepared to see a gunman, then a second as Tommy joined me, then a third. BT had not fired. He and Henry were heading straightaway for the building like I'd asked. Trip was the only near flaw in the plan, he started running towards the bikers. I reached out and spun him around, pointing for him to follow his frantic wife.

"Oh, I thought they were here to help," he said as he ran off.

Gary and Justin were staying on their flanks as the main body of the small group headed in. The bikers were getting bolder as more and more of us headed off. They'd stopped as well and were getting ready to lay down some effective counter-fire.

"Time to go," I told Tommy. "Shit," I said immediately upon turning.

Gary and Justin were trying to help BT up, who was on all fours. Henry was by his side barking, I think in encouragement for his 'ride' to get up.

"Help him!" I shouted to Tommy, while I turned back around.

The bikers were already beginning to converge. I didn't even bother aiming as I laid down a spray of bullets; it was enough to get their attention. Bullets were flying by me, but what was worse was that the group in front of the building was being targeted as well. I saw Tommy spin slightly as he took a round. He was doing his best to shield the quartet from harm. Justin grabbed Henry as Tommy picked up BT. Gary sent a few rounds down range to get me some help. It was greatly appreciated.

Then I heard an explosion of glass and rifles being fired from within the apartment building. At first my heart sank thinking that perhaps those inside were now involved in a different battle; then I realized it was Tracy and Travis helping out as well. That was all the prodding I needed as I nearly caught up to Tommy. We were all breathing heavily in that small foyer. BT seemed to be getting slightly better.

I put my hand on his shoulder as he was hunched over.

"I'm good," he said with long runnels of drool hanging from his mouth.

"Good, 'cause you look a little like Henry right now," I told him.

"I hate you." It was difficult for him to talk, but he got it out.

The apartment was five full floors of squalor (alright a little poetic license there). How about 'meh'? It looked very utilitarian. There wasn't graffiti plastering the walls or crackheads shooting up in the hallways, it was just a shitload of cinderblocks. This looked more like something the Soviets would have built, that's all I'm saying. The place was a giant rectangle bisected by a main corridor on each floor and an enclosed stairwell on each end. The place could have been a fortress if there had been enough time to remove the cement stairs. It would be many hours with a sledgehammer and a jackhammer to get that done.

"What now, Talbot?" Tracy asked, joining us in the hallway we had just entered.

The bikers were coming; it would have been impossible to not hear the flood of their engines. I didn't like the idea of staying on this floor because the windows would become vulnerable to attack. I also didn't want to go too high up, because then we lost a potential avenue of escape through those windows.

"Second floor, let's go."

"Dad, I think there're zombies," Travis said.

And then I caught the caustic whiff of malodor.

"It's Henry." Tommy pointed.

Henry was busy trying to send carpet fibers over his latest creation as his back paws scraped at the industrial rug.

"That's as good a reason to get out of here as any," I said. We went down the full length of the hallway to the opposite stairwell and up. "I really hate closed doors." I grumbled as I went a couple of doors down and knocked.

I made sure to step to the side and avoid what I figured would be a hail of bullets punching through. My apprehension grew the longer we waited for a response. The first floor had been remarkably free of any sort of hint of the apocalypse, the second not so much. Blood and tissue had long since dried on a fair amount of the walls and doors. Casings and the resultant holes were all over the place. What wasn't there, were bodies, human or zombie. And that normally meant human inhabitants, and I can't imagine they'd be all that thrilled that I'd brought another fight to their door step.

After no response to my entreaty, I gingerly checked the doorknob, fully expecting a gunshot for my efforts. "Locked, dammit."

"Were you perhaps expecting an invite?" BT asked.

"That would have been nice and at least you're feeling good enough to give me shit."

"Want me to kick it in?" Gary asked.

"Whoa, whoa, hold on, Gambo," I said. "You kick it in, and they know exactly where we are."

"We stay in this hallway and we're going to have the same problem," BT said. We all nodded at that.

"Alright, fan out. Let's quickly work down the hallway. Knock first then check the door knob. First unlocked one…we're heading in."

We were about halfway down the corridor when the silence became deafening. It's like that moment when you've been at a rock concert and the band has concluded their show and are exiting stage right. The whole night you've been communicating with those around you on a different level with hand gestures (usually a drinking motion to signify 'more beer?') or yelling into each other's ear or enjoying the cocoon of noise that envelopes you so completely you can immerse yourself in the music. When it's over, you have to go through a readjustment period. The resultant silence is deafening, and that's what I meant. The bikers had shut off their engines which I had to figure meant they were coming in.

"Dude, open up, I've got some killer smoke," Trip said to apartment 221's door.

"As good a reason to let someone in as any," BT said as we all watched Trip twist the knob and head straight in.

My heart raced with visions of Trip being blown back by a shotgun. I ran down the hallway to hopefully prevent that, or at least catch him as he fell. Nothing happened except the sweet smell of some burning leaf.

"Looks like he decided to start without them." BT leaned up against the doorframe.

I could only shake my head. "Everyone in." Not gonna lie, it seemed weird that we would be making a last stand in a crappy apartment. I guess it's truly weird when you have to make a last stand anywhere, truth be told.

The apartment was cleaned out. Whatever provisions

it held were gone, could have been from the previous occupants or someone scavenging. It was nice at least that the place wasn't the site of any bloodshed, those were few and far between. Gary turned the lock once we made sure there were no surprises within. There was a small corridor that led to the main room, the kitchen was on the right as you came in. I just couldn't see it being worth the bikers' trouble getting in here. We'd already bled them so much. I guess when you have nothing more to lose, what's the difference? That's what made them scary. I almost got the feeling they wanted to die.

"Trav, Justin, you guys keep an eye on the windows. Stay back enough so that no one can see you just in case someone gets the grand idea to put a ladder up or something. Tracy, you and BT take the kitchen. Me, Tommy, and Gary will hold them from the front."

I figured they were in for a world of hurt. If they'd listen, I'd love to tell them it wasn't worth it. Especially not to me, maybe their leader didn't give a shit about his people, but everyone in this apartment was precious to me.

"What about us?" Stephanie asked.

Trip could be as big of a liability as an asset. I really didn't want to make that coin flip. "See if there is anything in this place that you think we can use, a roll-away fire escape ladder would be perfect. Barring that, maybe see if you can tie some sheets together for a makeshift get-away."

"Does that really work?" Stephanie asked.

"I really hope we don't have to find out. Anything less than a two thousand thread count isn't going to hold BT anyway."

"Talbot, I'm right fucking here, I can hear you," BT said.

Then, from below us, we heard, "I'm going to find you!"

"You're going to wish you hadn't," BT said.

There were gunshots below us, and then the

slamming open of doors. No subtlety there. We were all tense in anticipation. I can't even begin to tell how many times I've been shot at, and it never gets easier—you're always waiting for that stray bullet that catches you in the neck or face or straight through the heart. The body just starts pegging all of the senses to hyper-awareness. I could easily see why some men love this stuff so much that they become professional soldiers. It becomes its own drug, something that doing daily errands will never achieve, unless, of course, it's in Afghanistan or somewhere equally deadly.

The sound of gunfire followed a door slamming open changed into screams of alarm and then a near constant rate of fire. They'd stumbled on a heavily armed homestead or…

"Zombies!" someone screamed.

"Blaze, there's dozens of them coming up the stairwell!"

"Basement?" I asked, looking at Tommy.

"Dozens…sounds like a hive," Tracy said.

"Bikers and zombies, sounds like a horrible B-movie." I quipped.

"I've seen that one," Trip said, coming out of the bedroom with a pillowcase.

"Going trick-or-treating?" I asked him.

"It's Halloween?" he asked all excited.

"Shit, there are enough monsters out there for it to be," BT said.

Trip started to head to the door, apparently to go seek out some free sweet treats.

"Why are you egging him on?" I asked BT.

"You're the one that brought it up," he said in self-defense.

"Trip, buddy, it's not Halloween yet," I told him.

"Sure it is. I have a pillowcase."

"Steph!" I yelled. She came and grabbed her husband.

"Maybe we can get out of here while they're fighting the zombies," Tracy said.

It was plausible. It did sound like most of the fighting was happening on the far side of the building. But they'd be retreating to where we needed to go. Would bygones be bygones if we ran into each other now, the whole 'your enemy is my enemy thus we are friends' saying? I got up and went to the door, opening it slowly. I poked my head out, to the right it was clear, to the left were bikers being closely pursued.

"Shit, he saw me." I pulled back in and quickly shut the door.

A couple of seconds later, a trio of heavy pounds hit the door. "I know where you are, fucker!" he yelled as he raced by.

"What the hell is he going to do about it?" BT asked.

"Beats me," I said, then we heard bullets firing outside our doorway. For a split-second I thought they were directed at us. But they went by and then we heard the pitter patter of zombie feet—shitloads of zombie feet. It sounded like the beginnings of a marathon out there.

"How many are there?" Tracy mouthed the words.

"Like…five," I lied to her quietly.

Occasionally one would slam into the door as they were jostled into it. Or we'd hear fingernails drag across it as a zombie or two tried to regain their balance. It was horrifying.

Stephanie came up to me and shook her head, letting me know they didn't find anything worthwhile. "No sheets, nothing," she said as we heard the last of the zombies streak on by. Then we heard the pounding upstairs; the bikers were leading them up and more importantly away from us.

"We should go," BT said. "This is our window."

"Where?" I asked. "Our ride is busted, and if the zombies catch wind of us, we'll never be able to outrun them."

"I hate when you make a valid point," he said. "It just doesn't seem right when someone as unstable as you makes sense, kind of throws my whole world off-kilter a bit."

I flipped him the bird. We all looked up when we heard footsteps overhead. Blaze had apparently decided to take up residence above us. I could tell how poorly the apartments were made when I could hear every single one of their footfalls and the ensuing muffled conversations they were having. Must have been a blast living under an apartment of a family with a few kids.

"Hey, shithead, you down there?" he yelled.

That came through loud and clear.

"Against the walls!" I hissed, but loud enough that my message was received by everyone.

Within a few seconds, bullets punctured through the drywall above us and burrowed deeply into the floor.

"Two can play at that game, shit stain!" I yelled, sending a spray upwards. I was rewarded with a scream, a thud, and a heavy cascading of blood leaking through the holes I had just made.

"Okay! Truce, man, truce! No more shooting!" Blaze, or whom I figured to be Blaze, yelled. "We cool?"

I didn't answer.

"Listen, man, we're pinned down by zombies. How many of you are there?" he asked. I thought I could detect an edge of panic in his voice.

"Seriously?" I asked him.

"Sorry, sorry, it's this new world, man, makes people do stupid shit."

Unfortunately, I didn't think it was this 'new world' that brought out the shittier side of humans. We have always had it in us. Why is man so fundamentally flawed? Does it really go back to knowledge and that stupid apple Eve just had to have? I would have rather been a noble savage. Thanks, Eve, for ruining it for the rest of us. There was civilization before the zombies, but I truly think it hung on the precarious edge of a razor. Take the news for example; which stories were we as a people drawn to almost without fail? It was the murders, the rapes, and the large scale robberies. In some sick way, that stuff triggered things in us.

Now, that's not saying we didn't enjoy the occasional 'feel good' fluff story about Johnny and his dog raising money for poor kids in Africa or something. But it's the devastating and sick stories that really got us. If you want to sit there and act all indignant, go ahead, but it's in all of us. Haven't you ever wanted to murder someone on the roadway, or shove a pen through your boss's eye? Not to mention what you may or may not do if you were ever able to get a hold of a cheerleading squad. The question is WHY is wanting to do harm to our fellow human being hardwired into us?

The veneer of civilization and religion usually prevents us from doing this. We obviously don't want to go to jail, or be tried in the court of public perception. But, you strip the restraints away, and being kind to your neighbor goes out the door in a hurry. Zombies suck; don't get me wrong, but it's the living that are worse. In a time when we should be banding together, we get people like Blaze who are only concerned with the moment in which they find themselves, and making it to the next at any and all costs to any that fall along his path. Can it be Evil sensing an opportunity? If God gave us free will, he sure wasn't granting us any favors.

"Blaze, I can't hold the door much longer!" someone screamed up above.

"God, forgive me for what I'm about to do," I said as I walked up to our doorway.

I pointed my rifle up and blew a good ten holes through the ceiling, moving before the resultant blood began to spill down. Then the screams began in earnest as zombies began to flood into the apartment above us, pushing past the now-deceased door minder. Sounded like they were hosting a huge rave.

"Let's go," I said amidst the battle above us.

"I'll find you!" Blaze screamed.

"Only in the after-life," I murmured.

I heard glass breaking just as BT exited. He and I were the last ones out.

"Hard-core, man," he said.

"I'd like to say I feel remorse, but I don't."

"Understood."

I turned as I saw something go by our window. I think Blaze was taking the express route.

"Come on, we gotta go before the zombies finish up and go looking for dessert," I said.

BT was already moving. Tommy was by the stairwell door, I saw him look through the small safety window. He then opened the door slowly and fired off five or six quick shots.

"Three in the stairwell," he said.

"Did they post guards?" I asked, more to myself.

We got down the stairs and out without any further complications, but we hadn't made it more than a hundred yards from the building when we heard the door slam open. We'd been spotted, and they looked hungry. BT was looking better, but he was easily going to be the slowest in the bunch. Well...that was unless, of course, Trip stopped and started smelling the flowers. We had no options.

"The truck!" I bellowed.

Anywhere else was suicide. Although, so was the truck. In all reality, it would be just drawn out a lot longer. Nobody questioned my decision; there was no alternative. I stayed by BT's side as he labored, turning every few steps to take out or slow down some of the lead zombies. Their bodies contorted as I sent hot lead into them. Sometimes I got lucky and would send a spread of brain tissue into the air, dropping the zombie forever.

A Henry-carrying Tommy reached the truck first. As soon as he got my mutt inside the back of the truck, he moved to the side to get some shots off. Gary was second and started helping or tossing people into the back depending on their location.

"Let's go, Tommy!" I shouted when I realized BT and I should be able to make it comfortably, and by 'comfortably' I meant by the skin of our teeth. If he had another seizure, we were through. "Help me get him in!" I told Tommy as an ashen-faced BT gripped the lip of the truck bed. Tommy and I hoisted him up while Gary and Trip pulled on his arms.

"This is just like Da Nang," Trip said.

"Vietnam?" I asked as Tommy and I crawled in.

Gary pulled the rod that held the tailgate open. I thought my heart was going to burst when I saw nearly a dozen severed zombie fingers twitching inches away from my feet as they got stuck between the steel of the truck bed and the heavy tailgate.

"Finger food!" Trip laughed.

"I think I'm going to be sick," Gary said.

"Not in here!" BT and I said nearly simultaneously.

Fists and hands began to beat against the truck. The body was secure enough, even if it didn't quench the stench. The cab was a different story. In his haste to leave the truck and get to the apartment building, Gary had left his door open. I couldn't fault him for that; he, like the rest of us, figured we were never coming back to our armored vehicle. Now it was going to become the focal point of our defense.

"Move!" I began to push people out of my way.

I was heading up to the front and the Plexiglas window where even now a zombie was making his way inside. He was halfway through when I placed the muzzle of my weapon on the back of his head. He turned and hissed at me, pure unadulterated hatred burned in his eyes as I blew a hole in his head.

Even with my ears ringing I could hear Gary retching in the corner. Right now I'd take the stink of vomit over what leaked out of the zombie's head. I was going to push him back out and into the cab, but that was not going to happen as zombies were beginning to pile in up front. Two pressed their way into the rapidly diminishing space. I waited until they were good and stuck before I ended their existences, such as they were.

Trip came up and put his arm around my shoulder. "Kind of reminds me of the cave," he said, smiling.

And instantly I was transported back to that rock constricting vice-like grip that ensnared my entire body. "Thanks for that," I told him, doing my best to shake the imagery from my mind.

"Oh...you're welcome," he said, looking at the zombies. "Good times." He walked away.

The dead zombies next to me were twitching violently, but not from nerve endings still firing. The zombies behind them were attempting to get through the roadblock and the prizes beyond.

Travis was peering through one of the murder holes. "There's got to be hundreds," he said with just about no inflection in his voice. I'll admit, that was in itself unnerving. It sounded like he was packing it in.

"We've been in tighter spots." I hoped my false words would lend assurance to his deaf ear.

Then I thought, *Have we?* We were effectively trapped in a sardine can; it was just a matter of the zombies figuring out how to use that little key to peel the cover back. I wondered if they still used that little key. I've got to be honest, I can't even remember the last time I saw a can of sardines being opened.

"You hear that?" Trip asked.

I heard Gary's constant stomach gurgling, the jostling of zombies, the pounding of multiple hands on metal, a bunch of snarls and hissing—most from outside—and some apprehensive murmuring from within the truck, all normal things for this particular predicament. I did not know which one Trip was fixating on.

"I hear it too," Tommy said. "Sounds like a plane."

"So?" was my bitter response. "Fat lot of good that's going to do us! Might as well be an ice cream truck." I'd just had a momentary tailspin and apparently felt like raining on the improvised parade.

"That's not a plane," Trip said as I was even now beginning to hear the prop wash.

Whatever it was flew directly over our location.

"Drone," he clarified.

"Drone? How can you know?" BT asked.

"He has three," Stephanie said.

"Who's operating drones?" I asked, definitely needing the answer.

"I don't know, but it's safe to assume they know we're here," Gary said, picking up his head long enough to speak.

"And what are they going to do about it?" I asked sourly.

"Talbot!" Tracy said sternly.

***

"Sir, I've got a visual from Sparrow Four on that truck you wanted me to follow," Staff Sergeant Emerson said.

"Put it up on the main screen," Captain Najarian ordered. "Holy shit, they got themselves into a jam didn't they?" He surveyed the scene. Zombies surrounded the plow with more coming in from all angles. "I wonder why they're not moving. Are they injured? Switch to thermal," he said as the drone made a wide arc and came around, the gyroscopic camera mounted underneath the craft never straying from the turmoil below.

"Switching to thermal," the staff sergeant said. The screen turned a murky gray with the minimal heat index of the zombies around the truck, bright points of light inside.

"Ten heat signatures." Captain Najarian did a quick

count. "At least two of them may be sick, one is burning with fever, and he's a big one. And then two of them have a cooler core temperature. Dying maybe. What of the other six? Their temps looks fine, so either they're out of gas, or that rolling zombie slayer has broken down."

"Orders, sir? Sparrow Four is twenty-four minutes from splash down." The staff sergeant was referring to how much fuel the bird had left.

"Well, let's lighten her load. Send a sidewinder spinning," Captain Najarian said.

"Sir?"

"Close enough to the truck that they know help is coming, but not close enough to cause them any harm. See how many of the zeds you can take out. And then unleash the fifty cal into the horde. That should buy you some more fly time with the reduced weight and them some more life time. Then get the bird home. I'm sending some boots on the ground to retrieve them."

"Yes, sir."

***

"You hear that?" Trip asked again.

It would have been impossible to miss. I'd heard enough missiles being launched during my military days.

"Everyone down!" I yelled.

If the drone and the people operating it were targeting us, then the gesture was useless. I was angry. Frying in a damn metal box was not on my list of things to do for the day. The truck rocked heavily as the missile slammed into the ground. The left side of the body got hot as a wave of fire and debris smashed into us.

"Wow, someone needs a little practice at the range," Trip said.

"Um…Trip, maybe we should be hoping that they didn't want to hit us," I said to him.

"Oh! That makes WAY more sense!" he answered.

"Mike, what's going on?" Tracy asked.

She might as well have been asking me to translate a calculus problem into German and then explain how it related to the ancient Mayans. I had no fucking clue. I was saved the trouble of bullshitting an answer as the air just about ripped open. The drone started firing what I had to believe was a fifty-caliber machine gun. Even with my hands placed against my head, the sound was ear splitting. If none of our eardrums were ruptured, I would consider that a victory. The truck bed only amplified the sound, like a mini-echo chamber.

The whole affair was over in less than a minute. When I felt it was safe to remove my hands from my ears, I could just make out the sound of the retreating drone.

"What the fuck is going on?" I asked.

I looked out my shooting hole only to be greeted with the ugly mug of a zombie. I stuck my barrel out and into his mouth, adding the back of his head to the devastation on the ground around the truck. The mini-plane had killed a lot of zombies. An accurate count was out of the question as there were parts of all sizes and shapes strewn amid the wreckage.

"I have got to get me one of those drones," I said as I tried to get an angle to see which way it had gone.

"You do remember when I got you and the kids all those remote-control helicopters that one year, right?" Tracy asked, coming up to me.

"Yeah," I said, dejected.

I had just got mine fully charged and no sooner got it into flight when it slammed off the kitchen light and onto the floor where a helicopter-hating Henry pounced on it, ripping the machine in half. I'd never seen the dog move that fast in my life. One second he was drooling on the couch a room away, and the next, he's got a paw on the chopper's blades and his mouth wrapped around the cockpit. I could only look on in abject horror as his massive jaw clamped down and snuffed out my fun. Travis had said I could play with his helicopter, but Tracy wouldn't let me because we all knew how that would end up.

I looked over to Henry, his stub tail wagging. "You'd tear my drone in half too, wouldn't you?" I said to him.

His mouth was open wide. It was hard not to imagine he was smiling.

"Got to be military right?" Gary asked.

Odds were yes, but none of us knew for sure, and even though the machine and its operator had helped out greatly, we were still surrounded by zombies. I had to imagine that the noise was only going to bring more of them.

"Dad, we've got a problem," Justin said.

I wanted to tell him that we had way more than one. He was pointing towards the front of the truck; the zombies had figured out a solution to their problem. They were pulling the jammed, dead zombies out from the window. It was disconcerting as fuck to witness a thinking zombie; mindless brain eaters were bad enough. And almost as if it was coordinated, the moment the hole was free, we heard zombies on the roof. The same roof designed really to only be a protector against the elements—plywood and tarp were not very effective enemy shields.

"Funner and funner," I said, raising my rifle, waiting for the first zombie to attempt the breech.

"It's actually more fun and more fun," Trip said, attempting to hand me a lit joint.

"You're kidding, right?" I asked him. I didn't know which was stranger, that he was correcting my horrible use of English, or trying to get me stoned.

"How did this guy save your life, man?" BT asked, shaking his head. He was sitting in the bench seat closest to us, his rifle pointed upwards for the inevitable assault.

"What are they waiting for?" Tracy asked.

"I don't know," I told her.

The zombies in the cab were looking at us like it was

Christmas 1996 and we had just taken the last Tickle Me Elmo dolls off the shelf. They hated us; the look they gave us said it all. I love cheeseburgers, may just be one of my favorite foods of all time, and I can honestly say I've never hated a cow. In fact, I love them for how tasty they are. But to these new zombies, it was something more. Not only were we their food supply…we were the enemy. We were hated merely for being who we were. A new term had been coined: Humanism; definition - *hatred or intolerance of another bipedal, merely because of one's status of being alive as opposed to undead.*

"Well, fellas, I'm really not a fan of this détente shit," I said as I got closer to the window and blew a burst of rounds into the cab, killing two zombies as the third jumped out.

I was looking at the gap, wondering if I could get through it quick enough to shut the door before a zombie caught me in an awkward position and ripped my throat out. I wouldn't even have the luxury of someone being able to cover me while I did the foolhardy maneuver.

The reward was worth the risk, it gave the zombies one less avenue of entry. I stuck my rifle through first, then my head. When I was a little past my shoulders I turned and fired shots into the chest of a zombie who was standing right next to the driver's door. As he fell over, I scrambled into the cab. My boot somehow got hung up in between the two partitions, twisting me into an awkward position as I attempted to free myself. Well, wouldn't you know it, an opportunistic little zombie took that precise moment to come in after me.

She was hideous, her brown hair plastered to her head in a beehive of gristle. Long swaths of strands framed her face. Her eyes burned with intensity as she cautiously entered. She was looking all around her for any signs of a trap. My rifle was effectively pinned under my side, my boot was lodged, and my rifle sling was hung up as well. I was in trouble.

The zombie's hands grabbed onto the lip of the seat so she could pull herself up. Her head was now level with mine, her blood-coated tongue licked over her stained teeth. She was pulling herself closer. I don't know how fast in real time the scene was playing out, but in my head it was in super slow motion. I watched in frame-by-frame detail as her tongue outlined her cracked and pustule-filled lips. Even as her dirty, disease-laden hands moved closer to my face. Like a snake, her tongue was rapidly flicking in and out of her mouth. She was three-quarters in when she finally darted at me.

A few things happened at once, I felt powerful hands grab my boot, twist it slightly, and push with enough force to send me crashing into the dashboard. As my body twisted, I brought my rifle up. The zombie woman snapped down on my trigger guard. I felt her tooth scrape against my finger. Then there was a loud explosion as BT drilled her in the head.

"Saving your ass is a full time job, I just wish it paid more and maybe came with medical and dental," he said, keeping an eye out for any more intruders.

"Shit, BT, thanks."

"Shut the damn door," he said. "Crazy cracker." A deep cough racked his body. If I hadn't known the man for the last six months I would have assumed he was a three-pack-a-day smoker the way his body shivered from the violent expulsion. Although, now that I think of it, Mrs. Deneaux probably smoked that much and I'd not so much as heard her clear her throat.

I pushed Headless Henrietta out the door, followed immediately by the other three dead zombies; tossing them like a teenager tosses McDonald's wrappers out from their car. My hands were covered in all manner of matter I do not wish to discuss, and the front of the truck looked like a softball team's worth of virgins had been deflowered. Think about it for a moment. Yup, you've got the picture now, and yes, I did just write that down. I reached over and grabbed the door handle to pull the door shut just as a zombie smacked into my arm. I'd taken too much time cleaning house.

The teeth were pressing down on my arm, I pulled away quickly, leaving the zombie with a mouthful of cotton for its trouble. I grabbed the steering wheel and spun quickly, sending my boot smashing into the zombie's nose, crushing it almost flush with the rest of its facial features. It might not have been an improvement, but it wasn't detrimental either. Quasimodo would have made fun of the thing that was trying to eat me. I finally pulled the door shut when the zombie fell on its ass. Three new ones were at the window before the echo of the shutting sound died down in the cab. A couple were looking at me through the passenger side, and at least four were climbing up the front bumper and onto the hood.

"This is horrible," I said, looking at all the angry faces that wanted nothing more in their existence than to end mine. In man-versus-man war, the general mindset, contrary to popular belief, isn't 'I hate them and must destroy them!' it's more like 'I need to protect myself and my friends.' Very rarely will you find a soldier who wants to fight, they are few and far between—
anomalies amidst the regular. It's always the men in power, those that have not been to war, that are willing to wage them.

"Ma-maybe you should come back here." BT gazed upon the same thing I was.

"Yup, on this we are in agreement." I handed him my rifle. "Thank you," I told him when I was back in the 'safe-zone' and the Plexiglas was locked in to place.

"At this point, Talbot, I don't know how I'd get through my day if I wasn't somehow pulling you out of your latest scrape."

"Thanks, man. Now sit down, you look like shit."

He didn't protest; that was how I knew his condition was worsening.

"Mike, he's burning up," Tracy said, feeling BT's forehead.

I had figured that out by the cherry-sized beads of sweat on his forehead.

"I've got something for that," Trip said, reaching into his fanny pack.

BT grabbed my arm. "Please don't let him medicate me," he begged.

"Dude, you're being much too judgmental. There's nothing quite like tripping your trees off during a zombie invasion. Expand your mind, man," I told him.

"I'll fold you up like a paper airplane if you let him near me."

Trip stepped up next to us. Two white pills in his outstretched hands. "Aspirin," he said, smiling.

BT looked up at him suspiciously, when he seemed satisfied all was okay, he grabbed them. "That I can deal with."

I handed him a bottle of water. With some difficulty, he swallowed the pills.

Trip was looking at us funny. "Why'd you take those?" he asked.

"What do you mean? You said they were aspirin," BT said in alarm.

"I figured you needed some, but you just took my last two Quaaludes," Trip said.

"I'm gonna kill him," BT threatened as he began to stand. I grabbed him around the waist to halt his progress.

"Steph, the Indian took my last two 'ludes," Trip said, turning towards his wife. "Oh, there's the aspirin." He pulled his hand out of his pants pocket. "Need some?" he asked a cheek puffing BT.

"Well, at least you're not going to feel anything for the next couple of hours," I told BT.

"And if we need to run?" he asked.

"Ludes or not my friend, you're in no shape to run," I said to him.

We were running out of time. Even if we made it through the night, I wasn't convinced he would. And honestly, I couldn't feel any more fucking helpless. Then there was going to be the unenviable task of putting a bullet in his brain before he could harm anyone in the truck, and knowing BT, he'd make me do it while he was still human. Running from this and getting dragged down from the zombies sounded like a much better option.

Then, after I blew my best friend away, then what? I got to watch my oldest son slowly decline into the abyss of zombie-dom. Maybe this was the rapture, maybe the good souls had died those first few days and the rest of us were now dealt with this hell on earth.

Is that it, God? Am I being judged for past sins? That's fucking fine, really it is. But what the fuck did Tracy or my kids do? Are they guilty by association? If that's the case, you can shove the whole thing up your—

The ripping of the tarp interrupted my sour thoughts.

"Um, Mike?" Gary said.

"Told you to use sheet metal on the roof," I told him.

"No you didn't."

"I should have then." I looked up to the corner where the sound was coming from. As one, we all spun to the front when we heard a window shatter.

"Natives are getting restless," BT said with a slight slur.

At least one of us was going out with a smile. And that actually made me slightly happier. All of us dying at the same time was alright as well; at least it would save me from the nightmare of shooting BT. The truck was rocking as dozens of zombies piled on, either on the roof or up by the cab.

"Mike, I'm scared," Tracy said, grabbing my arm, her

eyes wide.

"Well that makes all of us."

"Ponch, you have a real bad squirrel problem here." Trip was sitting on the bench seat behind BT and would from time to time lean over and look at the big man. "Anything yet?" he asked.

"I'm going to pop your head off like a Barbie doll," BT would tell him every time he asked. I did notice that the response got a little mellower with each retelling.

I think the last time I heard it before the zombies started smashing the plywood in, it was 'Barbie's hair is soft' I could be wrong, there was a lot going on.

As I heard fists smacking against the Plexiglas, and three-quarter inch plywood cracking, I was wishing that we had just about any other mythical creature attacking us rather than zombies. Werewolves were only a monster during a full moon, vampires couldn't be out in the day, and clowns were only at circuses. Sure, I'd find out eventually that all of those misconceived notions from my youth and Hollywood were wrong, but they still seemed better than the relentless tenacity of the zombies who would never stop. They were the undead version of the Terminator. Night, day, cloudy, clear, full moon, new moon, snow, sleet, rain, earthquake, tornado, yup...they'd still come.

"Travis, you stay on the Plexi. Don't fire until they get through. Gary, Tommy, you ready?" I asked as I trained my rifle up towards where the loudest cracking sound was coming.

Our shots, coupled with the zombies on top, were going to cave the structure in quicker. There were no other options that I could see. And then I did. It wasn't great. (More like decent, or maybe just adequate, but it would buy us more time.) And time was the most precious commodity ever allotted.

"Tommy, help me," I said as I got over to the right side of the truck and placed my hands flat against the wood.

"What are you doing?" he asked.

"Gonna flip some pancakes."

"What? Did Trip get to you too?" he asked.

"I want to push the roof off."

"Mike, there's probably fifteen hundred pounds of zombies on that thing," Gary said. "Not to mention the two-inch roofing nails I used to secure that thing."

"Well then you'd better get your ass over here," I told him.

"I'll help too." Trip put one hand on the roof. In the other he was holding a joint to his lips. "Let's get this show on the road," he said around a plume of smoke. "I've got a concert to get to."

"Whoosh playing?" BT slurred.

I bent my knees and pressed against the wood. I slowly flexed my knees, attempting to keep my elbows from buckling as the wood groaned. Tommy was standing like Atlas as he tried to push the wood off. The wood started to bow and groan as we put more pressure on it. My initial concern was that Tommy was going to end up putting his hands through before the nails gave.

I swallowed hard as I heard a loud pop; at first I thought it was my left nut rupturing. Then, thankfully, I realized it was the nail closest to us finally yielding its prize. When we had that one up a good inch, I stayed where I was, bracing to keep the accumulated weight of the zombies from pushing it back down. Tommy went to the next support and began the same routine. It was the first time I'd ever seen him not lift something effortlessly. Beads of sweat to match BT's broke out across his head. His shirt was soaked as if we were involved in a water fight and not a fight for our lives.

I had locked my knees in place and was doing my best not to have my spine blow disks out through the back of me. I was wholly unprepared to see zombie fingers trying to poke through the stretched tarp. How had they known there was an opening? The board above me began to dip down as zombies rushed over.

"Hold it!" Tommy shouted, maybe in encouragement.

Trip still had one hand wrapped around the bone in his mouth, the other was still above his head on the wood, although I think he had completely forgotten what that hand was doing.

"I'm moving to the last support…going to need everyone to hold this up," Tommy said through clenched teeth.

Steph, Gary, Tracy, and Justin rushed in to take his spot. I don't think they realized how much weight he was actually pushing. They visibly sagged as he moved.

"Trav, help them," I croaked.

He didn't look too thrilled about leaving his station. Three zombies were peering through the glass trying to figure a way in. BT, who I figured had by this time passed out, got up off the couch. I was going to tell him to get his ass back on the seat, but whatever he could muster might be enough to turn the tide. BT with a fever and stoned was probably stronger than any two men.

BT propped his shoulder against the wood and pushed up. His legs were shaking, and he was grunting, but I'll be damned if he wasn't raising the roof.

"I'm glad we're friends," I told him.

"I'm not," he said.

Tommy had pushed the third and final support up and free. We still had the tarp, which was secured outside with bungee cords.

"Justin, get my knife cut the tarp…and hurry," I said.

Within thirty or so seconds, daylight was pouring into the truck, followed by dozens of fingers.

"Ready?" Tommy asked.

None of us could wait until the count of three. We just started walking from left to right in the truck bed, pushing up on the roof as we went. The first foot was sheer agony, and I did not think gravity was going to give it up, but we finally hit the point of equilibrium. It started to get marginally easier the further we went. Zombies began to spill off the slanted roof as we went. Justin ran back and forth to keep pace with the cutting of the tarp.

Travis literally saved my ass. I was closest to the front of the truck, and a zombie had climbed onto the roof of the cab. It was getting ready to pounce when he had enough room. The bullet from Travis' rifle wasn't more than six inches from the back of my head. I was always thankful I'd never spanked him much, because who knows when he might have felt the need for a little payback.

More zombies were clamoring up the roof as we pushed the wood over, sending any remaining hangers-on tumbling to the ground, although we'd given them a decent ramp to come back up on. I flipped my rifle off my back to help Travis as BT and Tommy pried the wood free from its moorings, sending the sheet to the ground. We were a small oasis of humanity adrift in a sea of zombies. And like Z-day, they were making a beachhead. The roof was easy enough to defend for now, we had ammo; once that factor was taken out of the equation, then it would become exceedingly difficult.

The zombies for the most part seemed much more intent on coming from the front than the sides. Oh, to be sure there were a few mavericks, but most were busy knocking each other out of the way on the hood in an attempt to get to us. Travis and I were on the balls of our feet, spinning and twisting to keep up with the onslaught. The zombies seemed to be redoubling their efforts once we were spotted.

"I'm out!" I shouted. Tommy immediately stepped in and started firing. Justin stepped in for Travis a few moments later. We were furiously reloading, and Gary would shoot from time to time as a zombie would step on the rear tires and throw his or her hands over the lip of the truck.

"I'll load," Tracy said, dragging the ammo cans to one of the seats.

"I can help," an exhausted BT said.

Trip still had one hand in the air. Now it just looked like he was trying to get a bored, distracted teacher's attention. I looked up in time to watch him as his gaze followed his arm in the air to his hand. A confused look came across him as he tried to figure out what he was doing.

Good luck with that, I thought.

I stood up and got ready to get behind Tommy when he ran out, although it ended up being Justin who did so first. He tossed his mother his magazine, pinging her on the side of the head. I thought she was going to blow a gasket. For once I was grateful I was on the front lines.

"How long can we do this?" Gary asked.

"As long as we have to," was what I told him. The only other way to have answered this would have been 'Until we die'. In the end, though, they very well could be the same.

Even Henry got in on the action. Whenever he saw a hand come over the lip, he would run under it and bark his strange seal-like sound until someone came over and got rid of it. At first I may have assumed he thought it was a game with the way he was enjoying himself, but the sheer amount of time he 'played' let me know that Henry knew the stakes were much higher than getting a cookie or not. Henry's ideal play revolved around lying around and having people bring him things, whether food or tummy rubs—both of which he would accept with equal gusto.

We were on the losing side; that was pre-determined. The harder we fought, the more zombies came to see what all the fuss was about. Zombies were crowding around the truck, completely overrunning the street and spilling onto the neighboring yards. Fighting our way through them was not a possibility.

"This can't be happening," I said as I looked out over all of them.

Trip stood on one of the seats and was looking over the same scene as I was. He lifted both of his hands in the air, spreading them wide. He threw his head back and screamed.

"I am the Lizard King!" Harkening back to the days of Jim Morrison and The Doors, I would imagine, or he truly thought he was the king of lizards; with Trip, it's always difficult to tell.

Stephanie was looking up at her husband. She wore the worrying like a cloak, probably because she had to do it for the both of them. I was thinking that Trip as a zombie would be a pretty funny sight. He'd always be hungry and would never remember to eat.

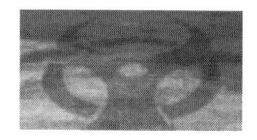

CHAPTER 25 – LIEUTENANT BARNES

"Captain Najarian, you asked me to apprise you if the situation changed," Staff Sergeant Emerson said as he knocked on his commanding officer's door and opened it.

"I know what I said, Staff Sergeant, what do you have?" he asked. "Holy shit!" he breathed when he saw the latest satellite imagery. "How many?"

The satellite that took the picture was designed for military crowd control purposes and had been equipped with powerful software technology that could count rioters or combatants with surprising accuracy.

"The computer says six hundred and sixty-six," the staff sergeant said.

Captain Najarian looked up. "Really? Well that doesn't bode well, does it."

"Didn't take you for a superstitious man."

"I'm not, I only sent ten men. Now, the question is, do I risk their lives for those lost souls in the truck? What's the ETA on the extraction team?"

The staff sergeant looked down at his watch. "Three hours forty-seven minutes, sir."

"And what do you put the odds of these people being alive that long?" the captain asked.

"Sir, I'm amazed they're not food now."

"So I'll put you down as doubtful. Alright, tell the men if they can't get to those people safely, to come back."

"Roger that."

"Remember, Staff Sergeant, I don't want any heroes. Those people mean nothing to me."

***

"Lieutenant Barnes, I'm in position." Corporal Godson said through the handset from the radio that PFC Vongim was carrying.

"Send me a feed," the lieutenant said, referring to the wireless video camera mounted on the corporal's helmet that would send a real-time image back to a monitor in the Humvee.

"How in the hell do they have a wireless vid and I'm stuck carrying this twenty pound radio? Does that make any sense to you, Godson?" Vongim asked.

"Listen, Gim, just do what PFCs are supposed to do; carry shit and be silent." The corporal fumbled around until he pushed in the power button.

"You seeing this, sir?" Godson asked his lieutenant.

"Well, now I know why the staff sergeant said 'No heroes,'" Barnes responded. "What a fuck fest. Looks like the whole town is out for the party. Stop panning around. I want to see the people in the truck."

The corporal and the PFC were on the roof of a home six or seven houses away from the melee below them, and even that was barely far enough. The lieutenant fiddled with a dial that gave him the ability to remotely zoom-in.

"Are you nervous, Corporal?" the lieutenant asked.

"Sir?" the corporal asked back.

"Your picture is jiggling around."

"Sorry, eating a candy bar, sir."

"Listen Godson, I know you have a tapeworm or some shit, but could you hold off for a minute?" the lieutenant asked.

"You've got it, sir," Godson answered. The picture moved rapidly as Godson chewed his last bite fast and then stilled.

"Well they sure as hell haven't given up," the lieutenant said as he watched the men and women in the truck fight. "How long did the staff sergeant say they've been out of ammo?"

"Couple of hours now, sir," Godson replied, wondering when he was going to be able to eat the other half of his Kit-Kat bar. He'd had to trade two bottles of whisky to get it.

"They should have been getting ready to fall on their swords by now," the lieutenant said softly.

"We're going in then?"

"Of course. I didn't come all this way just for your company."

"And the 'no heroes' part?" Godson asked.

"I didn't authorize any deaths today, Corporal. Pack up and get down here."

"Yes, sir. I fucking knew he was gonna want to go in," Godson said to the PFC.

"Corporal, the comm is still open," the lieutenant said. "Now bend your head down and let me see what you're so interested in eating. A Kit-Kat? That half is mine. I'll consider it your punishment for breach of military protocol. Now get your ass down here, I'm starving."

"Yes, sir. Shut the damn radio off this time will you, Gim. Dammit," he added at the end as he stuffed the remainder of his prized candy bar back into his pocket.

"Sir there's close to seven hundred of those ugly fuckers. How are you planning on getting through?" the corporal asked when he was once again face to face with the lieutenant.

"First things first." The lieutenant extended his hand.

"I was hoping you'd forgotten about that." Godson handed the candy bar over.

"Not a chance," the LT said as he savored the morsel. "That was delicious, thank you, Corporal. As for your initial question, why, we'll do it with superior firepower and potentially superior intellect. Although, in your case, that's questionable. Those people are fighting like demons. They've inspired me to join in the fun."

"Sir, we've got two Hummers, three RPG rounds, and some small arms. We're not really equipped to take on a horde that big," Corporal Godson said as he replayed the video he just shot.

"Relax, Godson, I know that. I've called in a helicopter for extraction," the lieutenant said.

"Oh thank God," Godson said. "I thought for sure you wanted to go in and get them."

"Not quite."

"Not quite, sir?" Godson asked.

"It's going to be a little over an hour before that chopper gets here, and we need to run interference, otherwise I don't think they're going to make it. Relax, Corporal, I'll make sure you get back to your woman in one piece."

"She'd appreciate that, sir," Godson said seriously.

"Doubtful, but I'll still get you home."

CHAPTER 26 – MIKE JOURNAL ENTRY 12

We were down to swinging and sticking things, on occasion even throwing punches and kicking. My worst nightmare was coming to fruition. Tommy had a tire iron that was shaped like an 'x' and was wielding it like a samurai. He was just about the only thing keeping us from being overrun. He would run around the truck to help out anyone who was in a mess. Something had clicked in Trip's head; the man looked like a stiff breeze could blow him over, but he was swinging a piece of two-by-four like Babe Ruth. Stephanie had been fighting side-by-side with him, but after a couple of near misses she figured it was safer to get a little further away.

"This is the most intense game of Whack-A-Mole I've ever played!" he shouted at one point. "The prize had better be worth it!"

Tracy and Steph were keeping their corner of the truck bed free and clear. Tracy had an ax handle and Steph was copying her husband's lead with the wood framing. Justin was in the corner opposite them, swatting at zombies with his rifle. Travis was next to him using a machete. Gary was next to Travis and they would switch off with other people in the truck as they got tired. BT, however, was my biggest concern. Here we were fighting off hundreds of zombies, and I couldn't help but take glances at him from time to time. He would join in the fight for a few minutes and need to rest for double that time. He looked like the walking dead, and I mean that in the absolute worst way.

I would greatly mourn my friend's passing when I got a quiet chance to do so. My concern now was that he was going to turn at any moment in that truck bed. Every time he hung his head down, I expected him to raise it up with that opaque glaze on his face. It would be my job to kill him before he could do any of us any harm; a job I did not take lightly. I noticed him more than once looking over at me, sometimes angrily, like maybe I should do him in now before he had the chance to cause harm. I think if he could have beaten his brains in himself, he would have done so.

I don't know what the fuck I was waiting for, the man was spiraling down the drain. Where he was going to end up was a foregone conclusion. The one thing I noticed that got more nerve wracking the longer it went on was that every time BT stood and fought for a little while, he would invariably move closer to me when he sat down. Either he wanted to see if he could get a bite of me when he turned, or he wanted to make sure that I was the one that did him in when the change happened. Both scenarios sucked wet diarrhea-laden ass.

I had the front of the truck where the majority of zombies were making their push. It was the easiest access, and more than once I'd felt arms on me before Tommy would rush in and help push back the onslaught. I jammed that blade into more heads than I could count. I had a hard time believing zombies could even get enough traction to get up towards me. The front end of the truck looked like we had plowed into the decomposing body of a brachiosaurus; chunks of tissue along with gallons of blood covered every available surface. I'd slammed the front of my rifle against so many of them, I'm not sure that, if I even had bullets, I'd be able to take the chance and shoot any of them. The barrel looked slightly off skew, although some might say that's just my natural perception of the world. Of course that was before my stock shattered and I switched weapons out.

My shoulders and forearms ached, and if I was hurting, I couldn't even begin to imagine what the others were going through. Nobody said anything as they went dutifully and diligently about their business. Okay…except for Trip, who would sometimes yell out things like. "Double combo!" or "When are we going to play table shuffleboard?"

"Does he think we're at Dave and Buster's?" BT asked from right behind me.

He startled me. I didn't know he had gotten so close. He was sitting, and his head was down. Sweat poured off his body in streams, it looked like he had a hose on him there was so much of it.

"It's almost time, Mike," he breathed out shallowly.

I wanted to tell him to fuck off and stop being so selfish, that maybe he should go jump into the crowd and save me the trouble of having to cave-in my best friend's head. It would save me a lot of nightmares if I survived. *Now* who was being selfish? I couldn't even pony up enough balls to give my friend the send-off he deserved.

"Fucking zombies!" I yelled, driving my machete into the nasal cavity of one and through the back of its skull.

I was pulling my knife blade back; I had to kick the zombie away to completely extract it from the steel, when I heard the chattering of gunfire.

"AKs?" BT asked.

"Sure sounds like it," I said. The AK had a louder, heavier, more ominous sound than that of the M-16, which sounded like a chirping canary in comparison.

"I wonder if they're as fucked as we are?" BT asked, looking up. That act alone seemed to drain him.

"Oh I doubt it. We've got some special sort of fuck going on up here," I told him as I drove the point of my large knife into the front of a zombie woman's forehead. I stirred the point around like I was performing a lobotomy for a second or two and then pulled out. The damage was done as she twitched and fell off to the side.

"Incoming!" Gary yelled.

I turned to see the telltale trail of smoke as someone

had let loose an RPG. It smashed into a house not more than fifty feet from us—a house that had been surrounded by zombies that were waiting patiently to get to us.

"Who are these guys?" Trip asked. "How can they miss a giant plow in the middle of the roadway?"

I was wondering who the guys were as well. It had to be the same men that were in charge of the drone, but why go through all of this trouble? Who were we to them? They were obviously a remnant of the military, their equipment lending credence to that assumption. While I was playing twenty questions, pieces of the burning house were raining down among all of us, zombies and humans alike. It may have not been a death peel to the zombies, but it did, for at least a little while, take the main focus off of our small group. The zombies on the periphery started to send out patrols to see where this new threat and food source was. Not enough to make a difference in our small brutal corner of the world, but it was still comforting in its own right.

More gunfire came from our right, it wasn't sustained, though. Whatever or whoever was out there, I was not getting the feeling that there were enough of them to make a difference. Which again began to raise the question: why bother? At this point, all they were really doing was wasting ammo and giving the other occupants of the truck some hope, even if it was of the false variety. And then another RPG slammed into a car not twenty feet from us. The truck swayed back and forth from the percussion.

"That's it!" Trip yelled encouragingly. "You're getting better!"

BT wrapped his face in his hands and shook slowly back and forth. "I truly thought you were as bad as it could get."

"Sorry to disappoint you," I told him.

I noticed Tracy leading Stephanie to the bench seat. The woman was so tired, I don't even think her eyes were open as my wife helped her sit down. Justin was fading fast as well; most of his last few swings had looked like an arthritic ninety-year-old's attempt. He was barely getting his gun past his hips.

"Justin, take a break!" I told him. He was no good to anybody that way. If even five minutes of sitting got him back in the game, then it was worth it.

***

"Sir, they're dropping like flies," Corporal Godson said into his handset. He had got into a house and was on the second floor looking down on the holdouts.

Lieutenant Barnes was about to call off the chopper. "Bitten?" he asked.

"I don't think so, but three of them look like they're out of the fight. The big black man, one of the women, and one of the younger men."

"Are you certain they're not bitten?" Barnes asked.

"I am, sir. I just think they're exhausted. Not that they could, but no one is attending to wounds of any kind. I don't see any blood. Something else isn't quite right here as well, sir."

"What is it, Godson?"

"Sir, two of the men, the way they're fighting, it just doesn't look…I don't know, it doesn't look natural. It's too quick. I feel like I'm watching those old time films where the speed was off and everything was moving faster than it should, especially the younger of the two. Are we sure we want to pick them up?"

"Scared of a few civilians?" Barnes asked.

"These ones I am," he said, making sure he was not depressing the send button.

***

I saw it before I heard it. It was a Huey helicopter,

something I'd gone for many a ride in during my Corps days. Were we the subject of the extraction, or were the men that were shooting around us the chosen few? Although that made no sense, they could have left on their own volition at any time. Chain-fire erupted from the side of the Huey as it sought position over us. Between the blades slicing through the air, and the bullets slicing through the zombies, it was impossible to hear anything. The rescue sled that was being lowered left little doubt of their intentions though.

"Justin!" I had to scream as loud as my throat was capable. When I realized he had heard me, I pointed to him then the basket. 'You first,' I mouthed. He shook his head and pointed to BT.

'You!' I mouthed and pointed angrily.

There was a good chance that, if I sent BT up there first, they would roll him out the chopper on the other side once they saw the condition he was in. I needed someone up there to fight for his safety. Plus, he was looking more and more of a liability the longer he stayed down here. I was concerned for his safety as well. The basket took an agonizingly long time to descend. I swear the more they dropped the bucket, the higher the copter went. Plus, the backwash from the rotors was no easy thing to contend with. It blew everything into the air and, invariably, the eyes of all of us.

"Looks like my helicopter!" Trip yelled.

I wanted to tell him 'No it didn't, this one was still airborne.'

I looked up in time to see the winch operator. He was making a two with his fingers.

"Justin, grab Stephanie!" I screamed.

She was shaking her head side to side when Justin grabbed her shoulder.

"Get your fucking ass up there!" I screeched. "The longer you delay, the more danger we're in!"

She looked at me like I had stomped on a brood of

kittens, but at least she went—albeit reluctantly. I can't say I blame her. I'm sure that on more than one occasion Trip had taken her up in his Tonka toy. And now she had a respectful fear of anything that even remotely resembled it. I think I celebrated another birthday by the time the basket made it down again.

"BT, you're up!" I told him.

"Not before Tracy and Travis," he said as loudly as he could, which wasn't that voluminous.

"You're taking my other kid up," I told him.

This was killing BT, but he dutifully grabbed Henry and got into the basket. Henry was like a board in BT's arms, I don't think the big dog was enjoying the ride. Then, upon closer inspection, I realized both BT and Henry were petrified. The duo were peering off into the horizon on some fixed spot, neither looking down at the horrendous scene below them. I thought it was kind of funny. Not that I'd say anything to BT about it…ever.

The basket began its third descent. This was where it was going to get interesting. Everyone that was left now was one less person manning the walls, so to speak.

"Travis, grab your mom!" I yelled, using a middleman as a buffer.

I knew Tracy would agree to this as much as she did that one time I tried to buy a cow. And not a butchered one, either. Long story short, we never did get Bessie. Hey, what pseudo prepper doesn't think about getting some livestock? Her argument was that we only had a fifteen-by-fifteen foot yard at the time. Always the pragmatist; or is it realist?

She gave a half-hearted fight, but she was exhausted and knew she was only moments away from collapsing as it was. I was thrilled when they were halfway up. No matter what happened now, the majority of my family was safe. It now came down to Gary, Tommy, Trip, and me to hold down the fort. Maybe not the optimum fighting force, but I was happy to be alongside them nonetheless.

"When do the tickets come out?" Trip asked, taking a moment to look into the side cutout in hopes that the prize redeeming coupons would begin to spit through. "I should be able to get a huge teddy bear after this game!"

"Gary, you and Trip next!" I yelled.

"What about you and Tommy?" he asked breathlessly.

"We've got this," I told him wearily. "Right?" I asked Tommy.

He nodded at me grimly.

By the time the bucket was down again, it nearly came down on Trip's head, he and Gary had been pushed back that far by the zombies. I cut in front of them, creating the room they would need to get up into the air.

***

"These guys are phenomenal," Barnes said, more to himself as he looked through his binoculars. "No wonder they're still alive."

"Keep an eye on the two that are still in the truck, sir," the corporal said. "If I hadn't seen it, I wouldn't believe it. He spins that tire iron like it's on a sprocket, and when it hits, I swear he goes halfway into the skull. And the older guy, he looks like he could be prior military because he knows how to use his weapon, but he's just too fast. I can't think of any other way to explain it. He shouldn't be moving with that much ease."

"Definitely interesting." The Lieutenant watched the two try to keep the converging zombies at bay. "We got anything that can help them?"

"We're low on everything, sir. Plus, we'd like to save a little for the ride home in case we encounter any trouble ourselves."

"Hate to see them fall now. I can't imagine they'll make it, though." He put down his glasses as zombies broke over every part of the truck bed. The two men left were now fighting back to back.

***

"Odds?" I asked when Tommy's back met mine.
"Odds? As in the chances we'll make it?"
"Yeah."
"You want to know what odds I would be giving on whether or not we survive? That's kind of inappropriate," he said.
"Not as much as mirrors on shoes."
"Please tell me you haven't done that."
"No," I told him. "I could never get the angle right and the glue wouldn't hold. Plus, I mean, unless you tack on some good-sized pieces of reflective glass, what are you really going to be able to see?"

The mounted thirty cal in the helo opened up again, but it was blowing zombies away too far from us to be of any immediate help. The basket finally made its way down to us. Unfortunately it was a good five feet and half a dozen zombies from our present location. It would be a life or death struggle just to get there.

Tommy had a much better weapon for the close-quarter combat we now found ourselves in, and unlike me, he looked like he had another couple of hours left in him. It was getting to the point where I could barely drive my blade through the skull plate anymore. It was much more jarring to the arms than one might imagine. I was slogging through the bodies of two dead zombies by the time I reached the basket. Tommy was inches from me; the basket began its ascent.

"Going up, lingerie, jewelry, perfume," I told him, hoping that the levity would break the spell of despair I was feeling even in the midst of a rescue.

Tommy jumped easily enough, the basket swaying drunkenly. He kicked out a few times, taking out some of the more rambunctious zombies that appeared to want to go for an aerial joyride themselves. We were about halfway up; the operator was guiding the cable onto the winch. I don't know what it was, but something didn't seem right, another crewman kept looking out over at us, but none of my family. I at least expected Trip to wave or something, or for Tracy to make sure I made it safely on board. I could only reason that they'd been made to strap themselves in and were telling them about our progress. I still didn't see that working on Tracy…or Trip for that matter.

We were three-quarters up as that second crewman peeked out again. Tommy looked over at me, I shrugged. He didn't appear to like my response. Hands reached out and grabbed me just as the basket was coming even with the skids of the helicopter. My eyes immediately went to BT as I stood and was being helped in. The big man was passed out on a stretcher. That was not a shock. It was when I panned around and noticed that everyone was passed out. I instinctively pulled back.

"Michael Talbot?" the man asked.

"Uh…yeah," I answered, still looking at my entire family.

It was then that the second crewman came up by my side. I felt rather than saw the prick of a needle going deep into my neck. I reached out and grabbed his windpipe, slowly constricting his airflow as I applied more pressure.

"What's going on here?" I asked. Whatever he had hit me with was already beginning to take effect as his image blurred and multiplied. All three of him were rapidly turning red as I kept squeezing.

I felt another needle on the side from the man that was working the cable. Tommy and the basket were just coming even with the opening to the craft. He saw as the second needle plunged into my neck and I would imagine, the status of everyone. His face twisted into a mask of anger as he grabbed the man that hit me the second time. He picked him up and threw him hard against the cockpit wall. The man slumped down. Two others that looked like Marines trained their weapons on Tommy. Before either of them could react Tommy hit the release on the basket; cable spun freely as he and the sled plummeted to the ground.

"Grab him!" someone shouted.

I thought they were talking about Tommy until I felt hands roughly grasp my arms and shoulders, dragging me the rest of the way into the helicopter before I rolled out and down. I was unconscious before I felt the hands leave me.

***

Lieutenant Barnes watched as the basket and the young man fell from the helicopter. "Dipshit air jockeys," he said as his heart skipped a beat. It was always difficult to watch someone die, and the more he saw, the worse it got. "Can't even pull off a simple rescue mission without killing someone. Alright, Godson, get everyone on the same page. We're out of here."

"We going to see if the kid is alright?" Godson asked.

"He just fell a hundred feet out of a helicopter into the waiting arms of several hundred zombies. I'm going to say the outcome is predetermined on this one. Let's saddle up and get out of here."

Barnes' radio crackled and came to life. "Pounder Four, Pounder Four, this is Wing Six, standby for orders."

"Shit, looks like we're going in after all," Barnes said.

"Pounder Four, this is Captain Emery. Do you still have an RPG?" he asked.

"Hello, Captain, this is Lieutenant Barnes, we've got one round left. You want us to go in and save the boy?"

"Negative, Lieutenant, I want you to put a round into that truck."

Barnes didn't say anything. He couldn't figure out the reasoning for the action.

"You still there, Lieutenant?"

"Uh...yes, sir, I think our last communication got garbled. I thought you said to light up the truck."

"You heard right. Put a round in the truck...now."

Godson was looking over at Barnes, he mouthed 'Why?'

"Lieutenant, put a round in that truck now or we will fire on your position."

"How about I just put the round in your ass," Barnes shot back. "Be a lot easier for me to hit a nice easy non-moving target like yourselves with a rocket."

"We'll talk when you get back," the captain said. The helicopter rose a little more and got to the side of the plow. Thirty caliber machine gun rounds plowed into the truck, shredding everything in and around it. By the time the gas tank was struck and ignited, nothing was living in a ten-foot perimeter of the DPW truck.

"Should I shoot him down?" Godson asked. He had grabbed the RPG and had it by his side.

"Normally I'd say yes, but he has all those civilians onboard. Just because Emery is an asshole doesn't mean they deserve to die."

A plume of flame erupted from the truck. The helicopter turned and the gunner was now pointing in the lieutenant's direction.

Godson shoulder mounted the tube and flipped the safety off.

"One damn round comes this way, blow that motherfucker out of the sky," the lieutenant said.

"With pleasure, sir."

Godson centered the helicopter in his sights. The last time he'd had such an easy flying target had been on the practice range a few years back. The copter would never be able to maneuver fast enough to get away from the rocket-propelled grenade. He'd feel slightly bad for the civvies, but they were nameless, faceless people to him right now. Tough to have nightmares about people you didn't even know.

The helicopter abruptly veered to the left and made a hasty departure.

"Ought to be a fun night on the base tonight," Barnes said. "Alright, let's try this again, round everyone up and let's get the hell out of here."

"I could still take them out," Godson replied.

Barnes thought about it for a moment. In the fog of war, all sorts of stuff went down that was never explained, and not too many people would miss Emery.

"As tempting as that sounds, I'd rather break that aristocratic nose of his with my fist instead."

Godson put the weapon on safe and quickly put it away without any more thought to the fact that he had his finger on the trigger of twelve human lives, and more importantly—in his opinion—one dog.

***

My head was splitting when I awoke. A harsh light from the ceiling shone down and, of course, directly into my eyes. I sat up slowly knowing to do it any faster would cause a serious case of vertigo. Sometimes it was alright to be a little older; at least I knew the limitations of my body.

"Tommy!?" I called out, sitting bolt upright quickly despite the pain. Last I had seen, he was plummeting to the ground. What had happened to me, to my family? It was then I realized I was in a cell. For just the briefest of moments I imagined that it was padded and everything that had happened that early December day last year was the result of some psychosis. I'd finally snapped and had been living a nightmare of zombies and vampires ever since. Typical Talbot shit, though. Why couldn't I get lost in a world of Hooters girls and unicorns? Nope, I had to go right for the shit storm. When I realized I wasn't in a straightjacket, holding on desperately to crayons, I got up to further inspect where I was.

"Hey, Mike," I heard off to my right. I whipped my head so fast it took the blinding white headache a second or two to catch up, but when it did, it took twice that long to be able to focus on the person in the cell next to mine.

"Wags?" I fairly sobbed. "Is that you?" I moved quickly to the heavy iron bars that separated us. I stuck my hand out and wrapped it around Dennis' head. "It's so good to see you, man. Have you seen the rest of my family?"

"No, I don't know where they are...they don't let me get out much."

I wasn't feeling all peachy-keen, but if they'd wanted us dead, they had ample opportunity to have done so. "How's your family?" I asked. His hangdog expression said everything. "I'm sorry, man." I quickly moved on. "What are you doing here? Were you 'rescued' too?" I asked with the air quotes. "They don't even know me and they already stuck me in jail. I mean, sure, once they get to know me, they'd probably figure out this is where I belong, but not yet. I should at least get the benefit of the doubt."

"My only crime is hitchhiking," he told me.

"Huh?"

"I was on my way up to Ron's when my car broke down. I flagged down this old bitch in a semi. One look at her and I knew I should have just walked away. I was desperate, though."

My worry over my family's safety began to compound on itself as I waited for him to give me an answer I already knew.

"The lady is one of the craziest, meanest snakes I'd ever come across," he continued.

"Yeah, that would be Deneaux," I said.

He paused for a moment as he raced to catch up to how I knew.

"Makes sense," he said. "Is what she said about your family and Paul true?" he asked. When he realized that I had no way of knowing what she'd said, he added, "That they're all dead."

"We've taken some losses," I said, not wanting to go into detail. They were all still too fresh.

"Paul?" he asked.

I nodded. "And I don't know how yet, but I know that bitch had something to do with it. I was going to beat it out of her, but she slipped through my hands and right into the arms of the enemy. She pulled a Benedict Arnold when she thought she could shake a better deal. If it's not for the betterment of Vivian Deneaux, don't expect any help."

"Wish I'd read that pamphlet before I got in the truck." Dennis replied.

"Maybe they should have had a film in our Health class back in school. Right after the Birds-and-the-Bees flick, they could have had one entitled *Deneaux and Deception*."

"Or maybe *Vicious Vivian: How to avoid a deadly strike*."

"I like that one. Do you know anything about this place?" I asked.

"Not much. I know it's a military base of some kind. I've heard some of the guards say something about the Demesne Group, but that means nothing to me. How about you?"

I shrugged my shoulders; it meant nothing to me either.

"That's really it. Deneaux comes down once a day; I think just to torment me. She talks a lot without really saying all that much. I get the feeling she's somewhat afraid here, but by the way the guards act around her, I think they're the ones who are scared."

"Naw, she must have power here, that's why the grunts are afraid. It's at the higher echelons where the shit is getting a little stickier. I wonder if she knows I'm here? I'd love to wrap my hands around her scrawny little wrinkly neck."

"Tell us how you really feel," Dennis said with a crooked smile.

"How long have I been here?" I asked, my pounding head once again making its presence known.

"Five…six hours maybe. They said you'd be out until tomorrow when they dropped you off."

"I'm glad you didn't try to take advantage of me."

"Bars were in the way."

"What is going on here? Makes absolutely no sense," I said. Just then, we heard the distinctive sound of a heavy lock being opened and the clanging of a metal door as it opened wide and struck something.

"You smell fried chicken?" Dennis asked me.

And I did. "Porkchop?" I asked when the poultry-wielding boy stepped in front of my cell.

"Want some?" he asked, sticking his hand out about halfway, looking more like he hoped I would refuse his generous offer.

"No, it's alright--I haven't eaten in about two days," I told him. "What are you doing here? Where's…Doc! Oh my God, it is so good to see you." I came up quickly to the bars. Porkchop backed up just in case it was a ruse for me to grab the chicken.

"Michael," he answered coolly as he approached. "Where's Tomas?" Doc asked in that same grave manner.

"Not here," I answered, trying to understand what was going on.

"You were with him?" It was phrased as a question, but that he already knew the answer was not in doubt.

"I was."

"Could you have killed him?"

"Probably not," I told him in all sincerity. Anything short of a second coming wouldn't kill him, I figured.

"He killed my family," Doc said with vacant eyes.

"I'm sorry, Doc. I loved them as well," I said, reaching out gently. My hand brushed against his arm before he backed up and out of reach, sticking his forearm out to block Porkchop from me as well.

"What are you now, Michael?" the doctor once again asked a question he already knew the answer to.

"What the hell does that mean?" Dennis asked.

"How many families have you killed, Michael?" the doc asked me.

"Mike, what's he talking about?" Dennis asked again.

"Mister, have some chicken," Porkchop said, sticking a half-eaten wing through Dennis' bars. It was clear this conversation was upsetting him.

"So it is true; you both do know each other. What a strange little world we find ourselves in," Doc said. "So much of what comes out of her mouth is a falsehood that it's difficult pulling the slivers of truth from the myriad of lies."

"Is that why I'm in this cell? Because she knows I'm here? Is she somehow running this place? What is this place? Where is my family? BT?" I was rapid-firing questions at him, none of which he seemed to want to answer…at least at first.

The doc smiled a little. "No, she doesn't know you're here. I do hope I'm around when she finds out, though. Seems she has a deep-rooted hatred for you."

"I did nothing but repeatedly save that old bitter bitch's life. Let us out of here, Doc, let me get to my family."

"Your family is fine. Apparently you're a better guardian than I am, Michael. Somehow you were able to kill Eliza where I failed."

"Technically it was Tracy," I said.

"Who'd Tracy kill?" Dennis asked. "The vampire chick?"

"You going to eat that?" Porkchop asked Dennis who was now holding a piece of chicken that he had seemingly forgotten about or never realized was there in the first place.

"I watched my whole family die. Butchered like farm animals really, and that traveling partner of yours drank them all."

"Mike, what the fuck?" Dennis asked. "That shit about the vampires Deneaux was telling me, that was real? I thought she was full of shit or at least a butt-load of Vicodin."

"I'm sorry, Doc, I truly am. But that doesn't change the fact that you need to get me out of here. I've got to get to my family and BT needs help," I said, ignoring Dennis.

"BT is dead," the doc said, looking hard at me.

I staggered away from the bars as if I'd been punched in the solar plexus from the very man…nay, the friend that had died. My world was spinning, I watched as Porkchop looked up to the doc and then to me.

"The giant man?" Porkchop asked. "He's okay. He was asking about you, Mr. Talbot," Porkchop said.

"What?" I asked, my eyes filled with salty tears.

"Hurts, doesn't it, Michael, when you realize that people you care for are dead. That small sample you just had is what I feel every waking moment. It never ceases, I see their accusation each and every time Eliza slices their throats…their cries of betrayal as I sit there, impotent to do anything. She made me watch as the blood flowed out of them. As their light of life left them, it left me as well, I'm an empty well inside." The Doc said.

"You're right, Doc, I can't imagine the pain you're going through. And maybe I'm selfish, because I never want to have to go through what you've been through," I said, truly empathizing with the man.

"Lawrence is responding well to the drugs. He was my first human trial. We weren't quite ready for that stage, but it didn't appear he was going to wait," Doc said, slipping from destroyed married man and father into the successful doctor persona.

If changing between the two roles is what kept him sane and operational, who the hell was I to say anything.

"Is he cured?" I asked, hoping.

"Not yet, but I believe that with aggressive treatment, he will be. I believe it will take a combination of drugs and radiation. Your grandfather made that intuitive leap almost a hundred years ago. The key is to hit them hard and fast or the virus adapts surprisingly well."

"And Justin?" I asked, swallowing hard.

"We should be weeks away from human test trials and I did not want to endanger him unless it becomes absolutely necessary, like it was with Lawrence."

"What about the shots that you were giving him?"

"I'm afraid those may have done more harm than good," he said. "The parasitic virus that now runs through him will be surprisingly immune to a lot of what we will attempt."

"Is there a chance?" I asked.

"There is…but it's significantly less than BT's."

"Thank you, Doc." I rested my head against the bars, letting the new information soak in. When I opened my eyes, Doc was staring intently at me.

"I've been working on a way to kill Tomas," he said, matter-of-factly. And with those last unsettling words to me, he turned. "Come on Porkchop, it's time for your lessons."

"I'll tell Henry you said hi," Porkchop whispered loudly to me.

"Thank you," I nearly sobbed.

"Mike, any chance you want to tell me what's going on?" Dennis asked.

"Not-fucking-really," I answered. "Sorry, man. Alright, here's the short version. Zombie apocalypse starts. This crazy zombie-slash-vampire chick decides I'm at the top of her shit list. Her half-vampire brother Tomas, with Ryan Seacrest as his spirit guide decides he's going to do his best to protect us. We end up on this roof fighting for our lives and it comes down to Tomas, infecting me with vampire blood so that I can beat down this über-asshole named Durgan. Yada, yada, yada, I lose my soul, win the fight.

Huge battle with Eliza and her minions, which we win, and now I'm on a quest to get my friend BT who was bitten and Justin who was scratched cured somehow."

Dennis' eyes were huge. "Dude, did you just 'yada, yada, yada' me with the zombie apocalypse?"

"Dude, listen, I know there's enough holes in that story you could fly a plane through. I promise if we get out of this I'll relate the whole thing. Plus I have a bunch of journals you can read. Just don't let Tracy see them. Right now, though, I've got to figure a way out of here."

Dennis' eyes were still huge, and now his mouth had dropped.

"You're going to start drooling soon," I told him.

Once again we heard the door open down at the end of the hall. I pulled back from the bars and deeper into the dark cell. I could smell the smoke from here. I retreated even deeper into my cell.

"Hello, Dennis," Mrs. Deneaux said in that oh-so-familiar raspy voice. "I brought you something." She placed a small flask on the floor and pushed it through the bottom of the bars.

Dennis turned towards her, his earlier facial expression not changing all that much.

"What's the matter with you?" Mrs. Deneaux asked, a large swirl of smog around her head. "I can be nice from time to time."

"Oh, I doubt it," I said, coming forward. I've got to admit it was extremely satisfying watching her stagger back, although the bitch recovered faster than humping rabbits.

"Michael? It's so good to see you," she said before spinning and quickly retreating.

"I'm going to take your cigarettes," I yelled down at her.

Bitch got spunk, had to admit that. She flipped me off.

***

Vivian entered Dixon's office. "Why did you not tell me you had apprehended Michael Talbot?" she demanded, interrupting the conversation between Dixon and Captain Najarian

"That will be all, Captain," Dixon said. "Vivian, so good to see you."

"Cut the shit, Dixon. What is he doing here, and why wasn't I told?"

"Vivian, it was a military operation. There was no need for you to know. And as for the reason why he is here, think about it, Viv. The man possesses the opportunity for immortality within the confines of his blood and body."

"He's not going to just give it to you, Dixon."

"Oh but he has. The lab is already working with the five vials they pulled from him while he was knocked out."

"Then kill him, Dixon. Kill him if you already have what you need."

"In time, Vivian, in time. There are still many things we can learn from him."

"He is dangerous and resourceful, Dixon. If given the opportunity, he will bring this place down."

"I did not realize you had a flair for the dramatic, Vivian. This is a military base with hundreds of military personnel and weaponry, I'm not overly concerned." Dixon laughed.

"You should be."

"We also have his family."

"You have the Talbots here?" she asked, pointing to the floor.

"Yes, Vivian. You act as if we let sharks loose in a fish tank. This Talbot will not do anything if he believes it could harm his family."

"You've got it wrong, Dixon, he will do something because you *are* threatening his family. Kill them, kill them all."

"I'm not a murderer of women and children, Vivian," he said indignantly.

"Oh…NOW you decide to employ a moral compass. Little late for that, don't you think? I'm going to pack so that when this goes to hell, which it will, I'll be able to leave that much quicker. I should have stayed on Michael's side," Mrs. Deneaux said sadly as she walked out of Dixon's office.

Dixon shook his head as she left. "Age has tempered her resolve."

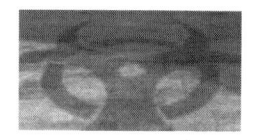

CHAPTER 27 – TALBOT FAMILY

"He's alright?" Tracy asked, hugging Porkchop.

"He seemed alright…but probably not, because he didn't want any of my chicken," Porkchop said.

"This is so exciting," Trip said, walking around the room, a glow seeming to emanate from him.

"Exciting?" Gary asked. "What's exciting?"

"Backstage, man," Trip said enthusiastically. "How many times can you say you've been backstage at a Dead show?"

"Ummm…still zero," Gary said.

"Leave him be," Tracy said. "At least one of us should be enjoying themselves."

She smiled. She was relieved to hear her husband was alright, even if he was in a cell, it wasn't his first time. Doc had been in earlier to tell them how BT was doing. The flat emotionless way he had talked was disturbing. Tracy couldn't blame him for that, though, not after all he'd been through. That he was still functioning at all was a testament to the strength of his will or his desire for revenge. She hoped for his and Porkchop's sake it was the former rather than the latter.

CHAPTER 28 – MIKE JOURNAL ENTRY 13

'Tommy?' I asked, feeling the boy around the peripheries of my mind. 'You're still alive? I thought I'd lost you.' The relief within me was palpable.

'You alright?' Tommy asked me back. 'I'm almost as hard to kill as you are.' Even though he was talking in my head I knew he said that last part with some mirth. 'When we were going up in that helicopter, I was just happy that all of you were safe. And then I saw everyone unconscious and you had just been given a shot. I hit the release on the winch. Crashing down onto the zombies bought me the time I needed as I jumped out of the truck and ran for cover. I got the distinct impression if they couldn't catch me they would attempt to kill me, and I wasn't wrong. They shot up the truck until it finally caught the fuel on fire.'

'How'd you get away from the zombies?' I asked.

'I can move faster than they can react.'

I was having a hard time with the concept and Tommy could tell.

'Just think about you walking around normally and everyone else is in super slow motion. That's what it's like for me with the zombies. What's this got to do with women's locker rooms?' Tommy asked, picking up on some stray thoughts.

'Ah…nothing…sorry. I'm glad you're here,' I changed the subject.

'I'm not quite there. I'm following the ground unit back. I just picked you up a few miles ago. How's everyone else doing?'

'Good as far as Porkchop says.'

'Porkchop's there?' I heard Tommy ask. It was a mixture of anguish and thankfulness.

'Doc's here too, Tommy,' I said. The boy went silent. I was picking up images of horrific detail. 'He may have found a cure for BT.'

'That's great,' Tommy said with true appreciation for that fact, but the thoughts of Doc's family dominated his attention.

'Tommy, he said he knows a way to kill you.'

'I would imagine,' Tommy said.

'I'm telling you this so you'll be careful,' I admonished.

'I've got it, you don't want me to die until I help you get out,' he said with some withdrawal in his voice.

And for the most part, he nailed it on the head. On some level, I did love the kid, but he had destroyed the foundation of trust from which our relationship was based. I hoped that someday we would get back to where we were, but it was going to take time. He had been lying to me the moment I had seen him on the Walmart roof.

'Tommy, would it help if I said I don't want you to die at all?' I asked.

'It would, Mr. T, it would.'

'Get us out of here kid, all of us.'

He pushed his darker thoughts down. 'I'll see you soon.'

'Looking forward to it.'

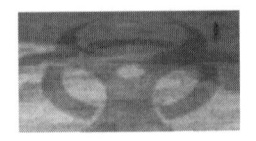

TALBOT-SODE #1

As it's been noted in previous journals, and from what goes unstated, I've not been a poster child for the law-abiding citizens of the world. I'd been caught in enough scrapes that I'd been forced to join the military or watch out if I dropped the soap. If I'd been caught in even a tenth of the things I'd truly done, I'm sure I'd still be doing hard time. And at the root of a lot of those things was Dennis. Now, I'm not saying it was his fault, not by any stretch of the imagination. It just so happened that when we got together, bad shit just kind of happened.

More than likely booze was the biggest mitigating factor. I don't know…when we got together it was like adding a flare to a gas can. I had just picked Dennis up from his house. Okay, shit, let me throw in a disclaimer. I am in NO way advocating Dennis' behavior or mine. If I caught any of my kids doing the shit I'd done, I'd kick their asses two ways to Sunday. Yeah, I know, I'm hypocritical. Any of you parents reading this know what I'm talking about, any of you without kids right now will eventually get it. Back to the…umm 'story' that's right…story, this is a piece of fiction that will not run afoul of jurisdictions, paroles, or statutes of limitations. So I had *mythically* picked up Dennis at his house, and he had *figuratively* pulled out a bottle of Southern Comfort—which is basically bottled diesel fuel. I took a pull on it like only an inexperienced drinker does, meaning I took in way too much of the fiery liquid.

"Good!" I lied. "Where'd you get this shit?" I looked at the bottle.

The 'shit' part I meant. I'm not really so sure why the majority of my youth revolved around booze and drugs. I grew up in a relatively stable environment. I wasn't abused, mentally, physically, or emotionally. I had no ailment that the drug companies had yet to create a moniker for. It was just what we did—partying I mean. This was before Nancy Reagan got on her high horse and started talking about 'Just Say No.' We were always pretty much 'Just Say Why Not.' It was an accepted part of our youth. It was as much a part of our growing up experience as was texting for my kids.

We had some time to kill before Linda Mahoney's party began, so we were basically riding around catching a hell of a buzz from the SoCo. It was then I noticed the cop lights, not behind me, but rather in front. We were on a side street and the cop had pulled up to someone's house on a call. I drove by slowly, making sure not to look over and make any sort of eye contact. Not that it would have mattered, the cop was inside the house.

"Nobody's in there," Dennis said.

"Good," I agreed as I cruised slowly past.

"Pull over up here a little bit." Dennis pointed to a darkened area on the street.

"This really isn't the best place to take a piss," I told him.

"You got any tools in your car?"

"Just you."

"You want any more of the SoCo?" he threatened.

"Fine, I've got a little roadside assistance kit or something my dad put in the trunk."

"Let me see it."

"Why?" I asked suspiciously.

"I want those lights."

I had no idea what he was talking about. At first I figured he meant a streetlight, but we were nowhere near that HIGH. Then I figured something on a house; still…nothing stood out.

"Dude, what are you talking about?"

"I want the cop lights," he said, sticking his hand out

for the keys so he could get in the trunk.

"What? Are you nuts? You want to steal the lights off a cop car with the lights going and the cop in the house?"

He thought for a moment. "Yeah…that's about it."

So then I thought for a moment. "Okay, let's go." I handed him the keys. I don't think the accumulated brainpower we shared that night could have powered an LED light.

"That'll work," Dennis said, grabbing a couple of screwdrivers and an adjustable wrench.

We walked up to that cruiser like we owned it, the red and blue lights playing havoc on my head. Vertigo was threatening to toss me on my ass—or maybe just my stomach contents onto someone's lawn.

"Hold this." Dennis directed my hand to the adjustable wrench.

There were two bolts on each side of the car that secured the lights to the roof. We spun the driver's side ones off in under a minute. Now came the more dangerous part, because we would be on the side that faced the house we figured the cop to be in. Although, in reality, he could be just about anywhere. I once again placed the wrench over the nut while Dennis worked furiously on the screw. I would alternate between closing my eyes from the nauseating lights and keeping lookout. The bracket clattered to the ground, bouncing off the top of my sneaker first.

"Ready?" he asked.

"For what?"

He tore the lights free from the car, snapping the wires that supplied the power. It took me a moment to get over the thrill that the stupid lights had finally stopped swirling before I sped to catch up with my fleeing partner-in-crime. I may have heard someone shout 'Hey you' or the much more scary 'I know your mother'. Either way, I wasn't stopping. Dennis tossed the lights into the backseat of my car and we both hopped in. My heart was slamming against my chest and it was all I could do to start the car. We hadn't driven more than a quarter mile away before we both started laughing so hard I had to pull over because I was tear-blind.

I drove around with those cop lights in my car for a good week. If I had gotten stopped for a broken taillight (which I had at the time) I would have been busted.

Of course it was big news in the small town. It made the front page of the local newspaper. There was a picture of the cruiser sans lights, and how they had some leads and suspects, but nothing ever came of it.

Dennis ended up putting the lights in his room, dragging them out a couple of times for parties. Hooked up to a car battery, they were just as obnoxious then as when they were mounted. I think he eventually ended up trading them for a bag of weed.

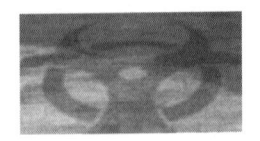

TALBOT-SODE #2

At this point I'd known Dennis nearly four years and we were driving around. I want to say we were going to Linda Mahoney's, again, for a party. Either her parents traveled a lot, or they just weren't much into supervision. All I knew was she had great parties and her kisses were nothing to sneeze at.

"Hey, pull over," Dennis said.

"Again, man? You just went. You've got the bladder of an eight-year-old," I told him.

"This is where my brother is buried," he said, getting out of the car before I could completely stop.

"Gonna be where you're buried if you do that again," I said when I finally was able to place the car in park.

He was walking up to the gates of the Plimpton Hill Cemetery. It was your typical start-to-a-scary-movie cemetery. A wrought iron gate held in place by stone wall, giant monoliths and even some earthen tombs dotted the uneven terrain. Brown leaves would occasionally swirl in the wind when it kicked up. You know, typical stuff.

"Come on, man, what are you doing?" I asked, not yet leaving the car. I thought he was full of shit. He had a younger brother and sister, and as far as I knew, they were at home.

"Talbot, my brother is buried here," he insisted, placing his hands on the gate.

He sounded so sincere. I might have been a self-absorbed teenager who may or may not have been drinking and smoking too much, but I'm pretty sure I would have known if my best friend's brother had suddenly passed. I reluctantly got out of the car to see what game he was playing. I felt like I was getting set up for a good scare. I took a quick leak by the side of my car just in case he scared me good and my bladder suddenly felt the need to release. At least this way the reservoir would be dry.

I stood next to him, my hands in my pockets. It was an early fall night not particularly cool, at least not until I approached the gate.

"I had a brother that died as a baby," he said, not looking over at me.

We'd known each other for years and not once did this come up. I mean, I guess it's not something you'd discuss all the time. 'Man, I was kissing Debbie Lynch and I have a dead brother.' Doesn't really mesh, but at some point, you'd think it would come up. Maybe not, though. We're guys; deep meaningful conversations are not really in our repertoire.

He pulled the gate open and slid through.

"They don't lock those?" I asked, sullenly following my friend in.

The night got darker the moment I crossed over that threshold, probably because the streetlights didn't stretch their protective shine that far, or maybe it couldn't penetrate the darkness that permeated that place. Breath plumed from my mouth, I would have said something to Dennis if my teeth weren't chattering as well. He'd noticed anyway--I watched as he tilted his head and purposefully blew into the air creating the same effect.

"You feel that?" I asked, beginning to seriously creep myself out. Prickles of ice climbed up my spine and to the base of my skull. It was a wholly unpleasant sensation.

"He's here," Dennis said.

"Who?" I asked, catching up to him.

"My brother Dan."

Goosed flesh sprang up on my arms. "Dude, it doesn't feel right in here."

I expected something along the lines of 'You pussy'

or 'Are you chicken?' The normal guy bluster. Instead, he said, "You feel that too?"

The quarter moon was playing hide and seek amongst the clouds and I was thankful and fearful every time it broke through. Thankful because I could see more of our immediate surroundings, and for that same reason, fearful.

"I think we're getting close," Dennis said.

I personally didn't think so, because the gate was further away. I wanted to grab Dennis' arm, certain my heart had gotten stuck for a handful of beats. A stiff wind had pushed the latest cloud cover away quickly, and as the moon shone down, I saw movement behind one of the grave markers. It was over to our left. It looked like a child's head had peeked around, and when it realized I had seen, it had pulled back quickly. Morbid curiosity warred with self-preservation within me. The false feeling of invincibility won out. I went over to where I had seen the figure.

Dennis came up beside me. "How did you know?"

It was then I looked down onto the gravestone itself and saw: Dan Waggoner, beloved child.

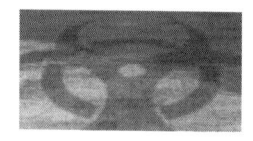

EPILOGUE 1 – DENEAUX - PRE-ZOMBIE APOCALYPSE

"What do you mean the North American shots are being shipped? Who's the idiot that gave the order?" a visibly flustered Winston Deneaux yelled into the handset of his phone. He dragged his hand across his face.

The Demesne Group would have him killed on principal for this failure if it were ever discovered how close to catastrophe they were. His only job, up to this point, in the destruction of the world's population was to house the tainted flu shots until he was given the order to release them. And now some wanna-be do-gooder maverick at his largest warehouse had taken it upon himself to single-handedly save the United States by releasing what he thought was forgotten about or misplaced vaccinations. The Third World supply had gone out the previous week.

"Sir, I don't know," Captain Najarian said. He was at the warehouse looking at an empty corner of the massive warehouse, talking on his cypher-encoded cell phone. "And I didn't say *being* shipped…they're gone."

"Get them back!" Deneaux screamed into the phone, spit flying from his mouth in anger.

"The authorization has to come from you. I tried right after I contacted Senator Wendelson."

"The senator knows about this?" Deneaux asked nervously, licking his lips.

"He does now, sir. I had no choice."

"So apparently any old dumbass can ship them, but I have to be the one that calls them back? Shit." Mr. Deneaux hung the phone up. He had picked it back up and was about to make a call when his doorbell rang. "Betty, could you get that!" he yelled to his full time maid. When she didn't respond, he came out of his office on the second ring.

"Vivian," a clearly flustered Winston said as he answered his door. "What are you doing here?"

"Winston, Winston, I thought you'd be thrilled to see your wife of thirty-something wonderful years." She placed her cool hand on his cheek and walked in.

"I'm in the middle of something, you should leave," he told her.

"What's her name?" Vivian asked as she strolled into the living room.

"I really don't have time for this." He followed.

"Oh, I think you'll make time," she said as she sat. "Sit." She motioned with her hand.

"Vivian—"

"I insist," she said as she brandished a weapon.

"Get out of here!" he roared.

"Raising your voice to a lady? What would high-society think of that? Oh, I guess they'd expect just about anything out of you at this point. Middle sixties and almost your entire world revolves around that little worm between your legs. I thank God every day that I wasn't cursed with that appendage."

"Get out," Winston said forcibly, pointing towards the door.

"Sit down," she answered in kind, pulling the hammer back on her revolver. "I'd listen to me if I were you. This isn't some thug nine millimeter, this is a .44 Magnum, and if I remember my pop culture correctly, it will blow your damn head clean off. And unlike Mr. Eastwood, I know exactly how many rounds are in it."

Winston looked visibly shaken, even more so than before he'd answered the door.

"Betty's here," he said, licking his lips again.

"Oh no, the sweet thing is out doing a bunch of

errands that I sent her on."

"What do you want, Vivian, more money?"

"It's ALL my money, husband, or did you forget that? I don't know what you did in that courtroom to get the judge to side with you. I still haven't figured it out. I know you have powerful friends, though, because I foolishly introduced you to them. Maybe I should have a little cock sewn on, then I could join the boys club you're in."

"Really, Vivian, where have you picked up this new vernacular?"

"You left me with so little, Winston, I'm nearly in the projects. Where do you think I learned it?"

"So little? People work their whole lives and don't accumulate half of what I gave you."

"Gave me?!" she shouted, standing up. "It was mine! All of it! You spineless little bitch. Without me, you'd still be tossing some selectman's salad."

"That's enough, you'll leave here now and I won't call the police," Winston said, nearly rising. He stopped when his ex-wife's knuckle began to whiten as she applied pressure to the trigger.

"I've always turned a blind eye when you went on your little dalliances. When you screwed our first maid, I said nothing. When I caught you doing Senator Tillman's wife in our bed, I went back down to the party and played the perfect hostess. I never cared who you stuck it in, because I didn't want that helmeted little shriveled up thing you called your manhood anywhere near me. Mr. Strongbone my ass, more like Miss Wet Noodle." She bent her pinkie finger. "I never said anything to you or to anyone because you and I had an understanding. I would show you how to rise to power. You had the penis and I had everything else. Then, in that pea-brained head of yours, the legend you thought you were got bigger than who you really are. You started to think you could do all of this without me. I guess it was that…and then you started parading what's-her-name around."

"Lori."

"I don't give a fuck. Don't interrupt me again. You start parading this girl that can't be a third of your age around, making me look like a fool in front of *our* circles! Do you really think she loves you? She's a damn yoga instructor for chrissakes. She's used to being around hard bodies all day and then she has to look at your pasty, paunchy ass. She's either an incredible actress or a world-class drinker. I haven't figured that out, although I do plan on visiting her right after I leave here."

"Don't you dare! I'll have you arrested."

"Oh, you'll be in no shape to pick up that phone when I'm done with you."

Winston looked hard at his wife, sweat beaded up on his brow. She'd never been one for idle threats. He'd always loved having her at his side as he'd climbed the ladder, because if she said she was going to get something done, there wasn't anything she wouldn't do to achieve that end. But now that he was on the other side of that equation, he was definitely feeling the heat. He wondered how he could have been so stupid as to leave this very dangerous variable outside of his control.

"What are you planning on doing? Listen, Vivian, we can work this out. There's no need to do anything rash."

"Rash? Dear husband, you've known me long enough to realize I've never done anything *rash* in my entire life."

Winston hadn't risen up more than an inch or two off the couch when a single shot rang out. Vivian looked through the haze of smoke to the look of terror etched forever on the face of her husband.

"A good mortician should be able to wipe that stupid look off your face." She placed the large revolver onto her lap. "Covering that giant hole in your head though, well that's going to take sheer genius," she quipped. "Maybe I should have just shot you years ago and shoved my hand up your ass like a puppet. It would have virtually been the same thing. I think I'll hire the same lawyers you did for our divorce, seems like poetic justice, I'd say. Well, one more stop before I call it a day." She walked over to her ex and kissed him tenderly on the lips. "We could have run the country, perhaps not from the Oval Office, but we could have ran it all the same. Such a shame."

Mrs. Deneaux walked to her car as if she didn't have a care in the world. The engine in her Mercedes roared to life as she hit the start button. She left a small trail of rubber on the cobblestone driveway as she peeled out. Pachelbel's *Canon in D* blared through her Bose sound system. The drive to Lori's home took less than fifteen minutes, but in that time, Mrs. Deneaux saw a police cruiser, a fire engine, and two ambulances heading in the opposite direction with their lights blazing. She knew there was no way her husband's body had already been discovered. And even if it had, it wouldn't have necessitated two ambulances. She wondered briefly what the commotion was all about and then forgot about it as she pulled up to the Palatial Estates.

"Looks like you've done alright for yourself, Lori," Mrs. Deneaux said as she pulled up to the building.

The gate guard did little more than look at her hundred and twenty thousand dollar ride before he pressed the button to lift the gate and allow the wolf into the sheep pasture.

Mrs. Deneaux waited until she saw a man approaching the front entryway before she grabbed a bag from the backseat of her car. She quickly departed the vehicle and made sure to get there a step or two ahead of him.

"Would you be a dear?" she asked him with a false smile that would have frozen a bear. "It seems my hands are full," she added when he didn't immediately move.

"Of course, of course," he said when his ingrained manners took over.

She let the bag drop to the floor the moment she was

inside, the man looked down at it and then up at her.

"Leave," she said to him, any hint of the earlier deception of niceness gone.

He knew trouble when he saw it and left without saying another word.

"Palatial Estates my ass. What kind of high-class place doesn't have an elevator? And of course Little-Miss-Flexible-Bitch lives on the top floor." Which in this case was the fourth. "Probably gets off walking up all these stairs," Mrs. Deneaux said angrily. "I should shoot her just for this."

Mrs. Deneaux rapped lightly on the door to apartment 4D and waited patiently. She heard soft footfalls come towards the door.

"Who is it?" sang out, not in a frightened way, but more of a way she'd been taught since she was old enough to answer a door.

"Package," Mrs. Deneaux said in her deepest voice.

"Great!" Lori pulled the door open enthusiastically. "What?" she asked as Mrs. Deneaux shoved her backwards.

"You really are beautiful. I can see what my husband sees in you. I mean, it is all superficial, though, because you're about as smart as toast."

"What?" Lori repeated, recovering from her near tumble.

"Is that all you can manage? Too bad your mind isn't as flexible as your body. Let me try and dumb this down for you. You were doing my ex-husband and now I've come for my sixpence."

"Sixpence?"

"Payment, you twit. I've come to collect."

"I...I don't have any money," Lori said indignantly.

She stood a good five or six inches taller than Mrs. Deneaux and her body was as honed as any statue ever sculpted. She had fully intended on using that as a form of intimidation right up until Mrs. Deneaux pulled her widow-maker out and shoved it in her face. The girl withered faster than a lilac in the desert.

"Go sit, dear girl. I'm afraid I've got some bad news for you," Mrs. Deneaux said.

"He...he said you two had an understanding," Lori pleaded as she sat.

"Oh, we did. He just changed the rules without letting me know. I'm curious, though. Besides the money and the power, what else could you see in him? He's almost as old as your own grandfather. You into that kind of thing?"

"It's not like that." Lori said. "We're...we're in love."

"You don't lie very convincingly. I bet you make him shut the lights off every time he screws you. Oh, I can tell by your eyes I'm right. There wasn't much to see when we were younger, and he has not aged gracefully I'm afraid."

"I'm going to tell Winston about this," Lori said, trying to prop herself up.

"That will fall on deaf ears, I'm afraid. I came here to tell you that your relationship with my former husband has come to an end."

"What...what do you mean? He promised that we'd be getting married."

"It is easier when you're married, isn't it, dear? Don't have to put out nearly as much—or in my case, at all—once you have that ring on your finger. Why churn the sweet cream when you already have the butter?" She laughed. "Did you know I once thought I was a lesbian? No of course not, how could you? Just the sight of that little dangling thing between a man's legs made me want to laugh. The last thing I wanted was the damned thing inside of me ferreting around like a gopher, doing God knows what. My girlfriends, though, I think they really enjoyed it--sex I mean," she said with a faraway look. "It was never a cock that got me off. Oh, I'm sorry, did that word give you offense? How about prick?"

Lori flinched.

"It was never the sex. I just don't like other people enough for them to touch me. It was, and still is, the power. I don't care in the least that you took Winston from my bedroom; in fact I welcomed it. I do however have a problem with you taking him from my house. You see, we've worked together for years to achieve what was nearly within our grasp and then your tight little ass clouds his mind to the point where he had forgotten how he has gotten to where he is. AND I WILL NOT BE LEFT BEHIND!" Mrs. Deneaux shrieked. "I have worked too damn hard and endured too many hardships to be cast to the side just as all my work is about to bear fruit."

"I'm calling him." Lori reached over to the phone on the table next to her couch.

"Go ahead. I don't think he's going to have much to say. I placed a rather large bullet in his brain."

Lori gasped. "You lie!" she said vehemently. "You wouldn't tell me that! I'll be able to tell the police."

"Are you truly that stupid? I thought the old adage about getting your brains screwed out was figurative…now you go and prove it's literal. Funny what you can learn."

"You'll never get away with this."

"I have some pretty highly placed friends, Lori. Plus, now with Winston out of the way, affording some top-notch lawyers won't be a problem. Who can even begin to imagine what sort of defense they will come up with? And none of it will matter in the least, I'll have at the minimum three jurors in my pocket. They'll be rich and it's not like I'm an at-large threat to society. I'm just some sweet old lady that went temporarily insane when her husband stepped out with a Girl Scout. I won't even have to pay off any of the women jurists; they'll be on my side anyway. At the most I'll get five years for manslaughter, but it'll be too late for me to serve it by the time this goes to trial anyway."

"Too late?" Lori asked resignedly.

"End of times is coming, Lori. I'm doing you a favor

here today. A pretty, stupid little thing like yourself wouldn't make it a day in the new world that's about to come."

Lori's face began to wrinkle up in confusion.

"Oh, I just can't take that look of ignorance anymore." Mrs. Deneaux said as she grabbed a pillow and blew a large hole through it, the exiting bullet leaving the sobakowa-filled pillow and perforating Lori's slender neck. Her hands did not even have a chance to stem the flow of blood before she fell over, her head hitting the coffee table.

"Do you have any Fresca?" Mrs. Deneaux asked, going into the rapidly cooling woman's kitchen. "Should have known." Mrs. Deneaux said, staring into a fridge full of bottled water and vegetable juices. "Oh ho! What do we have here?" Mrs. Deneaux said gleefully as she moved some bottles out of the way. "Glen Livet? That has to be for the nights you expect Winston over."

Mrs. Deneaux spun the top off and took a large swallow. She took two more swigs before she put the bottle on the counter and walked out, never once glancing at the body of her victim.

She was in one of the best moods she could recall as she pulled into her complex. Usually just pulling into the sub-standard housing area was enough to dampen her mood; not today, though. As she turned the corner to the straightaway that led to her townhome, she had to slam on her brakes, causing the heavy car to leave a skid mark. She had almost taken out her third and fourth casualties of the day. A man had been walking some sort of animal on the back roadway.

"There are laws about having livestock within the city limits!" she shouted at the man once she opened her window.

"Yeah, we're fine thanks for asking," the man said, looking at his knees and how very close the car had been to making them bend the opposite way that God had intended. "And for your information Henry here is an English Bulldog."

"Looks like a pig. Now get the hell out of my way," Mrs. Deneaux said as she drove past.

For two days she had sat in her apartment drinking expensive wine and listening to music, expecting a heavy rapping on her door at any moment. Even if she had performed a professional hit and left not a trace of evidence at her husband's, her image would show up extremely well in a half dozen of the high-definition video cameras he'd had installed a few years previous.

Maybe it would take longer if Lori was discovered first to put all the pieces of the puzzle together. But Winston was extremely rich and perceived as powerful. His absence would not go unnoticed for long.

"I wonder if I should have hidden his body?" Mrs. Deneaux said as she took a sip of her wine. "No, that would have looked premeditated, I suppose."

It was on the third day that she heard the plethora of sirens approaching. "Are they really going to make a spectacle of this?" she asked, looking through her window.

It was then that she noticed the shuffling abomination directly across from her house. She grabbed her pistol, which she had unloaded so as not to appear as a threat to the police, she grabbed it and reloaded. Then she closed her curtains and shut off all the lights, dimming the music until it was barely audible. The wine and the gun she kept close to her.

"So it has started." She took a swig directly from the bottle.

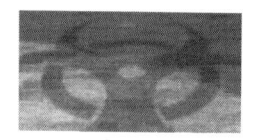

EPILOGUE 2

"Will, have you ever stopped and wondered why we're doing this?" June the biochemist asked as she peered into the heavy glass cage that housed their latest experiment.

"June, you think too much. We're some of the last humans left on the planet and we're absolutely safe in this underground bunker with enough supplies to grow old with. We get to do our work without any governmental agencies auditing us or some watch group raising the alarm."

"Just because we can do a thing doesn't mean we should," she said, still peering into the cage.

"That's not what you said last night. Sorry, sorry," he said, placating her when she turned an angry eye on him. "You're forgetting something, June. We do what they ask because if we don't we become just another expendable mouth to feed."

June had turned back to the cage and the grotesque animals within. The ashen gray-skinned monkeys looked at the pair; gray, intelligent eyes peered at the humans in a longingly hungry way.

"No good can come from creating zombie animals, Will. You have to see that don't you?"

"I see scientific advancement!" Will exclaimed, slamming the side of the case, causing a microscopic fracture to form. The bigger monkey in the front licked his lips as the man's hand came in contact with their enclosure. June shuddered.

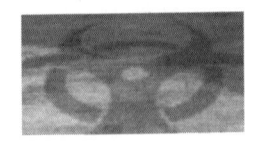

EPILOGUE 3

"It's been too long, my friend," my best friend Paul of close to thirty years said as we sat on the couch.

My wife Tracy and Paul's wife Erin had gone into the kitchen, to get more wine. It was my birthday and the missus had invited some friends over. It was a nice, quiet, subdued sort of party; nothing like the wild ones of my youth. Oh how I missed those! Being an adult had its perks, but if there was one thing I yearned for in regards to the past, a party was probably the biggest; the unknown of what the night was going to bring. Each one a blank slate in my mind, waiting for a memory to be indelibly carved into my ripples.

"It has been," I said to Paul. "How is it that we live ten miles apart and we never see each other?"

He shrugged. "Come on, man, want to go outside for a second? I could use some air."

"Sounds good...me too. Henry, hold my spot," I said as I nearly tripped over the big dog.

"Don't know what it is about you and dogs, Mike. Cats are so much easier to deal with."

I didn't answer. We'd been having this debate for years. I'd tell him how loyal dogs were and he'd tell me how independent cats were.

"How's work going?" I asked as we stepped out onto my back patio.

"It's work. Want a hit?" he asked as he produced a marijuana filled bowl.

"Man, I really don't smoke anymore. This new shit they have out is so friggin' potent, I have a hard time finding my feet after taking a toke."

Paul laughed; he'd gotten his medicinal marijuana

card some six months previous and had been telling me I should get mine as well. When we'd been in college, one of our biggest fantasies had revolved around the ability to walk into a store and choose from all different types of weed like someone would a pack of smokes. And now that it was a reality, I wasn't grasping at it.

"This stuff's not bad," Paul said as he exhaled a large plume of sweet smelling smoke.

"You smoke nearly every day, man. I haven't touched it since last June when Widespread was in town…and even then I thought I'd gone for a rocket ride."

"It's your birthday, man." Paul placed the bowl in my hand.

"Fucking peer pressure," I told him as I brought the bowl to my lips. I took a larger hit than was wise for someone who rarely partook.

"Shit's called Time Traveler."

"What?" I asked, coughing out a plume of smoke.

Paul's words stretched and elongated as he spoke, almost like he was saying them in a car that was racing by. I felt a fundamental shift in my reality, like it had been knocked askew. My eyes rolled back in my head momentarily.

"Oh shit, dude." Paul laughed. "You look fucked up!" He helped me to sit down.

Henry had come out to investigate. He was looking up at me; his barks also had that in-out, in-out reverberation.

My eyes were spinning like I was a slot machine at a Vegas casino.

"Oh, Paul, please tell him you didn't have him try the Time Traveler," Erin said as she came out back.

"Whoa." I tried to steady my movement despite the fact that I was sitting still in a chair.

"Talbot, your eyes are shining," Tracy said as she came out; she was smiling.

"I freel frunny."

"Yeah, well you sound funny too, buddy." Paul took another drag and then handed the bowl over to his wife.

And then, like an elastic band that has snapped back into place, I felt fine…like whatever had been sent out had now come home. "That was intense," I said as I looked around.

"You good now?" Paul once again had the bowl and was attempting to hand it to me.

"Fuck no, man, I'd rather give myself a root canal. Now my mouth is as dry as sand. Tracy, do we have any more beer up here?"

"I don't think so. Want me to go down into the basement and get you some?"

"No, no, stay here I'll grab them. Paul, you want one."

"What do you think?" He asked taking the last sip off of his.

I walked back into the house, the brightness of the lights had me grab on to the counter for a moment as I reestablished equilibrium. It was like my left and right eye were working independent of each other, each absorbing an image and attempting to overlap them; the effect was disconcerting. One was always slightly behind the other.

"That is the last fucking time I smoke."

I used the counter as a handrail. I smiled because I knew it for the lie it was. I just wished that they still had the ragweed of my youth. Not this super-hybrid high TCH stuff. I reached my hand out, having to wave it around a few times until it collided with the basement door handle.

"Stereographic vision would be spectacular right now," I said aloud; I guess asking the patron saint of vision…if there was such a person.

I was halfway down the steps when the change took place. The sixth step from the top was the plush, brownish cut-Berber rug of my home, and the seventh from the top was unadorned wood—and not finished wood, but rather, utilitarian plywood.

"What the…"

I took another step down; both my feet now on the new rug-less stairs and then I began to hear noise—and not the soft scurrying sound of mice, this was a full-blown party, loud music and raucous laughter. Smoke swirled around my eyes.

"What the…" I started again.

Most of the people Tracy invited had already filed out for the evening. This had to be my kids, but none of them were home…unless one of them snuck back in. But to what purpose? To have a raging party right under my feet? Did they think I wouldn't find out?

I hastily went down the rest of the steps to put the kibosh on it. I got to the landing expecting kids to go scurrying like mice caught on the open floor when the lights go on. Nothing.

"Hey, man, what took you so long? You got the beer?" Paul asked.

He was about ten feet away sitting at a table that I'd last seen in my parent's basement. A small glass was in the middle of the table and he was holding a quarter getting ready to shoot it in. He looked a good twenty pounds lighter and twenty-five years younger.

"What the fuck is going on?" I asked softly.

"Hey, babe. You alright?"

"Be-Beth? What are you doing here?"

Her eyebrows furrowed as she looked at me. "Did you take mescaline without me?" she asked, grabbing my hand.

"I loved you once," I told her as I pulled our co-joined hands up to look at them. With my free hand I touched them. "Is this real?" I asked her.

"You loved me once? Mike, are you alright?"

"Do I look alright? Do I look older to you?"

"You just turned nineteen not forty," she said.

"I just came down here to get beer. Wait…what? I'm nineteen? My oldest child Nicole is twenty-two."

"You have kids now? And somehow one of them is older than you. What's going on upstairs? Maybe I should go check it out," she said, making a move for the basement steps.

I got in front of her. "Um…no that would be a bad idea…my w-wine is up there." I'd nearly said wife, I wonder how that would have gone?

"Wine? You don't drink wine."

"I'm nineteen now, I want to become more sophisticated."

"Mike, get over here, I'm on fire. I want to kick your ass," Paul shouted from the quarters table.

"Come on, let's get some air." Beth led me to the bulkhead that went outside.

"This is my folks' house," I said as I really started to take a look at my surroundings.

"Yeah, Mike, remember? They left for the weekend. We came home to watch Dusty for them."

"Dusty's alive! I loved that dog! Where is she!"

"Again with the past tense. Dusty's fine, she's sleeping up in your folks' bedroom. Don't you remember?"

We went outside; the cool night air was invigorating. "It was warmer upstairs."

"What do you expect for October in New England?"

"It's March in Colorado," I whispered.

Beth wrapped her jacket tighter around herself. "Don't you want to keep me warm?" she said as she pulled me in close.

"Uh…" I was turned so that I could see the side of my townhome out of my peripheral vision. Tracy walked by the window. I quickly stepped back from Beth. "Did you see that?" I asked, pointing to the window.

"Are you just messing with me now, Mike?"

I turned to look at her. "Once upon a time, I was head

over heels for you…couldn't think of much else as a matter of fact. Then, slowly but surely, I began to see what others did."

"Oh? And what's that?" she said as she released my hand.

"That you're a very selfish person."

"Why are you saying such hurtful things?"

"I got my first true indication when my sister was working at that travel agency. I told you that she could get us two tickets anywhere in the Continental US or one ticket anywhere in the world. My first and only thought was where would we like to go. I remember you said to me before you had a chance to think about it that you always wanted to visit Egypt. If it had been your sister I'm convinced you would have gone to the Pyramids by yourself."

"That never happened," she said indignantly.

"It will," I told her. "The kicker, though…the real kicker is that next year you are going to get an internship with an ABC affiliate and then you're going to cheat on me with one of the producers. And not because you have any true feelings for him, but rather as a way to get your foot in the door regardless of the devastation it is going to cause me. I'm going to try and drown my liver in alcohol after you do that. I join the Marines to dry out. Do you believe that shit? Me in the Corps."

"I'm going to get going, Mike. Whatever you took tonight, I'm just going to wait until it has run its course."

"Okay," I told her, not even watching as she walked away.

Tracy was staring out the window in my general direction, but I'm pretty sure I could have had a roman candle shooting from my ass and she wouldn't have seen it…or me. I went back into my parents' basement; the same cellar that had seen so many get-togethers.

"Where's Beth?" Dennis asked, coming up to me. He was holding a cold beer that he handed to me.

"Dennis, you're alive! I've missed you, man." I hugged him fiercely.

"Dude, people are going to talk," he said, looking around like he was hoping no one was witnessing the event. Odds were none of them would remember it the next day anyway.

"Dennis," I gripped each shoulder hard, "you need to listen to me, man. You are one of my best friends."

"Is this drunk talk, Mike? I love you too, man," he said uncomfortably as he continued to look around.

"Dude, yes I am fucking wasted beyond comprehension, but you need to fucking listen to me. Write this shit down if you have to."

"Mike, I didn't carry a pen and paper in high school, what makes you think I'm going to have one now?"

"Fine, fine…are you paying the fuck attention."

"Listen, man, you're like five inches from my face, I promise I'm paying attention."

"How eff'd up are you?"

"Not too bad. Stomach has been a little iffy, so I've only been smoking mostly."

"Alright, man, in your thirties—"

He interrupted me. "My thirties? What the fuck are you talking about? I'm eighteen."

"Just shut up and listen, for some reason I'll probably never figure out, I was given a chance here to change some shit. In your thirties you are going to get diagnosed with diabetes, and like the asshole that you are, you aren't going to do anything about it, and it's going to kill you."

"Diabetes?"

"Yes! Now fucking promise me when you get that news that you will do everything in your power to live a long and normal life."

"Dude, you're freaking me out," he said as he tried to pull away.

I gripped him tighter. "Promise me, man, and I'll let

you go." I was staring at him intensely.

He dropped his gaze and promised.

"No, man, look me in the eye when you promise. Swear on your mother this time." He was getting angry. "Do it," I said, pulling him in closer.

Through gritted teeth he spoke. "I promise, now let me the fuck go." He shrugged me away.

"One more thing," I said to his retreating back, "invest in Microsoft."

"Hey, buddy," Paul said as I approached the quarters table.

"Want to see something crazy?" I asked him.

"Love to," he replied as he followed me to the basement stairs.

He was a step below me, I had one foot on the plywood and the other on carpet. For the briefest of moments the older Paul was above me looking down and the younger Paul was below me looking up. Both versions of Paul had their mouths agape as they stared at who they once were and who they were to become.

My next step brought me to the present; Paul was still looking past me.

"Some killer weed, huh?" I asked as I patted his back and moved on by.

"What the f…" He turned to follow.

"Yeah…welcome to my world. Next time, leave your crazy marijuana at home," I said as I opened the basement stairs door.

"Shit, you almost busted my nose," Dennis yelped from hallway.

Now it was my turn for my mouth to drop open. "You're…you're alive?" I asked, stepping back. I probably would have gone tumbling down the stairs if not for Paul directly behind me.

"I told you not to smoke that shit," Dennis laughed at me.

"The diabetes?"

"Under control for like the last five years, Mike. You alright? I always wanted to ask you how you knew about that."

"What…what about Microsoft?" I asked.

"Oh, Microsoft! That would have made *way* more sense. I thought you said Hasbro. Done all right with them, though.

"It's good to see you, man," I said, hugging him tight, neither of us embarrassed.

"Happy Birthday, man, may the gods shine down upon you."

"They already have, brother," I told him honestly.

Check out these other titles by Mark Tufo

Zombie Fallout Boxed Set

All the books you love in one easy to go e-box! Perfect for when you have to leave your house in a hurry! TAKE YOUR EREADER!

Zombie Fallout

It was a flu season like no other. With the H1N1 virus running rampant through the country, people lined up in droves to try and attain one of the coveted vaccines. What was not known, was the effect this largely untested inoculation was to have on the unsuspecting throngs. Within days, feverish folk throughout the country, convulsed, collapsed and died, only to be re-born. With a taste for brains, blood and bodies, hordes of modern-day zombies began scouring the lands for their next meal.

This is the story of Michael Talbot, his family and his friends: a band of ordinary people trying to get by in extraordinary times. When disaster strikes, Mike a self-proclaimed survivalist, does his best to ensure the safety and security of those he cares for. What he encounters along the way leads him down a long dark road, always skirting on the edge of insanity. Ensconced in a seemingly safe haven called Little Turtle, Mike and his family, together with the remnants of a tattered community, must fight against a relentless, ruthless, unstoppable force. This last bastion of civilization has made its final stand. God help them all.

Zombie Fallout 2: A Plague Upon Your Family

The Talbots are evacuating their home amidst a zombie apocalypse. Mankind is on the edge of extinction as a new dominant, mindless opponent scours the landscape in search of food, which just so happens to be non-infected humans. This book follows the journey of Michael Talbot, his wife, Tracy, and their three kids - Nicole, Justin and Travis. Accompanying them are Brendon, Nicole's fiancée and Tommy, a former Wal-Mart door greeter who may be more than he seems. Together they struggle against a ruthless, relentless enemy that has singled them out above all others.

As they travel across the war-torn country side the Talbots soon learn that there are more than just zombies to be fearful of: with law and order a long-distant memory some humans have decided to take any and all matters into their own hands. It's not just brains versus brain-eaters anymore. And the stakes may be higher than merely life and death, with eternal souls on the line.

Zombie Fallout 3: The End…

As the world spirals even further down into the abyss of apocalypse, one man struggles to keep those around him safe. Michael stands side by side with his wife, their children, his friends and Henry the wonder Bulldog along with the Wal-Mart greeter Tommy who is infinitely more than he appears. Whether Tommy is leading Mike and his family to salvation or death remains to be seen...

Zombie Fallout 3.5 - Dr. Hugh Mann – Prequel

Before there were zombies there was the virus...
In this Zombie Fallout prequel, Mark Tufo tells the story of the virus that started it all.

Zombie Fallout IV: The End…Has Come and

Gone

"The End...has come and gone. This is the new beginning, the new world order and it sucks. The end for humanity came the moment the U.S. government sent out the infected flu shots. My name is Michael Talbot and this is my journal. I'm writing this because no one's tomorrow is guaranteed, and I have to leave something behind to those who may follow." - From Mike Talbot's Journal

So continues Mike's journey, will he give up all that he is in a desperate bid to save his family and friends? Eliza is coming, can anyone be prepared?

Zombie Fallout V: Alive In A Dead World

Eliza turned to Tomas: "This is the end...he is no longer alive in a dead world."

In this installment of Mark Tufo's action-packed Zombie Fallout series, Mike Talbot and his family continue their fight for survival as Eliza plots their demise.

Zombie Fallout VI: 'Til Death Do Us Part

Mark Tufo's Zombie Fallout novels have their share of memorable characters. Throughout the series, we have become acquainted with Michael Talbot. We've gotten to know Mike's wife, Tracy, their children, and several other characters, including Mrs. Deneaux, BT, and Tommy.

One character here, however, deserves special mention - that of Eliza. In Zombie Fallout 2, we discovered the queen's origins. In particular, we learned of her transformation from human to vampire. Subsequent novels in the series, indeed, affirm this villain's bloodthirsty nature. Eliza will not rest until she sees to the destruction of the entire Talbot clan.

Now, in the latest novel in the Zombie Fallout series, the moment has come for the final showdown. But as BT, Gary, and Mrs. Deneaux prepare to face Eliza, they have other worries. With Mike still missing, they cannot help but fear the worst.

Is Mike alive? Will the Talbot's defeat their nemesis once and for all? Readers will learn the answers to these questions and more in the much-anticipated sixth installment of the Zombie Fallout series.

Indian Hill

This first story is about an ordinary boy growing up in relatively normal times who finds himself thrust into an extraordinary position. Growing up in suburban Boston, Mike Talbot undergoes the trials and tribulations of all teenagers, from the seemingly tyrannical mother, to girl problems to run-ins with the law. From there, he escapes to college in Colorado with his best friend, Paul, where they begin to forge new relationships. It is one girl in particular that has caught Mike's eye, and he alternately pines for her and laments ever meeting her.

It is on their true "first" date that things go strangely askew. Mike finds himself captive aboard an alien vessel, fighting for his very survival. The aliens have devised gladiator-type games - games of twofold importance that they use both for entertainment value and to learn about human strengths and weaknesses. The aliens want to better learn how to attack and defeat humans, and the battles are to the death on varying computer-generated terrains.

Follow Mike and Paul as they battles for their lives and try to keep the United States safe.

Indian Hill II: Reckoning

Reckoning starts where the first book in the series left off. After escaping from the Progerian alien vessel, Michael Talbot is given the opportunity to hide in obscurity with the rest of the human race or rise to the occasion and once again find himself immersed in a battle that he wants nothing to do with.

Mike goes home and decides to join whatever resistance force can be mustered to repel the oncoming invasion. As humanity gets thrust towards the abyss of extinction, two women in love with the same man make a desperate bid to travel across the country to reunite with him.

Mike will suffer the ultimate betrayal from those he loves the most. Will mankind fall and be ground to dust like so many other civilizations, or will the tiny humans thwart a takeover? Only time and shed blood will tell.

Indian Hill III: Conquest

And so the end begins...Indian Hill introduced us to Michael Talbot, an ordinary boy thrust into extraordinary circumstances when he finds himself captive aboard an alien vessel and forced to battle for his very survival in gladiator-type games. As Michael learns, the aliens were using him to learn about human weaknesses in preparation for an impending invasion.

In Indian Hill 2, Michael escaped from the alien ship and joined whatever resistance forces could be mustered to repel the oncoming alien invasion.

Now in the final chapter of the Indian Hill trilogy, Michael joins forces with an unlikely alliance in a desperate attempt to head off humanity's mass extinction. This is the long awaited conclusion to man's very struggle to survive against overwhelming odds and an aggressive alien species hell-bent on enslaving the entire world.

Timothy

Timothy was not a good man in life, and being undead did little to improve his disposition. What will a man trapped in his own mind do to survive when he wakes up to find himself a zombie controlled by a self-aware virus?

Tim 2

Timothy lived a life only a psychopathic sociopath could enjoy and understand. When he was bitten on the first day of the zombie-apocalypse he turned the tides on a single-minded virus he affectionately called Hugh. Together they terrorized a city before seemingly meeting their untimely demise. Nobody could have foreseen his resurrection, Tim's close call with death has done nothing to temper his missions in life, to live, to eat and to rule the world.

Tim is back and he's an asshole.

The Book of Riley: Part 1 - My Name is Riley

When the zombie apocalypse strikes without warning, one dog will hold the fate of her pack in her paws. This is the story of Riley, an American Bulldog who takes charge when the dead begin to walk. Follow along as she struggles to protect her pack from danger. Traveling with Riley are Ben-Ben, the high-strung Yorkie; Riley's favorite two-legger, Jessie; Jessie's younger brother, Zachary; and Riley's arch-enemy, Patches the cat. They are a rag-tag group of survivors who, when pushed to the limit, realize they are all that each other has.

The Book of Riley: Part 2 - My Name is Riley

In the second part of this unique horror tale from acclaimed author Mark Tufo, Riley, an American bulldog, continues to defend her pack in the midst of a zombie apocalypse. When the zombie apocalypse struck, intrepid American bulldog Riley quickly discovered it was up to her to keep the pack safe. Together with Yorkshire Terrier Ben-Ben and former archenemy Patches the cat, Riley helped to keep the zombies at bay while favorite human Jessie traveled cross-country to find safety for herself and her baby brother, Zachary.

But after a long journey, Riley and the gang arrive in Las Vegas - one of the few remaining inhabited cities - only to find that it has been taken over by a group of thugs who rule through fear and brutality. Making matters worse, ruler Icely and his gang have taken to staging dog fights as popular entertainment, and Riley catches their eye. With Riley forced to fight for her life and Jessie locked up in the home of Icely himself, the future is uncertain. Will Riley save the day once more and help her pack escape?

The Book of Riley: Part 3 - My Name is Riley

In this third installment, Jess aided by her four legged friends escapes the self-proclaimed King of Vegas and flees across state lines in a desperate bid to stay one step ahead of the vengeance seeking mad man.

Riley and company come a cross a unique ally that helps them on their quest to avoid recapture from Icely and his gang. Jess is one step closer to finding her way to Justin but is dogged each step of the way, by zombies and thugs. Can Riley and the ever petulant Patches along with the bacon loving Ben-Ben be able to keep her safe?

The Ravin
This is book one of the Indian Hill series in a more youth friendly version.

Coming Soon - The Prey! Book Two in the Youth Adventures of Michael Talbot.

Zombie Fallout VII: For the Fallen

The Spirit Clearing

Mark Tufo's novels often center upon a single figure - that of Michael Talbot. Fans have joined this unforgettable character in numerous adventures. They've accompanied Mike in his struggle to navigate the apocalyptic world of the Zombie Fallout series. They've cheered him on his quest to save mankind from an alien threat in the Indian Hill books.

Now, in The Spirit Clearing, Tufo presents a Michael Talbot adventure like no other. Our hero wakes one morning to find himself in the hospital. Blind in one eye, he is the sole survivor in a horrific car accident. Soon Mike discovers that his injured eye allows him to see what others cannot. When he tells others of his visions, no one believes him.

Overcome by confusion, Mike feels as if he's caught between one world and another. Then, hope arrives in the form of the beautiful Jandilyn Hollow. Will she be able to pull him out of the depths of his despair? Can love transcend even death?

Join Mike as he embarks on his latest adventure, in this eerie, well-paced tale. Full of twists and turns, The Spirit Clearing will keep readers guessing until the very end.

Callis Rose

Callis Rose is a girl blessed with a gift from above or cursed with a ruthless power she barely understands, it's really just a matter of degrees. As her family life is turned asunder she is thrown into an indifferent Social Services program where she defends herself the only way she knows how. Callis is moved from home to home until she finally settles at the Lowries. As she starts her first day of high school she meets both her favorite and least favorite person, both happen to reside at the same household.

Mindy Denton makes it her single mission in life to destroy Callis, even as her brother Kevin falls deeper into love with the mysterious and beautiful girl who is hiding something from them all. Follow along in Mark Tufo's newest adventure.

Lycan Fallout

The world of man was brought to its knees with the zombie apocalypse. A hundred and fifty years have passed since man has clawed and climbed his way from the brink of extinction. Civilization has rebooted, man has begun to rebuild, to create communities and society. It is on this fragile new shaky ground that a threat worse than the scourge of the dead has sprung. One man finds himself once again thrust into the forefront of a war he wants nothing to do with and seemingly cannot win. Follow along as Michael Talbot attempts to thwart the rise of the werewolf.

Zombie Fallout available in Spanish and Hindi

Mark Tufo

Zombie Fallout VII: For the Fallen

CUSTOMERS ALSO PURCHASED:

ARMAND ROSAMILLIA
DYING DAYS SERIES

SHAWN CHESSER
SURVIVING THE ZOMBIE APOCALYPSE SERIES

T.W. BROWN
THE DEAD SERIES

JOHN O'BRIEN
NEW WORLD SERIES

JAMES N. COOK
SURVIVING THE DEAD SERIES

HEATH STALLCUP
THE MONSTER SQUAD

Printed in Great Britain
by Amazon.co.uk, Ltd.,
Marston Gate.